THE WAR OF THE WORLDS

◆

THE WAR IN THE AIR
and Particularly How Mr Bert Smallways
Fared While it Lasted

The War of the Worlds

◆

The War in the Air

and Particularly How Mr Bert Smallways
Fared While It lasted

———— ◆ ————

H. G. WELLS

with an Introduction and Notes by
ANDREW FRAYN
Edinburgh Napier University

WORDSWORTH CLASSICS

For my husband
ANTHONY JOHN RANSON
with love from your wife, the publisher.
Eternally grateful for your unconditional love.

Readers who are interested in other titles from
Wordsworth Editions are invited to visit our website at
www.wordsworth-editions.com

First published in 2017 by Wordsworth Editions Limited
8B East Street, Ware, Hertfordshire SG12 9HJ

ISBN 978 1 84022 742 0

Text © Wordsworth Editions Limited, 2017
Introduction and Notes © Andrew Frayn, 2017

Wordsworth® is a registered trademark of
Wordsworth Editions Limited

Wordsworth Editions
is the company founded in 1987 by
MICHAEL TRAYLER

Typeset in Great Britain by Antony Gray
Printed and bound by Clays Ltd, St Ives plc

Contents

The War of the Worlds

page 29

The War in the Air

*and Particularly How Mr Bert Smallways
Fared While It Lasted*

page 175

GENERAL INTRODUCTION

Wordsworth Classics are inexpensive editions designed to appeal to the general reader and students. We commissioned teachers and specialists to write wide-ranging, jargon-free Introductions and to provide Notes that would assist the understanding of our readers rather than interpret the stories for them. In the same spirit, because the pleasures of reading are inseparable from the surprises, secrets and revelations that all narratives contain, we strongly advise you to enjoy this book before turning to the Introduction.

KEITH CARABINE
General Adviser
Rutherford College, University of Kent at Canterbury

BIOGRAPHY OF THE AUTHOR

Herbert George Wells, known as 'Bertie' or 'H. G.', was born on 21 September 1866 in Atlas House, on the High Street of what was then the Kentish market town of Bromley. His father Joseph, a former gardener, kept a shop and played professional cricket; after his father broke his leg when Wells was ten, Wells's mother Sarah returned to domestic service at the country house Uppark, near Midhurst, in Sussex.

Wells's elder brothers had both been apprenticed to drapers, a trade that Sarah Wells considered to be highly respectable. Wells was apprenticed to drapers in Windsor and Southsea but was much keener to continue to be educated, and he persuaded his mother to let him become a pupil-teacher at Midhurst Grammar School. Wells's exam results at Midhurst were so strong that he won a scholarship, aimed at increasing the number of science teachers in Britain, at the Normal School (now Imperial College London), under 'Darwin's bulldog', the biologist T. H. Huxley. Wells drew extensively on his experiences as a student for his 1900 novel *Love and Mr Lewisham*. Ill-fed, poor and increasingly discontented by both the quality of the teaching he received and the social organisation of the world, Wells became more and more interested in politics and in imaginative literature, especially Plato, Blake and Carlyle. He also began writing, providing articles and a time-travel story, 'The Chronic Argonauts', for the college magazine, the *Science Schools Journal*.

Wells failed his final exams and found work as a teacher in Wales. After being fouled in a rugby game, he suffered severe kidney damage, and for much of the 1890s Wells feared he would die prematurely. Returning to London and completing his degree, he worked as a correspondence tutor and in 1893 wrote his first books *Honours Physiography* and *A Textbook of Biology*. His writing branched out into literary journalism and popular scientific writing, and in 1895 alone Wells published four further books: *Select Conversations with an Uncle, The Wonderful Visit, The Stolen Bacillus and Other Incidents* and his masterpiece, *The Time Machine*. This first 'scientific romance' was swiftly followed by *The Island of Doctor Moreau* (1896), *The Invisible Man* (1897) and *The War of the Worlds* (1898). None has ever been out of print since; Wells was swiftly hailed as a man of genius by his contemporaries. Both sociable and irascible, Wells became friends, and fell out with, other writers such as George Gissing, Joseph Conrad, Stephen Crane, George Bernard Shaw, Arnold Bennett, Ford Madox Ford and Henry James, whom Wells would later cruelly lampoon in his 1915 novel *Boon*, the climax of a long disagreement between the two writers about the purpose and nature of the novel.

Wells never wanted to be limited to writing scientific romances, and during this period he also wrote realistic prose fiction set in a recognisable real world, whose disorganisation and unfairness these novels sought to diagnose: *The Wheels of Chance* (1896), *Kipps* (1905), *Tono-Bungay, Ann Veronica* (both 1909) and *The History of Mr Polly* (1910). Wells's early-twentieth-century science fiction, such as *The Food of the Gods* (1905) and *In the Days of the Comet* (1906), increasingly showed a vision of the world as Wells would want to order it. His political and utopian writing from *Anticipations of the Reactions of Mechanical and Scientific Progress upon Human Life and Thought* (1901) to *A Modern Utopia* (1905) also demonstrated Wells's commitment to creating a utopian government, a World State that would ensure that mankind would never go to war.

Following the First World War, Wells's passion for this project intensified, and he embarked on an ambitious collaborative project to write the first history of the world, hoping that if future generations were better educated, then rivalries between nations would be unnecessary, and world government would follow. *The Outline of*

History (1919) was Wells's best-selling book in his own lifetime, selling millions of copies internationally, and was followed by the school version *A Short History of the World* (1922) and by equivalents for science, *The Science of Life* (1930), and social science, *The Work, Wealth and Happiness of Mankind* (1931). At its height, Wells's fame was as much as a thinker and public intellectual as a novelist. He met or corresponded with the greatest figures of the first half of the twentieth century, notably Winston Churchill, Lenin and Stalin, Theodore and Franklin Roosevelt, Albert Einstein and Sigmund Freud. His later novels from *The New Machiavelli* (1911) onward tend to be more overtly engaged with Wells's 'Open Conspiracy' to convert his readership to his own political point of view, often at a cost to these books' literary merit and subsequent afterlife.

Wells had married his cousin Isabel in 1891, but the couple proved incompatible and he left her for his pupil Amy Catherine Robbins, whom he rechristened 'Jane'. In spite of Wells's many infidelities, which Jane seemed prepared to tolerate, the couple were happily married until Jane's death from cancer in 1928; and they had two sons, Gip and Frank. An affair with the writer Amber Reeves produced a daughter, Anna Jane, and Wells's long affair with novelist Rebecca West led to the birth of a further son, Anthony West. Wells also enjoyed liaisons with, among others, Dorothy Richardson, Elizabeth von Arnim, Margaret Sanger and, following Jane's death, Odette Keun and Moura Budberg.

Wells's writing was prophetic in both senses of the term: as exhorting humankind to mend its ways, and in foreseeing the future. His writing imagined before they existed the aeroplane, the tank, space travel, the atomic bomb and the internet. In later life, the emphasis of his political writing turned more towards the rights of the individual, and his 1940 book *The Rights of Man: Or, What Are We Fighting For?* is a key text in the history of human rights.

Wells often despaired of his warnings ever being sufficiently heeded, declaring that his epitaph should be: 'God *damn* you, you fools – I told you so.' None the less, the influence of his hundred and fifty books and pamphlets of science fiction, novels, politics, utopia, history, biography and autobiography has been enormous throughout the twentieth century and into the twenty-first.

SIMON J. JAMES
Professor of English Literature at Durham University
and author of *Maps of Utopia: H. G. Wells,
Modernity and the End of Culture*

INTRODUCTION

Published a decade apart and spanning the end of the nineteenth century, *The War of the Worlds* (1898) and *The War in the Air* (1908) are brought together in one volume for the first time in this Wordsworth edition. By the time he published *The War of the Worlds*, which has become ingrained in popular culture by iconic versions such as Orson Welles's radio drama (1938) and Jeff Wayne's musical (1978), H. G. Wells was already a popular novelist. The fact that his novels are still widely-read today attests to the power of his storytelling, and these two science fictions or, as Wells called them, 'scientific romances', address the possibilities and problems of technological progress, the relationship between science and society, and the impact of war on the individual. If the *War of the Worlds* tends towards the fantastic, with its tentacled Martians and futuristic heat-rays, *The War in the Air* cuts much closer to the bone in its vivid depictions of the evisceration of civilisation by bombs dropped from the then-nascent flying machines. The central concern of each novel with developing technologies and the relationships between countries and racial groups ensures that the substance, not merely the story, remains important over a hundred years later.

Fears of invasion

These novels address imperial rivalries at the height of the age of empire. The British Empire on the cusp of the twentieth century was in a position of great strength. Famously a commonwealth on which the sun never set, it was the wealth of resources brought back from its farthest reaches to be processed in manufacturing that ensured the great wealth of the nation. Shipping was vital to the continuing success of the empire, both for transport and defence. Naval strength continued to grow with a hectic programme of construction according to the Two Power Standard, made official by the Naval Defence Act of 1889. It is worth remembering that at the time the law was passed the next two largest navies, whose strength the law required Britain to match, were in fact France and Russia; Germany's strength came later. The outcome of this attempt to show unparalleled strength was, inevitably, a naval arms race that led to ever-greater fears about the security of the nation. The combination of national confidence and apparently reluctant antagonism is exemplified by the music-hall success 'McDermott's War Song' (1878), whose chorus proclaims: 'We don't want to fight, but by jingo if we do; / We've got the ships, we've got the men, and got the money too!' With imperial power came the threat of overthrow by another one of the far-reaching and abundantly resourced empires of the day.

The War of the Worlds and *The War in the Air* should be seen in the context of the invasion novels that were especially popular in the latter part of the nineteenth and the early twentieth centuries. The tradition stretches back to George Tomkins Chesney's *The Battle of Dorking* (1871), first published by *Blackwood's Magazine* just after the conclusion of the Franco-Prussian War, the most recent major conflict between European great powers. Chesney's novel worried about an invasion from the sea by a Germanic people (although their nationality is never explicitly stated). The genre is founded on a paradox, demanding bullishness about the status and ability of the protagonist, standing in for and up for the nation, but predicated on fears about its strength. Michael Paris sees it as a form of socialisation, imposing a narrative of imperial might and personal heroism that instilled the 'right' attitude for young Britons.[1] *The Battle of Dorking* spawned a mass of responses, ripostes and imitators. In the same year there was *What Happened After the Battle of Dorking; or, the Victory of Tunbridge Wells* and *Mrs Brown on the Battle of Dorking*; over a decade later came *The Battle off Worthing; Why the Invaders Never Got to Dorking* (1887). The noted militarist and imperialist F. N. Maude was still casting nervous glances across the channel in *The New Battle of Dorking* (1900).[2]

It cannot be entirely coincidental that Leatherhead, the town to which the narrator's wife retreats in *The War of the Worlds*, is just north of Dorking. Wells's novels constitute part of a second wave of invasion fiction around the turn of the century. Scores of now long-forgotten popular novels appeared, with utterly predictable titles such as *The Coming Waterloo* (1901), *A New Trafalgar* (1902) and *Seaward for the Foe* (1903). The most prominent author of invasion fiction at this time was William Le Queux, who feared French and Russian invasion in *The Great War in England in 1897* (1894) and German invasion in the shrill *The Invasion of 1910* (1906). The latter was commissioned by Alfred Harmsworth for the *Daily Mail*, who ensured that the towns named in

---

1 Michael Paris, *Over the Top*, pp. xii–xiii. For full publication details see the Bibliography following this Introduction.

2 A. Michael Matin, 'The Hun is at the Gate!', p. 318

the novel had high readerships of the newspaper.[3] The shift from Chesney's publication in the middle-class *Blackwood's* to Le Queux's in the popular press illustrates the widening readership, linked in part to increasing literacy following the Education Acts of the late nineteenth century.

In the novels in this volume Wells trades similarly on the immediacy of the danger by contrast to, for example, 'A Story of the Days to Come' (1897) and *When the Sleeper Wakes* (1898–9, rewritten as *The Sleeper Awakes*, 1910), which look to distant, dystopian futures. That immediacy is one of the strategies by which Wells works to ensure their realism. *The War of the Worlds* operates in a geography that is realist almost to a fault – so realistic that the very keen reader could reconstruct the narrator's steps as he walks through specific districts and past London's iconic landmarks. This is exemplified by the opening of Book Two, Chapter Eight, pointedly entitled 'Dead London'. The narrator walks down the Fulham Road through eerily still suburbs into a London haunted by the wailing of 'that superhuman note' (p. 161). His journey continues through South Kensington, along Exhibition Road past Hyde Park, contemplating the Natural History Museum, passing through the Marble Arch to Oxford Street, walking through Portman Square to Baker Street, before finally arriving at the wailing Martian in Regent's Park. This relentless accumulation of geographical detail clearly states that these events are never far away, particularly if one is in the south-east of England. The narrators, in differing ways, are key to the believability of the novels, despite the literally outlandish appearance of the Martians. The narrator of *The War of the Worlds* is a stoical and pragmatic British man who endures the trials put before him; but he is barely a developed character, more a set of eyes through which the reader can experience the invasion. The mostly-honest cockney Bert Smallways in *The War in the Air*, to whom we will return, is a better-developed everyman figure, a simultaneously naïve and savvy representative of mass culture who has similarities with Wells's other lower-middle-class protagonists such as the title characters of *Kipps* (1905) and *The History of Mr Polly* (1910). Until 1908 Wells was a member of the left-wing reformist Fabian Society, which believes in progress through dialogue and gradual change. The popularity of these novels certainly contributed to an ongoing national conversation about Britain's military preparedness, and the imperial behaviour of Europeans in their colonies.

3 Cecil D. Eby, *The Road to Armageddon*, p. 33

Complacency, belief and disbelief

The War of the Worlds makes clear the danger of complacency from its opening sentence. Apart from the alert and perceptive narrator, the general public is unable and/or unwilling to believe in the dangers of the Martian invasion. Wells trades on a fascination with Mars and Martians in the last quarter of the nineteenth century, alluding in the first chapter to the Italian astronomer Giovanni Schiaparelli, who named the 'seas', 'continents' and 'channels' of Mars.[4] That hubristic certainty about the strength of the nation and the efficacy of the current moment makes peril seem impossibly distant, a common trope of dystopian fiction that Margaret Atwood trades on notably in *The Handmaid's Tale* (1985). In Wells's novel a telegram revealing the appearance of the Martians from their craft 'was judged to be a canard' (p. 58). The narrator subsequently reports:

> Even within the five-mile circle the great majority of people were inert. I have already described the behaviour of the men and women to whom I spoke. All over the district people were dining and supping; working men were gardening after the labours of the day, children were being put to bed, young people were wandering through the lanes love-making, students sat over their books.   [p. 58]

The insistent continuation of normality is a harbinger of doom, but it mirrors the experience of civilians proximate to war: life tends to continue as normal until there is immediate danger. That inertness is contrasted pointedly by the narrator with the Martians 'hammering and stirring, sleepless, indefatigable, at work' (p. 60). Noises like that of contemporary industry pass for everyday activities, and the action rises as Book One, Chapter Eight ends with the landing of the second Martian cylinder; Wells's pacing of his material has all the hallmarks of the man accustomed to writing in serial form, as the pithy reveal carries the reader into the equally snappy chapter opening. The inability to recognise a new form of danger was a theme Wells picked up three years later in his successful non-fiction *Anticipations of the Reaction of Mechanical and Scientific Progress upon Human Life and Thought* (1901), usually more concisely known as *Anticipations*. He continued to warn about the move away from 'the old war [, which] was a matter of long dreary marches, great hardships of campaigning, but also of heroic

4 Robert Crossley, 'Percival Lowell and the History of Mars'

conclusive moments'.[5] Anticipating the development of mechanised warfare over the coming decades, the technology used by the Martians reduces the possibility for human agency in this war to a point where all that sensible humans can do is flee.

The novel wrestles with the difficulty of reconciling scientific developments with religious belief. The publication of Charles Darwin's *On the Origin of Species* (1859) had revised the history of life on earth: it led many readers to question their faith in Christianity and the biblical story of creation. Darwin's work was influential for Wells's thought and writing: Mars was seen as a superannuated version of Earth, and the Martians are therefore a projection of what humans might become.[6] Nevertheless, Britain was still predominantly a Christian country at the end of the nineteenth century. Both of these novels are eschatological – about the apparent end of days. After the narrator encounters for the first time the dead body of someone familiar to him, we see the Surrey countryside flaming from the Martians' heat-ray:

> It seemed indeed as if the whole country in that direction was on fire – a broad hillside set with minute tongues of flame, swaying and writhing with the gusts of the dying storm, and throwing a red reflection upon the cloud-scud above [. . .] I could not see [. . .] the nearer fire, though the reflections of it danced on the wall and ceiling of the study. A sharp, resinous tang of burning was in the air.
>
> [p. 70]

The apocalyptic image is one from Dante or Hieronymus Bosch. Wells cleverly makes it sensory for his narrator, the acrid smell and/or taste of burning heightening the realism that he strives to achieve. As the masses flee London, including the narrator's brother, this sense of judgement is reinforced by 'a blind man in the uniform of the Salvation Army, gesticulating with his crooked fingers and bawling, "Eternity! Eternity!" ' (p. 107).

This challenge to faith is represented conveniently – Wells does not shy away from coincidence, but he does it with such bravura that it passes quickly – when the narrator ends up travelling, and then hiding, with a curate who is experiencing doubts. Anxieties about the ability of religion to compete with the dominance of rationalism were being expressed at the time in the Catholic Church: Pope Pius X (1903–14) was the first to speak out against 'modernism'. The curate is not spared

5 Wells, *Anticipations*, p. 177
6 Frank McConnell, *The Science Fiction of H.G. Wells*, p. 130

the vitriol of the narrator, who balances rational action with a strong sense of morality:

> I had already come to hate the curate's trick of helpless exclamation, his stupid rigidity of mind. His endless muttering monologue vitiated every effort I made to think out a line of action, and drove me at times, thus pent up and intensified, almost to the verge of craziness. He was as lacking in restraint as a silly woman. He would weep for hours together, and I verily believe that to the very end this spoiled child of life thought his weak tears in some way efficacious. And I would sit in the darkness unable to keep my mind off him by reason of his importunities.   [p. 136]

Wells satirises the fallacy of rigid dogma. Already tested by the increasing dominance of the rationalist worldview in the late nineteenth century, for him this plague on Britain was the straw that broke the curate's back. However, the curate does not stand directly for religion. He represents the impact of concerns about degeneration that were prevalent at the time, often, as in this case, represented in terms of effeminacy and the failure to uphold Christian values.[7] *The War of the Worlds* shares an overarching structure with many nineteenth-century narratives: it is written in a Christian tradition in which fortitude in adversity is prized and the endurance of hardships leads ultimately to reward.

Science, civilisation and progress

Wells highlights the precariousness of scientific rationalism and the doctrine of progress, as well as its dominance. In his seminal account of the invasion novel *Voices Prophesying War*, I. F. Clarke highlights the ways in which the genre draws on Victorian notions of progress; the critic Fredric Jameson sees teleological progress as crucial to science fiction.[8] In *The War of the Worlds*, as the whole population of the capital rises up in terror, the narrator reports the 'stampede gigantic and terrible – without order and without a goal, six million people unarmed and unprovisioned, driving headlong. It was the beginning of the rout of civilisation, of the massacre of mankind' (p. 112). The Port of London epitomises the chaos as the men and women of the city take to

7 Daniel Pick, *Faces of Degeneration*
8 I. F. Clarke, *Voices Prophesying War*, pp. 69–70; Fredric Jameson, *The Political Unconscious*, pp. 86–90. See also John Rieder, 'Science Fiction, Colonialism, and the Plot of Invasion'.

the very seas that were supposed to defend the 'sea-walled garden'. Here, however, the invaders have arrived by other means. Reporting his brother's experiences, the narrator recounts:

> an astonishing scene. Steamboats and shipping of all sorts lay there, tempted by the enormous sums of money offered by fugitives, and it is said that many who swam out to these vessels were thrust off with boathooks and drowned. About one o'clock in the afternoon the thinning remnant of a cloud of the black vapour appeared between the arches of Blackfriars Bridge. At that the Pool became a scene of mad confusion, fighting, and collision, and for some time a multitude of boats and barges jammed in the northern arch of the Tower Bridge, and the sailors and lightermen had to fight savagely against the people who swarmed upon them from the riverfront. People were actually clambering down the piers of the bridge from above.
>
> When, an hour later, a Martian appeared beyond the Clock Tower and waded down the river, nothing but wreckage floated above Lime-house.   [p. 112]

Technology is unlinked from teleology: we see clearly that progress is not inexorable. In the panic-stricken chaos, liberal and democratic laws and ideals are left behind. Commerce becomes bribery, the social contract is broken, and life is no longer sacred. The brutally short paragraph that follows evokes the hidden violence of war, seen only in the wreckage left in the Martian's wake. While warfare occasions advances in practical development, it fatally arrests social and moral progress.

The mess of immediacy brought about by exposure to the dangers of invasion creates the fevered tone of the novel, and makes its puncturing by the appearance of the Martians beyond the familiar Clock Tower inevitable. The scramble at the Pool of London is just one example of how order collapses in the panic, and brutality becomes commonplace in the scramble for merely a chance at safety. Laws created for the common good no longer hold, and property is abandoned in favour of more immediately pressing concerns, alongside efforts to haul the civilisation back from the brink. The narrator hears from an artilleryman:

> 'One night last week,' he said, 'some fools got the electric light in order, and there was all Regent Street and the Circus ablaze, crowded with painted and ragged drunkards, men and women, dancing and shouting till dawn. A man who was there told me. And as the day came they became aware of a fighting-machine standing near by the Langham and looking down at them. Heaven knows how long he

had been there. It must have given some of them a nasty turn. He came down the road towards them, and picked up nearly a hundred too drunk or frightened to run away.'

Grotesque gleam of a time no history will ever fully describe!

[p. 158]

The electric light is a recent invention, a symbol of modernity for the original readers. The *carpe diem* attitude shown by the rash restoration of one of the luxuries of the preceding life as a palliative to the current situation is halted brutally by the invaders. The single sentence conclusion, which stands alone as a paragraph, makes the electric light seem uncanny, encapsulating terror and excitement in the 'grotesque gleam', but also highlighting the skewed relationship with normality in wartime. Wells also points out the disconnect between history and lived experience, a point on the road between Thomas Carlyle's histories of great men and Virginia Woolf's complaint against them.[9]

The description of the Martians highlights the precision of Wells's narrative technique. The narrator overcomes his initial terror, and the nausea that results, to give a quasi-scientific account of their appearance. Building on speculations made in his essay 'The Man of the Year Million' (1893) about the bodies of men and women in the distant future, Wells describes memorably the giant Martian heads that apparently only feature dark eyes, and the tentacle-hands near the part that functions as their mouth. The description has coloured the depiction of Martians in subsequent images, from the 1953 US feature film to UK advertisements for freeze-dried mashed potato in the 1970s and 1980s. The ill-fittedness of the Martians' bodies to the Earth is pointed out, before reaching the real horror:

all the complex apparatus of digestion, which makes up the bulk of our bodies, did not exist in the Martians. They were heads – merely heads. Entrails they had none. They did not eat, much less digest. Instead, they took the fresh, living blood of other creatures, and *injected* it into their own veins [. . . B]lood obtained from a still living animal, in most cases from a human being, was run directly by means of a little pipette into the recipient canal . . .

The bare idea of this is no doubt horribly repulsive to us, but at

9 Thomas Carlyle, *On Heroes, Hero-Worship and the Heroic in History*; Virginia Woolf, *Jacob's Room*, p. 145; and particularly Woolf's discussion of a fictional sister of Shakespeare in *A Room of One's Own*, pp. 36–42, pp. 85–6

the same time I think that we should remember how repulsive our carnivorous habits would seem to an intelligent rabbit.   (p. 131)

The chilling feeding on the warm blood of live mammals is brought into focus by the witty analogy between the Martians' feeding habits and our own: we, and particularly Wells's Victorian contemporaries, are invited to imagine being a subject race.[10] The comparisons made in this description epitomise the lines that Wells treads throughout the novel. The short sentences draw attention to the singularity of the Martians, but their extreme difference allows the threat to be disregarded. The warning against all invaders can be read as escapism because of the implausibility of the foe.

THE WAR IN THE AIR

There can be no doubt that *The War in the Air* is plausible and eerily prescient to the twenty-first-century reader. All but the very worst of its fears came true in the Second World War, as Wells noted in his Preface to the 1941 edition, published as Britain was under sustained aerial attack from Germany:

Again I ask the reader to note the warnings I gave [in the Preface to the 1921 edition] twenty years ago. Is there anything to add to that preface now? Nothing except my epitaph. That, when the time comes, will manifestly have to be: 'I told you so. You *damned* fools.' (The italics are mine.)[11]

Wells's frustration and despair at the failure to heed his warnings is palpable: his italics suggest not only the extent of the foolishness, but the damnation of the world. However, it is important to remember that as Wells was writing the novel in 1907–8, air power was far from certain to become a dominant force. While the Wright Brothers had flown at Kitty Hawk, North Carolina, in December 1903, *The War in the Air* was written, as its author pointed out in his Preface to the 1921 edition, 'before the days of the flying machine; Blériot did not cross the Channel

10 See also McConnell, *Science Fiction of H.G. Wells*, pp. 128–30.

11 Wells, Preface to the 1941 edition, in *The War in the Air*, edited by Patrick Parrinder and Andy Sawyer, p. 279. See also Wells, *Experiment in Autobiography*, 2, p. 666.

12 Wells, Preface to the 1921 edition, in *The War in the Air*, edited by Parrinder and Sawyer, p. 277. See also the first chapter of *An Englishman Looks at the World*.

until July 1909; and the Zeppelin airship was still in its infancy.'[12] He reflected in his entertaining *Experiment in Autobiography* on the development of air travel, having flown in 1934 to Moscow, that in 1900 'this would have been as incredible a journey as a trip on Prince Houssain's carpet'.[13] In 1901, though, Wells had seen aerial warfare coming. Even before the Wright Brothers flew, Wells wrote in *Anticipations* that 'the nature of the things that will ultimately fight in the sky is a matter for curious speculation'.[14] As the technology developed, he made remarkably far-sighted fictional speculations.

The protagonist of *The War in the Air* is Bert Smallways, a persevering cockney everyman who is a street-smart survivor, accustomed to making his entrepreneurial way in the world with his business partner, but naïve about wider political workings. The unnamed narrator of *The War of the Worlds* seems merely a pair of eyes at times, but Bert is at the opposite end of the spectrum – a character in (in)glorious technicolour. Wells stated that his focus was not on believable characterisation: 'I sketch out scenes and individuals, often quite crudely, and resort even to conventional types and symbols, in order to get on to a discussion of relationships.'[15] Bert's first name suggests a kinship with his author: Herbert George Wells was known as Bertie by friends and family. His surname tells us about his limited but representative experience of the 'small ways' in which most people live and think, while their local concerns are buffeted by unseen legislative and political forces. The opening to Chapter Three establishes his credentials, such as they are:

> Bert Smallways was a vulgar little creature, the sort of pert, limited soul that the old civilisation of the early twentieth century produced by the million in every country of the world. He had lived all his life in narrow streets, and between mean houses he could not look over, and in a narrow circle of ideas from which there was no escape [. . .] He was, in fact, the sort of man who had made England and America what they were. The luck had been against him so far, but that was by the way. He was a mere aggressive and acquisitive individual with no sense of the State, no habitual loyalty, no devotion, no code of honour, no code even of courage. Now by a curious accident he found himself lifted out of his marvellous modern world for a time, out of all the rush and confused appeals of it, and floating like a thing dead

13 Wells, *Experiment in Autobiography*, 2, p. 799
14 Wells, *Anticipations*, p. 191
15 Wells, *Experiment in Autobiography*, 2, p. 493

and disembodied between sea and sky. It was as if Heaven was experimenting with him, had picked him out as a sample from the
English millions, to look at him more nearly, and to see what was
happening to the soul of man.   [p. 219]

The harshness of this early dismissal of Bert softens as the novel
progresses: Bert remains a caricature, but he is well-intentioned and
loyal, and increasingly affectionately drawn. Wells seems to change his
mind as Bert becomes the key figure not only for the novel but, by a
series of remarkable coincidences, the rapidly developing world war. As
the world seems to be on the brink of war, he and his colleague Grubb
decide to give up their business and tour their proposed act singing
gently comedic songs. As they perform to a small and underwhelmed
audience on Dymchurch sands, the 'imperial Englishman' inventor
Alfred Butteridge lands in his hot-air balloon to seek help for his fainting
companion, who is 'no light woman' (p. 217). Bert enters the basket to
help as she, coming to, steps out of it, and the release of weight sends
him skywards with Butteridge's designs for his flying machines. Unable
to control the balloon, he is shot down in Germany by the military,
where it is assumed because of circumstance that Bert is Butteridge.
With this in mind, the narrator reconsiders:

Bert Smallways was by no means a stupid person, and up to a certain
limit he had not been badly educated. His board school had taught
him to draw up to certain limits, taught him to calculate and understand a specification. If at that point his country had tired of its
efforts, and handed him over unfinished to scramble for a living in an
atmosphere of advertisements and individual enterprise, that was
really not his fault. He was as his State had made him, and the reader
must not imagine because he was a little cockney cad, that he was
absolutely incapable of grasping the idea of the Butteridge flying-
machine. But he found it stiff and perplexing.   [p. 217]

The narrator begins to see someone making the best of his circumstances, with his limited agency. The critique of Bert becomes a critique
of the civilisation that has produced him as it is stripped away, an
individual swept along by the great processes of history, which are
themselves shown to be the product of momentary decisions and
remarkable coincidences. The criticism of advertisements anticipates
the reaction by modernist authors against gaudy commercial images
and the popular press in such disparate literary works as Conrad's *Chance*
(1913) and *Victory* (1915), Imagist poetry, and F. Scott Fitzgerald's *The*

Great Gatsby (1925). *The War in the Air* is part of the development of Wells's thinking towards perhaps his greatest comment on the condition of England, the following year's *Tono-Bungay*, and participates in an ongoing conversation about the condition of the working and lower-middle classes.

Technologies of war

The world of *The War in the Air* takes the technological developments of the early twentieth-century and pushes them to extremes. Aircraft and gyroscopic monorails proliferate, and there is a bridge over the English Channel. The flying machine that Bert tries to understand is designed by the eccentric Mr Alfred Butteridge. Wells offers us in this novel the possibility of a radically different line of development for the aeroplane, wondering what if the fixed-wing aeroplane had been a dead end:

> His machine was [. . .] neither birdlike nor butterfly-like, nor had it the wide, lateral expansion of the ordinary aeroplane. The effect upon the observer was rather something in the nature of a bee or wasp. Parts of the apparatus were spinning very rapidly, and gave one a hazy effect of transparent wings; but parts, including two peculiarly curved 'wing-cases' – if one may borrow a figure from the flying beetles – remained expanded stiffly. In the middle was a long rounded body like the body of a moth, and on this Mr Butteridge could be seen sitting astride, much as a man bestrides a horse. The wasplike resemblance was increased by the fact that the apparatus flew with a deep booming hum, exactly the sound made by a wasp at a window-pane.   [p. 192]

To borrow from nature for the development of the flying machine makes sense, as engineers strove to move beyond the short ranges and unreliable mechanics of the dangerous early phase of flight. The analogy with the bee and wasp suggests a greater nimbleness than the fixed lateral wing aeroplane, and also evokes their sting; perhaps the lights of the modern cities attract the moth-like aeroplanes.

Wasps and moths are a nuisance. But this analogy, early in the novel, hardly prepares the reader for the carnage of total war that arises as a result of the development of flying machines. Even in 1908 there was a sense of what warfare in the modern world would look like. The Franco-Prussian War was in living memory, and further clues came from the development and use of automatic weapons in the US Civil War (1861–5) and the development of entrenchment in the Second

Boer War (1899–1902). The recent Russo-Japanese War (1904–5) saw brutal artillery fighting at the initial Siege of Port Arthur (now Lüshunkou, China); later, as the Russian troops moved between battles with the opposing Japanese forces, they also destroyed Chinese villages, raping civilian women and slaughtering anyone in their path. In *The War in the Air*, the ability to move munitions in the air at speeds of several hundred miles an hour means that the civilian is no longer safe, as Bert discovers: 'I saw that dead chap in the passage. I seen too much smashing and killing today. That's the matter. I don't like it. I didn't know war was this sort of thing. I'm a civilian. I don't like it' (p. 280). Wells presciently sees the impact on the civilian of aerial warfare. Smallways witnesses the destruction of the emblematic city of the age and, by his presence in the German airship fleet, is complicit. The German destruction of Manhattan that precipitates the global war is an allegory for the destruction of modern civilisation, and New York is described as 'the supreme type of the City of the Scientific Commercial Age'[16] (p. 282). The narrator's enumeration of the great landmarks of the city and reflections on the 'large ways' of thinking (to reverse the pun in Bert's name) are deftly counterpointed by the protagonist's response: 'Gaw! *What* a place!' (p. 288). These shifts of register between the insightful, impassioned rhetoric of the narrator's warnings and Bert's awestruck demotic reactions give the novel much of its power.

The Americans fight back, and their inferior aircraft manage to disable the German flagship in which Bert is flying. He and the surviving German crew are rescued and taken to the new German base at Niagara Falls. Before long, however, the Asiatic air fleet attacks, leaving Bert stranded on Goat Island, in the middle of the Niagara River next to the Falls, as racist crimes are committed throughout the now overwhelmed United States. It is only when Bert is no longer in the midst of the battle, in Chapter Ten, that he begins to comprehend fully the scale of what has happened. When he finally manages to return to what remains of civilisation, Bert listens to two small-town Americans talking:

> They spoke of fire and massacre, of cruelties and counter cruelties, of things that had been done to harmless Asiatics by race-mad men, of the wholesale burning and smashing up of towns, railway junctions, bridges, of whole populations in hiding and exodus [. . .]
> Slowly, broadly, invincibly, there grew upon Bert's mind realisation

16 See also Wells, 'The Expansion of the United States', in *A Short History of the World*, Chapter 60.

of the immense tragedy of humanity into which his life was flowing; the appalling and universal nature of the epoch that had arrived; the conception of an end to security and order and habit. The whole world was at war and it could not get back to peace, it might never recover peace. [p. 375]

Once everywhere can be considered a war zone nothing is safe, and things unravel rapidly. The premonition of long-range death in Britain came true within six years: Scarborough was bombed from the sea by Germany in December 1914, and air warfare quickly developed during the First World War from reconnaissance to more destructive practices. Wells later wrote that 'the air offensive was the most revolutionary of all the new methods [. . .]. Hitherto in the history of mankind war had gone on only where the armies marched and met. Now it went on everywhere.'[17] We are returned to the point in *The War of the Worlds* about complacency: progress is not benign, and the stakes are high.

In *The War in the Air* the endgame is more brutal and longer-lasting than in *The War of the Worlds*. The Martians die because of their vulnerability to disease, luckily for the Britons of the novel, whereas when the empires of the Earth take each other on with equipment from the vanguard of progress, there is no escape. The narrator puts it pithily: 'It was the dissolution of an age; it was the collapse of the civilisation that had trusted to machinery, and the instruments of its destruction were machines' (p. 324). We are reminded emphatically that progress is not secure:

The accidental balance on the side of Progress was far slighter and infinitely more complex and delicate in its adjustments than the people of that time suspected; but that did not alter the fact that it was an effective balance. They did not realise that this age of relative good fortune was an age of immense but temporary opportunity for their kind. They complacently assumed a necessary progress towards which they had no moral responsibility. They did not realise that this security of progress was a thing still to be won or lost, and that the time to win it was a time that passed. [p. 382]

The most fluent and passionate passage of the novel, this cavalcade of warnings continues for all of the first section of Chapter Eleven, 'The Great Collapse'. Wells warns against complacency, situating progress not as continual and inevitable, but itself a battle to be fought and won.

17 Wells, *A Short History of the World*, p. 332

Wells's assured formulations illustrate that he is at his best as a social analyst and commentator: the polemical power of the philosophical passages is counterbalanced by the understated realism. He also returns to the intersection between technology and faith, asserting, despite his scepticism about the value of religion, the need to preserve and apply moral values. Socialisation cannot keep pace with technological progress, and underlying both these novels is Wells's implicit assertion that as great a focus must be placed on the correspondingly rapid development of moral and legal frameworks. This tension was later exemplified in discussions about the ultimate aerial weapon, the atomic bomb, as J. Robert Oppenheimer felt grave reservations about its development. Wells's passionate warnings continue to be relevant today, as little responsibility is taken for man's impact on the natural world, from the destruction of the rainforests to the pollution of the seas, and the extinction and near-extinction of numerous animals.

Scientific romances

Wells described this genre as the 'scientific romance', using romance in the sense of a fiction remote from everyday life. Both of these novels also feature romance in the more conventional sense of a love plot. In each the war separates the protagonist from his partner: in *The War of the Worlds* the narrator sends his wife to the safety of Leatherhead, and in *The War in the Air* Bert is separated from Edna, his intended, by his accidental balloon trip and the cataclysm it causes. Their journeys are to return to the security of the relationship, and it is this element of the texts that offers hope. In *The War of the Worlds*, the reunion of the couple is the first sign that things will return to normal. The ending of *The War in the Air* is much more ambiguous. Bert is returned to Edna, offering hope for the future, but it is only after civilisation has been all but eradicated, almost instantly pushed back several centuries. His journey to her takes him through the 'countryside at that time [, which] presented the strangest mingling of the assurance and wealth of the opening twentieth century with a sort of Düreresque medievalism' (p. 389), and when he arrives he has to murder the amorous vigilante chief of the area. Local concerns take primacy, and it is unclear whether the war continues; it was ever thus, the novel seems to conclude. The neatness and familiarity of the resolution of each novel allows the reader who seeks it an escape from the vitally important and serious social questions that Wells asks, which is undoubtedly just as strong a reason for their popularity as the acuity of their social commentary. The terrifying and blood-curdling aspects of *The War of the Worlds* simultaneously shock the reader and allow their dismissal as implausible; the fact that Bert is a comedic figure in *The War in the Air* means that he is engaging, but also allows the seriousness of his situation to be overlooked.

Wells continued to polemicise, watch and warn. In an article of July 1909 he wrote that 'within a year we shall have [. . .] aeroplanes capable of starting from Calais, let us say, circling over London, dropping a hundredweight or so of explosive upon the printing machines of *The Times*, and returning securely to Calais for another similar parcel'.[18] The 'parcel' of explosives is a reminder that Wells is describing something we now know to exist, but for which a vocabulary had yet to be created. *The War in the Air* was the beginning, even by his standards, of a prolific period: he published seven novels in the next five years, and a further eight books from 1914 to 1918. As if to emphasise his prescience, in the year of the First World War's outbreak he published *The World Set Free*, which anticipated the end of the Second World War. Wells's anticipation of and urgent commentary on the later horrors of the twentieth century inspired his pleas for international cooperation. He wondered in *Anticipations* about the possibility of an English-speaking New Republic, and by 1928 was arguing in *The Open Conspiracy* for a scientifically-led 'world commonwealth': Wells's ideal extended far beyond the organisations founded in the wake of each of the World Wars, the League of Nations (1920) and its successor, the United Nations (1945). He offered more detailed plans in *The New World Order* (1940), by which time the possibility seemed both imperative and for- lorn. These novels take us back to an historical moment at which Britain was attempting to secure its position on the world stage, while casting anxious glances overseas. Wells's proposals and warnings seem just as valuable today.

ANDREW FRAYN
Edinburgh Napier University

18 Wells, 'The Coming of Blériot', in *An Englishman Looks at the World*, p. 4

BIBLIOGRAPHY

Paul Alkon, *Science Fiction before 1900*, Routledge, New York, 2002

Thomas Carlyle, *On Heroes, Hero-Worship, and the Heroic in History*, edited by David R. Sorensen and Brent E. Kinser, Yale University Press, New Haven, CT, 2013 [1840]

I. F. Clarke, *Voices Prophesying War: Future Wars 1763–3749*, Oxford University Press, Oxford 1992

Robert Crossley, 'Percival Lowell and the History of Mars', in *Massachusetts Review*, Vol. 41, 1994, pp. 297–318

Cecil D. Eby, *The Road to Armageddon: The Martial Spirit in English Popular Literature 1870–1914*, Duke University Press, Durham, NC, 1988

Fredric Jameson, *The Political Unconscious: Narrative as a Socially Symbolic Act*, Routledge, London, 2002

Frank McConnell, *The Science Fiction of H. G. Wells*, Oxford University Press, Oxford, 1981

Steven McLean, *The Early Fiction of H. G. Wells: Fantasies of Science*, Palgrave Macmillan, Basingstoke, 2009

A. Michael Matin, ' "The Hun is at the Gate!": Historicizing Kipling's Militaristic Rhetoric, from the Imperial Periphery to the National Center: Part One: The Russian Threat to British India', in *Studies in the Novel*, Vol. 31, 1999, pp. 317–56

Michael Paris, *Over the Top: The Great War and Juvenile Literature in Britain*, Praeger, Westport, CT, 2004

Patrick Parrinder, *Shadows of the Future: H. G. Wells, Science Fiction and Prophecy*, Liverpool University Press, Liverpool, 1995

Daniel Pick, *Faces of Degeneration: A European Disorder, c.1848–1918*, Cambridge University Press, Cambridge, 1993

John Rieder, 'Science Fiction, Colonialism, and the Plot of Invasion', in *Extrapolation*, Vol. 46, 2005, pp. 373–94

H. G. Wells, *Anticipations of the Reaction of Mechanical and Scientific Progress Upon Human Life and Thought*, Chapman & Hall, London 1902 [1900]

H. G. Wells, *The War in the Air*, edited by Patrick Parrinder and Andy Sawyer, with an Introduction by Jay Winter, Penguin, London, 2005 [1908]

H. G. Wells, *An Englishman Looks at the World: Being a Series of Unrestrained Remarks upon Contemporary Matters*, Cassell, London, 1914

H. G. Wells, *A Short History of the World*, edited by Michael Sherborne; with an Introduction by Norman Stone, Penguin, London, 2006 [1922]

H. G. Wells, *Experiment in Autobiography: Discoveries and Conclusions of a Very Ordinary Brain (Since 1866)*, 2 vols, Gollancz and Cresset Press, London, 1934

Virginia Woolf, *Jacob's Room*, edited by Kate Flint, Oxford University Press, Oxford, 2008 [1922]

Virginia Woolf, *A Room of One's Own* and *Three Guineas*, edited by Anna Snaith, Oxford University Press, Oxford, 2015 [1929/1938]

The War of the Worlds

But who shall dwell in these worlds if they
be inhabited? . . . Are we or they Lords of the
World? . . . And how are all things made for
man?[1]

KEPLER
quoted in *The Anatomy of Melancholy*

The War of the Worlds

H. G. WELLS

The War of the Worlds was first published in Great Britain
in serial form in 1897 by *Pearson's Magazine* and
in the United States by *Cosmopolitan*.
First published in hardback in Great Britain in 1898
by William Heinemann, London
and by Harper & Brothers, New York

Contents

BOOK ONE
The Coming of the Martians

BOOK TWO
The Earth Under the Martians

BOOK ONE

The Coming of the Martians

CHAPTER ONE

The Eve of the War

NO ONE WOULD HAVE BELIEVED in the last years of the nineteenth century that this world was being watched keenly and closely by intelligences greater than man's and yet as mortal as his own; that as men busied themselves about their various concerns they were scrutinised and studied, perhaps almost as narrowly as a man with a microscope might scrutinise the transient creatures that swarm and multiply in a drop of water. With infinite complacency men went to and fro over this globe about their little affairs, serene in their assurance of their empire over matter. It is possible that the infusoria under the microscope do the same. No one gave a thought to the older worlds of space as sources of human danger, or thought of them only to dismiss the idea of life upon them as impossible or improbable. It is curious to recall some of the mental habits of those departed days. At most terrestrial men fancied there might be other men upon Mars, perhaps inferior to themselves and ready to welcome a missionary enterprise. Yet across the gulf of space, minds that are to our minds as ours are to those of the beasts[2] that perish, intellects vast and cool and unsympathetic, regarded this earth with envious eyes, and slowly and surely drew their plans against us. And early in the twentieth century came the great disillusionment.

The planet Mars,[3] I scarcely need remind the reader, revolves about the sun at a mean distance of 140,000,000 miles, and the light and heat it receives from the sun is barely half of that received by this world. It must be, if the nebular hypothesis[4] has any truth, older than our world; and long before this earth ceased to be molten, life upon its surface must have begun its course. The fact that it is scarcely one-seventh of the volume of the earth must have accelerated its cooling to the temperature at which life could begin. It has air and water and all that is necessary for the support of animated existence.

Yet so vain is man, and so blinded by his vanity, that no writer, up to the very end of the nineteenth century, expressed any idea that intelligent life might have developed there far, or indeed at all, beyond its earthly level. Nor was it generally understood that since Mars is older than our earth, with scarcely a quarter of the superficial area and remoter from the sun, it necessarily follows that it is not only more distant from time's beginning but nearer its end.

The secular cooling[5] that must someday overtake our planet has already gone far indeed with our neighbour. Its physical condition is still largely a mystery, but we know now that even in its equatorial region the midday temperature barely approaches that of our coldest winter. Its air is much more attenuated than ours, its oceans have shrunk until they cover but a third of its surface, and as its slow seasons change huge snowcaps gather and melt about either pole and periodically inundate its temperate zones. That last stage of exhaustion, which to us is still incredibly remote, has become a present-day problem for the inhabitants of Mars. The immediate pressure of necessity has brightened their intellects, enlarged their powers, and hardened their hearts. And looking across space with instruments, and intelligences such as we have scarcely dreamed of, they see, at its nearest distance only 35,000,000 of miles sunward of them, a morning star of hope, our own warmer planet, green with vegetation and grey with water, with a cloudy atmosphere eloquent of fertility, with glimpses through its drifting cloud wisps of broad stretches of populous country and narrow, navy-crowded seas.

And we men, the creatures who inhabit this earth, must be to them at least as alien and lowly as are the monkeys and lemurs to us. The intellectual side of man already admits that life is an incessant struggle for existence, and it would seem that this too is the belief of the minds upon Mars. Their world is far gone in its cooling and this world is still crowded with life, but crowded only with what they regard as inferior animals. To carry warfare sunward is, indeed, their only escape from the destruction that, generation after generation, creeps upon them.

And before we judge of them too harshly we must remember what ruthless and utter destruction our own species has wrought, not only upon animals, such as the vanished bison and the dodo,[6] but upon its inferior races. The Tasmanians, in spite of their human likeness,[7] were entirely swept out of existence in a war of extermination waged by European immigrants, in the space of fifty years. Are we such apostles of mercy as to complain if the Martians warred in the same spirit?

The Martians seem to have calculated their descent with amazing subtlety – their mathematical learning is evidently far in excess of ours – and to have carried out their preparations with a well-nigh perfect unanimity. Had our instruments permitted it, we might have seen the gathering trouble far back in the nineteenth century. Men like Schiaparelli[8] watched the red planet – it is odd, by the by, that for countless centuries Mars has been the star of war – but failed to interpret the fluctuating appearances of the markings they mapped so well. All that time the Martians must have been getting ready.

During the opposition of 1894[9] a great light was seen on the illuminated part of the disk, first at the Lick Observatory,[10] then by Perrotin of Nice,[11] and then by other observers. English readers heard of it first in the issue of *Nature* dated August 2.[12] I am inclined to think that this blaze may have been the casting of the huge gun, in the vast pit sunk into their planet, from which their shots were fired at us. Peculiar markings, as yet unexplained, were seen near the site of that outbreak during the next two oppositions.

The storm burst upon us six years ago now. As Mars approached opposition, Lavelle of Java set the wires of the astronomical exchange palpitating with the amazing intelligence of a huge outbreak of in-candescent gas upon the planet. It had occurred towards midnight of the twelfth; and the spectroscope, to which he had at once resorted, indicated a mass of flaming gas, chiefly hydrogen, moving with an enormous velocity towards this earth. This jet of fire had become invisible about a quarter past twelve. He compared it to a colossal puff of flame suddenly and violently squirted out of the planet, 'as flaming gases rushed out of a gun'.

A singularly appropriate phrase it proved. Yet the next day there was nothing of this in the papers except a little note in the *Daily Telegraph*,[13] and the world went in ignorance of one of the gravest dangers that ever threatened the human race. I might not have heard of the eruption at all had I not met Ogilvy, the well-known astronomer, at Ottershaw.[14] He was immensely excited at the news, and in the excess of his feelings invited me up to take a turn with him that night in a scrutiny of the red planet.

In spite of all that has happened since, I still remember that vigil very distinctly: the black and silent observatory, the shadowed lantern throwing a feeble glow upon the floor in the corner, the steady ticking of the clockwork of the telescope, the little slit in the roof – an oblong profundity with the stardust streaked across it. Ogilvy moved about, invisible but audible. Looking through the telescope, one saw a circle of deep blue and the little round planet swimming in the field. It seemed such a little thing, so bright and small and still, faintly marked with transverse stripes, and slightly flattened from the perfect round. But so little it was, so silvery warm – a pin's-head of light! It was as if it quivered, but really this was the telescope vibrating with the activity of the clock-work that kept the planet in view.

As I watched, the planet seemed to grow larger and smaller and to advance and recede, but that was simply that my eye was tired. Forty millions of miles it was from us – more than forty millions of miles of void. Few people realise the immensity of vacancy in which the dust of the material universe swims.

Near it in the field, I remember, were three faint points of light, three telescopic stars infinitely remote, and all around it was the unfathomable darkness of empty space. You know how that blackness looks on a frosty starlight night. In a telescope it seems far profounder. And invisible to me because it was so remote and small, flying swiftly and steadily towards me across that incredible distance, drawing nearer every minute by so many thousands of miles, came the Thing they were sending us, the Thing that was to bring so much struggle and calamity and death to the earth. I never dreamed of it then as I watched; no one on earth dreamed of that unerring missile.

That night, too, there was another jetting out of gas from the distant planet. I saw it. A reddish flash at the edge, the slightest projection of the outline just as the chronometer struck midnight; and at that I told Ogilvy and he took my place. The night was warm and I was thirsty, and I went stretching my legs clumsily and feeling my way in the darkness, to the little table where the siphon stood, while Ogilvy exclaimed at the streamer of gas that came out towards us.

That night another invisible missile started on its way to the earth from Mars, just a second or so under twenty-four hours after the first one. I remember how I sat on the table there in the blackness, with patches of green and crimson swimming before my eyes. I wished I had a light to smoke by, little suspecting the meaning of the minute gleam I had seen and all that it would presently bring me. Ogilvy watched till one, and then gave it up; and we lit the lantern and walked over to his house. Down below in the darkness were Ottershaw and Chertsey and all their hundreds of people, sleeping in peace.

He was full of speculation that night about the condition of Mars, and scoffed at the vulgar idea of its having inhabitants who were signalling us. His idea was that meteorites might be falling in a heavy shower upon the planet, or that a huge volcanic explosion was in progress. He pointed out to me how unlikely it was that organic evolution had taken the same direction in the two adjacent planets.

'The chances against anything manlike on Mars are a million to one,' he said.

Hundreds of observers saw the flame that night and the night after about midnight, and again the night after; and so for ten nights, a flame each night. Why the shots ceased after the tenth no one on earth has attempted to explain. It may be the gases of the firing caused the Martians inconvenience. Dense clouds of smoke or dust, visible through a powerful telescope on earth as little grey, fluctuating patches, spread through the clearness of the planet's atmosphere and obscured its more familiar features.

Even the daily papers woke up to the disturbances at last, and popular notes appeared here, there, and everywhere concerning the volcanoes upon Mars. The serio-comic periodical *Punch*,[15] I remember, made a happy use of it in the political cartoon. And, all unsuspected, those missiles the Martians had fired at us drew earthward, rushing now at a pace of many miles a second through the empty gulf of space, hour by hour and day by day, nearer and nearer. It seems to me now almost incredibly wonderful that, with that swift fate hanging over us, men could go about their petty concerns as they did. I remember how jubilant Markham was at securing a new photograph of the planet for the illustrated paper he edited in those days. People in these latter times scarcely realise the abundance and enterprise of our nineteenth-century papers. For my own part, I was much occupied in learning to ride the bicycle, and busy upon a series of papers discussing the probable developments of moral ideas as civilisation progressed.

One night (the first missile then could scarcely have been 10,000,000 miles away) I went for a walk with my wife. It was starlight and I explained the Signs of the Zodiac to her, and pointed out Mars, a bright dot of light creeping zenithward, towards which so many telescopes were pointed. It was a warm night. Coming home, a party of excursionists from Chertsey or Isleworth passed us singing and playing music. There were lights in the upper windows of the houses as the people went to bed. From the railway station in the distance came the sound of shunting trains, ringing and rumbling, softened almost into melody by the distance. My wife pointed out to me the brightness of the red, green, and yellow signal lights hanging in a framework against the sky. It seemed so safe and tranquil.

CHAPTER TWO

The Falling Star

Then came the night of the first falling star. It was seen early in the morning, rushing over Winchester eastward, a line of flame high in the atmosphere. Hundreds must have seen it, and taken it for an ordinary falling star. Albin described it as leaving a greenish streak behind it that glowed for some seconds. Denning, our greatest authority on meteorites,[16] stated that the height of its first appearance was about ninety or one hundred miles. It seemed to him that it fell to earth about one hundred miles east of him.

I was at home at that hour and writing in my study; and although my French windows face towards Ottershaw and the blind was up (for I loved in those days to look up at the night sky), I saw nothing of it. Yet this strangest of all things that ever came to earth from outer space must have fallen while I was sitting there, visible to me had I only looked up as it passed. Some of those who saw its flight say it travelled with a hissing sound. I myself heard nothing of that. Many people in Berkshire, Surrey, and Middlesex must have seen the fall of it, and, at most, have thought that another meteorite had descended. No one seems to have troubled to look for the fallen mass that night.

But very early in the morning poor Ogilvy, who had seen the shooting star and who was persuaded that a meteorite lay somewhere on the common between Horsell, Ottershaw, and Woking, rose early with the idea of finding it. Find it he did, soon after dawn, and not far from the sand pits. An enormous hole had been made by the impact of the projectile, and the sand and gravel had been flung violently in every direction over the heath, forming heaps visible a mile and a half away. The heather was on fire eastward, and a thin blue smoke rose against the dawn.

The Thing itself lay almost entirely buried in sand, amidst the scattered splinters of a fir tree it had shivered to fragments in its descent. The uncovered part had the appearance of a huge cylinder, caked over and its outline softened by a thick scaly dun-coloured incrustation. It had a diameter of about thirty yards. He approached the mass, surprised at the size and more so at the shape, since most meteorites are rounded more or less completely. It was, however, still so hot from its flight through the air as to forbid his near approach. A stirring noise within its cylinder he ascribed to the unequal cooling of its surface; for at that time it had not occurred to him that it might be hollow.

He remained standing at the edge of the pit that the Thing had made for itself, staring at its strange appearance, astonished chiefly at its unusual shape and colour, and dimly perceiving even then some evidence of design in its arrival. The early morning was wonderfully still, and the sun, just clearing the pine trees towards Weybridge, was already warm. He did not remember hearing any birds that morning, there was certainly no breeze stirring, and the only sounds were the faint movements from within the cindery cylinder. He was all alone on the common.

Then suddenly he noticed with a start that some of the grey clinker, the ashy incrustation that covered the meteorite, was falling off the circular edge of the end. It was dropping off in flakes and raining down upon the sand. A large piece suddenly came off and fell with a sharp noise that brought his heart into his mouth.

For a minute he scarcely realised what this meant, and, although the heat was excessive, he clambered down into the pit close to the bulk to see the Thing more clearly. He fancied even then that the cooling of the body might account for this, but what disturbed that idea was the fact that the ash was falling only from the end of the cylinder.

And then he perceived that, very slowly, the circular top of the cylinder was rotating on its body. It was such a gradual movement that he discovered it only through noticing that a black mark that had been near him five minutes ago was now at the other side of the circumference. Even then he scarcely understood what this indicated, until he heard a muffled grating sound and saw the black mark jerk forward an inch or so. Then the thing came upon him in a flash. The cylinder was artificial – hollow – with an end that screwed out! Something within the cylinder was unscrewing the top!

'Good heavens!' said Ogilvy. 'There's a man in it – men in it! Half roasted to death! Trying to escape!'

At once, with a quick mental leap, he linked the Thing with the flash upon Mars.

The thought of the confined creature was so dreadful to him that he forgot the heat and went forward to the cylinder to help turn. But luckily the dull radiation arrested him before he could burn his hands on the still-glowing metal. At that he stood irresolute for a moment, then turned, scrambled out of the pit, and set off running wildly into Woking. The time then must have been somewhere about six o'clock.

He met a waggoner and tried to make him understand, but the tale he told and his appearance were so wild – his hat had fallen off in the pit – that the man simply drove on. He was equally unsuccessful with the potman who was just unlocking the doors of the public-house by Horsell Bridge. The fellow thought he was a lunatic at large and made an unsuccessful attempt to shut him into the taproom. That sobered him a little; and when he saw Henderson, the London journalist, in his garden, he called over the palings and made himself understood.

'Henderson,' he called, 'you saw that shooting star last night?'

'Well?' said Henderson.

'It's out on Horsell Common now.'

'Good Lord!' said Henderson. 'Fallen meteorite! That's good.'

'But it's something more than a meteorite. It's a cylinder – an artificial cylinder, man! And there's something inside.'

Henderson stood up with his spade in his hand.

'What's that?' he said. He was deaf in one ear.

Ogilvy told him all that he had seen. Henderson was a minute or so taking it in. Then he dropped his spade, snatched up his jacket, and came out into the road. The two men hurried back at once to the common, and found the cylinder still lying in the same position. But now the sounds inside had ceased, and a thin circle of bright metal showed between the top and the body of the cylinder. Air was either entering or escaping at the rim with a thin, sizzling sound.

They listened, rapped on the scaly burnt metal with a stick, and, meeting with no response, they both concluded the man or men inside must be insensible or dead.

Of course the two were quite unable to do anything. They shouted consolation and promises, and went off back to the town again to get help. One can imagine them, covered with sand, excited and disordered, running up the little street in the bright sunlight just as the shop folks were taking down their shutters and people were opening their bedroom windows. Henderson went into the railway station at once, in order to telegraph the news to London. The newspaper articles had prepared men's minds for the reception of the idea.

By eight o'clock a number of boys and unemployed men had already started for the common to see the 'dead men from Mars'. That was the form the story took. I heard of it first from my newspaper boy about a quarter to nine when I went out to get my *Daily Chronicle*.[17] I was naturally startled, and lost no time in going out and across the Ottershaw bridge to the sand pits.

CHAPTER THREE

On Horsell Common

I found a little crowd of perhaps twenty people surrounding the huge hole in which the cylinder lay. I have already described the appearance of that colossal bulk, embedded in the ground. The turf and gravel about it seemed charred as if by a sudden explosion. No doubt its impact had caused a flash of fire. Henderson and Ogilvy were not there. I think they perceived that nothing was to be done for the present, and had gone away to breakfast at Henderson's house.

There were four or five boys sitting on the edge of the pit, with their feet dangling, and amusing themselves – until I stopped them – by throwing stones at the giant mass. After I had spoken to them about it, they began playing at 'touch' in and out of the group of bystanders.

Among these were a couple of cyclists, a jobbing gardener I employed sometimes, a girl carrying a baby, Gregg the butcher and his little boy, and two or three loafers and golf caddies who were accustomed to hang about the railway station. There was very little talking. Few of the common people in England had anything but the vaguest astronomical ideas in those days. Most of them were staring quietly at the big table-ike end of the cylinder, which was still as Ogilvy and Henderson had left it. I fancy the popular expectation of a heap of charred corpses was disappointed at this inanimate bulk. Some went away while I was there, and other people came. I clambered into the pit and fancied I heard a faint movement under my feet. The top had certainly ceased to rotate.

It was only when I got thus close to it that the strangeness of this object was at all evident to me. At the first glance it was really no more exciting than an overturned carriage or a tree blown across the road. Not so much so, indeed. It looked like a rusty gas float.[18] It required a certain amount of scientific education to perceive that the grey scale of the Thing was no common oxide, that the yellowish-white metal that gleamed in the crack between the lid and the cylinder had an unfamiliar hue. 'Extraterrestrial' had no meaning for most of the onlookers.

At that time it was quite clear in my own mind that the Thing had come from the planet Mars, but I judged it improbable that it contained any living creature. I thought the unscrewing might be automatic. In spite of Ogilvy, I still believed that there were men in Mars. My mind ran fancifully on the possibilities of its containing manuscript, on the difficulties in translation that might arise, whether we should find coins and models in it, and so forth. Yet it was a little too large for assurance on this idea. I felt an impatience to see it opened. About eleven, as nothing seemed happening, I walked back, full of such thought, to my home in Maybury. But I found it difficult to get to work upon my abstract investigations.

In the afternoon the appearance of the common had altered very much. The early editions of the evening papers had startled London with enormous headlines:

A MESSAGE RECEIVED FROM MARS.

REMARKABLE STORY FROM WOKING,

and so forth. In addition, Ogilvy's wire to the Astronomical Exchange[19] had roused every observatory in the three kingdoms.[20]

There were half a dozen flys[21] or more from the Woking station standing in the road by the sand pits, a basket-chaise[22] from Chobham, and a rather lordly carriage. Besides that, there was quite a heap of bicycles. In addition, a large number of people must have walked, in spite of the heat of the day, from Woking and Chertsey, so that there was altogether quite a considerable crowd – one or two gaily dressed ladies among the others.

It was glaringly hot, not a cloud in the sky nor a breath of wind, and the only shadow was that of the few scattered pine trees. The burning heather had been extinguished, but the level ground towards Ottershaw was blackened as far as one could see, and still giving off vertical streamers of smoke. An enterprising sweet-stuff dealer in the Chobham Road had sent up his son with a barrow-load of green apples and ginger beer.

Going to the edge of the pit, I found it occupied by a group of about half a dozen men – Henderson, Ogilvy, and a tall, fair-haired man that I afterwards learned was Stent, the Astronomer Royal,[23] with several workmen wielding spades and pickaxes. Stent was giving directions in a clear, high-pitched voice. He was standing on the cylinder, which was now evidently much cooler; his face was crimson and streaming with perspiration, and something seemed to have irritated him.

A large portion of the cylinder had been uncovered, though its lower end was still embedded. As soon as Ogilvy saw me among the staring crowd on the edge of the pit he called to me to come down, and asked me if I would mind going over to see Lord Hilton, the lord of the manor.

The growing crowd, he said, was becoming a serious impediment to their excavations, especially the boys. They wanted a light railing put up, and help to keep the people back. He told me that a faint stirring was occasionally still audible within the case, but that the workmen had failed to unscrew the top, as it afforded no grip to them. The case appeared to be enormously thick, and it was possible that the faint sounds we heard represented a noisy tumult in the interior.

I was very glad to do as he asked, and so become one of the privileged spectators within the contemplated enclosure. I failed to find Lord Hilton at his house, but I was told he was expected from London by the six o'clock train from Waterloo; and as it was then about a quarter past five, I went home, had some tea, and walked up to the station to waylay him.

CHAPTER FOUR

The Cylinder Opens

When I returned to the common the sun was setting. Scattered groups were hurrying from the direction of Woking, and one or two persons were returning. The crowd about the pit had increased, and stood out black against the lemon yellow of the sky – a couple of hundred people, perhaps. There were raised voices, and some sort of struggle appeared to be going on about the pit. Strange imaginings passed through my mind. As I drew nearer I heard Stent's voice: 'Keep back! Keep back!'

A boy came running towards me.

'It's a-movin',' he said to me as he passed; 'a-screwin' and a-screwin' out. I don't like it. I'm a-goin' 'ome, I am.'

I went on to the crowd. There were really, I should think, two or three hundred people elbowing and jostling one another, the one or two ladies there being by no means the least active.

'He's fallen in the pit!' cried someone.

'Keep back!' said several.

The crowd swayed a little, and I elbowed my way through. Everyone seemed greatly excited. I heard a peculiar humming sound from the pit.

'I say!' said Ogilvy; 'help keep these idiots back. We don't know what's in the confounded thing, you know!'

I saw a young man, a shop assistant in Woking I believe he was, standing on the cylinder and trying to scramble out of the hole again. The crowd had pushed him in.

The end of the cylinder was being screwed out from within. Nearly two feet of shining screw projected. Somebody blundered against me, and I narrowly missed being pitched on to the top of the screw. I turned, and as I did so the screw must have come out, for the lid of the cylinder fell upon the gravel with a ringing concussion. I stuck my elbow into the person behind me, and turned my head towards the Thing again. For a moment that circular cavity seemed perfectly black. I had the sunset in my eyes.

I think everyone expected to see a man emerge – possibly something a little unlike us terrestrial men, but in all essentials a man. I know I did. But, looking, I presently saw something stirring within the shadow: greyish billowy movements, one above another, and then two luminous disks – like eyes. Then something resembling a little grey snake, about the thickness of a walking stick, coiled up out of the writing middle, and wriggled in the air towards me – and then another.

A sudden chill came over me. There was a loud shriek from a woman behind. I half turned, keeping my eyes fixed upon the cylinder still, from which other tentacles were now projecting, and began pushing my way back from the edge of the pit. I saw astonishment giving place to horror on the faces of the people about me. I heard inarticulate exclamations on all sides. There was a general movement backwards. I saw the shopman struggling still on the edge of the pit. I found myself alone, and saw the people on the other side of the pit running off, Stent among them. I looked again at the cylinder, and ungovernable terror gripped me. I stood petrified and staring.

A big greyish rounded bulk, the size, perhaps, of a bear, was rising slowly and painfully out of the cylinder. As it bulged up and caught the light, it glistened like wet leather.

Two large dark-coloured eyes were regarding me steadfastly. The mass that framed them, the head of the thing, was rounded, and had, one might say, a face. There was a mouth under the eyes, the lipless brim of which quivered and panted, and dropped saliva. The whole creature heaved and pulsated convulsively. A lank tentacular appendage gripped the edge of the cylinder, another swayed in the air.

Those who have never seen a living Martian can scarcely imagine the strange horror of its appearance. The peculiar V-shaped mouth with its pointed upper lip, the absence of brow ridges, the absence of a chin beneath the wedgelike lower lip, the incessant quivering of this mouth, the Gorgon groups of tentacles,[24] the tumultuous breathing of the lungs in a strange atmosphere, the evident heaviness and painfulness of movement due to the greater gravitational energy of the earth –

above all, the extraordinary intensity of the immense eyes – were at once vital, intense, inhuman, crippled and monstrous. There was something fungoid in the oily brown skin, something in the clumsy deliberation of the tedious movements unspeakably nasty. Even at this first encounter, this first glimpse, I was overcome with disgust and dread.

Suddenly the monster vanished. It had toppled over the brim of the cylinder and fallen into the pit, with a thud like the fall of a great mass of leather. I heard it give a peculiar thick cry, and forthwith another of these creatures appeared darkly in the deep shadow of the aperture.

I turned and, running madly, made for the first group of trees, perhaps a hundred yards away; but I ran slantingly and stumbling, for I could not avert my face from these things.

There, among some young pine trees and furze bushes, I stopped, panting, and waited further developments. The common round the sand pits was dotted with people, standing like myself in a half-fascinated terror, staring at these creatures, or rather at the heaped gravel at the edge of the pit in which they lay. And then, with a renewed horror, I saw a round, black object bobbing up and down on the edge of the pit. It was the head of the shopman who had fallen in, but showing as a little black object against the hot western sun. Now he got his shoulder and knee up, and again he seemed to slip back until only his head was visible. Suddenly he vanished, and I could have fancied a faint shriek had reached me. I had a momentary impulse to go back and help him that my fears overruled.

Everything was then quite invisible, hidden by the deep pit and the heap of sand that the fall of the cylinder had made. Anyone coming along the road from Chobham or Woking would have been amazed at the sight – a dwindling multitude of perhaps a hundred people or more standing in a great irregular circle, in ditches, behind bushes, behind gates and hedges, saying little to one another and that in short, excited shouts, and staring, staring hard at a few heaps of sand. The barrow of ginger beer stood, a queer derelict, black against the burning sky, and in the sand pits was a row of deserted vehicles with their horses feeding out of nosebags or pawing the ground.

CHAPTER FIVE

The Heat-Ray

After the glimpse I had had of the Martians emerging from the cylinder in which they had come to the earth from their planet, a kind of fascination paralysed my actions. I remained standing knee-deep in the heather, staring at the mound that hid them. I was a battleground of fear and curiosity.

I did not dare to go back towards the pit, but I felt a passionate longing to peer into it. I began walking, therefore, in a big curve, seeking some point of vantage and continually looking at the sand heaps that hid these new-comers to our earth. Once a leash of thin black whips, like the arms of an octopus, flashed across the sunset and was immediately withdrawn, and afterwards a thin rod rose up, joint by joint, bearing at its apex a circular disk that spun with a wobbling motion. What could be going on there?

Most of the spectators had gathered in one or two groups – one a little crowd towards Woking, the other a knot of people in the direction of Chobham. Evidently they shared my mental conflict. There were few near me. One man I approached – he was, I perceived, a neighbour of mine, though I did not know his name – and accosted. But it was scarcely a time for articulate conversation.

'What ugly *brutes*!' he said. 'Good God! What ugly brutes!' He repeated this over and over again.

'Did you see a man in the pit?' I said; but he made no answer to that. We became silent, and stood watching for a time side by side, deriving, I fancy, a certain comfort in one another's company. Then I shifted my position to a little knoll that gave me the advantage of a yard or more of elevation and when I looked for him presently he was walking towards Woking.

The sunset faded to twilight before anything further happened. The crowd far away on the left, towards Woking, seemed to grow, and I heard now a faint murmur from it. The little knot of people towards Chobham dispersed. There was scarcely an intimation of movement from the pit.

It was this, as much as anything, that gave people courage, and I suppose the new arrivals from Woking also helped to restore confidence. At any rate, as the dusk came on a slow, intermittent movement upon the sand pits began, a movement that seemed to gather force as the stillness of the evening about the cylinder remained unbroken. Vertical black figures in twos and threes would advance, stop, watch, and advance again, spreading out as they did so in a thin irregular crescent that promised to enclose the pit in its attenuated horns. I, too, on my side began to move towards the pit.

Then I saw some cabmen and others had walked boldly into the sand pits, and heard the clatter of hoofs and the gride of wheels. I saw a lad trundling off the barrow of apples. And then, within thirty yards of the pit, advancing from the direction of Horsell, I noted a little black knot of men, the foremost of whom was waving a white flag.

This was the Deputation. There had been a hasty consultation, and since the Martians were evidently, in spite of their repulsive forms, intelligent creatures, it had been resolved to show them, by approaching them with signals, that we too were intelligent.

Flutter, flutter, went the flag, first to the right, then to the left. It was too far for me to recognise anyone there, but afterwards I learned that Ogilvy, Stent, and Henderson were with others in this attempt at communication. This little group had in its advance dragged inward, so to speak, the circumference of the now almost complete circle of people, and a number of dim black figures followed it at discreet distances.

Suddenly there was a flash of light, and a quantity of luminous greenish smoke came out of the pit in three distinct puffs, which drove up, one after the other, straight into the still air.

This smoke (or flame, perhaps, would be the better word for it) was so bright that the deep blue sky overhead and the hazy stretches of brown common towards Chertsey, set with black pine trees, seemed to darken abruptly as these puffs arose, and to remain the darker after their dispersal. At the same time a faint hissing sound became audible.

Beyond the pit stood the little wedge of people with the white flag at its apex, arrested by these phenomena, a little knot of small vertical black shapes upon the black ground. As the green smoke arose, their faces flashed out pallid green, and faded again as it vanished. Then slowly the hissing passed into a humming, into a long, loud, droning noise. Slowly a humped shape rose out of the pit, and the ghost of a beam of light seemed to flicker out from it.

Forthwith flashes of actual flame, a bright glare leaping from one to another, sprang from the scattered group of men. It was as if some invisible jet impinged upon them and flashed into white flame. It was as if each man were suddenly and momentarily turned to fire.

Then, by the light of their own destruction, I saw them staggering and falling, and their supporters turning to run.

I stood staring, not as yet realising that this was death leaping from man to man in that little distant crowd. All I felt was that it was something very strange. An almost noiseless and blinding flash of light, and a man fell headlong and lay still; and as the unseen shaft of heat passed over them, pine trees burst into fire, and every dry furze bush became with one dull thud a mass of flames. And far away towards Knaphill I saw the flashes of trees and hedges and wooden buildings suddenly set alight.

It was sweeping round swiftly and steadily, this flaming death, this invisible, inevitable sword of heat. I perceived it coming towards me by the flashing bushes it touched, and was too astounded and stupefied to stir. I heard the crackle of fire in the sand pits and the sudden squeal of a horse that was as suddenly stilled. Then it was as if an invisible yet intensely heated finger were drawn through the heather between me and the Martians, and all along a curving line beyond the sand pits the dark ground smoked and crackled. Something fell with a crash far away to the left where the road from Woking station opens out on the common. Forthwith the hissing and humming ceased, and the black, domelike object sank slowly out of sight into the pit.

All this had happened with such swiftness that I had stood motionless, dumbfounded and dazzled by the flashes of light. Had that death swept through a full circle, it must inevitably have slain me in my surprise. But it passed and spared me, and left the night about me suddenly dark and unfamiliar.

The undulating common seemed now dark almost to blackness, except where its roadways lay grey and pale under the deep blue sky of the early night. It was dark, and suddenly void of men. Overhead the stars were mustering, and in the west the sky was still a pale, bright, almost greenish blue. The tops of the pine trees and the roofs of Horsell came out sharp and black against the western afterglow. The Martians and their appliances were altogether invisible, save for that thin mast upon which their restless mirror wobbled. Patches of bush and isolated trees here and there smoked and glowed still, and the houses towards Woking station were sending up spires of flame into the stillness of the evening air.

Nothing was changed save for that and a terrible astonishment. The little group of black specks with the flag of white had been swept out of existence, and the stillness of the evening, so it seemed to me, had scarcely been broken.

It came to me that I was upon this dark common, helpless, unprotected, and alone. Suddenly, like a thing falling upon me from without, came – fear.

With an effort I turned and began a stumbling run through the heather.

The fear I felt was no rational fear, but a panic terror not only of the Martians, but of the dusk and stillness all about me. Such an extraordinary effect in unmanning me it had that I ran weeping silently as a child might do. Once I had turned, I did not dare to look back.

I remember I felt an extraordinary persuasion that I was being played with, that presently, when I was upon the very verge of safety, this mysterious death – as swift as the passage of light – would leap after me from the pit about the cylinder and strike me down.

CHAPTER SIX

The Heat-Ray in the Chobham Road

It is still a matter of wonder how the Martians are able to slay men so swiftly and so silently. Many think that in some way they are able to generate an intense heat in a chamber of practically absolute non-conductivity. This intense heat they project in a parallel beam against any object they choose, by means of a polished parabolic mirror of unknown composition, much as the parabolic mirror of a lighthouse[25] projects a beam of light. But no one has absolutely proved these details. However it is done, it is certain that a beam of heat is the essence of the matter. Heat, and invisible, instead of visible, light. Whatever is combustible flashes into flame at its touch, lead runs like water, it softens iron, cracks and melts glass, and when it falls upon water, incontinently that explodes into steam.

That night nearly forty people lay under the starlight about the pit, charred and distorted beyond recognition, and all night long the common from Horsell to Maybury was deserted and brightly ablaze.

The news of the massacre probably reached Chobham, Woking, and Ottershaw about the same time. In Woking the shops had closed when the tragedy happened, and a number of people, shop people and so forth, attracted by the stories they had heard, were walking over the Horsell Bridge and along the road between the hedges that runs out at last upon the common. You may imagine the young people brushed up after the labours of the day, and making this novelty, as they would make any novelty, the excuse for walking together and enjoying a trivial flirtation. You may figure to yourself the hum of voices along the road in the gloaming . . .

As yet, of course, few people in Woking even knew that the cylinder had opened, though poor Henderson had sent a messenger on a bicycle to the post office with a special wire to an evening paper.

As these folks came out by twos and threes upon the open, they found little knots of people talking excitedly and peering at the spinning mirror over the sand pits, and the newcomers were, no doubt, soon infected by the excitement of the occasion.

By half-past eight, when the Deputation was destroyed, there may have been a crowd of three hundred people or more at this place, besides those who had left the road to approach the Martians nearer. There were three policemen too, one of whom was mounted, doing their best, under instructions from Stent, to keep the people back and deter them from approaching the cylinder. There was some booing from those more thoughtless and excitable souls to whom a crowd is always an occasion for noise and horseplay.

Stent and Ogilvy, anticipating some possibilities of a collision, had telegraphed from Horsell to the barracks as soon as the Martians emerged, for the help of a company of soldiers to protect these strange creatures from violence. After that they returned to lead that ill-fated advance. The description of their death, as it was seen by the crowd, tallies very closely with my own impressions: the three puffs of green smoke, the deep humming note, and the flashes of flame.

But that crowd of people had a far narrower escape than mine. Only the fact that a hummock of heathery sand intercepted the lower part of the Heat-Ray saved them. Had the elevation of the parabolic mirror been a few yards higher, none could have lived to tell the tale. They saw the flashes and the men falling and an invisible hand, as it were, lit the bushes as it hurried towards them through the twilight. Then, with a whistling note that rose above the droning of the pit, the beam swung close over their heads, lighting the tops of the beech trees that line the road, and splitting the bricks, smashing the windows, firing the window frames, and bringing down in crumbling ruin a portion of the gable of the house nearest the corner.

In the sudden thud, hiss, and glare of the igniting trees, the panic-stricken crowd seems to have swayed hesitatingly for some moments. Sparks and burning twigs began to fall into the road, and single leaves like puffs of flame. Hats and dresses caught fire. Then came a crying from the common. There were shrieks and shouts, and suddenly a mounted policeman came galloping through the confusion with his hands clasped over his head, screaming.

'They're coming!' a woman shrieked, and incontinently everyone was turning and pushing at those behind, in order to clear their way to Woking again. They must have bolted as blindly as a flock of sheep. Where the road grows narrow and black between the high banks the crowd jammed, and a desperate struggle occurred. All that crowd did not escape; three persons at least, two women and a little boy, were crushed and trampled there, and left to die amid the terror and the darkness.

CHAPTER SEVEN

How I Reached Home

For my own part, I remember nothing of my flight except the stress of blundering against trees and stumbling through the heather. All about me gathered the invisible terrors of the Martians; that pitiless sword of heat seemed whirling to and fro, flourishing overhead before it descended and smote me out of life. I came into the road between the crossroads and Horsell, and ran along this to the crossroads.

At last I could go no further; I was exhausted with the violence of my emotion and of my flight, and I staggered and fell by the wayside. That was near the bridge that crosses the canal by the gasworks. I fell and lay still.

I must have remained there some time.

I sat up, strangely perplexed. For a moment, perhaps, I could not clearly understand how I came there. My terror had fallen from me like a garment. My hat had gone, and my collar had burst away from its fastener. A few minutes before, there had only been three real things before me – the immensity of the night and space and nature, my own feebleness and anguish, and the near approach of death. Now it was as if something turned over, and the point of view altered abruptly. There was no sensible transition from one state of mind to the other. I was immediately the self of every day again – a decent, ordinary citizen. The silent common, the impulse of my flight, the starting flames, were as if they had been in a dream. I asked myself had these latter things indeed happened? I could not credit it.

I rose and walked unsteadily up the steep incline of the bridge. My mind was blank wonder. My muscles and nerves seemed drained of their strength. I dare say I staggered drunkenly. A head rose over the arch, and the figure of a workman carrying a basket appeared. Beside him ran a little boy. He passed me, wishing me good-night. I was minded to speak to him, but did not. I answered his greeting with a meaningless mumble and went on over the bridge.

Over the Maybury arch a train, a billowing tumult of white, firelit smoke, and a long caterpillar of lighted windows, went flying south – clatter, clatter, clap, rap, and it had gone. A dim group of people talked in the gate of one of the houses in the pretty little row of gables that was called Oriental Terrace. It was all so real and so familiar. And that behind me! It was frantic, fantastic! Such things, I told myself, could not be.

Perhaps I am a man of exceptional moods. I do not know how far my experience is common. At times I suffer from the strangest sense of detachment from myself and the world about me; I seem to watch it all from the outside, from somewhere inconceivably remote, out of time, out of space, out of the stress and tragedy of it all. This feeling was very strong upon me that night. Here was another side to my dream.

But the trouble was the blank incongruity of this serenity and the swift death flying yonder, not two miles away. There was a noise of business from the gasworks, and the electric lamps[26] were all alight. I stopped at the group of people.

'What news from the common?' said I.

There were two men and a woman at the gate.

'Eh?' said one of the men, turning.

'What news from the common?' I said.

' 'Ain't yer just *been* there?' asked the men.

'People seem fair silly about the common,' said the woman over the gate. 'What's it all abart?'

'Haven't you heard of the men from Mars?' said I; 'the creatures from Mars?'

'Quite enough,' said the woman over the gate. 'Thenks'; and all three of them laughed.

I felt foolish and angry. I tried and found I could not tell them what I had seen. They laughed again at my broken sentences.

'You'll hear more yet,' I said, and went on to my home.

I startled my wife at the doorway, so haggard was I. I went into the dining room, sat down, drank some wine, and so soon as I could collect myself sufficiently I told her the things I had seen. The dinner, which

was a cold one, had already been served, and remained neglected on the
table while I told my story.

'There is one thing,' I said, to allay the fears I had aroused; 'they are
the most sluggish things I ever saw crawl. They may keep the pit and
kill people who come near them, but they cannot get out of it . . . But
the horror of them!'

'Don't, dear!' said my wife, knitting her brows and putting her hand
on mine.

'Poor Ogilvy!' I said. 'To think he may be lying dead there!'

My wife at least did not find my experience incredible. When I saw
how deadly white her face was, I ceased abruptly.

'They may come here,' she said again and again.

I pressed her to take wine, and tried to reassure her.

'They can scarcely move,' I said.

I began to comfort her and myself by repeating all that Ogilvy had
told me of the impossibility of the Martians establishing themselves
on the earth. In particular I laid stress on the gravitational difficulty.
On the surface of the earth the force of gravity is three times what it
is on the surface of Mars. A Martian, therefore, would weigh three
times more than on Mars, albeit his muscular strength would be the
same. His own body would be a cope of lead to him. That, indeed, was
the general opinion. Both *The Times*[27] and the *Daily Telegraph*, for
instance, insisted on it the next morning, and both overlooked, just as
I did, two obvious modifying influences.

The atmosphere of the earth, we now know, contains far more oxygen
or far less argon (whichever way one likes to put it) than does Mars.
The invigorating influences of this excess of oxygen upon the Martians
indisputably did much to counterbalance the increased weight of their
bodies. And, in the second place, we all overlooked the fact that such
mechanical intelligence as the Martian possessed was quite able to
dispense with muscular exertion at a pinch.

But I did not consider these points at the time, and so my reasoning
was dead against the chances of the invaders. With wine and food, the
confidence of my own table, and the necessity of reassuring my wife, I
grew by insensible degrees courageous and secure.

'They have done a foolish thing,' said I, fingering my wineglass. 'They
are dangerous because, no doubt, they are mad with terror. Perhaps
they expected to find no living things – certainly no intelligent living
things.'

'A shell in the pit,' said I, 'if the worst comes to the worst, will kill
them all.'

The intense excitement of the events had no doubt left my perceptive powers in a state of erethism. I remember that dinner table with extraordinary vividness even now. My dear wife's sweet anxious face peering at me from under the pink lampshade, the white cloth with its silver and glass table furniture – for in those days even philosophical writers had many little luxuries – the crimson-purple wine in my glass, are photographically distinct. At the end of it I sat, tempering nuts with a cigarette, regretting Ogilvy's rashness, and denouncing the short-sighted timidity of the Martians.

So some respectable dodo in the Mauritius might have lorded it in his nest, and discussed the arrival of that shipful of pitiless sailors in want of animal food. 'We will peck them to death tomorrow, my dear.'

I did not know it, but that was the last civilised dinner I was to eat for very many strange and terrible days.

CHAPTER EIGHT

Friday Night

The most extraordinary thing to my mind, of all the strange and wonderful things that happened upon that Friday, was the dovetailing of the commonplace habits of our social order with the first beginnings of the series of events that was to topple that social order headlong. If on Friday night you had taken a pair of compasses and drawn a circle with a radius of five miles round the Woking sand pits, I doubt if you would have had one human being outside it, unless it were some relation of Stent or of the three or four cyclists or London people lying dead on the common, whose emotions or habits were at all affected by the new-comers. Many people had heard of the cylinder, of course, and talked about it in their leisure, but it certainly did not make the sensation that an ultimatum to Germany would have done.

In London that night poor Henderson's telegram describing the gradual unscrewing of the shot was judged to be a canard, and his evening paper, after wiring for authentication from him and receiving no reply – the man was killed – decided not to print a special edition.

Even within the five-mile circle the great majority of people were inert. I have already described the behaviour of the men and women to whom I spoke. All over the district people were dining and supping; working men were gardening after the labours of the day, children were being put to bed, young people were wandering through the lanes love-making, students sat over their books.

Maybe there was a murmur in the village streets, a novel and dominant topic in the public-houses, and here and there a messenger, or even an eye-witness of the later occurrences, caused a whirl of excitement, a shouting, and a running to and fro; but for the most part the daily routine of working, eating, drinking, sleeping, went on as it had done for countless years – as though no planet Mars existed in the sky. Even at Woking station and Horsell and Chobham that was the case.

In Woking junction, until a late hour, trains were stopping and going on, others were shunting on the sidings, passengers were alighting and waiting, and everything was proceeding in the most ordinary way. A boy from the town, trenching on Smith's monopoly,[28] was selling papers with the afternoon's news. The ringing impact of trucks, the sharp whistle of the engines from the junction, mingled with their shouts of 'Men from Mars!' Excited men came into the station about nine o'clock with incredible tidings, and caused no more disturbance than drunkards might have done. People rattling Londonwards peered into the darkness outside the carriage windows, and saw only a rare, flickering, vanishing spark dance up from the direction of Horsell, a red glow and a thin veil of smoke driving across the stars, and thought that nothing more serious than a heath fire was happening. It was only round the edge of the common that any disturbance was perceptible. There were half a dozen villas burning on the Woking border. There were lights in all the houses on the common side of the three villages, and the people there kept awake till dawn.

A curious crowd lingered restlessly, people coming and going but the crowd remaining, both on the Chobham and Horsell bridges. One or two adventurous souls, it was afterwards found, went into the darkness and crawled quite near the Martians; but they never returned, for now and again a light-ray, like the beam of a warship's searchlight, swept the common, and the Heat-Ray was ready to follow. Save for such, that big area of common was silent and desolate, and the charred bodies lay about on it all night under the stars, and all the next day. A noise of hammering from the pit was heard by many people.

So you have the state of things on Friday night. In the centre, sticking into the skin of our old planet Earth like a poisoned dart, was this cylinder. But the poison was scarcely working yet. Around it was a patch of silent common, smouldering in places, and with a few dark, dimly seen objects lying in contorted attitudes here and there. Here and there was a burning bush or tree. Beyond was a fringe of excitement, and farther than that fringe the inflammation had not crept as yet. In the rest of the world the stream of life still flowed as it had flowed for immemorial years. The fever of war that would presently clog vein and artery, deaden nerve and destroy brain, had still to develop.

All night long the Martians were hammering and stirring, sleepless, indefatigable, at work upon the machines they were making ready, and ever and again a puff of greenish-white smoke whirled up to the starlit sky.

About eleven a company of soldiers came through Horsell, and deployed along the edge of the common to form a cordon. Later a second company marched through Chobham to deploy on the north side of the common. Several officers from the Inkerman barracks had been on the common earlier in the day, and one, Major Eden, was reported to be missing. The colonel of the regiment came to the Chobham bridge and was busy questioning the crowd at midnight. The military authorities were certainly alive to the seriousness of the business. About eleven, the next morning's papers were able to say, a squadron of hussars, two Maxims,[29] and about four hundred men of the Cardigan regiment[30] started from Aldershot.

A few seconds after midnight the crowd in the Chertsey road, Woking, saw a star fall from heaven into the pine woods to the north-west. It had a greenish colour, and caused a silent brightness like summer lightning. This was the second cylinder.

CHAPTER NINE

The Fighting Begins

Saturday lives in my memory as a day of suspense. It was a day of lassitude too, hot and close, with, I am told, a rapidly fluctuating barometer. I had slept but little, though my wife had succeeded in sleeping, and I rose early. I went into my garden before breakfast and stood listening, but towards the common there was nothing stirring but a lark.

The milkman came as usual. I heard the rattle of his chariot and I went round to the side gate to ask the latest news. He told me that during the night the Martians had been surrounded by troops, and that guns were expected. Then – a familiar, reassuring note – I heard a train running towards Woking.

'They aren't to be killed,' said the milkman, 'if that can possibly be avoided.'

I saw my neighbour gardening, chatted with him for a time, and then strolled in to breakfast. It was a most unexceptional morning. My neighbour was of opinion that the troops would be able to capture or to destroy the Martians during the day.

'It's a pity they make themselves so unapproachable,' he said. 'It would be curious to know how they live on another planet; we might learn a thing or two.'

He came up to the fence and extended a handful of strawberries, for his gardening was as generous as it was enthusiastic. At the same time he told me of the burning of the pine woods about the Byfleet Golf Links.

'They say,' said he, 'that there's another of those blessed things fallen there – number two. But one's enough, surely. This lot'll cost the insurance people a pretty penny before everything's settled.' He laughed with an air of the greatest good humour as he said this. The woods, he said, were still burning, and pointed out a haze of smoke to me. 'They will be hot under foot for days, on account of the thick soil of pine needles and turf,' he said, and then grew serious over 'poor Ogilvy'.

After breakfast, instead of working, I decided to walk down towards the common. Under the railway bridge I found a group of soldiers – sappers, I think, men in small round caps, dirty red jackets unbuttoned, and showing their blue shirts, dark trousers, and boots coming to the calf. They told me no one was allowed over the canal, and, looking along the road towards the bridge, I saw one of the Cardigan men standing sentinel there. I talked with these soldiers for a time; I told them of my sight of the Martians on the previous evening. None of them had seen the Martians, and they had but the vaguest ideas of them, so that they plied me with questions. They said that they did not know who had authorised the movements of the troops; their idea was that a dispute had arisen at the Horse Guards.[31] The ordinary sapper is a great deal better educated than the common soldier, and they discussed the peculiar conditions of the possible fight with some acuteness. I described the Heat-Ray to them, and they began to argue among themselves.

'Crawl up under cover and rush 'em, say I,' said one.

'Get aht!' said another. 'What's cover against this 'ere 'eat? Sticks to cook yer! What we got to do is to go as near as the ground'll let us, and then drive a trench.'

'Blow yer trenches! You always want trenches; you ought to ha' been born a rabbit, Snippy.'

' 'Ain't they got any necks, then?' said a third, abruptly – a little, contemplative, dark man, smoking a pipe.

I repeated my description.

'Octopuses,' said he, 'that's what I calls 'em. Talk about fishers of men[32] – fighters of fish it is this time!'

'It ain't no murder killing beasts like that,' said the first speaker.

'Why not shell the darned things strite off and finish 'em?' said the little dark man. 'You carn tell what they might do.'

'Where's your shells?' said the first speaker. 'There ain't no time. Do it in a rush, that's my tip, and do it at once.'

So they discussed it. After a while I left them, and went on to the railway station to get as many morning papers as I could.

But I will not weary the reader with a description of that long morning and of the longer afternoon. I did not succeed in getting a glimpse of the common, for even Horsell and Chobham church towers were in the hands of the military authorities. The soldiers I addressed didn't know anything; the officers were mysterious as well as busy. I found people in the town quite secure again in the presence of the military, and I heard for the first time from Marshall, the tobacconist, that his son was among the dead on the common. The soldiers had made the people on the outskirts of Horsell lock up and leave their houses.

I got back to lunch about two, very tired for, as I have said, the day was extremely hot and dull; and in order to refresh myself I took a cold bath in the afternoon. About half-past four I went up to the railway station to get an evening paper, for the morning papers had contained only a very inaccurate description of the killing of Stent, Henderson, Ogilvy, and the others. But there was little I didn't know. The Martians did not show an inch of themselves. They seemed busy in their pit, and there was a sound of hammering and an almost continuous streamer of smoke. Apparently they were busy getting ready for a struggle. 'Fresh attempts have been made to signal, but without success,' was the stereo-typed formula of the papers. A sapper told me it was done by a man in a ditch with a flag on a long pole. The Martians took as much notice of such advances as we should of the lowing of a cow.

I must confess the sight of all this armament, all this preparation, greatly excited me. My imagination became belligerent, and defeated the invaders in a dozen striking ways; something of my schoolboy dreams of battle and heroism came back. It hardly seemed a fair fight to me at that time. They seemed very helpless in that pit of theirs.

About three o'clock there began the thud of a gun at measured intervals from Chertsey or Addlestone. I learned that the smouldering pine wood into which the second cylinder had fallen was being shelled, in the hope of destroying that object before it opened. It was only about five, however, that a field gun reached Chobham for use against the first body of Martians.

About six in the evening, as I sat at tea with my wife in the summer-house talking vigorously about the battle that was lowering upon us, I heard a muffled detonation from the common, and immediately after a gust of firing. Close on the heels of that came a violent rattling crash, quite close to us, that shook the ground; and, starting out upon the lawn, I saw the tops of the trees about the Oriental Colleg[33]e burst into smoky red flame, and the tower of the little church beside it slide down into ruin. The pinnacle of the mosque had vanished, and the roof line of the college itself looked as if a hundred-ton gun had been at work upon it. One of our chimneys cracked as if a shot had hit it, flew, and a piece of it came clattering down the tiles and made a heap of broken red fragments upon the flower bed by my study window.

I and my wife stood amazed. Then I realised that the crest of Maybury Hill must be within range of the Martians' Heat-Ray now that the college was cleared out of the way.

At that I gripped my wife's arm, and without ceremony ran her out into the road. Then I fetched out the servant, telling her I would go upstairs myself for the box she was clamouring for.

'We can't possibly stay here,' I said; and as I spoke the firing reopened for a moment upon the common.

'But where are we to go?' said my wife in terror.

I thought perplexed. Then I remembered her cousins at Leatherhead.

'Leatherhead!' I shouted above the sudden noise.

She looked away from me downhill. The people were coming out of their houses, astonished.

'How are we to get to Leatherhead?' she said.

Down the hill I saw a bevy of hussars ride under the railway bridge; three galloped through the open gates of the Oriental College; two others dismounted, and began running from house to house. The sun, shining through the smoke that drove up from the tops of the trees, seemed blood red, and threw an unfamiliar lurid light upon everything.

'Stop here,' said I; 'you are safe here'; and I started off at once for the Spotted Dog, for I knew the landlord had a horse and dogcart.[34] I ran, for I perceived that in a moment everyone upon this side of the hill would be moving. I found him in his bar, quite unaware of what was going on behind his house. A man stood with his back to me, talking to him.

'I must have a pound,' said the landlord, 'and I've no one to drive it.'

'I'll give you two,' said I, over the stranger's shoulder.

'What for?'

'And I'll bring it back by midnight,' I said.

'Lord!' said the landlord; 'what's the hurry? I'm selling my bit of a pig. Two pounds, and you bring it back? What's going on now?'

I explained hastily that I had to leave my home, and so secured the dog cart. At the time it did not seem to me nearly so urgent that the landlord should leave his. I took care to have the cart there and then, drove it off down the road, and, leaving it in charge of my wife and servant, rushed into my house and packed a few valuables, such plate as we had, and so forth. The beech trees below the house were burning while I did this, and the palings up the road glowed red. While I was occupied in this way, one of the dismounted hussars came running up. He was going from house to house, warning people to leave. He was going on as I came out of my front door, lugging my treasures, done up in a tablecloth. I shouted after him: 'What news?'

He turned, stared, bawled something about 'crawling out in a thing like a dish cover', and ran on to the gate of the house at the crest. A sudden whirl of black smoke driving across the road hid him for a moment. I ran to my neighbour's door and rapped to satisfy myself of what I already knew, that his wife had gone to London with him and had locked up their house. I went in again, according to my promise, to get my servant's box, lugged it out, clapped it beside her on the tail of the dog cart, and then caught the reins and jumped up into the driver's seat beside my wife. In another moment we were clear of the smoke and noise, and spanking down the opposite slope of Maybury Hill towards Old Woking.

In front was a quiet sunny landscape, a wheat field ahead on either side of the road, and the Maybury Inn with its swinging sign. I saw the doctor's cart ahead of me. At the bottom of the hill I turned my head to look at the hillside I was leaving. Thick streamers of black smoke shot with threads of red fire were driving up into the still air, and throwing dark shadows upon the green treetops eastward. The smoke already extended far away to the east and west – to the Byfleet pine woods eastward, and to Woking on the west. The road was dotted with people running towards us. And very faint now, but very distinct through the hot, quiet air, one heard the whirr of a machine-gun that was presently stilled, and an intermittent cracking of rifles. Apparently the Martians were setting fire to everything within range of their Heat-Ray.

I am not an expert driver, and I had immediately to turn my attention to the horse. When I looked back again the second hill had hidden the black smoke. I slashed the horse with the whip, and gave him a loose rein until Woking and Send lay between us and that quivering tumult. I overtook and passed the doctor between Woking and Send.

CHAPTER TEN

In the Storm

Leatherhead is about twelve miles from Maybury Hill. The scent of hay was in the air through the lush meadows beyond Pyrford, and the hedges on either side were sweet and gay with multitudes of dog-roses. The heavy firing that had broken out while we were driving down Maybury Hill ceased as abruptly as it began, leaving the evening very peaceful and still. We got to Leatherhead without misadventure about nine o'clock, and the horse had an hour's rest while I took supper with my cousins and commended my wife to their care.

My wife was curiously silent throughout the drive, and seemed oppressed with forebodings of evil. I talked to her reassuringly, pointing out that the Martians were tied to the pit by sheer heaviness, and at the utmost could but crawl a little out of it; but she answered only in monosyllables. Had it not been for my promise to the innkeeper, she would, I think, have urged me to stay in Leatherhead that night. Would that I had! Her face, I remember, was very white as we parted.

For my own part, I had been feverishly excited all day. Something very like the war fever that occasionally runs through a civilised community had got into my blood, and in my heart I was not so very sorry that I had to return to Maybury that night. I was even afraid that that last fusillade I had heard might mean the extermination of our invaders from Mars. I can best express my state of mind by saying that I wanted to be in at the death.

It was nearly eleven when I started to return. The night was unexpectedly dark; to me, walking out of the lighted passage of my cousins' house, it seemed indeed black, and it was as hot and close as the day. Overhead the clouds were driving fast, albeit not a breath stirred the shrubs about us. My cousins' man lit both lamps. Happily, I knew the road intimately. My wife stood in the light of the doorway, and watched me until I jumped up into the dog cart. Then abruptly she turned and went in, leaving my cousins side by side wishing me good hap.

I was a little depressed at first with the contagion of my wife's fears, but very soon my thoughts reverted to the Martians. At that time I was absolutely in the dark as to the course of the evening's fighting. I did not know even the circumstances that had precipitated the conflict. As I came through Ockham (for that was the way I returned, and not through Send and Old Woking) I saw along the western horizon a blood-red glow, which as I drew nearer, crept slowly up the sky. The driving clouds of the gathering thunderstorm mingled there with masses of black and red smoke.

Ripley Street was deserted, and except for a lighted window or so the village showed not a sign of life; but I narrowly escaped an accident at the corner of the road to Pyrford, where a knot of people stood with their backs to me. They said nothing to me as I passed. I do not know what they knew of the things happening beyond the hill, nor do I know if the silent houses I passed on my way were sleeping securely, or deserted and empty, or harassed and watching against the terror of the night.

From Ripley until I came through Pyrford I was in the valley of the Wey, and the red glare was hidden from me. As I ascended the little hill beyond Pyrford Church the glare came into view again, and the trees about me shivered with the first intimation of the storm that was upon me. Then I heard midnight pealing out from Pyrford Church behind me, and then came the silhouette of Maybury Hill, with its treetops and roofs black and sharp against the red.

Even as I beheld this a lurid green glare lit the road about me and showed the distant woods towards Addlestone. I felt a tug at the reins. I saw that the driving clouds had been pierced as it were by a thread of green fire, suddenly lighting their confusion and falling into the field to my left. It was the third falling star!

Close on its apparition, and blindingly violet by contrast, danced out the first lightning of the gathering storm, and the thunder burst like a rocket overhead. The horse took the bit between his teeth and bolted.

A moderate incline runs towards the foot of Maybury Hill, and down this we clattered. Once the lightning had begun, it went on in as rapid a succession of flashes as I have ever seen. The thunderclaps, treading one on the heels of another and with a strange crackling accompaniment, sounded more like the working of a gigantic electric machine than the usual detonating reverberations. The flickering light was blinding and confusing, and a thin hail smote gustily at my face as I drove down the slope.

At first I regarded little but the road before me, and then abruptly my attention was arrested by something that was moving rapidly down the opposite slope of Maybury Hill. At first I took it for the wet roof of a house, but one flash following another showed it to be in swift rolling movement. It was an elusive vision – a moment of bewildering darkness, and then, in a flash like daylight, the red masses of the Orphanage near the crest of the hill, the green tops of the pine trees, and this problematical object came out clear and sharp and bright.

And this Thing I saw! How can I describe it? A monstrous tripod, higher than many houses, striding over the young pine trees, and smashing them aside in its career; a walking engine of glittering metal, striding now across the heather; articulate ropes of steel dangling from it, and the clattering tumult of its passage mingling with the riot of the thunder. A flash, and it came out vividly, heeling over one way with two feet in the air, to vanish and reappear almost instantly as it seemed, with the next flash, a hundred yards nearer. Can you imagine a milking stool tilted and bowled violently along the ground? That was the impression those instant flashes gave. But instead of a milking stool imagine it a great body of machinery on a tripod stand.

Then suddenly the trees in the pine wood ahead of me were parted, as brittle reeds are parted by a man thrusting through them; they were snapped off and driven headlong, and a second huge tripod appeared, rushing, as it seemed, headlong towards me. And I was galloping hard to meet it! At the sight of the second monster my nerve went altogether. Not stopping to look again, I wrenched the horse's head hard round to the right and in another moment the dog cart had heeled over upon the horse; the shafts smashed noisily, and I was flung sideways and fell heavily into a shallow pool of water.

I crawled out almost immediately, and crouched, my feet still in the water, under a clump of furze. The horse lay motionless (his neck was broken, poor brute!) and by the lightning flashes I saw the black bulk of the overturned dog cart and the silhouette of the wheel still spinning slowly. In another moment the colossal mechanism went striding by me, and passed uphill towards Pyrford.

Seen nearer, the Thing was incredibly strange, for it was no mere insensate machine driving on its way. Machine it was, with a ringing metallic pace, and long, flexible, glittering tentacles (one of which gripped a young pine tree) swinging and rattling about its strange body. It picked its road as it went striding along, and the brazen hood that surmounted it moved to and fro with the inevitable suggestion of a head looking about. Behind the main body was a huge mass of white metal like a gigantic fisherman's basket, and puffs of green smoke squirted out from the joints of the limbs as the monster swept by me. And in an instant it was gone.

So much I saw then, all vaguely for the flickering of the lightning, in blinding highlights and dense black shadows.

As it passed it set up an exultant deafening howl that drowned the thunder – 'Aloo! Aloo!' – and in another minute it was with its companion, half a mile away, stooping over something in the field. I have no doubt this Thing in the field was the third of the ten cylinders they had fired at us from Mars.

For some minutes I lay there in the rain and darkness watching, by the intermittent light, these monstrous beings of metal moving about in the distance over the hedge tops. A thin hail was now beginning, and as it came and went their figures grew misty and then flashed into clearness again. Now and then came a gap in the lightning, and the night swallowed them up.

I was soaked with hail above and puddle water below. It was some time before my blank astonishment would let me struggle up the bank to a drier position, or think at all of my imminent peril.

Not far from me was a little one-roomed squatter's hut of wood, surrounded by a patch of potato garden. I struggled to my feet at last, and, crouching and making use of every chance of cover, I made a run for this. I hammered at the door, but I could not make the people hear (if there were any people inside), and after a time I desisted, and, availing myself of a ditch for the greater part of the way, succeeded in crawling, unobserved by these monstrous machines, into the pine woods towards Maybury.

Under cover of this I pushed on, wet and shivering now, towards my own house. I walked among the trees trying to find the footpath. It was very dark indeed in the wood, for the lightning was now becoming infrequent, and the hail, which was pouring down in a torrent, fell in columns through the gaps in the heavy foliage.

If I had fully realised the meaning of all the things I had seen I should have immediately worked my way round through Byfleet to Street Cobham, and so gone back to rejoin my wife at Leatherhead. But that night the strangeness of things about me, and my physical wretchedness, prevented me, for I was bruised, weary, wet to the skin, deafened and blinded by the storm.

I had a vague idea of going on to my own house, and that was as much motive as I had. I staggered through the trees, fell into a ditch and bruised my knees against a plank, and finally splashed out into the lane that ran down from the College Arms. I say splashed, for the storm water was sweeping the sand down the hill in a muddy torrent. There in the darkness a man blundered into me and sent me reeling back.

He gave a cry of terror, sprang sideways, and rushed on before I could gather my wits sufficiently to speak to him. So heavy was the stress of the storm just at this place that I had the hardest task to win my way up the hill. I went close up to the fence on the left and worked my way along its palings.

Near the top I stumbled upon something soft, and, by a flash of lightning, saw between my feet a heap of black broadcloth and a pair of boots. Before I could distinguish clearly how the man lay, the flicker of light had passed. I stood over him waiting for the next flash. When it came, I saw that he was a sturdy man, cheaply but not shabbily dressed; his head was bent under his body, and he lay crumpled up close to the fence, as though he had been flung violently against it.

Overcoming the repugnance natural to one who had never before touched a dead body, I stooped and turned him over to feel for his heart. He was quite dead. Apparently his neck had been broken. The lightning flashed for a third time, and his face leaped upon me. I sprang to my feet. It was the landlord of the Spotted Dog, whose conveyance I had taken.

I stepped over him gingerly and pushed on up the hill. I made my way by the police station and the College Arms towards my own house. Nothing was burning on the hillside, though from the common there still came a red glare and a rolling tumult of ruddy smoke beating up against the drenching hail. So far as I could see by the flashes, the houses about me were mostly uninjured. By the College Arms a dark heap lay in the road.

Down the road towards Maybury Bridge there were voices and the sound of feet, but I had not the courage to shout or to go to them. I let myself in with my latchkey, closed, locked and bolted the door, staggered to the foot of the staircase, and sat down. My imagination was full of those striding metallic monsters, and of the dead body smashed against the fence.

I crouched at the foot of the staircase with my back to the wall, shivering violently.

CHAPTER ELEVEN

At the Window

I have already said that my storms of emotion have a trick of exhausting themselves. After a time I discovered that I was cold and wet, and with little pools of water about me on the stair carpet. I got up almost mechanically, went into the dining room and drank some whisky, and then I was moved to change my clothes.

After I had done that I went upstairs to my study, but why I did so I do not know. The window of my study looks over the trees and the railway towards Horsell Common. In the hurry of our departure this window had been left open. The passage was dark, and, by contrast with the picture the window frame enclosed, the side of the room seemed impenetrably dark. I stopped short in the doorway.

The thunderstorm had passed. The towers of the Oriental College and the pine trees about it had gone, and very far away, lit by a vivid red glare, the common about the sand pits was visible. Across the light huge black shapes, grotesque and strange, moved busily to and fro.

It seemed indeed as if the whole country in that direction was on fire – a broad hillside set with minute tongues of flame, swaying and writhing with the gusts of the dying storm, and throwing a red reflection upon the cloud-scud above. Every now and then a haze of smoke from some nearer conflagration drove across the window and hid the Martian shapes. I could not see what they were doing, nor the clear form of them, nor recognise the black objects they were busied upon. Neither could I see the nearer fire, though the reflections of it danced on the wall and ceiling of the study. A sharp, resinous tang of burning was in the air.

I closed the door noiselessly and crept towards the window. As I did so, the view opened out until, on the one hand, it reached to the houses about Woking station, and on the other to the charred and blackened pine woods of Byfleet. There was a light down below the hill, on the railway, near the arch, and several of the houses along the Maybury road and the streets near the station were glowing ruins. The light upon the railway puzzled me at first; there were a black heap and a vivid glare, and to the right of that a row of yellow oblongs. Then I perceived this was a wrecked train, the fore part smashed and on fire, the hinder carriages still upon the rails.

Between these three main centres of light – the houses, the train, and the burning county towards Chobham – stretched irregular patches of dark country, broken here and there by intervals of dimly glowing and smoking ground. It was the strangest spectacle, that black expanse set with fire. It reminded me, more than anything else, of the Potteries[35] at night. At first I could distinguish no people at all, though I peered intently for them. Later I saw against the light of Woking station a number of black figures hurrying one after the other across the line.

And this was the little world in which I had been living securely for years, this fiery chaos! What had happened in the last seven hours I still did not know; nor did I know, though I was beginning to guess, the relation between these mechanical colossi and the sluggish lumps I had seen disgorged from the cylinder. With a queer feeling of impersonal interest I turned my desk chair to the window, sat down, and stared at the blackened country, and particularly at the three gigantic black things that were going to and fro in the glare about the sand pits.

They seemed amazingly busy. I began to ask myself what they could be. Were they intelligent mechanisms? Such a thing I felt was impossible. Or did a Martian sit within each, ruling, directing, using, much as a man's brain sits and rules in his body? I began to compare the things to human machines, to ask myself for the first time in my life how an ironclad[36] or a steam engine would seem to an intelligent lower animal.

The storm had left the sky clear, and over the smoke of the burning land the little fading pinpoint of Mars was dropping into the west, when a soldier came into my garden. I heard a slight scraping at the fence, and rousing myself from the lethargy that had fallen upon me, I looked down and saw him dimly, clambering over the palings. At the sight of another human being my torpor passed, and I leaned out of the window eagerly.

'Hist!' said I, in a whisper.

He stopped astride of the fence in doubt. Then he came over and across the lawn to the corner of the house. He bent down and stepped softly.

'Who's there?' he said, also whispering, standing under the window and peering up.

'Where are you going?' I asked.

'God knows.'

'Are you trying to hide?'

'That's it.'

'Come into the house,' I said.

I went down, unfastened the door, and let him in, and locked the door again. I could not see his face. He was hatless, and his coat was unbuttoned.

'My God!' he said, as I drew him in.

'What has happened?' I asked.

'What hasn't?' In the obscurity I could see he made a gesture of despair. 'They wiped us out – simply wiped us out,' he repeated again and again.

He followed me, almost mechanically, into the dining room.

'Take some whisky,' I said, pouring out a stiff dose.

He drank it. Then abruptly he sat down before the table, put his head on his arms, and began to sob and weep like a little boy, in a perfect passion of emotion, while I, with a curious forgetfulness of my own recent despair, stood beside him, wondering.

It was a long time before he could steady his nerves to answer my questions, and then he answered perplexingly and brokenly. He was a driver in the artillery, and had only come into action about seven. At that time firing was going on across the common, and it was said the first party of Martians were crawling slowly towards their second cylinder under cover of a metal shield.

Later this shield staggered up on tripod legs and became the first of the fighting-machines I had seen. The gun he drove had been unlimbered near Horsell, in order to command the sand pits, and its arrival it was that had precipitated the action. As the limber gunners went to the rear, his horse trod in a rabbit hole and came down, throwing him into a depression of the ground. At the same moment the gun exploded behind him, the ammunition blew up, there was fire all about him, and he found himself lying under a heap of charred dead men and dead horses.

'I lay still,' he said, 'scared out of my wits, with the fore quarter of a horse atop of me. We'd been wiped out. And the smell – good God! Like burnt meat! I was hurt across the back by the fall of the horse, and there I had to lie until I felt better. Just like parade it had been a minute before – then stumble, bang, swish!

'Wiped out!' he said.

He had hid under the dead horse for a long time, peeping out furtively across the common. The Cardigan men had tried a rush, in skirmishing order, at the pit, simply to be swept out of existence. Then the monster had risen to its feet and had begun to walk leisurely to and fro across the common among the few fugitives, with its headlike hood turning about exactly like the head of a cowled human being. A kind of arm carried a complicated metallic case, about which green flashes scintillated, and out of the funnel of this there smoked the Heat-Ray.

In a few minutes there was, so far as the soldier could see, not a living thing left upon the common, and every bush and tree upon it that was not already a blackened skeleton was burning. The hussars had been on the road beyond the curvature of the ground, and he saw nothing of them. He heard the Martians rattle for a time and then become still. The giant saved Woking station and its cluster of houses until the last; then in a moment the Heat-Ray was brought to bear, and the town became a heap of fiery ruins. Then the Thing shut off the Heat-Ray, and turning its back upon the artilleryman, began to waddle away towards the smouldering pine woods that sheltered the second cylinder. As it did so a second glittering Titan built itself up out of the pit.

The second monster followed the first, and at that the artilleryman began to crawl very cautiously across the hot heather ash towards Horsell. He managed to get alive into the ditch by the side of the road, and so escaped to Woking. There his story became ejaculatory. The place was impassable. It seems there were a few people alive there, frantic for the most part and many burned and scalded. He was turned aside by the fire, and hid among some almost scorching heaps of broken wall as one of the Martian giants returned. He saw this one pursue a man, catch him up in one of its steely tentacles, and knock his head against the trunk of a pine tree. At last, after nightfall, the artilleryman made a rush for it and got over the railway embankment.

Since then he had been skulking along towards Maybury, in the hope of getting out of danger Londonward. People were hiding in trenches and cellars, and many of the survivors had made off towards Woking village and Send. He had been consumed with thirst until he found one of the water mains near the railway arch smashed, and the water bubbling out like a spring upon the road.

That was the story I got from him, bit by bit. He grew calmer telling me and trying to make me see the things he had seen. He had eaten no food since midday, he told me early in his narrative, and I found some mutton and bread in the pantry and brought it into the room. We lit no lamp for fear of attracting the Martians, and ever and again our hands would touch upon bread or meat. As he talked, things about us came darkly out of the darkness, and the trampled bushes and broken rose trees outside the window grew distinct. It would seem that a number of men or animals had rushed across the lawn. I began to see his face, blackened and haggard, as no doubt mine was also.

When we had finished eating we went softly upstairs to my study, and I looked again out of the open window. In one night the valley had become a valley of ashes.[37] The fires had dwindled now. Where flames had been there were now streamers of smoke; but the countless ruins of shattered and gutted houses and blasted and blackened trees that the night had hidden stood out now gaunt and terrible in the pitiless light of dawn.[38] Yet here and there some object had had the luck to escape – a white railway signal here, the end of a greenhouse there, white and fresh amid the wreckage. Never before in the history of warfare had destruction been so indiscriminate and so universal. And shining with the growing light of the east, three of the metallic giants stood about the pit, their cowls rotating as though they were surveying the desolation they had made.

It seemed to me that the pit had been enlarged, and ever and again puffs of vivid green vapour streamed up and out of it towards the brightening dawn – streamed up, whirled, broke, and vanished.

Beyond were the pillars of fire[39] about Chobham. They became pillars of bloodshot smoke at the first touch of day.

CHAPTER TWELVE

What I Saw of the Destruction of Weybridge and Shepperton

As the dawn grew brighter we withdrew from the window from which we had watched the Martians, and went very quietly downstairs.

The artilleryman agreed with me that the house was no place to stay in. He proposed, he said, to make his way Londonward, and thence rejoin his battery – No. 12, of the Horse Artillery. My plan was to return at once to Leatherhead; and so greatly had the strength of the Martians impressed me that I had determined to take my wife to Newhaven, and go with her out of the country forthwith. For I already perceived clearly that the country about London must inevitably be the scene of a disastrous struggle before such creatures as these could be destroyed.

Between us and Leatherhead, however, lay the third cylinder, with its guarding giants. Had I been alone, I think I should have taken my chance and struck across country. But the artilleryman dissuaded me: 'It's no kindness to the right sort of wife,' he said, 'to make her a widow'; and in the end I agreed to go with him, under cover of the woods, northward as far as Street Cobham before I parted with him. Thence I would make a big detour by Epsom to reach Leatherhead.

I should have started at once, but my companion had been in active service and he knew better than that. He made me ransack the house for a flask, which he filled with whisky; and we lined every available pocket with packets of biscuits and slices of meat. Then we crept out of the house, and ran as quickly as we could down the ill-made road by which I had come overnight. The houses seemed deserted. In the road lay a group of three charred bodies close together, struck dead by the Heat-Ray; and here and there were things that people had dropped – a clock, a slipper, a silver spoon, and the like poor valuables. At the corner turning up towards the post office a little cart, filled with boxes and furniture, and horseless, heeled over on a broken wheel. A cash box had been hastily smashed open and thrown under the debris.

Except the lodge at the Orphanage, which was still on fire, none of the houses had suffered very greatly here. The Heat-Ray had shaved the chimney tops and passed. Yet, save ourselves, there did not seem to be a living soul on Maybury Hill. The majority of the inhabitants had escaped, I suppose, by way of the Old Woking road – the road I had taken when I drove to Leatherhead – or they had hidden.

We went down the lane, by the body of the man in black, sodden now from the overnight hail, and broke into the woods at the foot of the hill. We pushed through these towards the railway without meeting a soul. The woods across the line were but the scarred and blackened ruins of woods; for the most part the trees had fallen, but a certain proportion still stood, dismal grey stems, with dark brown foliage instead of green.

On our side the fire had done no more than scorch the nearer trees; it had failed to secure its footing. In one place the woodmen had been at work on Saturday; trees, felled and freshly trimmed, lay in a clearing, with heaps of sawdust by the sawing-machine and its engine. Hard by was a temporary hut, deserted. There was not a breath of wind this morning, and everything was strangely still. Even the birds were hushed, and as we hurried along I and the artilleryman talked in whispers and looked now and again over our shoulders. Once or twice we stopped to listen.

After a time we drew near the road, and as we did so we heard the clatter of hoofs and saw through the tree stems three cavalry soldiers riding slowly towards Woking. We hailed them, and they halted while we hurried towards them. It was a lieutenant and a couple of privates of the 8th Hussars,[40] with a stand like a theodolite, which the artilleryman told me was a heliograph.

'You are the first men I've seen coming this way this morning,' said the lieutenant. 'What's brewing?'

His voice and face were eager. The men behind him stared curiously. The artilleryman jumped down the bank into the road and saluted.

'Gun destroyed last night, sir. Have been hiding. Trying to rejoin battery, sir. You'll come in sight of the Martians, I expect, about half a mile along this road.'

'What the dickens are they like?' asked the lieutenant.

'Giants in armour, sir. Hundred feet high. Three legs and a body like 'luminium, with a mighty great head in a hood, sir.'

'Get out!' said the lieutenant. 'What confounded nonsense!'

'You'll see, sir. They carry a kind of box, sir, that shoots fire and strikes you dead.'

'What d'ye mean – a gun?'

'No, sir,' and the artilleryman began a vivid account of the Heat-Ray. Halfway through, the lieutenant interrupted him and looked up at me. I was still standing on the bank by the side of the road.

'It's perfectly true,' I said.

'Well,' said the lieutenant, 'I suppose it's my business to see it too. Look here' – to the artilleryman – 'we're detailed here clearing people out of their houses. You'd better go along and report yourself to Brigadier-General Marvin, and tell him all you know. He's at Wey-bridge. Know the way?'

'I do,' I said; and he turned his horse southward again.

'Half a mile, you say?' said he.

'At most,' I answered, and pointed over the treetops southward. He thanked me and rode on, and we saw them no more.

Farther along we came upon a group of three women and two children in the road, busy clearing out a labourer's cottage. They had got hold of a little hand truck, and were piling it up with unclean-looking bundles and shabby furniture. They were all too assiduously engaged to talk to us as we passed.

By Byfleet station we emerged from the pine trees, and found the country calm and peaceful under the morning sunlight. We were far beyond the range of the Heat-Ray there, and had it not been for the silent desertion of some of the houses, the stirring movement of packing in others, and the knot of soldiers standing on the bridge over the railway and staring down the line towards Woking, the day would have seemed very like any other Sunday.

Several farm waggons and carts were moving creakily along the road to Addlestone, and suddenly through the gate of a field we saw, across a stretch of flat meadow, six twelve-pounders standing neatly at equal distances pointing towards Woking. The gunners stood by the guns waiting, and the ammunition waggons were at a businesslike distance. The men stood almost as if under inspection.

'That's good!' said I. 'They will get one fair shot, at any rate.'

The artilleryman hesitated at the gate.

'I shall go on,' he said.

Farther on towards Weybridge, just over the bridge, there were a number of men in white fatigue jackets throwing up a long rampart, and more guns behind.

'It's bows and arrows against the lightning, anyhow,' said the artillery-man. 'They 'aven't seen that fire-beam yet.'

The officers who were not actively engaged stood and stared over the treetops south-westward, and the men digging would stop every now and again to stare in the same direction.

Byfleet was in a tumult; people packing, and a score of hussars, some of them dismounted, some on horseback, were hunting them about. Three or four black government waggons, with crosses in white circles, and an old omnibus, among other vehicles, were being loaded in the village street. There were scores of people, most of them sufficiently sabbatical[41] to have assumed their best clothes. The soldiers were having the greatest difficulty in making them realise the gravity of their position. We saw one shrivelled old fellow with a huge box and a score or more of flower pots containing orchids, angrily expostulating with the corporal who would leave them behind. I stopped and gripped his arm.

'Do you know what's over there?' I said, pointing at the pine tops that hid the Martians.

'Eh?' said he, turning. 'I was explainin' these is vallyble.'

'Death!' I shouted. 'Death is coming! Death!' and leaving him to digest that if he could, I hurried on after the artilleryman. At the corner I looked back. The soldier had left him, and he was still standing by his box, with the pots of orchids on the lid of it, and staring vaguely over the trees.

No one in Weybridge could tell us where the headquarters were established; the whole place was in such confusion as I had never seen in any town before. Carts, carriages everywhere, the most astonishing miscellany of conveyances and horseflesh. The respectable inhabitants of the place, men in golf and boating costumes, wives prettily dressed, were packing, riverside loafers energetically helping, children excited, and, for the most part, highly delighted at this astonishing variation of their Sunday experiences. In the midst of it all the worthy vicar was very pluckily holding an early celebration, and his bell was jangling out above the excitement.

I and the artilleryman, seated on the step of the drinking fountain, made a very passable meal upon what we had brought with us. Patrols of soldiers – here no longer hussars, but grenadiers in white – were warning people to move now or to take refuge in their cellars as soon as the firing began. We saw as we crossed the railway bridge that a growing crowd of people had assembled in and about the railway station, and the swarming platform was piled with boxes and packages. The ordinary traffic had been stopped, I believe, in order to allow of the passage of troops and guns to Chertsey, and I have heard since that a savage struggle occurred for places in the special trains that were put on at a later hour.

We remained at Weybridge until midday, and at that hour we found ourselves at the place near Shepperton Lock where the Wey and Thames join. Part of the time we spent helping two old women to pack a little cart. The Wey has a treble mouth, and at this point boats are to be hired, and there was a ferry across the river. On the Shepperton side was an inn with a lawn, and beyond that the tower of Shepperton Church – it has been replaced by a spire – rose above the trees.

Here we found an excited and noisy crowd of fugitives. As yet the flight had not grown to a panic, but there were already far more people than all the boats going to and fro could enable to cross. People came panting along under heavy burdens; one husband and wife were even carrying a small outhouse door between them, with some of their household goods piled thereon. One man told us he meant to try to get away from Shepperton station.

There was a lot of shouting, and one man was even jesting. The idea people seemed to have here was that the Martians were simply formidable human beings, who might attack and sack the town, to be certainly destroyed in the end. Every now and then people would glance nervously across the Wey, at the meadows towards Chertsey, but everything over there was still.

Across the Thames, except just where the boats landed, everything was quiet, in vivid contrast with the Surrey side. The people who landed there from the boats went tramping off down the lane. The big ferryboat had just made a journey. Three or four soldiers stood on the lawn of the inn, staring and jesting at the fugitives, without offering to help. The inn was closed, as it was now within prohibited hours.

'What's that?' cried a boatman, and 'Shut up, you fool!' said a man near me to a yelping dog. Then the sound came again, this time from the direction of Chertsey, a muffled thud – the sound of a gun.

The fighting was beginning. Almost immediately unseen batteries across the river to our right, unseen because of the trees, took up the chorus, firing heavily one after the other. A woman screamed. Everyone stood arrested by the sudden stir of battle, near us and yet invisible to us. Nothing was to be seen save flat meadows, cows feeding unconcernedly for the most part, and silvery pollard willows motionless in the warm sunlight.

'The sojers'll stop 'em,' said a woman beside me, doubtfully. A haziness rose over the treetops.

Then suddenly we saw a rush of smoke far away up the river, a puff of smoke that jerked up into the air and hung; and forthwith the ground heaved underfoot and a heavy explosion shook the air, smashing two or three windows in the houses near, and leaving us astonished.

'Here they are!' shouted a man in a blue jersey. 'Yonder! D'yer see them? Yonder!'

Quickly, one after the other, one, two, three, four of the armoured Martians appeared, far away over the little trees, across the flat meadows that stretched towards Chertsey, and striding hurriedly towards the river. Little cowled figures they seemed at first, going with a rolling motion and as fast as flying birds.

Then, advancing obliquely towards us, came a fifth. Their armoured bodies glittered in the sun as they swept swiftly forward upon the guns, growing rapidly larger as they drew nearer. One on the extreme left, the remotest that is, flourished a huge case high in the air, and the ghostly, terrible Heat-Ray I had already seen on Friday night smote towards Chertsey, and struck the town.

At sight of these strange, swift, and terrible creatures the crowd near the water's edge seemed to me to be for a moment horror-struck. There was no screaming or shouting, but a silence. Then a hoarse murmur and a movement of feet – a splashing from the water. A man, too frightened to drop the portmanteau he carried on his shoulder, swung round and sent me staggering with a blow from the corner of his burden. A woman thrust at me with her hand and rushed past me. I turned with the rush of the people, but I was not too terrified for thought. The terrible Heat-Ray was in my mind. To get under water! That was it!

'Get under water!' I shouted, unheeded.

I faced about again, and rushed towards the approaching Martian, rushed right down the gravelly beach and headlong into the water. Others did the same. A boatload of people putting back came leaping out as I rushed past. The stones under my feet were muddy and slippery, and the river was so low that I ran perhaps twenty feet scarcely waist-deep. Then, as the Martian towered overhead scarcely a couple of hundred yards away, I flung myself forward under the surface. The splashes of the people in the boats leaping into the river sounded like thunderclaps in my ears. People were landing hastily on both sides of the river. But the Martian machine took no more notice for the moment of the people running this way and that than a man would of the confusion of ants in a nest against which his foot has kicked. When, half suffocated, I raised my head above water, the Martian's hood pointed at the batteries that were still firing across the river, and as it advanced it swung loose what must have been the generator of the Heat-Ray.

In another moment it was on the bank, and in a stride wading halfway across. The knees of its foremost legs bent at the farther bank, and in another moment it had raised itself to its full height again, close to the village of Shepperton. Forthwith the six guns which, unknown to anyone on the right bank, had been hidden behind the outskirts of that village, fired simultaneously. The sudden near concussion, the last close upon the first, made my heart jump. The monster was already raising the case generating the Heat-Ray as the first shell burst six yards above the hood.

I gave a cry of astonishment. I saw and thought nothing of the other four Martian monsters; my attention was riveted upon the nearer incident. Simultaneously two other shells burst in the air near the body as the hood twisted round in time to receive, but not in time to dodge, the fourth shell.

The shell burst clean in the face of the Thing. The hood bulged, flashed, was whirled off in a dozen tattered fragments of red flesh and glittering metal.

'Hit!' shouted I, with something between a scream and a cheer.

I heard answering shouts from the people in the water about me. I could have leaped out of the water with that momentary exultation.

The decapitated colossus reeled like a drunken giant; but it did not fall over. It recovered its balance by a miracle, and, no longer heeding its steps and with the camera that fired the Heat-Ray now rigidly upheld, it reeled swiftly upon Shepperton. The living intelligence, the Martian within the hood, was slain and splashed to the four winds of heaven, and the Thing was now but a mere intricate device of metal whirling to destruction. It drove along in a straight line, incapable of guidance. It struck the tower of Shepperton Church, smashing it down as the impact of a battering ram might have done, swerved aside, blundered on and collapsed with tremendous force into the river out of my sight.

A violent explosion shook the air, and a spout of water, steam, mud, and shattered metal shot far up into the sky. As the camera of the

Heat-Ray hit the water, the latter had immediately flashed into steam. In another moment a huge wave, like a muddy tidal bore but almost scaldingly hot, came sweeping round the bend upstream. I saw people struggling shorewards, and heard their screaming and shouting faintly above the seething and roar of the Martian's collapse.

For a moment I heeded nothing of the heat, forgot the patent need of self-preservation. I splashed through the tumultuous water, pushing aside a man in black to do so, until I could see round the bend. Half a dozen deserted boats pitched aimlessly upon the confusion of the waves. The fallen Martian came into sight downstream, lying across the river, and for the most part submerged.

Thick clouds of steam were pouring off the wreckage, and through the tumultuously whirling wisps I could see, intermittently and vaguely, the gigantic limbs churning the water and flinging a splash and spray of mud and froth into the air. The tentacles swayed and struck like living arms, and, save for the helpless purposelessness of these movements, it was as if some wounded thing were struggling for its life amid the waves. Enormous quantities of a ruddy-brown fluid were spurting up in noisy jets out of the machine.

My attention was diverted from this death flurry by a furious yelling, like that of the thing called a siren in our manufacturing towns. A man, knee-deep near the towing path, shouted inaudibly to me and pointed. Looking back, I saw the other Martians advancing with gigantic strides down the riverbank from the direction of Chertsey. The Shepperton guns spoke this time unavailingly.

At that I ducked at once under water, and, holding my breath until movement was an agony, blundered painfully ahead under the surface as long as I could. The water was in a tumult about me, and rapidly growing hotter.

When for a moment I raised my head to take breath and throw the hair and water from my eyes, the steam was rising in a whirling white fog that at first hid the Martians altogether. The noise was deafening. Then I saw them dimly, colossal figures of grey, magnified by the mist. They had passed by me, and two were stooping over the frothing, tumultuous ruins of their comrade.

The third and fourth stood beside him in the water, one perhaps two hundred yards from me, the other towards Laleham. The generators of the Heat-Rays waved high, and the hissing beams smote down this way and that.

The air was full of sound, a deafening and confusing conflict of noises – the clangorous din of the Martians, the crash of falling houses, the thud of trees, fences, sheds flashing into flame, and the crackling and roaring of fire. Dense black smoke was leaping up to mingle with the steam from the river, and as the Heat-Ray went to and fro over Weybridge its impact was marked by flashes of incandescent white, that gave place at once to a smoky dance of lurid flames. The nearer houses still stood intact, awaiting their fate, shadowy, faint and pallid in the steam, with the fire behind them going to and fro.

For a moment perhaps I stood there, breast-high in the almost boiling water, dumbfounded at my position, hopeless of escape. Through the reek I could see the people who had been with me in the river scrambling out of the water through the reeds, like little frogs hurrying through grass from the advance of a man, or running to and fro in utter dismay on the towing path.

Then suddenly the white flashes of the Heat-Ray came leaping towards me. The houses caved in as they dissolved at its touch, and darted out flames; the trees changed to fire with a roar. The Ray flickered up and down the towing path, licking off the people who ran this way and that, and came down to the water's edge not fifty yards from where I stood. It swept across the river to Shepperton, and the water in its track rose in a boiling weal crested with steam. I turned shoreward.

In another moment the huge wave, well-nigh at the boiling-point, had rushed upon me. I screamed aloud, and scalded, half blinded, agonised, I staggered through the leaping, hissing water towards the shore. Had my foot stumbled, it would have been the end. I fell helplessly, in full sight of the Martians, upon the broad, bare gravelly spit that runs down to mark the angle of the Wey and Thames. I expected nothing but death.

I have a dim memory of the foot of a Martian coming down within a score of yards of my head, driving straight into the loose gravel, whirling it this way and that and lifting again; of a long suspense, and then of the four carrying the debris of their comrade between them, now clear and then presently faint through a veil of smoke, receding interminably, as it seemed to me, across a vast space of river and meadow. And then, very slowly, I realised that by a miracle I had escaped.

CHAPTER THIRTEEN

How I Fell in with the Curate

After getting this sudden lesson in the power of terrestrial weapons, the Martians retreated to their original position upon Horsell Common; and in their haste, and encumbered with the debris of their smashed companion, they no doubt overlooked many such a stray and negligible victim as myself. Had they left their comrade and pushed on forthwith, there was nothing at that time between them and London but batteries of twelve-pounder guns, and they would certainly have reached the capital in advance of the tidings of their approach; as sudden, dreadful, and destructive their advent would have been as the earthquake that destroyed Lisbon[42] a century ago.

But they were in no hurry. Cylinder followed cylinder on its interplanetary flight; every twenty-four hours brought them reinforcement. And meanwhile the military and naval authorities, now fully alive to the tremendous power of their antagonists, worked with furious energy. Every minute a fresh gun came into position until, before twilight, every copse, every row of suburban villas on the hilly slopes about Kingston and Richmond, masked an expectant black muzzle. And through the charred and desolated area – perhaps twenty square miles altogether – that encircled the Martian encampment on Horsell Common, through charred and ruined villages among the green trees, through the blackened and smoking arcades that had been but a day ago pine spinneys, crawled the devoted scouts with the heliographs that were presently to warn the gunners of the Martian approach. But the Martians now understood our command of artillery and the danger of human proximity, and not a man ventured within a mile of either cylinder, save at the price of his life.

It would seem that these giants spent the earlier part of the afternoon in going to and fro, transferring everything from the second and third cylinders – the second in Addlestone Golf Links and the third at Pyrford – to their original pit on Horsell Common. Over that, above the blackened heather and ruined buildings that stretched far and wide, stood one as sentinel, while the rest abandoned their vast fighting-machines and descended into the pit. They were hard at work there far into the night, and the towering pillar of dense green smoke that rose therefrom could be seen from the hills about Merrow, and even, it is said, from Banstead and Epsom Downs.

And while the Martians behind me were thus preparing for their next sally, and in front of me Humanity gathered for the battle, I made my way with infinite pains and labour from the fire and smoke of burning Weybridge towards London.

I saw an abandoned boat, very small and remote, drifting downstream; and throwing off the most of my sodden clothes, I went after it, gained it, and so escaped out of that destruction. There were no oars in the boat, but I contrived to paddle, as well as my parboiled hands would allow, down the river towards Halliford and Walton, going very tediously and continually looking behind me, as you may well understand. I followed the river, because I considered that the water gave me my best chance of escape should these giants return.

The hot water from the Martian's overthrow drifted downstream with me, so that for the best part of a mile I could see little of either bank. Once, however, I made out a string of black figures hurrying across the meadows from the direction of Weybridge. Halliford, it seemed, was deserted, and several of the houses facing the river were on fire. It was strange to see the place quite tranquil, quite desolate under the hot blue sky, with the smoke and little threads of flame going straight up into the heat of the afternoon. Never before had I seen houses burning without the accompaniment of an obstructive crowd. A little farther on the dry reeds up the bank were smoking and glowing, and a line of fire inland was marching steadily across a late field of hay.

For a long time I drifted, so painful and weary was I after the violence I had been through, and so intense the heat upon the water. Then my fears got the better of me again, and I resumed my paddling. The sun scorched my bare back. At last, as the bridge at Walton was coming into sight round the bend, my fever and faintness overcame my fears, and I landed on the Middlesex bank and lay down, deadly sick, amid the long grass. I suppose the time was then about four or five o'clock. I got up presently, walked perhaps half a mile without meeting a soul, and then lay down again in the shadow of a hedge. I seem to remember talking, wanderingly, to myself during that last spurt. I was also very thirsty, and bitterly regretful I had drunk no more water. It is a curious thing that I felt angry with my wife; I cannot account for it, but my impotent desire to reach Leatherhead worried me excessively.

I do not clearly remember the arrival of the curate, so that probably I dozed. I became aware of him as a seated figure in soot-smudged shirt sleeves, and with his upturned, clean-shaven face staring at a faint flickering that danced over the sky. The sky was what is called a mackerel sky – rows and rows of faint down-plumes of cloud, just tinted with the midsummer sunset.

I sat up, and at the rustle of my motion he looked at me quickly.

'Have you any water?' I asked abruptly.

He shook his head.

'You have been asking for water for the last hour,' he said.

For a moment we were silent, taking stock of each other. I dare say he found me a strange enough figure, naked, save for my water-soaked trousers and socks, scalded, and my face and shoulders blackened by the smoke. His face was a fair weakness, his chin retreated, and his hair lay in crisp, almost flaxen curls on his low forehead; his eyes were rather large, pale blue, and blankly staring. He spoke abruptly, looking vacantly away from me.

'What does it mean?' he said. 'What do these things mean?'

I stared at him and made no answer.

He extended a thin white hand and spoke in almost a complaining tone.

'Why are these things permitted? What sins have we done? The morning service was over, I was walking through the roads to clear my brain for the afternoon, and then – fire, earthquake, death! As if it were Sodom and Gomorrah![43] All our work undone, all the work – What are these Martians?'

'What are we?' I answered, clearing my throat.

He gripped his knees and turned to look at me again. For half a minute, perhaps, he stared silently.

'I was walking through the roads to clear my brain,' he said. 'And suddenly – fire, earthquake, death!'

He relapsed into silence, with his chin now sunken almost to his knees.

Presently he began waving his hand.

'All the work – all the Sunday schools – What have we done – what has Weybridge done? Everything gone – everything destroyed. The church! We rebuilt it only three years ago. Gone! Swept out of existence! Why?'

Another pause, and he broke out again like one demented.

'The smoke of her burning goeth up for ever and ever!'[44] he shouted.

His eyes flamed, and he pointed a lean finger in the direction of Weybridge.

By this time I was beginning to take his measure. The tremendous tragedy in which he had been involved – it was evident he was a fugitive from Weybridge – had driven him to the very verge of his reason.

'Are we far from Sunbury?' I said, in a matter-of-fact tone.

'What are we to do?' he asked. 'Are these creatures everywhere? Has the earth been given over to them?'

'Are we far from Sunbury?'

'Only this morning I officiated at early celebration – '

'Things have changed,' I said, quietly. 'You must keep your head. There is still hope.'

'Hope!'

'Yes. Plentiful hope – for all this destruction!'

I began to explain my view of our position. He listened at first, but as I went on the interest dawning in his eyes gave place to their former stare, and his regard wandered from me.

'This must be the beginning of the end,' he said, interrupting me. 'The end! The great and terrible day of the Lord! When men shall call upon the mountains and the rocks to fall upon them and hide them – hide them from the face of Him that sitteth upon the throne!'[45]

I began to understand the position. I ceased my laboured reasoning, struggled to my feet, and, standing over him, laid my hand on his shoulder.

'Be a man!' said I. 'You are scared out of your wits! What good is religion if it collapses under calamity? Think of what earthquakes and floods, wars and volcanoes, have done before to men! Did you think God had exempted Weybridge? He is not an insurance agent.'

For a time he sat in blank silence.

'But how can we escape?' he asked, suddenly. 'They are invulnerable, they are pitiless.'

'Neither the one nor, perhaps, the other,' I answered. 'And the mightier they are the more sane and wary should we be. One of them was killed yonder not three hours ago.'

'Killed!' he said, staring about him. 'How can God's ministers be killed?'

'I saw it happen.' I proceeded to tell him. 'We have chanced to come in for the thick of it,' said I, 'and that is all.'

'What is that flicker in the sky?' he asked abruptly.

I told him it was the heliograph signalling – that it was the sign of human help and effort in the sky.

'We are in the midst of it,' I said, 'quiet as it is. That flicker in the sky tells of the gathering storm. Yonder, I take it, are the Martians, and Londonward, where those hills rise about Richmond and Kingston and the trees give cover, earthworks are being thrown up and guns are being placed. Presently the Martians will be coming this way again.'

And even as I spoke he sprang to his feet and stopped me by a gesture. 'Listen!' he said.

From beyond the low hills across the water came the dull resonance of distant guns and a remote weird crying. Then everything was still. A cockchafer came droning over the hedge and past us. High in the west the crescent moon hung faint and pale above the smoke of Weybridge and Shepperton and the hot, still splendour of the sunset.

'We had better follow this path,' I said, 'northward.'

CHAPTER FOURTEEN

In London

My younger brother was in London when the Martians fell on Woking. He was a medical student working for an imminent examination, and he heard nothing of the arrival until Saturday morning. The morning papers on Saturday contained, in addition to lengthy special articles on the planet Mars, on life in the planets, and so forth, a brief and vaguely worded telegram, all the more striking for its brevity.

The Martians, alarmed by the approach of a crowd, had killed a number of people with a quick-firing gun, so the story ran. The telegram concluded with the words: 'Formidable as they seem to be, the Martians have not moved from the pit into which they have fallen, and, indeed, seem incapable of doing so. Probably this is due to the relative strength of the earth's gravitational energy.'[46] On that last text their leader-writer expanded very comfortingly.

Of course all the students in the crammer's biology class, to which my brother went that day, were intensely interested, but there were no signs of any unusual excitement in the streets. The afternoon papers puffed scraps of news under big headlines. They had nothing to tell beyond the movements of troops about the common, and the burning of the pine woods between Woking and Weybridge, until eight. Then the *St James's Gazette*,[47] in an extra-special edition, announced the bare fact of the interruption of telegraphic communication. This was thought to be due to the falling of burning pine trees across the line. Nothing more of the fighting was known that night, the night of my drive to Leatherhead and back.

My brother felt no anxiety about us, as he knew from the description in the papers that the cylinder was a good two miles from my house.

He made up his mind to run down that night to me, in order, as he says, to see the Things before they were killed. He dispatched a telegram, which never reached me, about four o'clock, and spent the evening at a music hall.

In London, also, on Saturday night there was a thunderstorm, and my brother reached Waterloo in a cab. On the platform from which the midnight train usually starts he learned, after some waiting, that an accident prevented trains from reaching Woking that night. The nature of the accident he could not ascertain; indeed, the railway authorities did not clearly know at that time. There was very little excitement in the station, as the officials, failing to realise that anything further than a breakdown between Byfleet and Woking junction had occurred, were running the theatre trains[48] which usually passed through Woking round by Virginia Water or Guildford. They were busy making the necessary arrangements to alter the route of the Southampton and Portsmouth Sunday League excursions.[49] A nocturnal newspaper reporter, mistaking my brother for the traffic manager, to whom he bears a slight resemblance, waylaid and tried to interview him. Few people, excepting the railway officials, connected the breakdown with the Martians.

I have read, in another account of these events, that on Sunday morning 'all London was electrified by the news from Woking'. As a matter of fact, there was nothing to justify that very extravagant phrase. Plenty of Londoners did not hear of the Martians until the panic of Monday morning. Those who did took some time to realise all that the hastily worded telegrams in the Sunday papers conveyed. The majority of people in London do not read Sunday papers.

The habit of personal security, moreover, is so deeply fixed in the Londoner's mind, and startling intelligence so much a matter of course in the papers, that they could read without any personal tremors: 'About seven o'clock last night the Martians came out of the cylinder, and, moving about under an armour of metallic shields, have completely wrecked Woking station with the adjacent houses, and massacred an entire battalion of the Cardigan Regiment. No details are known. Maxims have been absolutely useless against their armour; the field guns have been disabled by them. Flying hussars have been galloping into Chertsey. The Martians appear to be moving slowly towards Chertsey or Windsor. Great anxiety prevails in West Surrey, and earthworks are being thrown up to check the advance Londonward.' That was how the *Sunday Sun*[50] put it, and a clever and remarkably prompt 'handbook' article in the *Referee*[51] compared the affair to a menagerie suddenly let loose in a village.

No one in London knew positively of the nature of the armoured Martians, and there was still a fixed idea that these monsters must be sluggish: 'crawling', 'creeping painfully' – such expressions occurred in almost all the earlier reports. None of the telegrams could have been written by an eyewitness of their advance. The Sunday papers printed separate editions as further news came to hand, some even in default of it. But there was practically nothing more to tell people until late in the afternoon, when the authorities gave the press agencies the news in their possession. It was stated that the people of Walton and Weybridge, and all the district were pouring along the roads Londonward, and that was all.

My brother went to church at the Foundling Hospital[52] in the morning, still in ignorance of what had happened on the previous night. There he heard allusions made to the invasion, and a special prayer for peace. Coming out, he bought a *Referee*. He became alarmed at the news in this, and went again to Waterloo station to find out if communication were restored. The omnibuses,[53] carriages, cyclists, and innumerable people walking in their best clothes seemed scarcely affected by the strange intelligence that the news vendors were disseminating. People were interested, or, if alarmed, alarmed only on account of the local residents. At the station he heard for the first time that the Windsor and Chertsey lines were now interrupted. The porters told him that several remarkable telegrams had been received in the morning from Byfleet and Chertsey stations, but that these had abruptly ceased. My brother could get very little precise detail out of them. 'There's fighting going on about Weybridge' was the extent of their information.

The train service was now very much disorganised. Quite a number of people who had been expecting friends from places on the South-Western network were standing about the station. One grey-headed old gentleman came and abused the South-Western Company[54] bitterly to my brother. 'It wants showing up,' he said.

One or two trains came in from Richmond, Putney, and Kingston, containing people who had gone out for a day's boating and found the locks closed and a feeling of panic in the air. A man in a blue and white blazer addressed my brother, full of strange tidings.

'There's hosts of people driving into Kingston in traps and carts and things, with boxes of valuables and all that,' he said. 'They come from Molesey and Weybridge and Walton, and they say there's been guns heard at Chertsey, heavy firing, and that mounted soldiers have told them to get off at once because the Martians are coming. We heard guns firing at Hampton Court station, but we thought it was thunder.

What the dickens does it all mean? The Martians can't get out of their pit, can they?'

My brother could not tell him.

Afterwards he found that the vague feeling of alarm had spread to the clients of the underground railway, and that the Sunday excursionists began to return from all over the South-Western 'lungs'[55] – Barnes, Wimbledon, Richmond Park, Kew, and so forth – at unnaturally early hours; but not a soul had anything more than vague hearsay to tell of. Everyone connected with the terminus seemed ill-tempered.

About five o'clock the gathering crowd in the station was immensely excited by the opening of the line of communication, which is almost invariably closed, between the South-Eastern and the South-Western stations, and the passage of carriage trucks bearing huge guns and carriages crammed with soldiers. These were the guns that were brought up from Woolwich and Chatham to cover Kingston. There was an exchange of pleasantries: 'You'll get eaten!' 'We're the beast-tamers!' and so forth. A little while after that a squad of police came into the station and began to clear the public off the platforms, and my brother went out into the street again.

The church bells were ringing for evensong, and a squad of Salvation Army lassies[56] came singing down Waterloo Road. On the bridge a number of loafers were watching a curious brown scum that came drifting down the stream in patches. The sun was just setting, and the Clock Tower and the Houses of Parliament rose against one of the most peaceful skies it is possible to imagine, a sky of gold, barred with long transverse stripes of reddish-purple cloud. There was talk of a floating body. One of the men there, a reservist he said he was, told my brother he had seen the heliograph flickering in the west.

In Wellington Street my brother met a couple of sturdy roughs who had just been rushed out of Fleet Street with still-wet newspapers and staring placards. 'Dreadful catastrophe!' they bawled one to the other down Wellington Street. 'Fighting at Weybridge! Full description! Repulse of the Martians! London in Danger!' He had to give threepence for a copy of that paper.

Then it was, and then only, that he realised something of the full power and terror of these monsters. He learned that they were not merely a handful of small sluggish creatures, but that they were minds swaying vast mechanical bodies; and that they could move swiftly and smite with such power that even the mightiest guns could not stand against them.

They were described as 'vast spiderlike machines, nearly a hundred feet high, capable of the speed of an express train, and able to shoot out a beam of intense heat'. Masked batteries, chiefly of field guns, had been planted in the country about Horsell Common, and especially between the Woking district and London. Five of the machines had been seen moving towards the Thames, and one, by a happy chance, had been destroyed. In the other cases the shells had missed, and the batteries had been at once annihilated by the Heat-Rays. Heavy losses of soldiers were mentioned, but the tone of the dispatch was optimistic.

The Martians had been repulsed; they were not invulnerable. They had retreated to their triangle of cylinders again, in the circle about Woking. Signallers with heliographs were pushing forward upon them from all sides. Guns were in rapid transit from Windsor, Portsmouth, Aldershot, Woolwich – even from the north; among others, long wire-guns of ninety-five tons from Woolwich. Altogether one hundred and sixteen were in position or being hastily placed, chiefly covering London. Never before in England had there been such a vast or rapid concentration of military material.

Any further cylinders that fell, it was hoped, could be destroyed at once by high explosives, which were being rapidly manufactured and distributed. No doubt, ran the report, the situation was of the strangest and gravest description, but the public was exhorted to avoid and dis-courage panic. No doubt the Martians were strange and terrible in the extreme, but at the outside there could not be more than twenty of them against our millions.

The authorities had reason to suppose, from the size of the cylinders, that at the outside there could not be more than five in each cylinder – fifteen altogether. And one at least was disposed of – perhaps more. The public would be fairly warned of the approach of danger, and elaborate measures were being taken for the protection of the people in the threatened south-western suburbs. And so, with reiterated assurances of the safety of London and the ability of the authorities to cope with the difficulty, this quasi-proclamation closed.

This was printed in enormous type on paper so fresh that it was still wet, and there had been no time to add a word of comment. It was curious, my brother said, to see how ruthlessly the usual contents of the paper had been hacked and taken out to give this place.

All down Wellington Street people could be seen fluttering out the pink sheets and reading, and the Strand was suddenly noisy with the voices of an army of hawkers following these pioneers. Men came scrambling off buses to secure copies. Certainly this news excited people intensely, whatever their previous apathy. The shutters of a map shop in the Strand were being taken down, my brother said, and a man in his Sunday raiment, lemon-yellow gloves even, was visible inside the window hastily fastening maps of Surrey to the glass.

Going on along the Strand to Trafalgar Square, the paper in his hand, my brother saw some of the fugitives from West Surrey. There was a man with his wife and two boys and some articles of furniture in a cart such as greengrocers use. He was driving from the direction of Westminster Bridge; and close behind him came a hay waggon with five or six respectable-looking people in it, and some boxes and bundles. The faces of these people were haggard, and their entire appearance contrasted conspicuously with the Sabbath-best appearance of the people on the omnibuses. People in fashionable clothing peeped at them out of cabs. They stopped at the Square as if undecided which way to take, and finally turned eastward along the Strand. Some way behind these came a man in workday clothes, riding one of those old-fashioned tricycles with a small front wheel. He was dirty and white in the face.

My brother turned down towards Victoria, and met a number of such people. He had a vague idea that he might see something of me. He noticed an unusual number of police regulating the traffic. Some of the refugees were exchanging news with the people on the omnibuses. One was professing to have seen the Martians. 'Boilers on stilts, I tell you, striding along like men.' Most of them were excited and animated by their strange experience.

Beyond Victoria the public-houses were doing a lively trade with these arrivals. At all the street corners groups of people were reading papers, talking excitedly, or staring at these unusual Sunday visitors. They seemed to increase as night drew on, until at last the roads, my brother said, were like Epsom High Street on a Derby Day.[57] My brother addressed several of these fugitives and got unsatisfactory answers from most.

None of them could tell him any news of Woking except one man, who assured him that Woking had been entirely destroyed on the previous night.

'I come from Byfleet,' he said; 'a man on a bicycle came through the place in the early morning, and ran from door to door warning us to come away. Then came soldiers. We went out to look, and there were clouds of smoke to the south – nothing but smoke, and not a soul coming that way. Then we heard the guns at Chertsey, and folks coming from Weybridge. So I've locked up my house and come on.'

At the time there was a strong feeling in the streets that the authorities were to blame for their incapacity to dispose of the invaders without all this inconvenience.

About eight o'clock a noise of heavy firing was distinctly audible all over the south of London. My brother could not hear it for the traffic in the main thoroughfares, but by striking through the quiet back streets to the river he was able to distinguish it quite plainly.

He walked from Westminster to his apartments near Regent's Park, about two. He was now very anxious on my account, and disturbed at the evident magnitude of the trouble. His mind was inclined to run, even as mine had run on Saturday, on military details. He thought of all those silent, expectant guns, of the suddenly nomadic countryside; he tried to imagine 'boilers on stilts' a hundred feet high.

There were one or two cartloads of refugees passing along Oxford Street, and several in the Marylebone Road, but so slowly was the news spreading that Regent Street and Portland Place were full of their usual Sunday-night promenaders, albeit they talked in groups, and along the edge of Regent's Park there were as many silent couples 'walking out' together under the scattered gas lamps as ever there had been. The night was warm and still, and a little oppressive; the sound of guns continued intermittently, and after midnight there seemed to be sheet lightning in the south.

He read and reread the paper, fearing the worst had happened to me. He was restless, and after supper prowled out again aimlessly. He returned and tried in vain to divert his attention to his examination notes. He went to bed a little after midnight, and was awakened from lurid dreams in the small hours of Monday by the sound of door knockers, feet running in the street, distant drumming, and a clamour of bells. Red reflections danced on the ceiling. For a moment he lay astonished, wondering whether day had come or the world gone mad. Then he jumped out of bed and ran to the window.

His room was an attic and as he thrust his head out, up and down the street there were a dozen echoes to the noise of his window sash, and heads in every kind of night disarray appeared. Enquiries were being shouted. 'They are coming!' bawled a policeman, hammering at the door; 'the Martians are coming!' and hurried to the next door.

The sound of drumming and trumpeting came from the Albany Street Barracks, and every church within earshot was hard at work killing sleep with a vehement disorderly tocsin. There was a noise of doors opening, and window after window in the houses opposite flashed from darkness into yellow illumination.

Up the street came galloping a closed carriage, bursting abruptly into noise at the corner, rising to a clattering climax under the window, and dying away slowly in the distance. Close on the rear of this came a couple of cabs, the forerunners of a long procession of flying vehicles, going for the most part to Chalk Farm station, where the North-Western special trains[58] were loading up, instead of coming down the gradient into Euston.

For a long time my brother stared out of the window in blank astonishment, watching the policemen hammering at door after door, and delivering their incomprehensible message. Then the door behind him opened, and the man who lodged across the landing came in, dressed only in shirt, trousers, and slippers, his braces loose about his waist, his hair disordered from his pillow.

'What the devil is it?' he asked. 'A fire? What a devil of a row!'

They both craned their heads out of the window, straining to hear what the policemen were shouting. People were coming out of the side streets, and standing in groups at the corners talking.

'What the devil is it all about?' said my brother's fellow lodger.

My brother answered him vaguely and began to dress, running with each garment to the window in order to miss nothing of the growing excitement. And presently men selling unnaturally early newspapers came bawling into the street: 'London in danger of suffocation! The Kingston and Richmond defences forced! Fearful massacres in the Thames Valley!'

And all about him – in the rooms below, in the houses on each side and across the road, and behind in the Park Terraces and in the hundred other streets of that part of Marylebone, and the Westbourne Park district and St Pancras, and westward and northward in Kilburn and St John's Wood and Hampstead, and eastward in Shoreditch and Highbury and Haggerston and Hoxton, and, indeed, through all the vastness of London from Ealing to East Ham – people were rubbing their eyes, and opening windows to stare out and ask aimless questions, dressing hastily as the first breath of the coming storm of Fear blew through the streets. It was the dawn of the great panic. London, which had gone to bed on Sunday night oblivious and inert, was awakened, in the small hours of Monday morning, to a vivid sense of danger.

Unable from his window to learn what was happening, my brother went down and out into the street, just as the sky between the parapets of the houses grew pink with the early dawn. The flying people on foot and in vehicles grew more numerous every moment. 'Black smoke!' he heard people crying, and again 'Black smoke!' The contagion of such a unanimous fear was inevitable. As my brother hesitated on the doorstep, he saw another news vendor approaching, and got a paper forthwith. The man was running away with the rest, and selling his papers for a shilling each as he ran – a grotesque mingling of profit and panic.

And from this paper my brother read that catastrophic dispatch of the Commander-in-Chief:

> The Martians are able to discharge enormous clouds of a black and poisonous vapour by means of rockets. They have smothered our batteries, destroyed Richmond, Kingston, and Wimbledon, and are advancing slowly towards London, destroying everything on the way. It is impossible to stop them. There is no safety from the Black Smoke but in instant flight.

That was all, but it was enough. The whole population of the great six-million city was stirring, slipping, running; presently it would be pouring *en masse* northward.

'Black smoke!' the voices cried. 'Fire!'

The bells of the neighbouring church made a jangling tumult, a cart carelessly driven smashed, amid shrieks and curses, against the water trough up the street. Sickly yellow lights went to and fro in the houses, and some of the passing cabs flaunted unextinguished lamps. And overhead the dawn was growing brighter, clear and steady and calm.

He heard footsteps running to and fro in the rooms, and up and down stairs behind him. His landlady came to the door, loosely wrapped in dressing gown and shawl; her husband followed ejaculating.

As my brother began to realise the import of all these things, he turned hastily to his own room, put all his available money – some ten pounds altogether – into his pockets, and went out again into the streets.

CHAPTER FIFTEEN

What Happened in Surrey

It was while the curate had sat and talked so wildly to me under the hedge in the flat meadows near Halliford, and while my brother was watching the fugitives stream over Westminster Bridge, that the Martians had resumed the offensive. So far as one can ascertain from the conflicting accounts that have been put forth, the majority of them remained busied with preparations in the Horsell pit until nine that night, hurrying on some operation that disengaged huge volumes of green smoke.

But three certainly came out about eight o'clock and, advancing slowly and cautiously, made their way through Byfleet and Pyrford towards Ripley and Weybridge, and so came in sight of the expectant batteries against the setting sun. These Martians did not advance in a body, but in a line, each perhaps a mile and a half from his nearest fellow. They communicated with one another by means of siren-like howls, running up and down the scale from one note to another.

It was this howling and firing of the guns at Ripley and St George's Hill that we had heard at Upper Halliford. The Ripley gunners, unseasoned artillery volunteers who ought never to have been placed in such a position, fired one wild, premature, ineffectual volley, and bolted on horse and foot through the deserted village, while the Martian, without using his Heat-Ray, walked serenely over their guns, stepped gingerly among them, passed in front of them, and so came unexpectedly upon the guns in Painshill Park, which he destroyed.

The St George's Hill men, however, were better led or of a better mettle. Hidden by a pine wood as they were, they seem to have been quite unsuspected by the Martian nearest to them. They laid their guns as deliberately as if they had been on parade, and fired at about a thousand yards' range.

The shells flashed all round him, and he was seen to advance a few paces, stagger, and go down. Everybody yelled together, and the guns were reloaded in frantic haste. The overthrown Martian set up a prolonged ululation, and immediately a second glittering giant, answering him, appeared over the trees to the south. It would seem that a leg of the tripod had been smashed by one of the shells. The whole of the second volley flew wide of the Martian on the ground, and, simultaneously, both his companions brought their Heat-Rays to bear on the battery. The ammunition blew up, the pine trees all about the guns flashed into fire, and only one or two of the men who were already running over the crest of the hill escaped.

After this it would seem that the three took counsel together and halted, and the scouts who were watching them report that they remained absolutely stationary for the next half-hour. The Martian who had been overthrown crawled tediously out of his hood, a small brown figure, oddly suggestive from that distance of a speck of blight, and apparently engaged in the repair of his support. About nine he had finished, for his cowl was then seen above the trees again.

It was a few minutes past nine that night when these three sentinels were joined by four other Martians, each carrying a thick black tube. A similar tube was handed to each of the three, and the seven proceeded to distribute themselves at equal distances along a curved line between St George's Hill, Weybridge, and the village of Send, south-west of Ripley.

A dozen rockets sprang out of the hills before them so soon as they began to move, and warned the waiting batteries about Ditton and Esher. At the same time four of their fighting machines, similarly armed with tubes, crossed the river, and two of them, black against the western sky, came into sight of myself and the curate as we hurried wearily and painfully along the road that runs northward out of Halliford. They moved, as it seemed to us, upon a cloud, for a milky mist covered the fields and rose to a third of their height.

At this sight the curate cried faintly in his throat, and began running; but I knew it was no good running from a Martian, and I turned aside and crawled through dewy nettles and brambles into the broad ditch by the side of the road. He looked back, saw what I was doing, and turned to join me.

The two halted, the nearer to us standing and facing Sunbury, the remoter being a grey indistinctness towards the evening star, away towards Staines.

The occasional howling of the Martians had ceased; they took up their positions in the huge crescent about their cylinders in absolute silence. It was a crescent with twelve miles between its horns. Never since the devising of gunpowder was the beginning of a battle so still. To us and to an observer about Ripley it would have had precisely the same effect – the Martians seemed in solitary possession of the darkling night, lit only as it was by the slender moon, the stars, the afterglow of the daylight, and the ruddy glare from St George's Hill and the woods of Painshill.

But facing that crescent everywhere – at Staines, Hounslow, Ditton, Esher, Ockham, behind hills and woods south of the river, and across the flat grass meadows to the north of it, wherever a cluster of trees or village houses gave sufficient cover – the guns were waiting. The signal rockets burst and rained their sparks through the night and vanished, and the spirit of all those watching batteries rose to a tense expectation. The Martians had but to advance into the line of fire, and instantly those motionless black forms of men, those guns glittering so darkly in the early night, would explode into a thunderous fury of battle.

No doubt the thought that was uppermost in a thousand of those vigilant minds, even as it was uppermost in mine, was the riddle – how much they understood of us. Did they grasp that we in our millions were organised, disciplined, working together? Or did they interpret our spurts of fire, the sudden stinging of our shells, our steady investment of their encampment, as we should the furious unanimity of onslaught in a disturbed hive of bees? Did they dream they might exterminate us? (At that time no one knew what food they needed.) A hundred such questions struggled together in my mind as I watched that vast sentinel shape. And in the back of my mind was the sense of all the huge unknown and hidden forces Londonward. Had they prepared pitfalls? Were the powder mills at Hounslow ready as a snare? Would the Londoners have the heart and courage to make a greater Moscow[59] of their mighty province of houses?

Then, after an interminable time, as it seemed to us, crouching and peering through the hedge, came a sound like the distant concussion of a gun. Another nearer, and then another. And then the Martian beside us raised his tube on high and discharged it, gunwise, with a heavy report that made the ground heave. The one towards Staines answered him. There was no flash, no smoke, simply that loaded detonation.

I was so excited by these heavy minute-guns following one another that I so far forgot my personal safety and my scalded hands as to clamber up into the hedge and stare towards Sunbury. As I did so a second report followed, and a big projectile hurtled overhead towards Hounslow. I expected at least to see smoke or fire, or some such evidence of its work. But all I saw was the deep blue sky above, with one solitary star, and the white mist spreading wide and low beneath. And there had been no crash, no answering explosion. The silence was restored; the minute lengthened to three.

'What has happened?' said the curate, standing up beside me.

'Heaven knows!' said I.

A bat flickered by and vanished. A distant tumult of shouting began and ceased. I looked again at the Martian, and saw he was now moving eastward along the riverbank, with a swift, rolling motion.

Every moment I expected the fire of some hidden battery to spring upon him; but the evening calm was unbroken. The figure of the Martian grew smaller as he receded, and presently the mist and the gathering night had swallowed him up. By a common impulse we clambered higher. Towards Sunbury was a dark appearance, as though a conical hill had suddenly come into being there, hiding our view of the farther country; and then, remoter across the river, over Walton, we saw another such summit. These hill-like forms grew lower and broader even as we stared.

Moved by a sudden thought, I looked northward, and there I perceived a third of these cloudy black kopjes[60] had risen.

Everything had suddenly become very still. Far away to the southeast, marking the quiet, we heard the Martians hooting to one another, and then the air quivered again with the distant thud of their guns. But the earthly artillery made no reply.

Now at the time we could not understand these things, but later I was to learn the meaning of these ominous kopjes that gathered in the twilight. Each of the Martians, standing in the great crescent I have described, had discharged, by means of the gunlike tube he carried, a huge canister over whatever hill, copse, cluster of houses, or other possible cover for guns, chanced to be in front of him. Some fired only one of these, some two – as in the case of the one we had seen; the one at Ripley is said to have discharged no fewer than five at that time. These canisters smashed on striking the ground – they did not explode – and incontinently disengaged an enormous volume of heavy, inky vapour, coiling and pouring upward in a huge and ebony cumulus cloud, a gaseous hill that sank and spread itself slowly over the surrounding country. And the touch of that vapour, the inhaling of its pungent wisps, was death to all that breathes.

It was heavy, this vapour, heavier than the densest smoke, so that, after the first tumultuous uprush and outflow of its impact, it sank down through the air and poured over the ground in a manner rather liquid than gaseous, abandoning the hills, and streaming into the valleys and ditches and watercourses even as I have heard the carbonic-acid gas[61] that pours from volcanic clefts is wont to do. And where it came upon water some chemical action occurred, and the surface would be instantly covered with a powdery scum that sank slowly and made way for more.

The scum was absolutely insoluble, and it is a strange thing, seeing the instant effect of the gas, that one could drink without hurt the water from which it had been strained. The vapour did not diffuse as a true gas would do. It hung together in banks, flowing sluggishly down the slope of the land and driving reluctantly before the wind, and very slowly it combined with the mist and moisture of the air, and sank to the earth in the form of dust. Save that an unknown element giving a group of four lines in the blue of the spectrum is concerned, we are still entirely ignorant of the nature of this substance.

Once the tumultuous upheaval of its dispersion was over, the Black Smoke clung so closely to the ground, even before its precipitation, that fifty feet up in the air, on the roofs and upper storeys of high houses and on great trees, there was a chance of escaping its poison altogether, as was proved even that night at Street Cobham and Ditton.

The man who escaped at the former place tells a wonderful story of the strangeness of its coiling flow, and how he looked down from the church spire and saw the houses of the village rising like ghosts out of its inky nothingness. For a day and a half he remained there, weary, starving and sun-scorched, the earth under the blue sky and against the prospect of the distant hills a velvet-black expanse, with red roofs, green trees, and, later, black-veiled shrubs and gates, barns, outhouses, and walls, rising here and there into the sunlight.

But that was at Street Cobham, where the black vapour was allowed to remain until it sank of its own accord into the ground. As a rule the Martians, when it had served its purpose, cleared the air of it again by wading into it and directing a jet of steam upon it.

This they did with the vapour banks near us, as we saw in the starlight from the window of a deserted house at Upper Halliford, whither we had returned. From there we could see the searchlights on Richmond Hill and Kingston Hill going to and fro, and about eleven the windows rattled, and we heard the sound of the huge siege guns that had been put in position there. These continued intermittently for the space of a quarter of an hour, sending chance shots at the invisible Martians at Hampton and Ditton, and then the pale beams of the electric light vanished, and were replaced by a bright red glow.

Then the fourth cylinder fell – a brilliant green meteor – as I learned afterwards, in Bushey Park. Before the guns on the Richmond and Kingston line of hills began, there was a fitful cannonade far away in the south-west, due, I believe, to guns being fired haphazard before the black vapour could overwhelm the gunners.

So, setting about it as methodically as men might smoke out a wasps' nest, the Martians spread this strange stifling vapour over the London-ward country. The horns of the crescent slowly moved apart, until at last they formed a line from Hanwell to Coombe and Malden. All night through their destructive tubes advanced. Never once, after the Martian at St George's Hill was brought down, did they give the artillery the ghost of a chance against them. Wherever there was a possibility of guns being laid for them unseen, a fresh canister of the black vapour was discharged, and where the guns were openly displayed the Heat-Ray was brought to bear.

By midnight the blazing trees along the slopes of Richmond Park and the glare of Kingston Hill threw their light upon a network of Black Smoke, blotting out the whole valley of the Thames and extending as far as the eye could reach. And through this two Martians slowly waded, and turned their hissing steam jets this way and that.

They were sparing of the Heat-Ray that night, either because they had but a limited supply of material for its production or because they did not wish to destroy the country but only to crush and overawe the opposition they had aroused. In the latter aim they certainly succeeded. Sunday night was the end of the organised opposition to their movements. After that no body of men would stand against them, so hopeless was the enterprise. Even the crews of the torpedo-boats and destroyers that had brought their quick-firers up the Thames refused to stop, mutinied, and went down again. The only offensive operation men ventured upon after that night was the preparation of mines and pitfalls, and even in that their energies were frantic and spasmodic.

One has to imagine, as well as one may, the fate of those batteries towards Esher, waiting so tensely in the twilight. Survivors there were none. One may picture the orderly expectation, the officers alert and watchful, the gunners ready, the ammunition piled to hand, the limber gunners with their horses and waggons, the groups of civilian spectators standing as near as they were permitted, the evening stillness, the ambulances and hospital tents with the burned and wounded from Weybridge; then the dull resonance of the shots the Martians fired, and the clumsy projectile whirling over the trees and houses and smashing amid the neighbouring fields.

One may picture, too, the sudden shifting of the attention, the swiftly spreading coils and bellyings of that blackness advancing headlong, towering heavenward, turning the twilight to a palpable darkness, a strange and horrible antagonist of vapour striding upon its victims, men and horses near it seen dimly, running, shrieking, falling headlong, shouts of dismay, the guns suddenly abandoned, men choking and writhing on the ground, and the swift broadening-out of the opaque cone of smoke. And then night and extinction – nothing but a silent mass of impenetrable vapour hiding its dead.

Before dawn the black vapour was pouring through the streets of Richmond, and the disintegrating organism of government was, with a last expiring effort, rousing the population of London to the necessity of flight.

CHAPTER SIXTEEN

The Exodus from London

So you understand the roaring wave of fear that swept through the greatest city in the world just as Monday was dawning – the stream of flight rising swiftly to a torrent, lashing in a foaming tumult round the railway stations, banked up into a horrible struggle about the shipping in the Thames, and hurrying by every available channel northward and eastward. By ten o'clock the police organisation, and by midday even the railway organisations, were losing coherency, losing shape and efficiency, guttering, softening, running at last in that swift liquefaction of the social body.

All the railway lines north of the Thames and the South-Eastern people at Cannon Street had been warned by midnight on Sunday, and trains were being filled. People were fighting savagely for standing-room in the carriages even at two o'clock. By three, people were being trampled and crushed even in Bishopsgate Street, a couple of hundred yards or more from Liverpool Street station; revolvers were fired, people stabbed, and the policemen who had been sent to direct the traffic, exhausted and infuriated, were breaking the heads of the people they were called out to protect.

And as the day advanced and the engine drivers and stokers refused to return to London, the pressure of the flight drove the people in an ever-thickening multitude away from the stations and along the north-ward-running roads. By midday a Martian had been seen at Barnes, and a cloud of slowly sinking black vapour drove along the Thames and across the flats of Lambeth, cutting off all escape over the bridges in its sluggish advance. Another bank drove over Ealing, and surrounded a little island of survivors on Castle Hill, alive, but unable to escape.

After a fruitless struggle to get aboard a North-Western train at Chalk

Farm – the engines of the trains that had loaded in the goods yard there *ploughed* through shrieking people, and a dozen stalwart men fought to keep the crowd from crushing the driver against his furnace – my brother emerged upon the Chalk Farm road, dodged across through a hurrying swarm of vehicles, and had the luck to be foremost in the sack of a cycle shop. The front tire of the machine he got was punctured in dragging it through the window, but he got up and off, notwithstanding, with no further injury than a cut wrist. The steep foot of Haverstock Hill was impassable owing to several overturned horses, and my brother struck into Belsize Road.

So he got out of the fury of the panic, and, skirting the Edgware Road, reached Edgware about seven, fasting and wearied, but well ahead of the crowd. Along the road people were standing in the roadway, curious, wondering. He was passed by a number of cyclists, some horsemen, and two motor cars. A mile from Edgware the rim of the wheel broke, and the machine became unridable. He left it by the roadside and trudged through the village. There were shops half opened in the main street of the place, and people crowded on the pavement and in the doorways and windows, staring astonished at this extraordinary procession of fugitives that was beginning. He succeeded in getting some food at an inn.

For a time he remained in Edgware not knowing what next to do. The flying people increased in number. Many of them, like my brother, seemed inclined to loiter in the place. There was no fresh news of the invaders from Mars.

At that time the road was crowded, but as yet far from congested. Most of the fugitives at that hour were mounted on cycles, but there were soon motor cars, hansom cabs, and carriages hurrying along, and the dust hung in heavy clouds along the road to St Albans.

It was perhaps a vague idea of making his way to Chelmsford, where some friends of his lived, that at last induced my brother to strike into a quiet lane running eastward. Presently he came upon a stile, and, crossing it, followed a footpath north-eastward. He passed near several farmhouses and some little places whose names he did not learn. He saw few fugitives until, in a grass lane towards High Barnet, he happened upon two ladies who became his fellow travellers. He came upon them just in time to save them.

He heard their screams, and, hurrying round the corner, saw a couple of men struggling to drag them out of the little pony-chaise[62] in which they had been driving, while a third with difficulty held the frightened pony's head. One of the ladies, a short woman dressed in white, was simply screaming; the other, a dark, slender figure, slashed at the man who gripped her arm with a whip she held in her disengaged hand.

My brother immediately grasped the situation, shouted, and hurried towards the struggle. One of the men desisted and turned towards him, and my brother, realising from his antagonist's face that a fight was unavoidable, and being an expert boxer, went into him forthwith and sent him down against the wheel of the chaise.

It was no time for pugilistic chivalry and my brother laid him quiet with a kick, and gripped the collar of the man who pulled at the slender lady's arm. He heard the clatter of hoofs, the whip stung across his face, a third antagonist struck him between the eyes, and the man he held wrenched himself free and made off down the lane in the direction from which he had come.

Partly stunned, he found himself facing the man who had held the horse's head, and became aware of the chaise receding from him down the lane, swaying from side to side, and with the women in it looking back. The man before him, a burly rough, tried to close, and he stopped him with a blow in the face. Then, realising that he was deserted, he dodged round and made off down the lane after the chaise, with the sturdy man close behind him, and the fugitive, who had turned now, following remotely.

Suddenly he stumbled and fell; his immediate pursuer went headlong, and he rose to his feet to find himself with a couple of antagonists again. He would have had little chance against them had not the slender lady very pluckily pulled up and returned to his help. It seems she had had a revolver all this time, but it had been under the seat when she and her companion were attacked. She fired at six yards' distance, narrowly missing my brother. The less courageous of the robbers made off, and his companion followed him, cursing his cowardice. They both stopped in sight down the lane, where the third man lay insensible.

'Take this!' said the slender lady, and she gave my brother her revolver.

'Go back to the chaise,' said my brother, wiping the blood from his split lip.

She turned without a word – they were both panting – and they went back to where the lady in white struggled to hold back the frightened pony.

The robbers had evidently had enough of it. When my brother looked again they were retreating.

'I'll sit here,' said my brother, 'if I may'; and he got upon the empty front seat. The lady looked over her shoulder.

'Give me the reins,' she said, and laid the whip along the pony's side. In another moment a bend in the road hid the three men from my brother's eyes.

So, quite unexpectedly, my brother found himself, panting, with a cut mouth, a bruised jaw, and bloodstained knuckles, driving along an unknown lane with these two women.

He learned they were the wife and the younger sister of a surgeon living at Stanmore, who had come in the small hours from a dangerous case at Pinner, and heard at some railway station on his way of the Martian advance. He had hurried home, roused the women – their servant had left them two days before – packed some provisions, put his revolver under the seat – luckily for my brother – and told them to drive on to Edgware, with the idea of getting a train there. He stopped behind to tell the neighbours. He would overtake them, he said, at about half-past four in the morning, and now it was nearly nine and they had seen nothing of him. They could not stop in Edgware because of the growing traffic through the place, and so they had come into this side lane.

That was the story they told my brother in fragments when presently they stopped again, nearer to New Barnet. He promised to stay with them, at least until they could determine what to do, or until the missing man arrived, and professed to be an expert shot with the revolver – a weapon strange to him – in order to give them confidence.

They made a sort of encampment by the wayside, and the pony became happy in the hedge. He told them of his own escape out of London, and all that he knew of these Martians and their ways. The sun crept higher in the sky, and after a time their talk died out and gave place to an uneasy state of anticipation. Several wayfarers came along the lane, and of these my brother gathered such news as he could. Every broken answer he had deepened his impression of the great disaster that had come on humanity, deepened his persuasion of the immediate necessity for prosecuting this flight. He urged the matter upon them.

'We have money,' said the slender woman, and hesitated.

Her eyes met my brother's, and her hesitation ended.

'So have I,' said my brother.

She explained that they had as much as thirty pounds in gold,[63] besides a five-pound note, and suggested that with that they might get upon a train at St Albans or New Barnet. My brother thought that was hopeless, seeing the fury of the Londoners to crowd upon the trains, and broached his own idea of striking across Essex towards Harwich and thence escaping from the country altogether.

Mrs Elphinstone – that was the name of the woman in white – would listen to no reasoning, and kept calling upon 'George'; but her sister-in-law was astonishingly quiet and deliberate, and at last agreed to my brother's suggestion. So, designing to cross the Great North Road, they went on towards Barnet, my brother leading the pony to save it as much as possible. As the sun crept up the sky the day became excessively hot, and under foot a thick, whitish sand grew burning and blinding, so that they travelled only very slowly. The hedges were grey with dust. And as they advanced towards Barnet a tumultuous murmuring grew stronger.

They began to meet more people. For the most part these were staring before them, murmuring indistinct questions, jaded, haggard, unclean. One man in evening dress passed them on foot, his eyes on the ground. They heard his voice, and, looking back at him, saw one hand clutched in his hair and the other beating invisible things. His paroxysm of rage over, he went on his way without once looking back.

As my brother's party went on towards the crossroads to the south of Barnet they saw a woman approaching the road across some fields on their left, carrying a child and with two other children; and then passed a man in dirty black, with a thick stick in one hand and a small portmanteau in the other. Then round the corner of the lane, from between the villas that guarded it at its confluence with the high road, came a little cart drawn by a sweating black pony and driven by a sallow youth in a bowler hat, grey with dust. There were three girls, East End factory girls, and a couple of little children crowded in the cart.

'This'll tike us rahnd Edgware?' asked the driver, wild-eyed, white-faced; and when my brother told him it would if he turned to the left, he whipped up at once without the formality of thanks.

My brother noticed a pale grey smoke or haze rising among the houses in front of them, and veiling the white façade of a terrace beyond the road that appeared between the backs of the villas. Mrs Elphinstone suddenly cried out at a number of tongues of smoky red flame leaping up above the houses in front of them against the hot, blue sky. The tumultuous noise resolved itself now into the disorderly mingling of many voices, the gride of many wheels, the creaking of waggons, and the staccato of hoofs. The lane came round sharply not fifty yards from the crossroads.

'Good heavens!' cried Mrs Elphinstone. 'What is this you are driving us into?'

My brother stopped.

For the main road was a boiling stream of people, a torrent of human beings rushing northward, one pressing on another. A great bank of dust, white and luminous in the blaze of the sun, made everything within twenty feet of the ground grey and indistinct and was perpetually renewed by the hurrying feet of a dense crowd of horses and of men and women on foot, and by the wheels of vehicles of every description.

'Way!' my brother heard voices crying. 'Make way!'

It was like riding into the smoke of a fire to approach the meeting point of the lane and road; the crowd roared like a fire, and the dust was hot and pungent. And, indeed, a little way up the road a villa was burning and sending rolling masses of black smoke across the road to add to the confusion.

Two men came past them. Then a dirty woman, carrying a heavy bundle and weeping. A lost retriever dog, with hanging tongue, circled dubiously round them, scared and wretched, and fled at my brother's threat.

So much as they could see of the road Londonward between the houses to the right was a tumultuous stream of dirty, hurrying people, pent in between the villas on either side; the black heads, the crowded forms, grew into distinctness as they rushed towards the corner, hurried past, and merged their individuality again in a receding multitude that was swallowed up at last in a cloud of dust.

'Go on! Go on!' cried the voices. 'Way! Way!'

One man's hands pressed on the back of another. My brother stood at the pony's head. Irresistibly attracted, he advanced slowly, pace by pace, down the lane.

Edgware had been a scene of confusion, Chalk Farm a riotous tumult, but this was a whole population in movement. It is hard to imagine that host. It had no character of its own. The figures poured out past the corner, and receded with their backs to the group in the lane. Along the margin came those who were on foot threatened by the wheels, stumbling in the ditches, blundering into one another.

The carts and carriages crowded close upon one another, making little way for those swifter and more impatient vehicles that darted forward every now and then when an opportunity showed itself of doing so, sending the people scattering against the fences and gates of the villas.

'Push on!' was the cry. 'Push on! They are coming!'

In one cart stood a blind man in the uniform of the Salvation Army, gesticulating with his crooked fingers and bawling, 'Eternity! Eternity!' His voice was hoarse and very loud so that my brother could hear him long after he was lost to sight in the dust. Some of the people who crowded in the carts whipped stupidly at their horses and quarrelled with other drivers; some sat motionless, staring at nothing with miserable eyes; some gnawed their hands with thirst, or lay prostrate in the bottoms of their conveyances. The horses' bits were covered with foam, their eyes bloodshot.

There were cabs, carriages, shop cars, waggons, beyond counting; a mail cart, a road-cleaner's cart marked 'Vestry of St Pancras',[64] a huge timber waggon crowded with roughs. A brewer's dray rumbled by with its two near wheels splashed with fresh blood.

'Clear the way!' cried the voices. 'Clear the way!'

'Eter–nity! Eter–nity!' came echoing down the road.

There were sad, haggard women tramping by, well dressed, with children that cried and stumbled, their dainty clothes smothered in dust, their weary faces smeared with tears. With many of these came men, sometimes helpful, sometimes lowering and savage. Fighting side by side with them pushed some weary street outcast in faded black rags, wide-eyed, loud-voiced, and foul-mouthed. There were sturdy work-men thrusting their way along, wretched, unkempt men, clothed like clerks or shopmen, struggling spasmodically; a wounded soldier my brother noticed, men dressed in the clothes of railway porters, one wretched creature in a nightshirt with a coat thrown over it.

But varied as its composition was, certain things all that host had in common. There were fear and pain on their faces, and fear behind them. A tumult up the road, a quarrel for a place in a waggon, sent the whole host of them quickening their pace; even a man so scared and broken that his knees bent under him was galvanised for a moment into renewed activity. The heat and dust had already been at work upon this multitude. Their skins were dry, their lips black and cracked. They were all thirsty, weary, and footsore. And amid the various cries one heard disputes, reproaches, groans of weariness and fatigue; the voices of most of them were hoarse and weak. Through it all ran a refrain: 'Way! Way! The Martians are coming!'

Few stopped and came aside from that flood. The lane opened slantingly into the main road with a narrow opening, and had a delusive appearance of coming from the direction of London. Yet a kind of eddy of people drove into its mouth; weaklings elbowed out of the stream, who for the most part rested but a moment before plunging into it again. A little way down the lane, with two friends bending over him, lay a man with a bare leg, wrapped about with bloody rags. He was a lucky man to have friends.

A little old man, with a grey military moustache and a filthy black frock coat, limped out and sat down beside the trap, removed his boot –

his sock was blood-stained – shook out a pebble, and hobbled on again; and then a little girl of eight or nine, all alone, threw herself under the hedge close by my brother, weeping.

'I can't go on! I can't go on!'

My brother woke from his torpor of astonishment and lifted her up, speaking gently to her, and carried her to Miss Elphinstone. So soon as my brother touched her she became quite still, as if frightened.

'Ellen!' shrieked a woman in the crowd, with tears in her voice – 'Ellen!' And the child suddenly darted away from my brother, crying 'Mother!'

'They are coming,' said a man on horseback, riding past along the lane.

'Out of the way, there!' bawled a coachman, towering high; and my brother saw a closed carriage turning into the lane.

The people crushed back on one another to avoid the horse. My brother pushed the pony and chaise back into the hedge, and the man drove by and stopped at the turn of the way. It was a carriage, with a pole for a pair of horses, but only one was in the traces. My brother saw dimly through the dust that two men lifted out something on a white stretcher and put it gently on the grass beneath the privet hedge.

One of the men came running to my brother.

'Where is there any water?' he said. 'He is dying fast, and very thirsty. It is Lord Garrick.'

'Lord Garrick!' said my brother – 'the Chief Justice?'[65]

'The water?' he said.

'There may be a tap,' said my brother, 'in some of the houses. We have no water. I dare not leave my people.'

The man pushed against the crowd towards the gate of the corner house.

'Go on!' said the people, thrusting at him. 'They are coming! Go on!'

Then my brother's attention was distracted by a bearded, eagle-faced man lugging a small handbag, which split even as my brother's eyes rested on it and disgorged a mass of sovereigns that seemed to break up into separate coins as it struck the ground. They rolled hither and thither among the struggling feet of men and horses. The man stopped and looked stupidly at the heap, and the shaft of a cab struck his shoulder and sent him reeling. He gave a shriek and dodged back, and a cartwheel shaved him narrowly.

'Way!' cried the men all about him. 'Make way!'

So soon as the cab had passed, he flung himself, with both hands open, upon the heap of coins, and began thrusting handfuls in his pocket. A horse rose close upon him, and in another moment, half rising, he had been borne down under the horse's hoofs.

'Stop!' screamed my brother, and pushing a woman out of his way, tried to clutch the bit of the horse.

Before he could get to it, he heard a scream under the wheels, and saw through the dust the rim passing over the poor wretch's back. The driver of the cart slashed his whip at my brother, who ran round behind the cart. The multitudinous shouting confused his ears. The man was writhing in the dust among his scattered money, unable to rise, for the wheel had broken his back, and his lower limbs lay limp and dead. My brother stood up and yelled at the next driver, and a man on a black horse came to his assistance.

'Get him out of the road,' said he; and, clutching the man's collar with his free hand, my brother lugged him sideways. But he still clutched after his money, and regarded my brother fiercely, hammering at his arm with a handful of gold. 'Go on! Go on!' shouted angry voices behind. 'Way! Way!'

There was a smash as the pole of a carriage crashed into the cart that the man on horseback stopped. My brother looked up, and the man with the gold twisted his head round and bit the wrist that held his collar. There was a concussion, and the black horse came staggering sideways, and the carthorse pushed beside it. A hoof missed my brother's foot by a hair's breadth. He released his grip on the fallen man and jumped back. He saw anger change to terror on the face of the poor wretch on the ground, and in a moment he was hidden and my brother was borne backward and carried past the entrance of the lane, and had to fight hard in the torrent to recover it.

He saw Miss Elphinstone covering her eyes, and a little child, with all a child's want of sympathetic imagination, staring with dilated eyes at a dusty something that lay black and still, ground and crushed under the rolling wheels. 'Let us go back!' he shouted, and began turning the pony round. 'We cannot cross this – hell,' he said; and they went back a hundred yards the way they had come, until the fighting crowd was hidden. As they passed the bend in the lane my brother saw the face of the dying man in the ditch under the privet, deadly white and drawn, and shining with perspiration. The two women sat silent, crouching in their seat and shivering.

Then beyond the bend my brother stopped again. Miss Elphinstone was white and pale, and her sister-in-law sat weeping, too wretched even to call upon 'George'. My brother was horrified and perplexed. So soon as they had retreated he realised how urgent and unavoidable it was to attempt this crossing. He turned to Miss Elphinstone, suddenly resolute.

'We must go that way,' he said, and led the pony round again.

For the second time that day this girl proved her quality. To force their way into the torrent of people, my brother plunged into the traffic and held back a cab horse, while she drove the pony across its head. A waggon locked wheels for a moment and ripped a long splinter from the chaise. In another moment they were caught and swept forward by the stream. My brother, with the cabman's whip marks red across his face and hands, scrambled into the chaise and took the reins from her.

'Point the revolver at the man behind,' he said, giving it to her, 'if he presses us too hard. No! – point it at his horse.'

Then he began to look out for a chance of edging to the right across the road. But once in the stream he seemed to lose volition, to become a part of that dusty rout. They swept through Chipping Barnet with the torrent; they were nearly a mile beyond the centre of the town before they had fought across to the opposite side of the way. It was din and confusion indescribable; but in and beyond the town the road forks repeatedly, and this to some extent relieved the stress.

They struck eastward through Hadley, and there on either side of the road, and at another place farther on they came upon a great multitude of people drinking at the stream, some fighting to come at the water. And farther on, from a lull near East Barnet, they saw two trains running slowly one after the other without signal or order – trains swarming with people, with men even among the coals behind the engines – going northward along the Great Northern Railway.[66] My brother supposes they must have filled outside London, for at that time the furious terror of the people had rendered the central termini impossible.

Near this place they halted for the rest of the afternoon, for the violence of the day had already utterly exhausted all three of them. They began to suffer the beginnings of hunger; the night was cold, and none of them dared to sleep. And in the evening many people came hurrying along the road nearby their stopping place, fleeing from unknown dangers before them, and going in the direction from which my brother had come.

CHAPTER SEVENTEEN

The Thunder Child

Had the Martians aimed only at destruction, they might on Monday have annihilated the entire population of London, as it spread itself slowly through the home counties. Not only along the road through Barnet, but also through Edgware and Waltham Abbey, and along the roads eastward to Southend and Shoeburyness, and south of the Thames to Deal and Broadstairs, poured the same frantic rout. If one could have hung that June morning in a balloon in the blazing blue above London every northward and eastward road running out of the tangled maze of streets would have seemed stippled black with the streaming fugitives, each dot a human agony of terror and physical distress. I have set forth at length in the last chapter my brother's account of the road through Chipping Barnet, in order that my readers may realise how that swarming of black dots appeared to one of those concerned. Never before in the history of the world had such a mass of human beings moved and suffered together. The legendary hosts of Goths and Huns,[67] the hugest armies Asia has ever seen, would have been but a drop in that current. And this was no disciplined march; it was a stampede – a stampede gigantic and terrible – without order and without a goal, six million people unarmed and unprovisioned, driving headlong. It was the beginning of the rout of civilisation, of the massacre of mankind.

Directly below him the balloonist would have seen the network of streets far and wide, houses, churches, squares, crescents, gardens – already derelict – spread out like a huge map, and in the southward *blotted*. Over Ealing, Richmond, Wimbledon, it would have seemed as if some monstrous pen had flung ink upon the chart. Steadily, incessantly, each black splash grew and spread, shooting out ramifications this way and that, now banking itself against rising ground, now pouring swiftly over a crest into a new-found valley, exactly as a gout of ink would spread itself upon blotting paper.

And beyond, over the blue hills that rise southward of the river, the glittering Martians went to and fro, calmly and methodically spreading their poison cloud over this patch of country and then over that, laying it again with their steam jets when it had served its purpose, and taking possession of the conquered country. They do not seem to have aimed at extermination so much as at complete demoralisation and the destruction of any opposition. They exploded any stores of powder they came upon, cut every telegraph, and wrecked the railways here and there. They were hamstringing mankind. They seemed in no hurry to extend the field of their operations, and did not come beyond the central part of London all that day. It is possible that a very considerable number of people in London stuck to their houses through Monday morning. Certain it is that many died at home suffocated by the Black Smoke.

Until about midday the Pool of London[68] was an astonishing scene. Steamboats and shipping of all sorts lay there, tempted by the enormous sums of money offered by fugitives, and it is said that many who swam out to these vessels were thrust off with boathooks and drowned. About one o'clock in the afternoon the thinning remnant of a cloud of the black vapour appeared between the arches of Blackfriars Bridge. At that the Pool became a scene of mad confusion, fighting, and collision, and for some time a multitude of boats and barges jammed in the northern arch of the Tower Bridge, and the sailors and lightermen[69] had to fight savagely against the people who swarmed upon them from the river-front. People were actually clambering down the piers of the bridge from above.

When, an hour later, a Martian appeared beyond the Clock Tower and waded down the river, nothing but wreckage floated above Limehouse.

Of the falling of the fifth cylinder I have presently to tell. The sixth star fell at Wimbledon. My brother, keeping watch beside the women in the chaise in a meadow, saw the green flash of it far beyond the hills. On Tuesday the little party, still set upon getting across the sea, made its way through the swarming country towards Colchester. The news that the Martians were now in possession of the whole of London was confirmed. They had been seen at Highgate, and even, it was said, at Neasden. But they did not come into my brother's view until the morrow.

That day the scattered multitudes began to realise the urgent need of provisions. As they grew hungry the rights of property ceased to be regarded. Farmers were out to defend their cattle-sheds, granaries, and ripening root crops with arms in their hands. A number of people now, like my brother, had their faces eastward, and there were some desperate souls even going back towards London to get food. These were chiefly people from the northern suburbs, whose knowledge of the Black Smoke came by hearsay. He heard that about half the members of the government had gathered at Birmingham, and that enormous quantities of high explosives were being prepared to be used in automatic mines across the Midland counties.

He was also told that the Midland Railway Company[70] had replaced the desertions of the first day's panic, had resumed traffic, and was running northward trains from St Albans to relieve the congestion of the home counties. There was also a placard in Chipping Ongar announcing that large stores of flour were available in the northern towns and that within twenty-four hours bread would be distributed among the starving people in the neighbourhood. But this intelligence did not deter him from the plan of escape he had formed, and the three pressed eastward all day, and heard no more of the bread distribution than this promise. Nor, as a matter of fact, did anyone else hear more of it. That night fell the seventh star, falling upon Primrose Hill. It fell while Miss Elphinstone was watching, for she took that duty alternately with my brother. She saw it.

On Wednesday the three fugitives – they had passed the night in a field of unripe wheat – reached Chelmsford, and there a body of the inhabitants, calling itself the Committee of Public Supply,[71] seized the pony as provisions, and would give nothing in exchange for it but the promise of a share in it the next day. Here there were rumours of Martians at Epping, and news of the destruction of Waltham Abbey Powder Mills[72] in a vain attempt to blow up one of the invaders.

People were watching for Martians here from the church towers. My brother, very luckily for him as it chanced, preferred to push on at once to the coast rather than wait for food, although all three of them were very hungry. By midday they passed through Tillingham, which, strangely enough, seemed to be quite silent and deserted, save for a few furtive plunderers hunting for food. Near Tillingham they suddenly came in sight of the sea, and the most amazing crowd of shipping of all sorts that it is possible to imagine.

For after the sailors could no longer come up the Thames, they came on to the Essex coast, to Harwich and Walton and Clacton, and afterwards to Foulness and Shoebury, to bring off the people. They lay in a huge sickle-shaped curve that vanished into mist at last towards the Naze. Close inshore was a multitude of fishing smacks – English, Scotch, French, Dutch, and Swedish; steam launches from the Thames, yachts, electric boats; and beyond were ships of large burden, a multitude of filthy colliers, trim merchantmen, cattle ships, passenger boats, petroleum tanks, ocean tramps, an old white transport even, neat white and grey liners from Southampton and Hamburg; and along the blue coast across the Blackwater my brother could make out dimly a dense swarm of boats chaffering with the people on the beach, a swarm which also extended up the Blackwater almost to Maldon.

About a couple of miles out lay an ironclad, very low in the water, almost, to my brother's perception, like a waterlogged ship. This was the ram *Thunder Child*. It was the only warship in sight, but far away to the right over the smooth surface of the sea – for that day there was a dead calm – lay a serpent of black smoke to mark the next ironclads of the Channel Fleet, which hovered in an extended line, steam up and ready for action, across the Thames estuary during the course of the Martian conquest, vigilant and yet powerless to prevent it.

At the sight of the sea, Mrs Elphinstone, in spite of the assurances of her sister-in-law, gave way to panic. She had never been out of England before, she would rather die than trust herself friendless in a foreign country, and so forth. She seemed, poor woman, to imagine that the French and the Martians might prove very similar. She had been growing increasingly hysterical, fearful, and depressed during the two days' journeyings. Her great idea was to return to Stanmore. Things had been always well and safe at Stanmore. They would find George at Stanmore.

It was with the greatest difficulty they could get her down to the beach, where presently my brother succeeded in attracting the attention of some men on a paddle steamer from the Thames. They sent a boat and drove a bargain for thirty-six pounds for the three. The steamer was going, these men said, to Ostend.

It was about two o'clock when my brother, having paid their fares at the gangway, found himself safely aboard the steamboat with his charges. There was food aboard, albeit at exorbitant prices, and the three of them contrived to eat a meal on one of the seats forward.

There were already a couple of score of passengers aboard, some of whom had expended their last money in securing a passage, but the captain lay off the Blackwater until five in the afternoon, picking up passengers until the seated decks were even dangerously crowded. He would probably have remained longer had it not been for the sound of guns that began about that hour in the south. As if in answer, the ironclad seaward fired a small gun and hoisted a string of flags. A jet of smoke sprang out of her funnels.

Some of the passengers were of opinion that this firing came from Shoeburyness, until it was noticed that it was growing louder. At the same time, far away in the south-east the masts and upperworks of three ironclads rose one after the other out of the sea, beneath clouds of black smoke. But my brother's attention speedily reverted to the distant firing in the south. He fancied he saw a column of smoke rising out of the distant grey haze.

The little steamer was already flapping her way eastward of the big crescent of shipping, and the low Essex coast was growing blue and hazy, when a Martian appeared, small and faint in the remote distance, advancing along the muddy coast from the direction of Foulness. At that the captain on the bridge swore at the top of his voice with fear and anger at his own delay, and the paddles seemed infected with his terror. Every soul aboard stood at the bulwarks or on the seats of the steamer and stared at that distant shape, higher than the trees or church towers inland, and advancing with a leisurely parody of a human stride.

It was the first Martian my brother had seen, and he stood, more amazed than terrified, watching this Titan advancing deliberately towards the shipping, wading farther and farther into the water as the coast fell away. Then, far away beyond the Crouch, came another, striding over some stunted trees, and then yet another, still farther off, wading deeply through a shiny mudflat that seemed to hang halfway up between sea and sky. They were all stalking seaward, as if to intercept the escape of the multitudinous vessels that were crowded between Foulness and the Naze. In spite of the throbbing exertions of the engines of the little paddle-boat, and the pouring foam that her wheels flung behind her, she receded with terrifying slowness from this ominous advance.

Glancing north-westward, my brother saw the large crescent of shipping already writhing with the approaching terror; one ship passing behind another, another coming round from broadside to end on, steamships whistling and giving off volumes of steam, sails being let out, launches rushing hither and thither. He was so fascinated by this and by the creeping danger away to the left that he had no eyes for anything seaward. And then a swift movement of the steamboat (she had suddenly come round to avoid being run down) flung him headlong from the seat upon which he was standing. There was a shouting all about him, a trampling of feet, and a cheer that seemed to be answered faintly. The steamboat lurched and rolled him over upon his hands.

He sprang to his feet and saw to starboard, and not a hundred yards from their heeling, pitching boat, a vast iron bulk like the blade of a plough tearing through the water, tossing it on either side in huge waves of foam that leaped towards the steamer, flinging her paddles helplessly in the air, and then sucking her deck down almost to the waterline.

A douche of spray blinded my brother for a moment. When his eyes were clear again he saw the monster had passed and was rushing landward. Big iron upperworks rose out of this headlong structure, and from that twin funnels projected and spat a smoking blast shot with fire. It was the torpedo ram,[73] *Thunder Child*, steaming headlong, coming to the rescue of the threatened shipping.

Keeping his footing on the heaving deck by clutching the bulwarks, my brother looked past this charging leviathan at the Martians again, and he saw the three of them now close together, and standing so far out to sea that their tripod supports were almost entirely submerged. Thus sunken, and seen in remote perspective, they appeared far less formidable than the huge iron bulk in whose wake the steamer was pitching so helplessly. It would seem they were regarding this new antagonist with astonishment. To their intelligence, it may be, the giant was even such another as themselves. The *Thunder Child* fired no gun, but simply drove full speed towards them. It was probably her not firing that enabled her to get so near the enemy as she did. They did not know what to make of her. One shell, and they would have sent her to the bottom forthwith with the Heat-Ray.

She was steaming at such a pace that in a minute she seemed halfway between the steamboat and the Martians – a diminishing black bulk against the receding horizontal expanse of the Essex coast.

Suddenly the foremost Martian lowered his tube and discharged a canister of the black gas at the ironclad. It hit her larboard side and glanced off in an inky jet that rolled away to seaward, an unfolding torrent of Black Smoke, from which the ironclad drove clear. To the watchers from the steamer, low in the water and with the sun in their eyes, it seemed as though she were already among the Martians.

They saw the gaunt figures separating and rising out of the water as they retreated shoreward, and one of them raised the camera-like generator of the Heat-Ray. He held it pointing obliquely downward, and a bank of steam sprang from the water at its touch. It must have driven through the iron of the ship's side like a white-hot iron rod through paper.

A flicker of flame went up through the rising steam, and then the Martian reeled and staggered. In another moment he was cut down, and a great body of water and steam shot high in the air. The guns of the *Thunder Child* sounded through the reek, going off one after the other, and one shot splashed the water high close by the steamer, ricocheted towards the other flying ships to the north, and smashed a smack to matchwood.

But no one heeded that very much. At the sight of the Martian's collapse the captain on the bridge yelled inarticulately, and all the crowding passengers on the steamer's stern shouted together. And then they yelled again. For, surging out beyond the white tumult, drove something long and black, the flames streaming from its middle parts, its ventilators and funnels spouting fire.

She was alive still; the steering gear, it seems, was intact and her engines working. She headed straight for a second Martian, and was within a hundred yards of him when the Heat-Ray came to bear. Then with a violent thud, a blinding flash, her decks, her funnels, leaped upward. The Martian staggered with the violence of her explosion, and in another moment the flaming wreckage, still driving forward with the impetus of its pace, had struck him and crumpled him up like a thing of cardboard. My brother shouted involuntarily. A boiling tumult of steam hid everything again.

'Two!' yelled the captain.

Everyone was shouting. The whole steamer from end to end rang with frantic cheering that was taken up first by one and then by all in the crowding multitude of ships and boats that was driving out to sea.

The steam hung upon the water for many minutes, hiding the third Martian and the coast altogether. And all this time the boat was paddling steadily out to sea and away from the fight; and when at last the confusion cleared, the drifting bank of black vapour intervened, and nothing of the *Thunder Child* could be made out, nor could the third Martian be seen. But the ironclads to seaward were now quite close and standing in towards shore past the steamboat.

The little vessel continued to beat its way seaward, and the ironclads receded slowly towards the coast, which was hidden still by a marbled bank of vapour, part steam, part black gas, eddying and combining in the strangest way. The fleet of refugees was scattering to the north-east; several smacks were sailing between the ironclads and the steamboat. After a time, and before they reached the sinking cloud bank, the warships turned northward, and then abruptly went about and passed into the thickening haze of evening southward. The coast grew faint, and at last indistinguishable amid the low banks of clouds that were gathering about the sinking sun.

Then suddenly out of the golden haze of the sunset came the vibration of guns, and a form of black shadows moving. Everyone struggled to the rail of the steamer and peered into the blinding furnace of the west, but nothing was to be distinguished clearly. A mass of smoke rose slanting and barred the face of the sun. The steamboat throbbed on its way through an interminable suspense.

The sun sank into grey clouds, the sky flushed and darkened, the evening star trembled into sight. It was deep twilight when the captain cried out and pointed. My brother strained his eyes. Something rushed up into the sky out of the greyness – rushed slantingly upward and very swiftly into the luminous clearness above the clouds in the western sky; something flat and broad, and very large, that swept round in a vast curve, grew smaller, sank slowly, and vanished again into the grey mystery of the night. And as it flew it rained down darkness upon the land.[74]

BOOK TWO

The Earth Under the Martians

CHAPTER ONE

Under Foot

In the first book I have wandered so much from my own adventures to tell of the experiences of my brother that all through the last two chapters I and the curate have been lurking in the empty house at Halliford whither we fled to escape the Black Smoke. There I will resume. We stopped there all Sunday night and all the next day – the day of the panic – in a little island of daylight, cut off by the Black Smoke from the rest of the world. We could do nothing but wait in aching inactivity during those two weary days.

My mind was occupied by anxiety for my wife. I figured her at Leatherhead, terrified, in danger, mourning me already as a dead man. I paced the rooms and cried aloud when I thought of how I was cut off from her, of all that might happen to her in my absence. My cousin I knew was brave enough for any emergency, but he was not the sort of man to realise danger quickly, to rise promptly. What was needed now was not bravery, but circumspection. My only consolation was to believe that the Martians were moving Londonward and away from her. Such vague anxieties keep the mind sensitive and painful. I grew very weary and irritable with the curate's perpetual ejaculations; I tired of the sight of his selfish despair. After some ineffectual remonstrance I kept away from him, staying in a room – evidently a children's schoolroom – containing globes, forms, and copybooks. When he followed me thither, I went to a box room at the top of the house and, in order to be alone with my aching miseries, locked myself in.

We were hopelessly hemmed in by the Black Smoke all that day and the morning of the next. There were signs of people in the next house on Sunday evening – a face at a window and moving lights, and later the slamming of a door. But I do not know who these people were, nor what became of them. We saw nothing of them next day. The Black Smoke drifted slowly riverward all through Monday morning, creeping nearer and nearer to us, driving at last along the roadway outside the house that hid us.

A Martian came across the fields about midday, laying the stuff with a jet of superheated steam that hissed against the walls, smashed all the windows it touched, and scalded the curate's hand as he fled out of the front room. When at last we crept across the sodden rooms and looked out again, the country northward was as though a black snowstorm had passed over it. Looking towards the river, we were astonished to see an unaccountable redness mingling with the black of the scorched meadows.

For a time we did not see how this change affected our position, save that we were relieved of our fear of the Black Smoke. But later I perceived that we were no longer hemmed in, that now we might get away. So soon as I realised that the way of escape was open, my dream of action returned. But the curate was lethargic, unreasonable.

'We are safe here,' he repeated; 'safe here.'

I resolved to leave him – would that I had! Wiser now for the artillery-man's teaching, I sought out food and drink. I had found oil and rags for my burns, and I also took a hat and a flannel shirt that I found in one of the bedrooms. When it was clear to him that I meant to go alone – had reconciled myself to going alone – he suddenly roused himself to come. And all being quiet throughout the afternoon, we started about five o'clock, as I should judge, along the blackened road to Sunbury.

In Sunbury, and at intervals along the road, were dead bodies lying in contorted attitudes, horses as well as men, overturned carts and luggage, all covered thickly with black dust. That pall of cindery powder made me think of what I had read of the destruction of Pompeii.[75] We got to Hampton Court without misadventure, our minds full of strange and unfamiliar appearances, and at Hampton Court[76] our eyes were relieved to find a patch of green that had escaped the suffocating drift. We went through Bushey Park, with its deer going to and fro under the chestnuts, and some men and women hurrying in the distance towards Hampton, and so we came to Twickenham. These were the first people we saw.

Away across the road the woods beyond Ham and Petersham were still afire. Twickenham was uninjured by either Heat-Ray or Black Smoke, and there were more people about here, though none could give us news. For the most part they were like ourselves, taking advantage of a lull to shift their quarters. I have an impression that many of the houses here were still occupied by scared inhabitants, too frightened even for flight. Here too the evidence of a hasty rout was abundant along the road. I remember most vividly three smashed bicycles in a heap, pounded into the road by the wheels of subsequent carts. We crossed Richmond Bridge about half-past eight. We hurried across the exposed bridge, of course, but I noticed floating down the stream a number of red masses, some many feet across. I did not know what these were – there was no time for scrutiny – and I put a more horrible interpretation on them than they deserved. Here again on the Surrey side were black dust that had once been smoke, and dead bodies – a heap near the approach to the station; but we had no glimpse of the Martians until we were some way towards Barnes.

We saw in the blackened distance a group of three people running down a side street towards the river, but otherwise it seemed deserted. Up the hill Richmond town was burning briskly; outside the town of Richmond there was no trace of the Black Smoke.

Then suddenly, as we approached Kew, came a number of people running, and the upperworks of a Martian fighting-machine loomed in sight over the housetops, not a hundred yards away from us. We stood aghast at our danger, and had the Martian looked down we must immediately have perished. We were so terrified that we dared not go on, but turned aside and hid in a shed in a garden. There the curate crouched, weeping silently, and refusing to stir again.

But my fixed idea of reaching Leatherhead would not let me rest, and in the twilight I ventured out again. I went through a shrubbery, and along a passage beside a big house standing in its own grounds, and so emerged upon the road towards Kew. The curate I left in the shed, but he came hurrying after me.

That second start was the most foolhardy thing I ever did. For it was manifest the Martians were about us. No sooner had the curate over-taken me than we saw either the fighting-machine we had seen before or another, far away across the meadows in the direction of Kew Lodge. Four or five little black figures hurried before it across the green-grey of the field, and in a moment it was evident this Martian pursued them. In three strides he was among them, and they ran radiating from his feet in all directions. He used no Heat-Ray to destroy them, but picked them up one by one. Apparently he tossed them into the great metallic carrier which projected behind him, much as a workman's basket hangs over his shoulder.

It was the first time I realised that the Martians might have any other purpose than destruction with defeated humanity. We stood for a moment petrified, then turned and fled through a gate behind us into a walled garden, fell into, rather than found, a fortunate ditch, and lay there, scarce daring to whisper to each other until the stars were out.

I suppose it was nearly eleven o'clock before we gathered courage to start again, no longer venturing into the road, but sneaking along hedgerows and through plantations, and watching keenly through the darkness, he on the right and I on the left, for the Martians, who seemed to be all about us. In one place we blundered upon a scorched and blackened area, now cooling and ashen, and a number of scattered dead bodies of men, burned horribly about the heads and trunks but with their legs and boots mostly intact; and of dead horses, fifty feet, perhaps, behind a line of four ripped guns and smashed gun carriages.

Sheen, it seemed, had escaped destruction, but the place was silent and deserted. Here we happened on no dead, though the night was too dark for us to see into the side roads of the place. In Sheen my companion suddenly complained of faintness and thirst, and we decided to try one of the houses.

The first house we entered, after a little difficulty with the window, was a small semi-detached villa, and I found nothing eatable left in the place but some mouldy cheese. There was, however, water to drink; and I took a hatchet, which promised to be useful in our next house-breaking.

We then crossed to a place where the road turns towards Mortlake. Here there stood a white house within a walled garden, and in the pantry of this domicile we found a store of food – two loaves of bread in a pan, an uncooked steak, and the half of a ham. I give this catalogue so precisely because, as it happened, we were destined to subsist upon this store for the next fortnight. Bottled beer stood under a shelf, and there were two bags of haricot beans and some limp lettuces. This pantry opened into a kind of wash-up kitchen, and in this was firewood; there was also a cupboard, in which we found nearly a dozen of burgundy, tinned soups and salmon, and two tins of biscuits.

We sat in the adjacent kitchen in the dark – for we dared not strike a light – and ate bread and ham, and drank beer out of the same bottle. The curate, who was still timorous and restless, was now, oddly enough, for pushing on, and I was urging him to keep up his strength by eating when the thing happened that was to imprison us.

'It can't be midnight yet,' I said, and then came a blinding glare of vivid green light. Everything in the kitchen leaped out, clearly visible in green and black, and vanished again. And then followed such a concussion as I have never heard before or since. So close on the heels of this as to seem instantaneous came a thud behind me, a clash of glass, a crash and rattle of falling masonry all about us, and the plaster of the ceiling came down upon us, smashing into a multitude of fragments upon our heads. I was knocked headlong across the floor against the oven handle and stunned. I was insensible for a long time, the curate told me, and when I came to we were in darkness again, and he, with a face wet, as I found afterwards, with blood from a cut forehead, was dabbing water over me.

For some time I could not recollect what had happened. Then things came to me slowly. A bruise on my temple asserted itself.

'Are you better?' asked the curate in a whisper.

At last I answered him. I sat up.

'Don't move,' he said. 'The floor is covered with smashed crockery from the dresser. You can't possibly move without making a noise, and I fancy *they* are outside.'

We both sat quite silent, so that we could scarcely hear each other breathing. Everything seemed deadly still, but once something near us, some plaster or broken brickwork, slid down with a rumbling sound. Outside and very near was an intermittent, metallic rattle.

'That!' said the curate, when presently it happened again.

'Yes,' I said. 'But what is it?'

'A Martian!' said the curate.

I listened again.

'It was not like the Heat-Ray,' I said, and for a time I was inclined to think one of the great fighting-machines had stumbled against the house, as I had seen one stumble against the tower of Shepperton Church.

Our situation was so strange and incomprehensible that for three or four hours, until the dawn came, we scarcely moved. And then the light filtered in, not through the window, which remained black, but through a triangular aperture between a beam and a heap of broken bricks in the wall behind us. The interior of the kitchen we now saw greyly for the first time.

The window had been burst in by a mass of garden mould, which flowed over the table upon which we had been sitting and lay about our feet. Outside, the soil was banked high against the house. At the top of the window frame we could see an uprooted drainpipe. The floor was littered with smashed hardware; the end of the kitchen towards the house was broken into, and since the daylight shone in there, it was evident the greater part of the house had collapsed. Contrasting vividly with this ruin was the neat dresser, stained in the fashion, pale green, and with a number of copper and tin vessels below it, the wallpaper imitating blue and white tiles, and a couple of coloured supplements[77] fluttering from the walls above the kitchen range.

As the dawn grew clearer, we saw through the gap in the wall the body of a Martian, standing sentinel, I suppose, over the still glowing cylinder. At the sight of that we crawled as circumspectly as possible out of the twilight of the kitchen into the darkness of the scullery.

Abruptly the right interpretation dawned upon my mind.

'The fifth cylinder,' I whispered, 'the fifth shot from Mars, has struck this house and buried us under the ruins!'

For a time the curate was silent, and then he whispered: 'God have mercy upon us!'

I heard him presently whimpering to himself.

Save for that sound we lay quite still in the scullery; I for my part scarce dared breathe, and sat with my eyes fixed on the faint light of the kitchen door. I could just see the curate's face, a dim, oval shape, and his collar and cuffs. Outside there began a metallic hammering, then a violent hooting, and then again, after a quiet interval, a hissing like the hissing of an engine. These noises, for the most part problematical, continued intermittently, and seemed if anything to increase in number as time wore on. Presently a measured thudding and a vibration that made everything about us quiver and the vessels in the pantry ring and shift, began and continued. Once the light was eclipsed, and the ghostly kitchen doorway became absolutely dark. For many hours we must have crouched there, silent and shivering, until our tired attention failed . . .

At last I found myself awake and very hungry. I am inclined to believe we must have spent the greater portion of a day before that awakening. My hunger was at a stride so insistent that it moved me to action. I told the curate I was going to seek food, and felt my way towards the pantry. He made me no answer, but so soon as I began eating the faint noise I made stirred him up and I heard him crawling after me.

CHAPTER TWO

What We Saw from the Ruined House

After eating we crept back to the scullery, and there I must have dozed again, for when presently I looked round I was alone. The thudding vibration continued with wearisome persistence. I whispered for the curate several times, and at last felt my way to the door of the kitchen. It was still daylight, and I perceived him across the room, lying against the triangular hole that looked out upon the Martians. His shoulders were hunched, so that his head was hidden from me.

I could hear a number of noises almost like those in an engine shed; and the place rocked with that beating thud. Through the aperture in the wall I could see the top of a tree touched with gold and the warm blue of a tranquil evening sky. For a minute or so I remained watching the curate, and then I advanced, crouching and stepping with extreme care amid the broken crockery that littered the floor.

I touched the curate's leg, and he started so violently that a mass of plaster went sliding down outside and fell with a loud impact. I gripped his arm, fearing he might cry out, and for a long time we crouched motionless. Then I turned to see how much of our rampart remained. The detachment of the plaster had left a vertical slit open in the debris, and by raising myself cautiously across a beam I was able to see out of this gap into what had been overnight a quiet suburban roadway. Vast, indeed, was the change that we beheld.

The fifth cylinder must have fallen right into the midst of the house we had first visited. The building had vanished, completely smashed, pulverised, and dispersed by the blow. The cylinder lay now far beneath the original foundations – deep in a hole, already vastly larger than the pit I had looked into at Woking. The earth all round it had splashed under that tremendous impact – 'splashed' is the only word – and lay in heaped piles that hid the masses of the adjacent houses. It had behaved exactly like mud under the violent blow of a hammer. Our house had collapsed backward; the front portion, even on the ground floor, had been destroyed completely; by a chance the kitchen and scullery had escaped, and stood buried now under soil and ruins, closed in by tons of earth on every side save towards the cylinder. Over that aspect we hung now on the very edge of the great circular pit the Martians were engaged in making. The heavy beating sound was evidently just behind us, and ever and again a bright green vapour drove up like a veil across our peephole.

The cylinder was already opened in the centre of the pit, and on the farther edge of the pit, amid the smashed and gravel-heaped shrubbery, one of the great fighting-machines, deserted by its occupant, stood stiff and tall against the evening sky. At first I scarcely noticed the pit and the cylinder, although it has been convenient to describe them first, on account of the extraordinary glittering mechanism I saw busy in the excavation, and on account of the strange creatures that were crawling slowly and painfully across the heaped mould near it.

The mechanism it certainly was that held my attention first. It was one of those complicated fabrics that have since been called handling-machines, and the study of which has already given such an enormous impetus to terrestrial invention. As it dawned upon me first, it presented a sort of metallic spider with five jointed, agile legs, and with an extra-ordinary number of jointed levers, bars, and reaching and clutching tentacles about its body. Most of its arms were retracted, but with three long tentacles it was fishing out a number of rods, plates, and bars which lined the covering and apparently strengthened the walls of the cylinder. These, as it extracted them, were lifted out and deposited upon a level surface of earth behind it.

Its motion was so swift, complex, and perfect that at first I did not see it as a machine, in spite of its metallic glitter. The fighting-machines were coordinated and animated to an extraordinary pitch, but nothing to compare with this. People who have never seen these structures, and have only the ill-imagined efforts of artists or the imperfect descriptions of such eye-witnesses as myself to go upon, scarcely realise that living quality.

I recall particularly the illustration of one of the first pamphlets to give a consecutive account of the war. The artist had evidently made a hasty study of one of the fighting-machines, and there his knowledge ended. He presented them as tilted, stiff tripods, without either flexibility or subtlety, and with an altogether misleading monotony of effect. The pamphlet containing these renderings had a considerable vogue, and I mention them here simply to warn the reader against the impression they may have created. They were no more like the Martians I saw in action than a Dutch doll is like a human being. To my mind, the pamphlet would have been much better without them.

At first, I say, the handling-machine did not impress me as a machine, but as a crablike creature with a glittering integument, the controlling Martian whose delicate tentacles actuated its movements seeming to be simply the equivalent of the crab's cerebral portion. But then I perceived the resemblance of its grey-brown, shiny, leathery integument to that of the other sprawling bodies beyond, and the true nature of this dexterous workman dawned upon me. With that realisation my interest shifted to those other creatures, the real Martians. Already I had had a transient impression of these, and the first nausea no longer obscured my observation. Moreover, I was concealed and motionless, and under no urgency of action.

They were, I now saw, the most unearthly creatures it is possible to conceive. They were huge round bodies – or, rather, heads – about four feet in diameter, each body having in front of it a face. This face had no nostrils – indeed, the Martians do not seem to have had any sense of smell, but it had a pair of very large dark-coloured eyes, and just beneath this a kind of fleshy beak. In the back of this head or body – I scarcely know how to speak of it – was the single tight tympanic surface, since known to be anatomically an ear, though it must have been almost useless in our dense air. In a group round the mouth were sixteen slender, almost whiplike tentacles, arranged in two bunches of eight each. These bunches have since been named rather aptly, by that distinguished anatomist, Professor Howes,[78] the *hands*. Even as I saw these Martians for the first time they seemed to be endeavouring to raise themselves on these hands, but of course, with the increased weight of terrestrial conditions, this was impossible. There is reason to suppose that on Mars they may have progressed upon them with some facility.

The internal anatomy, I may remark here, as dissection has since shown, was almost equally simple. The greater part of the structure was the brain, sending enormous nerves to the eyes, ear, and tactile tentacles. Besides this were the bulky lungs, into which the mouth opened, and the heart and its vessels. The pulmonary distress caused by the denser atmosphere and greater gravitational attraction was only too evident in the convulsive movements of the outer skin.

And this was the sum of the Martian organs. Strange as it may seem to a human being, all the complex apparatus of digestion, which makes up the bulk of our bodies, did not exist in the Martians. They were heads – merely heads. Entrails they had none. They did not eat, much less digest. Instead, they took the fresh, living blood of other creatures, and *injected* it into their own veins. I have myself seen this being done, as I shall mention in its place. But, squeamish as I may seem, I cannot bring myself to describe what I could not endure even to continue watching. Let it suffice to say, blood obtained from a still living animal, in most cases from a human being, was run directly by means of a little pipette into the recipient canal . . .

The bare idea of this is no doubt horribly repulsive to us, but at the same time I think that we should remember how repulsive our carnivorous habits would seem to an intelligent rabbit.

The physiological advantages of the practice of injection are undeniable, if one thinks of the tremendous waste of human time and energy occasioned by eating and the digestive process. Our bodies are half made up of glands and tubes and organs, occupied in turning heterogeneous food into blood. The digestive processes and their reaction upon the nervous system sap our strength and colour our minds. Men go happy or miserable as they have healthy or unhealthy livers, or sound gastric glands. But the Martians were lifted above all these organic fluctuations of mood and emotion.

Their undeniable preference for men as their source of nourishment is partly explained by the nature of the remains of the victims they had brought with them as provisions from Mars. These creatures, to judge from the shrivelled remains that have fallen into human hands, were bipeds with flimsy, silicious skeletons (almost like those of the silicious sponges) and feeble musculature, standing about six feet high and having round, erect heads, and large eyes in flinty sockets. Two or three of these seem to have been brought in each cylinder, and all were killed before earth was reached. It was just as well for them, for the mere attempt to stand upright upon our planet would have broken every bone in their bodies.

And while I am engaged in this description, I may add in this place certain further details which, although they were not all evident to us at the time, will enable the reader who is unacquainted with them to form a clearer picture of these offensive creatures.

In three other points their physiology differed strangely from ours. Their organisms did not sleep, any more than the heart of man sleeps. Since they had no extensive muscular mechanism to recuperate, that periodical extinction was unknown to them. They had little or no sense of fatigue, it would seem. On earth they could never have moved without effort, yet even to the last they kept in action. In twenty-four hours they did twenty-four hours of work, as even on earth is perhaps the case with the ants.

In the next place, wonderful as it seems in a sexual world, the Martians were absolutely without sex, and therefore without any of the tumultuous emotions that arise from that difference among men. A young Martian, there can now be no dispute, was really born upon earth during the war, and it was found attached to its parent, partially *budded* off, just as young lily-bulbs bud off, or like the young animals in the freshwater polyp.

In man, in all the higher terrestrial animals, such a method of increase has disappeared; but even on this earth it was certainly the primitive method. Among the lower animals, up even to those first cousins of the vertebrated animals, the Tunicates, the two processes occur side by side, but finally the sexual method superseded its competitor altogether. On Mars, however, just the reverse has apparently been the case.

It is worthy of remark that a certain speculative writer of quasi-scientific repute, writing long before the Martian invasion, did forecast for man a final structure not unlike the actual Martian condition. His prophecy, I remember, appeared in November or December 1893, in a long-defunct publication, the *Pall Mall Budget*,[79] and I recall a caricature of it in a pre-Martian periodical called *Punch*. He pointed out – writing in a foolish, facetious tone – that the perfection of mechanical appliances must ultimately supersede limbs; the perfection of chemical devices, digestion; that such organs as hair, external nose, teeth, ears, and chin were no longer essential parts of the human being, and that the tendency of natural selection would lie in the direction of their steady diminution through the coming ages. The brain alone remained a cardinal necessity. Only one other part of the body had a strong case for survival, and that was the hand, 'teacher and agent of the brain'. While the rest of the body dwindled, the hands would grow larger.

There is many a true word written in jest, and here in the Martians we have beyond dispute the actual accomplishment of such a suppression of the animal side of the organism by the intelligence. To me it is quite credible that the Martians may be descended from beings not unlike ourselves, by a gradual development of brain and hands (the latter giving rise to the two bunches of delicate tentacles at last) at the expense of the rest of the body. Without the body the brain would, of course, become a mere selfish intelligence, without any of the emotional substratum of the human being.

The last salient point in which the systems of these creatures differed from ours was in what one might have thought a very trivial particular. Micro-organisms, which cause so much disease and pain on earth, have either never appeared upon Mars or Martian sanitary science eliminated them ages ago. A hundred diseases, all the fevers and contagions of human life, consumption, cancers, tumours and such morbidities, never enter the scheme of their life. And speaking of the differences between the life on Mars and terrestrial life, I may allude here to the curious suggestions of the red weed.[80]

Apparently the vegetable kingdom in Mars, instead of having green for a dominant colour, is of a vivid blood-red tint. At any rate, the seeds which the Martians (intentionally or accidentally) brought with them gave rise in all cases to red-coloured growths. Only that known popularly as the red weed, however, gained any footing in competition with terrestrial forms. The red creeper was quite a transitory growth, and few people have seen it growing. For a time, however, the red weed grew with astonishing vigour and luxuriance. It spread up the sides of the pit by the third or fourth day of our imprisonment, and its cactus-like branches formed a carmine fringe to the edges of our triangular window. And afterwards I found it broadcast throughout the country, and especially wherever there was a stream of water.

The Martians had what appears to have been an auditory organ, a single round drum at the back of the head-body, and eyes with a visual range not very different from ours except that, according to Philips,[81] blue and violet were as black to them. It is commonly supposed that they communicated by sounds and tentacular gesticulations; this is asserted, for instance, in the able but hastily compiled pamphlet (written evidently by someone not an eye-witness of Martian actions) to which I have already alluded, and which, so far, has been the chief source of information concerning them. Now no surviving human being saw so much of the Martians in action as I did. I take no credit to myself for an accident, but the fact is so. And I assert that I watched them closely time after time, and that I have seen four, five, and (once) six of them sluggishly performing the most elaborately complicated operations together without either sound or gesture. Their peculiar hooting invariably preceded feeding; it had no modulation, and was, I believe, in no sense a signal, but merely the expiration of air preparatory to the suctional operation. I have a certain claim to at least an elementary knowledge of psychology, and in this matter I am convinced – as firmly as I am convinced of anything – that the Martians interchanged thoughts without any physical intermediation. And I have been convinced of this in spite of strong preconceptions. Before the Martian invasion, as an occasional reader here or there may remember, I had written with some little vehemence against the telepathic theory.[82]

The Martians wore no clothing. Their conceptions of ornament and decorum were necessarily different from ours; and not only were they evidently much less sensible of changes of temperature than we are, but changes of pressure do not seem to have affected their health at all seriously. Yet though they wore no clothing, it was in the other artificial additions to their bodily resources that their great superiority over man lay. We men, with our bicycles and road-skates,[83] our Lilienthal soaring-machines,[84] our guns and sticks and so forth, are just in the beginning of the evolution that the Martians have worked out. They have become practically mere brains, wearing different bodies according to their needs just as men wear suits of clothes and take a bicycle in a hurry or an umbrella in the wet. And of their appliances, perhaps nothing is more wonderful to a man than the curious fact that what is the dominant feature of almost all human devices in mechanism is absent – the *wheel* is absent; among all the things they brought to earth there is no trace or suggestion of their use of wheels. One would have at least expected it in locomotion. And in this connection it is curious to remark that even on this earth Nature has never hit upon the wheel, or has preferred other expedients to its development. And not only did the Martians either not know of (which is incredible), or abstain from, the wheel, but in their apparatus singularly little use is made of the fixed pivot or relatively fixed pivot, with circular motions thereabout confined to one plane. Almost all the joints of the machinery present a complicated system of sliding parts moving over small but beautifully curved friction bearings. And while upon this matter of detail, it is remarkable that the long leverages of their machines are in most cases actuated by a sort of sham musculature of the disks in an elastic sheath; these disks become polarised and drawn closely and powerfully together when traversed by a current of electricity. In this way the curious parallelism to animal motions, which was so striking and disturbing to the human beholder, was attained. Such quasi-muscles abounded in the crablike handling-machine which, on my first peeping out of the slit, I watched unpacking the cylinder. It seemed infinitely more alive than the actual Martians lying beyond it in the sunset light, panting, stirring ineffectual tentacles, and moving feebly after their vast journey across space.

While I was still watching their sluggish motions in the sunlight, and noting each strange detail of their form, the curate reminded me of his presence by pulling violently at my arm. I turned to a scowling face, and silent, eloquent lips. He wanted the slit, which permitted only one of us to peep through; and so I had to forgo watching them for a time while he enjoyed that privilege.

When I looked again, the busy handling-machine had already put together several of the pieces of apparatus it had taken out of the cylinder into a shape having an unmistakable likeness to its own; and down on the left a busy little digging mechanism had come into view, emitting jets of green vapour and working its way round the pit, excavating and embanking in a methodical and discriminating manner. This it was which had caused the regular beating noise, and the rhythmic shocks that had kept our ruinous refuge quivering. It piped and whistled as it worked. So far as I could see, the thing was without a directing Martian at all.

CHAPTER THREE

The Days of Imprisonment

The arrival of a second fighting-machine drove us from our peephole into the scullery, for we feared that from his elevation the Martian might see down upon us behind our barrier. At a later date we began to feel less in danger of their eyes, for to an eye in the dazzle of the sunlight outside our refuge must have been blank blackness, but at first the slightest suggestion of approach drove us into the scullery in heart-throbbing retreat. Yet terrible as was the danger we incurred, the attraction of peeping was for both of us irresistible. And I recall now with a sort of wonder that, in spite of the infinite danger in which we were between starvation and a still more terrible death, we could yet struggle bitterly for that horrible privilege of sight. We would race across the kitchen in a grotesque way between eagerness and the dread of making a noise, and strike each other, and thrust and kick, within a few inches of exposure.

The fact is that we had absolutely incompatible dispositions and habits of thought and action, and our danger and isolation only accentuated the incompatibility. At Halliford I had already come to hate the curate's trick of helpless exclamation, his stupid rigidity of mind. His endless muttering monologue vitiated every effort I made to think out a line of action, and drove me at times, thus pent up and intensified, almost to the verge of craziness. He was as lacking in restraint as a silly woman. He would weep for hours together, and I verily believe that to the very end this spoiled child of life thought his weak tears in some way efficacious. And I would sit in the darkness unable to keep my mind off him by reason of his importunities. He ate more than I did, and it was in vain I pointed out that our only chance of life was to stop in the house until the Martians had done with their pit, that in that long patience a time might presently come when we should need food. He ate and drank impulsively in heavy meals at long intervals. He slept little.

As the days wore on, his utter carelessness of any consideration so intensified our distress and danger that I had, much as I loathed doing it, to resort to threats, and at last to blows. That brought him to reason for a time. But he was one of those weak creatures, void of pride, timorous, anaemic, hateful souls, full of shifty cunning, who face neither God nor man, who face not even themselves.

It is disagreeable for me to recall and write these things, but I set them down that my story may lack nothing. Those who have escaped the dark and terrible aspects of life will find my brutality, my flash of rage in our final tragedy, easy enough to blame; for they know what is wrong as well as any, but not what is possible to tortured men. But those who have been under the shadow, who have gone down at last to elemental things, will have a wider charity.

And while within we fought out our dark, dim contest of whispers, snatched food and drink, and gripping hands and blows, without, in the pitiless sunlight of that terrible June, was the strange wonder, the unfamiliar routine of the Martians in the pit. Let me return to those first new experiences of mine. After a long time I ventured back to the peephole, to find that the new-comers had been reinforced by the occupants of no fewer than three of the fighting-machines. These last had brought with them certain fresh appliances that stood in an orderly manner about the cylinder. The second handling-machine was now completed, and was busied in serving one of the novel contrivances the big machine had brought. This was a body resembling a milk can in its general form, above which oscillated a pear-shaped receptacle, and from which a stream of white powder flowed into a circular basin below.

The oscillatory motion was imparted to this by one tentacle of the handling-machine. With two spatulate hands the handling-machine was digging out and flinging masses of clay into the pear-shaped receptacle above, while with another arm it periodically opened a door and removed rusty and blackened clinkers from the middle part of the machine. Another steely tentacle directed the powder from the basin along a ribbed channel towards some receiver that was hidden from me by the mound of bluish dust. From this unseen receiver a little thread of green smoke rose vertically into the quiet air. As I looked, the handling-machine, with a faint and musical clinking, extended, telescopic fashion, a tentacle that had been a moment before a mere blunt projection, until its end was hidden behind the mound of clay. In another second it had lifted a bar of white aluminium into sight, untarnished as yet, and shining dazzlingly, and deposited it in a growing stack of bars that stood at the side of the pit. Between sunset and starlight this dexterous machine must have made more than a hundred such bars out of the crude clay, and the mound of bluish dust rose steadily until it topped the side of the pit.

The contrast between the swift and complex movements of these contrivances and the inert panting clumsiness of their masters was acute, and for days I had to tell myself repeatedly that these latter were indeed the living of the two things.

The curate had possession of the slit when the first men were brought to the pit. I was sitting below, huddled up, listening with all my ears. He made a sudden movement backward, and I, fearful that we were observed, crouched in a spasm of terror. He came sliding down the rubbish and crept beside me in the darkness, inarticulate, gesticulating, and for a moment I shared his panic. His gesture suggested a resignation of the slit, and after a little while my curiosity gave me courage, and I rose up, stepped across him, and clambered up to it. At first I could see no reason for his frantic behaviour. The twilight had now come, the stars were little and faint, but the pit was illuminated by the flickering green fire that came from the aluminium-making. The whole picture was a flickering scheme of green gleams and shifting rusty black shadows, strangely trying to the eyes. Over and through it all went the bats, heeding it not at all. The sprawling Martians were no longer to be seen, the mound of blue-green powder had risen to cover them from sight, and a fighting-machine, with its legs contracted, crumpled, and abbreviated, stood across the corner of the pit. And then, amid the clangour of the machinery, came a drifting suspicion of human voices, that I entertained at first only to dismiss.

I crouched, watching this fighting-machine closely, satisfying myself now for the first time that the hood did indeed contain a Martian. As the green flames lifted I could see the oily gleam of his integument and the brightness of his eyes. And suddenly I heard a yell, and saw a long tentacle reaching over the shoulder of the machine to the little cage that hunched upon its back. Then something – something struggling violently – was lifted high against the sky, a black, vague enigma against the starlight; and as this black object came down again, I saw by the green brightness that it was a man. For an instant he was clearly visible. He was a stout, ruddy, middle-aged man, well dressed; three days before, he must have been walking the world, a man of considerable consequence. I could see his staring eyes and gleams of light on his studs and watch chain. He vanished behind the mound, and for a moment there was silence. And then began a shrieking and a sustained and cheerful hooting from the Martians.

I slid down the rubbish, struggled to my feet, clapped my hands over my ears, and bolted into the scullery. The curate, who had been crouching silently with his arms over his head, looked up as I passed, cried out quite loudly at my desertion of him, and came running after me.

That night, as we lurked in the scullery, balanced between our horror and the terrible fascination this peeping had, although I felt an urgent need of action I tried in vain to conceive some plan of escape; but afterwards, during the second day, I was able to consider our position with great clearness. The curate, I found, was quite incapable of discussion; this new and culminating atrocity had robbed him of all vestiges of reason or forethought. Practically he had already sunk to the level of an animal. But as the saying goes, I gripped myself with both hands. It grew upon my mind, once I could face the facts, that terrible as our position was, there was as yet no justification for absolute despair. Our chief chance lay in the possibility of the Martians making the pit nothing more than a temporary encampment. Or even if they kept it permanently, they might not consider it necessary to guard it, and a chance of escape might be afforded us. I also weighed very carefully the possibility of our digging a way out in a direction away from the pit, but the chances of our emerging within sight of some sentinel fighting-machine seemed at first too great. And I should have had to do all the digging myself. The curate would certainly have failed me.

It was on the third day, if my memory serves me right, that I saw the lad killed. It was the only occasion on which I actually saw the Martians feed. After that experience I avoided the hole in the wall for the better part of a day. I went into the scullery, removed the door, and spent some hours digging with my hatchet as silently as possible; but when I had made a hole about a couple of feet deep the loose earth collapsed noisily, and I did not dare continue. I lost heart, and lay down on the scullery floor for a long time, having no spirit even to move. And after that I abandoned altogether the idea of escaping by excavation.

It says much for the impression the Martians had made upon me that at first I entertained little or no hope of our escape being brought about by their overthrow through any human effort. But on the fourth or fifth night I heard a sound like heavy guns.

It was very late in the night, and the moon was shining brightly. The Martians had taken away the excavating-machine, and, save for a fighting-machine that stood in the remoter bank of the pit and a handling-machine that was buried out of my sight in a corner of the pit immediately beneath my peephole, the place was deserted by them. Except for the pale glow from the handling-machine and the bars and patches of white moonlight the pit was in darkness, and, except for the clinking of the handling-machine, quite still. That night was a beautiful serenity; save for one planet, the moon seemed to have the sky to herself. I heard a dog howling, and that familiar sound it was that made me listen. Then I heard quite distinctly a booming exactly like the sound of great guns. Six distinct reports I counted, and after a long interval six again. And that was all.

CHAPTER FOUR

The Death of the Curate

It was on the sixth day of our imprisonment that I peeped for the last time, and presently found myself alone. Instead of keeping close to me and trying to oust me from the slit, the curate had gone back into the scullery. I was struck by a sudden thought. I went back quickly and quietly into the scullery. In the darkness I heard the curate drinking. I snatched in the darkness, and my fingers caught a bottle of burgundy.

For a few minutes there was a tussle. The bottle struck the floor and broke, and I desisted and rose. We stood panting and threatening each other. In the end I planted myself between him and the food, and told him of my determination to begin a discipline. I divided the food in the pantry, into rations to last us ten days. I would not let him eat any more that day. In the afternoon he made a feeble effort to get at the food. I had been dozing, but in an instant I was awake. All day and all night we sat face to face, I weary but resolute, and he weeping and complaining of his immediate hunger. It was, I know, a night and a day, but to me it seemed – it seems now – an interminable length of time.

And so our widened incompatibility ended at last in open conflict. For two vast days we struggled in undertones and wrestling contests. There were times when I beat and kicked him madly, times when I cajoled and persuaded him, and once I tried to bribe him with the last bottle of burgundy, for there was a rainwater pump from which I could get water. But neither force nor kindness availed; he was indeed beyond reason. He would neither desist from his attacks on the food nor from his noisy babbling to himself. The rudimentary precautions to keep our imprisonment endurable he would not observe. Slowly I began to realise the complete overthrow of his intelligence, to perceive that my sole companion in this close and sickly darkness was a man insane.

From certain vague memories I am inclined to think my own mind wandered at times. I had strange and hideous dreams whenever I slept. It sounds paradoxical, but I am inclined to think that the weakness and insanity of the curate warned me, braced me, and kept me a sane man.

On the eighth day he began to talk aloud instead of whispering, and nothing I could do would moderate his speech.

'It is just, O God!' he would say, over and over again. 'It is just. On me and mine be the punishment laid. We have sinned, we have fallen short.[85] There was poverty, sorrow; the poor were trodden in the dust, and I held my peace. I preached acceptable folly – my God, what folly! – when I should have stood up, though I died for it, and called upon them to repent – repent! . . . Oppressors of the poor and needy[86] . . . ! The wine press of God!'[87]

Then he would suddenly revert to the matter of the food I withheld from him, praying, begging, weeping, at last threatening. He began to raise his voice – I prayed him not to. He perceived a hold on me – he threatened he would shout and bring the Martians upon us. For a time that scared me; but any concession would have shortened our chance of escape beyond estimating. I defied him, although I felt no assurance that he might not do this thing. But that day, at any rate, he did not. He talked with his voice rising slowly, through the greater part of the eighth and ninth days – threats, entreaties, mingled with a torrent of half-sane and always frothy repentance for his vacant sham of God's service, such as made me pity him. Then he slept awhile, and began again with renewed strength, so loudly that I must needs make him desist.

'Be still!' I implored.

He rose to his knees, for he had been sitting in the darkness near the copper.

'I have been still too long,' he said, in a tone that must have reached the pit, 'and now I must bear my witness. Woe unto this unfaithful city! Woe! Woe! Woe! Woe! Woe! To the inhabitants of the earth by reason of the other voices of the trumpet – '

'Shut up!' I said, rising to my feet, and in a terror lest the Martians should hear us. 'For God's sake – '

'Nay,' shouted the curate, at the top of his voice, standing likewise and extending his arms. 'Speak! The word of the Lord is upon me!'

In three strides he was at the door leading into the kitchen.

'I must bear my witness! I go! It has already been too long delayed.'

I put out my hand and felt the meat chopper hanging to the wall. In a flash I was after him. I was fierce with fear. Before he was halfway across the kitchen I had overtaken him. With one last touch of humanity I turned the blade back and struck him with the butt. He went headlong forward and lay stretched on the ground. I stumbled over him and stood panting. He lay still.

Suddenly I heard a noise without, the run and smash of slipping plaster, and the triangular aperture in the wall was darkened. I looked up and saw the lower surface of a handling-machine coming slowly across the hole. One of its gripping limbs curled amid the debris;

another limb appeared, feeling its way over the fallen beams. I stood petrified, staring. Then I saw through a sort of glass plate near the edge of the body the face, as we may call it, and the large dark eyes of a Martian, peering, and then a long metallic snake of tentacle came feeling slowly through the hole.

I turned by an effort, stumbled over the curate, and stopped at the scullery door. The tentacle was now some way, two yards or more, in the room, and twisting and turning, with queer sudden movements, this way and that. For a while I stood fascinated by that slow, fitful advance. Then, with a faint, hoarse cry, I forced myself across the scullery. I trembled violently; I could scarcely stand upright. I opened the door of the coal cellar, and stood there in the darkness staring at the faintly lit doorway into the kitchen, and listening. Had the Martian seen me? What was it doing now?

Something was moving to and fro there, very quietly; every now and then it tapped against the wall, or started on its movements with a faint metallic ringing, like the movements of keys on a split-ring. Then a heavy body – I knew too well what – was dragged across the floor of the kitchen towards the opening. Irresistibly attracted, I crept to the door and peeped into the kitchen. In the triangle of bright outer sunlight I saw the Martian, in its Briareus[88] of a handling-machine, scrutinising the curate's head. I thought at once that it would infer my presence from the mark of the blow I had given him.

I crept back to the coal cellar, shut the door, and began to cover myself up as much as I could, and as noiselessly as possible in the darkness, among the firewood and coal therein. Every now and then I paused, rigid, to hear if the Martian had thrust its tentacles through the opening again.

Then the faint metallic jingle returned. I traced it slowly feeling over the kitchen. Presently I heard it nearer – in the scullery, as I judged. I thought that its length might be insufficient to reach me. I prayed copiously. It passed, scraping faintly across the cellar door. An age of almost intolerable suspense intervened; then I heard it fumbling at the latch! It had found the door! The Martians understood doors!

It worried at the catch for a minute, perhaps, and then the door opened.

In the darkness I could just see the thing – like an elephant's trunk more than anything else – waving towards me and touching and examining the wall, coals, wood and ceiling. It was like a black worm swaying its blind head to and fro.

Once, even, it touched the heel of my boot. I was on the verge of screaming; I bit my hand. For a time the tentacle was silent. I could have fancied it had been withdrawn. Presently, with an abrupt click, it gripped something – I thought it had me! – and seemed to go out of the cellar again. For a minute I was not sure. Apparently it had taken a lump of coal to examine.

I seized the opportunity of slightly shifting my position, which had become cramped, and then listened. I whispered passionate prayers for safety.

Then I heard the slow, deliberate sound creeping towards me again. Slowly, slowly it drew near, scratching against the walls and tapping the furniture.

While I was still doubtful, it rapped smartly against the cellar door and closed it. I heard it go into the pantry, and the biscuit-tins rattled and a bottle smashed, and then came a heavy bump against the cellar door. Then silence that passed into an infinity of suspense.

Had it gone?

At last I decided that it had.

It came into the scullery no more; but I lay all the tenth day in the close darkness, buried among coals and firewood, not daring even to crawl out for the drink for which I craved. It was the eleventh day before I ventured so far from my security.

CHAPTER FIVE

The Stillness

My first act before I went into the pantry was to fasten the door between the kitchen and the scullery. But the pantry was empty; every scrap of food had gone. Apparently, the Martian had taken it all on the previous day. At that discovery I despaired for the first time. I took no food, or no drink either, on the eleventh or the twelfth day.

At first my mouth and throat were parched, and my strength ebbed sensibly. I sat about in the darkness of the scullery, in a state of despondent wretchedness. My mind ran on eating. I thought I had become deaf, for the noises of movement I had been accustomed to hear from the pit had ceased absolutely. I did not feel strong enough to crawl noiselessly to the peephole, or I would have gone there.

On the twelfth day my throat was so painful that, taking the chance of alarming the Martians, I attacked the creaking rainwater pump that stood by the sink, and got a couple of glassfuls of blackened and tainted rain-water. I was greatly refreshed by this, and emboldened by the fact that no enquiring tentacle followed the noise of my pumping.

During these days, in a rambling, inconclusive way, I thought much of the curate and of the manner of his death.

On the thirteenth day I drank some more water, and dozed and thought disjointedly of eating and of vague impossible plans of escape. Whenever I dozed I dreamt of horrible phantasms, of the death of the curate, or of sumptuous dinners; but, asleep or awake, I felt a keen pain that urged me to drink again and again. The light that came into the scullery was no longer grey, but red. To my disordered imagination it seemed the colour of blood.

On the fourteenth day I went into the kitchen, and I was surprised to find that the fronds of the red weed had grown right across the hole in the wall, turning the half-light of the place into a crimson-coloured obscurity.

It was early on the fifteenth day that I heard a curious, familiar sequence of sounds in the kitchen, and, listening, identified it as the snuffing and scratching of a dog. Going into the kitchen, I saw a dog's nose peering in through a break among the ruddy fronds. This greatly surprised me. At the scent of me he barked shortly.

I thought if I could induce him to come into the place quietly I should be able, perhaps, to kill and eat him; and in any case, it would be advisable to kill him, lest his actions attracted the attention of the Martians.

I crept forward, saying 'Good dog!' very softly; but he suddenly withdrew his head and disappeared.

I listened – I was not deaf – but certainly the pit was still. I heard a sound like the flutter of a bird's wings, and a hoarse croaking, but that was all.

For a long while I lay close to the peephole, but not daring to move aside the red plants that obscured it. Once or twice I heard a faint pitter-patter like the feet of the dog going hither and thither on the sand far below me, and there were more birdlike sounds, but that was all. At length, encouraged by the silence, I looked out.

Except in the corner, where a multitude of crows hopped and fought over the skeletons of the dead the Martians had consumed, there was not a living thing in the pit.

I stared about me, scarcely believing my eyes. All the machinery had gone. Save for the big mound of greyish-blue powder in one corner, certain bars of aluminium in another, the black birds, and the skeletons of the killed, the place was merely an empty circular pit in the sand.

Slowly I thrust myself out through the red weed, and stood upon the mound of rubble. I could see in any direction save behind me, to the north, and neither Martians nor sign of Martians were to be seen. The pit dropped sheerly from my feet, but a little way along the rubbish afforded a practicable slope to the summit of the ruins. My chance of escape had come. I began to tremble.

I hesitated for some time, and then, in a gust of desperate resolution, and with a heart that throbbed violently, I scrambled to the top of the mound in which I had been buried so long.

I looked about again. To the northward, too, no Martian was visible.

When I had last seen this part of Sheen in the daylight it had been a straggling street of comfortable white and red houses, interspersed with abundant shady trees. Now I stood on a mound of smashed brickwork, clay, and gravel, over which spread a multitude of red cactus-shaped plants, knee-high, without a solitary terrestrial growth to dispute their footing. The trees near me were dead and brown, but a further network of red thread scaled the still living stems.

The neighbouring houses had all been wrecked, but none had been burned; their walls stood, sometimes to the second storey, with smashed windows and shattered doors. The red weed grew tumultuously in their roofless rooms. Below me was the great pit, with the crows struggling for its refuse. A number of other birds hopped about among the ruins. Far away I saw a gaunt cat slink crouchingly along a wall, but traces of men there were none.

The day seemed, by contrast with my recent confinement, dazzlingly bright, the sky a glowing blue. A gentle breeze kept the red weed that covered every scrap of unoccupied ground gently swaying. And oh! the sweetness of the air!

CHAPTER SIX

The Work of Fifteen Days

For some time I stood tottering on the mound regardless of my safety. Within that noisome den from which I had emerged I had thought with a narrow intensity only of our immediate security. I had not realised what had been happening to the world, had not anticipated this startling vision of unfamiliar things. I had expected to see Sheen in ruins – I found about me the landscape, weird and lurid, of another planet.

For that moment I touched an emotion beyond the common range of men, yet one that the poor brutes we dominate know only too well. I felt as a rabbit might feel returning to his burrow and suddenly confronted by the work of a dozen busy navvies digging the foundations of a house. I felt the first inkling of a thing that presently grew quite clear in my mind, that oppressed me for many days, a sense of dethronement, a persuasion that I was no longer a master, but an animal among the animals, under the Martian heel. With us it would be as with them, to lurk and watch, to run and hide; the fear and empire of man had passed away.

But so soon as this strangeness had been realised it passed, and my dominant motive became the hunger of my long and dismal fast. In the direction away from the pit I saw, beyond a red-covered wall, a patch of garden ground unburied. This gave me a hint, and I went knee-deep, and sometimes neck-deep, in the red weed. The density of the weed gave me a reassuring sense of hiding. The wall was some six feet high, and when I attempted to clamber it I found I could not lift my feet to the crest. So I went along by the side of it, and came to a corner and a rockwork that enabled me to get to the top, and tumble into the garden I coveted. Here I found some young onions, a couple of gladiolus bulbs, and a quantity of immature carrots, all of which I secured, and, scrambling over a ruined wall, went on my way through scarlet and crimson trees towards Kew – it was like walking through an avenue of gigantic blood drops – possessed with two ideas: to get more food, and to limp, as soon and as far as my strength permitted, out of this accursed unearthly region of the pit.

Some way farther, in a grassy place, was a group of mushrooms which also I devoured, and then I came upon a brown sheet of flowing shallow water, where meadows used to be. These fragments of nourishment served only to whet my hunger. At first I was surprised at this flood in a hot, dry summer, but afterwards I discovered that it was caused by the tropical exuberance of the red weed. Directly this extraordinary growth encountered water it straightway became gigantic and of unparalleled fecundity. Its seeds were simply poured down into the water of the Wey and Thames, and its swiftly growing and Titanic water fronds speedily choked both those rivers.

At Putney,[89] as I afterwards saw, the bridge was almost lost in a tangle of this weed, and at Richmond, too, the Thames water poured in a broad and shallow stream across the meadows of Hampton and Twickenham. As the water spread the weed followed them, until the ruined villas of the Thames valley were for a time lost in this red swamp, whose margin I explored, and much of the desolation the Martians had caused was concealed.

In the end the red weed succumbed almost as quickly as it had spread. A cankering disease, due, it is believed, to the action of certain bacteria, presently seized upon it. Now by the action of natural selection, all terrestrial plants have acquired a resisting power against bacterial diseases – they never succumb without a severe struggle, but the red weed rotted like a thing already dead. The fronds became bleached, and then shrivelled and brittle. They broke off at the least touch, and the waters that had stimulated their early growth carried their last vestiges out to sea.

My first act on coming to this water was, of course, to slake my thirst. I drank a great deal of it and, moved by an impulse, gnawed some fronds of red weed; but they were watery, and had a sickly, metallic taste. I found the water was sufficiently shallow for me to wade securely, although the red weed impeded my feet a little; but the flood evidently got deeper towards the river, and I turned back to Mortlake. I managed to make out the road by means of occasional ruins of its villas and fences and lamps, and so presently I got out of this spate and made my way to the hill going up towards Roehampton and came out on Putney Common.

Here the scenery changed from the strange and unfamiliar to the wreckage of the familiar: patches of ground exhibited the devastation of a cyclone, and in a few score yards I would come upon perfectly undisturbed spaces, houses with their blinds trimly drawn and doors closed, as if they had been left for a day by the owners, or as if their inhabitants slept within. The red weed was less abundant; the tall trees along the lane were free from the red creeper. I hunted for food among the trees, finding nothing, and I also raided a couple of silent houses, but they had already been broken into and ransacked. I rested for the remainder of the daylight in a shrubbery, being, in my enfeebled condition, too fatigued to push on.

All this time I saw no human beings, and no signs of the Martians. I encountered a couple of hungry-looking dogs, but both hurried circuitously away from the advances I made them. Near Roehampton I had seen two human skeletons – not bodies, but skeletons, picked clean – and in the wood by me I found the crushed and scattered bones of several cats and rabbits and the skull of a sheep. But though I gnawed parts of these in my mouth, there was nothing to be got from them.

After sunset I struggled on along the road towards Putney, where I think the Heat-Ray must have been used for some reason. And in the garden beyond Roehampton I got a quantity of immature potatoes, sufficient to stay my hunger. From this garden one looked down upon Putney and the river. The aspect of the place in the dusk was singularly desolate: blackened trees, blackened, desolate ruins, and down the hill the sheets of the flooded river, red-tinged with the weed. And over all – silence. It filled me with indescribable terror to think how swiftly that desolating change had come.

For a time I believed that mankind had been swept out of existence, and that I stood there alone, the last man left alive. Hard by the top of Putney Hill I came upon another skeleton, with the arms dislocated and removed several yards from the rest of the body. As I proceeded I became more and more convinced that the extermination of mankind was, save for such stragglers as myself, already accomplished in this part of the world. The Martians, I thought, had gone on and left the country desolated, seeking food elsewhere. Perhaps even now they were destroying Berlin or Paris, or it might be they had gone northward.

CHAPTER SEVEN

The Man on Putney Hill

I spent that night in the inn that stands at the top of Putney Hill, sleeping in a made bed for the first time since my flight to Leatherhead. I will not tell the needless trouble I had breaking into that house – afterwards I found the front door was on the latch – nor how I ransacked every room for food, until just on the verge of despair, in what seemed to me to be a servant's bedroom, I found a rat-gnawed crust and two tins of pineapple. The place had been already searched and emptied. In the bar I afterwards found some biscuits and sandwiches that had been overlooked. The latter I could not eat, they were too rotten, but the former not only stayed my hunger, but filled my pockets. I lit no lamps, fearing some Martian might come beating that part of London for food in the night. Before I went to bed I had an interval of restlessness, and prowled from window to window, peering out for some sign of these monsters. I slept little. As I lay in bed I found myself thinking consecutively – a thing I do not remember to have done since my last argument with the curate. During all the intervening time my mental condition had been a hurrying succession of vague emotional states or a sort of stupid receptivity. But in the night my brain, reinforced, I suppose, by the food I had eaten, grew clear again, and I thought.

Three things struggled for possession of my mind: the killing of the curate, the whereabouts of the Martians, and the possible fate of my wife. The former gave me no sensation of horror or remorse to recall; I saw it simply as a thing done, a memory infinitely disagreeable but quite without the quality of remorse. I saw myself then as I see myself now, driven step by step towards that hasty blow, the creature of a sequence of accidents leading inevitably to that. I felt no condemnation; yet the memory, static, unprogressive, haunted me. In the silence of the night, with that sense of the nearness of God that sometimes comes into the stillness and the darkness, I stood my trial, my only trial, for that moment of wrath and fear. I retraced every step of our conversation from the moment when I had found him crouching beside me, heedless of my thirst, and pointing to the fire and smoke that streamed up from the ruins of Weybridge. We had been incapable of co-operation – grim chance had taken no heed of that. Had I foreseen, I should have left him at Halliford. But I did not foresee; and crime is to foresee and do. And I set this down as I have set all this story down, as it was. There were no witnesses – all these things I might have concealed. But I set it down, and the reader must form his judgement as he will.

And when, by an effort, I had set aside that picture of a prostrate body, I faced the problem of the Martians and the fate of my wife. For the former I had no data; I could imagine a hundred things, and so, unhappily, I could for the latter. And suddenly that night became terrible. I found myself sitting up in bed, staring at the dark. I found myself praying that the Heat-Ray might have suddenly and painlessly struck her out of being. Since the night of my return from Leatherhead I had not prayed. I had uttered prayers, fetish prayers, had prayed as heathens mutter charms when I was in extremity; but now I prayed indeed, pleading steadfastly and sanely, face to face with the darkness of God. Strange night! Strangest in this, that so soon as dawn had come, I, who had talked with God, crept out of the house like a rat leaving its hiding place – a creature scarcely larger, an inferior animal, a thing that for any passing whim of our masters might be hunted and killed. Perhaps they also prayed confidently to God. Surely, if we have learned nothing else, this war has taught us pity – pity for those witless souls that suffer our dominion.

The morning was bright and fine, and the eastern sky glowed pink, and was fretted with little golden clouds. In the road that runs from the top of Putney Hill to Wimbledon was a number of poor vestiges of the panic torrent that must have poured Londonward on the Sunday night after the fighting began. There was a little two-wheeled cart inscribed with the name of Thomas Lobb,[90] Greengrocer, New Malden, with a smashed wheel and an abandoned tin trunk; there was a straw hat trampled into the now hardened mud, and at the top of West Hill a lot of blood-stained glass about the overturned water trough. My movements were languid, my plans of the vaguest. I had an idea of going to Leatherhead, though I knew that there I had the poorest chance of finding my wife. Certainly, unless death had overtaken them suddenly, my cousins and she would have fled thence; but it seemed to me I might find or learn there whither the Surrey people had fled. I knew I wanted to find my wife, that my heart ached for her and the world of men, but I had no clear idea how the finding might be done. I was also sharply aware now of my intense loneliness. From the corner I went, under cover of a thicket of trees and bushes, to the edge of Wimbledon Common, stretching wide and far.

That dark expanse was lit in patches by yellow gorse and broom; there was no red weed to be seen, and as I prowled, hesitating, on the verge of the open, the sun rose, flooding it all with light and vitality. I came upon a busy swarm of little frogs in a swampy place among the trees. I stopped to look at them, drawing a lesson from their stout resolve to live. And presently, turning suddenly, with an odd feeling of being watched, I beheld something crouching amid a clump of bushes. I stood regarding this. I made a step towards it, and it rose up and became a man armed with a cutlass. I approached him slowly. He stood silent and motionless, regarding me.

As I drew nearer I perceived he was dressed in clothes as dusty and filthy as my own; he looked, indeed, as though he had been dragged through a culvert. Nearer, I distinguished the green slime of ditches mixing with the pale drab of dried clay and shiny, coaly patches. His black hair fell over his eyes, and his face was dark and dirty and sunken, so that at first I did not recognise him. There was a red cut across the lower part of his face.

'Stop!' he cried, when I was within ten yards of him, and I stopped. His voice was hoarse. 'Where do you come from?' he said.

I thought, surveying him.

'I come from Mortlake,' I said. 'I was buried near the pit the Martians made about their cylinder. I have worked my way out and escaped.'

'There is no food about here,' he said. 'This is my country. All this hill down to the river, and back to Clapham, and up to the edge of the common. There is only food for one. Which way are you going?'

I answered slowly.

'I don't know,' I said. 'I have been buried in the ruins of a house thirteen or fourteen days. I don't know what has happened.'

He looked at me doubtfully, then started, and looked with a changed expression.

'I've no wish to stop about here,' said I. 'I think I shall go to Leatherhead, for my wife was there.'

He shot out a pointing finger.

'It is you,' said he; 'the man from Woking. And you weren't killed at Weybridge?'

I recognised him at the same moment.

'You are the artilleryman who came into my garden.'

'Good luck!' he said. 'We are lucky ones! Fancy *you*!' He put out a hand, and I took it. 'I crawled up a drain,' he said. 'But they didn't kill everyone. And after they went away I got off towards Walton across the fields. But – It's not sixteen days altogether – and your hair is grey.' He looked over his shoulder suddenly. 'Only a rook,' he said. 'One gets to know that birds have shadows these days. This is a bit open. Let us crawl under those bushes and talk.'

'Have you seen any Martians?' I said. 'Since I crawled out – '

'They've gone away across London,' he said. 'I guess they've got a bigger camp there. Of a night, all over there, Hampstead way, the sky is alive with their lights. It's like a great city, and in the glare you can just see them moving. By daylight you can't. But nearer – I haven't seen them – ' (he counted on his fingers) 'five days. Then I saw a couple across Hammersmith way carrying something big. And the night before last' – he stopped and spoke impressively – 'it was just a matter of lights, but it was something up in the air. I believe they've built a flying-machine, and are learning to fly.'

I stopped, on hands and knees, for we had come to the bushes.

'Fly!'

'Yes,' he said, 'fly.'

I went on into a little bower, and sat down.

'It is all over with humanity,' I said. 'If they can do that they will simply go round the world.'

He nodded.

'They will. But – It will relieve things over here a bit. And besides – ' He looked at me. 'Aren't you satisfied it *is* up with humanity? I am. We're down; we're beat.'

I stared. Strange as it may seem, I had not arrived at this fact – a fact perfectly obvious so soon as he spoke. I had still held a vague hope;

rather, I had kept a lifelong habit of mind. He repeated his words, 'We're beat.' They carried absolute conviction.

'It's all over,' he said. 'They've lost *one* – just *one*. And they've made their footing good and crippled the greatest power in the world. They've walked over us. The death of that one at Weybridge was an accident. And these are only pioneers. They kept on coming. These green stars – I've seen none these five or six days, but I've no doubt they're falling somewhere every night. Nothing's to be done. We're under! We're beat!'

I made him no answer. I sat staring before me, trying in vain to devise some countervailing thought.

'This isn't a war,' said the artilleryman. 'It never was a war, any more than there's war between man and ants.'

Suddenly I recalled the night in the observatory.

'After the tenth shot they fired no more – at least, until the first cylinder came.'

'How do you know?' said the artilleryman. I explained. He thought. 'Something wrong with the gun,' he said. 'But what if there is? They'll get it right again. And even if there's a delay, how can it alter the end? It's just men and ants. There's the ants builds their cities, live their lives, have wars, revolutions, until the men want them out of the way, and then they go out of the way. That's what we are now – just ants. Only – '

'Yes,' I said.

'We're eatable ants.'

We sat looking at each other.

'And what will they do with us?' I said.

'That's what I've been thinking,' he said; 'that's what I've been thinking. After Weybridge I went south – thinking. I saw what was up. Most of the people were hard at it squealing and exciting themselves. But I'm not so fond of squealing. I've been in sight of death once or twice; I'm not an ornamental soldier, and at the best and worst, death – it's just death. And it's the man that keeps on thinking comes through. I saw everyone tracking away south. Says I, "Food won't last this way," and I turned right back. I went for the Martians like a sparrow goes for man. All round' – he waved a hand to the horizon – 'they're starving in heaps, bolting, treading on each other . . . '

He saw my face, and halted awkwardly.

'No doubt lots who had money have gone away to France,' he said. He seemed to hesitate whether to apologise, met my eyes, and went on: 'There's food all about here. Canned things in shops; wines, spirits, mineral waters; and the water mains and drains are empty. Well, I was telling you what I was thinking. "Here's intelligent things," I said, "and it seems they want us for food. First, they'll smash us up – ships, machines, guns, cities, all the order and organisation. All that will go. If we were the size of ants we might pull through. But we're not. It's all too bulky to stop. That's the first certainty." Eh?'

I assented.

'It is; I've thought it out. Very well, then – next; at present we're caught as we're wanted. A Martian has only to go a few miles to get a crowd on the run. And I saw one, one day, out by Wandsworth, picking houses to pieces and routing among the wreckage. But they won't keep on doing that. So soon as they've settled all our guns and ships, and smashed our railways, and done all the things they are doing over there, they will begin catching us systematic, picking the best and storing us in cages and things. That's what they will start doing in a bit. Lord! They haven't begun on us yet. Don't you see that?'

'Not begun!' I exclaimed.

'Not begun. All that's happened so far is through our not having the sense to keep quiet – worrying them with guns and such foolery. And losing our heads, and rushing off in crowds to where there wasn't any more safety than where we were. They don't want to bother us yet. They're making their things – making all the things they couldn't bring with them, getting things ready for the rest of their people. Very likely that's why the cylinders have stopped for a bit, for fear of hitting those who are here. And instead of our rushing about blind, on the howl, or getting dynamite on the chance of busting them up, we've got to fix ourselves up according to the new state of affairs. That's how I figure it out. It isn't quite according to what a man wants for his species, but it's about what the facts point to. And that's the principle I acted upon. Cities, nations, civilisation, progress – it's all over. That game's up. We're beat.'

'But if that is so, what is there to live for?'

The artilleryman looked at me for a moment.

'There won't be any more blessed concerts for a million years or so; there won't be any Royal Academy of Arts,[91] and no nice little feeds at restaurants. If it's amusement you're after, I reckon the game is up. If you've got any drawing-room manners or a dislike to eating peas with a knife or dropping aitches, you'd better chuck 'em away. They ain't no further use.'

'You mean – '

'I mean that men like me are going on living – for the sake of the breed. I tell you, I'm grim set on living. And if I'm not mistaken, you'll show what insides *you've* got, too, before long. We aren't going to be exterminated. And I don't mean to be caught either, and tamed and fattened and bred like a thundering ox. Ugh! Fancy those brown creepers!'

'You don't mean to say – '

'I do. I'm going on, under their feet. I've got it planned; I've thought it out. We men are beat. We don't know enough. We've got to learn before we've got a chance. And we've got to live and keep independent while we learn. See! That's what has to be done.'

I stared, astonished, and stirred profoundly by the man's resolution.

'Great God!' cried I. 'But you are a man indeed!' And suddenly I gripped his hand.

'Eh!' he said, with his eyes shining. 'I've thought it out, eh?'

'Go on,' I said.

'Well, those who mean to escape their catching must get ready. I'm getting ready. Mind you, it isn't all of us that are made for wild beasts; and that's what it's got to be. That's why I watched you. I had my doubts. You're slender. I didn't know that it was you, you see, or just how you'd been buried. All these – the sort of people that lived in these houses, and all those damn little clerks that used to live down that way – they'd be no good. They haven't any spirit in them – no proud dreams and no proud lusts; and a man who hasn't one or the other – Lord! What is he but funk and precautions? They just used to skedaddle off to work – I've seen hundreds of 'em, bit of breakfast in hand, running wild and shining to catch their little season-ticket train, for fear they'd get dismissed if they didn't; working at businesses they were afraid to take the trouble to understand; skedaddling back for fear they wouldn't be in time for dinner; keeping indoors after dinner for fear of the back streets, and sleeping with the wives they married, not because they wanted them, but because they had a bit of money that would make for safety in their one little miserable skedaddle through the world. Lives insured and a bit invested for fear of accidents. And on Sundays – fear of the hereafter. As if hell was built for rabbits! Well, the Martians will just be a godsend to these. Nice roomy cages, fattening food, careful breeding, no worry. After a week or so chasing about the fields and lands on empty stomachs, they'll come and be caught cheerful. They'll be quite glad after a bit. They'll wonder what people did before there were Martians to take care of them. And the bar loafers, and mashers, and singers – I can imagine them. I can imagine them,' he said, with a sort of sombre gratification. 'There'll be any amount of sentiment and religion loose among them. There's hundreds of things I saw with my eyes that I've only begun to see clearly these last few days. There's lots will take things as they are – fat and stupid; and lots will be worried by a sort of feeling that it's all wrong, and that they ought to be doing something. Now whenever things are so that a lot of people feel they ought to be doing something, the weak, and those who go weak with a lot of complicated thinking, always make for a sort of do-nothing religion, very pious and superior, and submit to persecution and the will of the Lord. Very likely you've seen the same thing. It's energy in a gale of funk, and turned clean inside out. These cages will be full of psalms and hymns and piety. And those of a less simple sort will work in a bit of – what is it? – eroticism.'

He paused.

'Very likely these Martians will make pets of some of them; train them to do tricks – who knows? – get sentimental over the pet boy who grew up and had to be killed. And some, maybe, they will train to hunt us.'

'No,' I cried, 'that's impossible! No human being – '

'What's the good of going on with such lies?' said the artilleryman. 'There's men who'd do it cheerful. What nonsense to pretend there isn't!'

And I succumbed to his conviction.

'If they come after me,' he said; 'Lord, if they come after me!' and subsided into a grim meditation.

I sat contemplating these things. I could find nothing to bring against this man's reasoning. In the days before the invasion no one would have questioned my intellectual superiority to his – I, a professed and recognised writer on philosophical themes, and he, a common soldier; and yet he had already formulated a situation that I had scarcely realised.

'What are you doing?' I said presently. 'What plans have you made?'

He hesitated.

'Well, it's like this,' he said. 'What have we to do? We have to invent a sort of life where men can live and breed, and be sufficiently secure to bring the children up. Yes – wait a bit, and I'll make it clearer what I think ought to be done. The tame ones will go like all tame beasts; in a few generations they'll be big, beautiful, rich-blooded, stupid – rubbish! The risk is that we who keep wild will go savage – degenerate into a sort of big, savage rat . . . You see, how I mean to live is underground. I've been thinking about the drains. Of course those who don't know drains think horrible things; but under this London are miles and miles – hundreds of miles – and a few days' rain and

London empty will leave them sweet and clean. The main drains are big enough and airy enough for anyone. Then there's cellars, vaults, stores, from which bolting passages may be made to the drains. And the railway tunnels and subways. Eh? You begin to see? And we form a band – able-bodied, clean-minded men. We're not going to pick up any rubbish that drifts in. Weaklings go out again.'

'As you meant me to go?'

'Well – I parleyed, didn't I?'

'We won't quarrel about that. Go on.'

'Those who stop obey orders. Able-bodied, clean-minded women we want also – mothers and teachers. No lackadaisical ladies – no blasted rolling eyes. We can't have any weak or silly. Life is real again, and the useless and cumbersome and mischievous have to die. They ought to die. They ought to be willing to die. It's a sort of disloyalty, after all, to live and taint the race. And they can't be happy. Moreover, dying's none so dreadful; it's the funking makes it bad. And in all those places we shall gather. Our district will be London. And we may even be able to keep a watch, and run about in the open when the Martians keep away. Play cricket, perhaps. That's how we shall save the race. Eh? It's a possible thing? But saving the race is nothing in itself. As I say, that's only being rats. It's saving our knowledge and adding to it is the thing. There men like you come in. There's books, there's models. We must make great safe places down deep, and get all the books we can; not novels and poetry swipes,[92] but ideas, science books. That's where men like you come in. We must go to the British Museum and pick all those books through. Especially we must keep up our science – learn more. We must watch these Martians. Some of us must go as spies. When it's all working, perhaps I will. Get caught, I mean. And the great thing is, we must leave the Martians alone. We mustn't even steal. If we get in their way, we clear out. We must show them we mean no harm. Yes, I know. But they're intelligent things, and they won't hunt us down if they have all they want, and think we're just harmless vermin.'

The artilleryman paused and laid a brown hand upon my arm.

'After all, it may not be so much we may have to learn before – Just imagine this: four or five of their fighting-machines suddenly starting off – Heat-Rays right and left, and not a Martian in 'em. Not a Martian in 'em, but men – men who have learned the way how. It may be in my time, even – those men. Fancy having one of them lovely things, with its Heat-Ray wide and free! Fancy having it in control! What would it matter if you smashed to smithereens at the end of the run, after a bust like that? I reckon the Martians'll open their beautiful eyes! Can't you see them, man? Can't you see them hurrying, hurrying – puffing and blowing and hooting to their other mechanical affairs? Something out of gear in every case. And swish, bang, rattle, swish! Just as they are fumbling over it, *swish* comes the Heat-Ray, and, behold! man has come back to his own.'

For a while the imaginative daring of the artilleryman, and the tone of assurance and courage he assumed, completely dominated my mind. I believed unhesitatingly both in his forecast of human destiny and in the practicability of his astonishing scheme, and the reader who thinks me susceptible and foolish must contrast his position, reading steadily with all his thoughts about his subject, and mine, crouching fearfully in the bushes and listening, distracted by apprehension. We talked in this manner through the early morning time, and later crept out of the bushes, and, after scanning the sky for Martians, hurried precipitately to the house on Putney Hill where he had made his lair. It was the coal cellar of the place, and when I saw the work he had spent a week upon – it was a burrow scarcely ten yards long, which he designed to reach to the main drain on Putney Hill – I had my first inkling of the gulf between his dreams and his powers. Such a hole I could have dug in a day. But I believed in him sufficiently to work with him all that morning until past midday at his digging. We had a garden barrow and shot the earth we removed against the kitchen range. We refreshed ourselves with a tin of mock-turtle soup[93] and wine from the neighbouring pantry. I found a curious relief from the aching strangeness of the world in this steady labour. As we worked, I turned his project over in my mind, and presently objections and doubts began to arise; but I worked there all the morning, so glad was I to find myself with a purpose again. After working an hour I began to speculate on the distance one had to go before the cloaca was reached, the chances we had of missing it altogether. My immediate trouble was why we should dig this long tunnel, when it was possible to get into the drain at once down one of the manholes, and work back to the house. It seemed to me, too, that the house was inconveniently chosen, and required a needless length of tunnel. And just as I was beginning to face these things, the artilleryman stopped digging, and looked at me.

'We're working well,' he said. He put down his spade. 'Let us knock off a bit,' he said. 'I think it's time we reconnoitred from the roof of the house.'

I was for going on, and after a little hesitation he resumed his spade; and then suddenly I was struck by a thought. I stopped, and so did he at once.

'Why were you walking about the common,' I said, 'instead of being here?'

'Taking the air,' he said. 'I was coming back. It's safer by night.'

'But the work?'

'Oh, one can't always work,' he said, and in a flash I saw the man plain. He hesitated, holding his spade. 'We ought to reconnoitre now,' he said, 'because if any come near they may hear the spades and drop upon us unawares.'

I was no longer disposed to object. We went together to the roof and stood on a ladder peeping out of the roof door. No Martians were to be seen, and we ventured out on the tiles, and slipped down under shelter of the parapet.

From this position a shrubbery hid the greater portion of Putney, but we could see the river below, a bubbly mass of red weed, and the low parts of Lambeth flooded and red. The red creeper swarmed up the trees about the old palace,[94] and their branches stretched gaunt and dead, and set with shrivelled leaves, from amid its clusters. It was strange how entirely dependent both these things were upon flowing water for their propagation. About us neither had gained a footing; laburnums, pink mays, snowballs, and trees of arbor-vitae, rose out of laurels and hydrangeas, green and brilliant into the sunlight. Beyond Kensington dense smoke was rising, and that and a blue haze hid the northward hills.

The artilleryman began to tell me of the sort of people who still remained in London.

'One night last week,' he said, 'some fools got the electric light in order, and there was all Regent Street and the Circus[95] ablaze, crowded with painted and ragged drunkards, men and women, dancing and shouting till dawn. A man who was there told me. And as the day came they became aware of a fighting-machine standing near by the Langham[96] and looking down at them. Heaven knows how long he had been there. It must have given some of them a nasty turn. He came down the road towards them, and picked up nearly a hundred too drunk or frightened to run away.'

Grotesque gleam of a time no history will ever fully describe!

From that, in answer to my questions, he came round to his grandiose plans again. He grew enthusiastic. He talked so eloquently of the possibility of capturing a fighting-machine that I more than half believed in him again. But now that I was beginning to understand something of his quality, I could divine the stress he laid on doing nothing precipitately. And I noted that now there was no question that he personally was to capture and fight the great machine.

After a time we went down to the cellar. Neither of us seemed disposed to resume digging, and when he suggested a meal, I was nothing loath. He became suddenly very generous, and when we had eaten he went away and returned with some excellent cigars. We lit these, and his optimism glowed. He was inclined to regard my coming as a great occasion.

'There's some champagne in the cellar,' he said.

'We can dig better on this Thames-side burgundy,' said I.

'No,' said he; 'I am host today. Champagne! Great God! We've a heavy enough task before us! Let us take a rest and gather strength while we may. Look at these blistered hands!'

And pursuant to this idea of a holiday, he insisted upon playing cards after we had eaten. He taught me euchre, and after dividing London between us, I taking the northern side and he the southern, we played for parish points.[97] Grotesque and foolish as this will seem to the sober reader, it is absolutely true, and what is more remarkable, I found the card game and several others we played extremely interesting.

Strange mind of man! that, with our species upon the edge of extermination or appalling degradation, with no clear prospect before us but the chance of a horrible death, we could sit following the chance of this painted pasteboard, and playing the 'joker' with vivid delight. Afterwards he taught me poker, and I beat him at three tough chess games. When dark came we decided to take the risk, and lit a lamp.

After an interminable string of games, we supped, and the artilleryman finished the champagne. We went on smoking the cigars. He was no longer the energetic regenerator of his species I had encountered in the morning. He was still optimistic, but it was a less kinetic, a more thoughtful optimism. I remember he wound up with my health, proposed in a speech of small variety and considerable intermittence. I took a cigar, and went upstairs to look at the lights of which he had spoken that blazed so greenly along the Highgate hills.

At first I stared unintelligently across the London valley. The northern hills were shrouded in darkness; the fires near Kensington glowed redly, and now and then an orange-red tongue of flame flashed up and vanished in the deep blue night. All the rest of London was black. Then, nearer, I perceived a strange light, a pale, violet-purple fluorescent glow, quivering under the night breeze. For a space I could not understand it, and then I knew that it must be the red weed from which this faint irradiation proceeded. With that realisation my dormant sense of wonder, my sense of the proportion of things, awoke again. I glanced from that to Mars, red and clear, glowing high in the west, and then gazed long and earnestly at the darkness of Hampstead and Highgate.

I remained a very long time upon the roof, wondering at the grotesque changes of the day. I recalled my mental states from the midnight prayer to the foolish card-playing. I had a violent revulsion of feeling. I remember I flung away the cigar with a certain wasteful symbolism. My folly came to me with glaring exaggeration. I seemed a traitor to my wife and to my kind; I was filled with remorse. I resolved to leave this strange undisciplined dreamer of great things to his drink and gluttony, and to go on into London. There, it seemed to me, I had the best chance of learning what the Martians and my fellow men were doing. I was still upon the roof when the late moon rose.

CHAPTER EIGHT

Dead London

After I had parted from the artilleryman, I went down the hill, and by the High Street across the bridge to Fulham. The red weed was tumultuous at that time, and nearly choked the bridge roadway; but its fronds were already whitened in patches by the spreading disease that presently removed it so swiftly.

At the corner of the lane that runs to Putney Bridge station I found a man lying. He was as black as a sweep with the black dust, alive, but helplessly and speechlessly drunk. I could get nothing from him but curses and furious lunges at my head. I think I should have stayed by him but for the brutal expression of his face.

There was black dust along the roadway from the bridge onwards, and it grew thicker in Fulham. The streets were horribly quiet. I got food – sour, hard, and mouldy, but quite eatable – in a baker's shop here. Some way towards Walham Green the streets became clear of powder, and I passed a white terrace of houses on fire; the noise of the burning was an absolute relief. Going on towards Brompton, the streets were quiet again.

Here I came once more upon the black powder in the streets and upon dead bodies. I saw altogether about a dozen in the length of the Fulham Road. They had been dead many days, so that I hurried quickly past them. The black powder covered them over, and softened their outlines. One or two had been disturbed by dogs.

Where there was no black powder, it was curiously like a Sunday in the City, with the closed shops, the houses locked up and the blinds drawn, the desertion, and the stillness. In some places plunderers had been at work, but rarely at other than the provision and wine shops. A jeweller's window had been broken open in one place, but apparently the thief had been disturbed, and a number of gold chains and a watch lay scattered on the pavement. I did not trouble to touch them. Farther on was a tattered woman in a heap on a doorstep; the hand that hung over her knee was gashed and bled down her rusty brown dress, and a smashed magnum of champagne formed a pool across the pavement. She seemed asleep, but she was dead.

The farther I penetrated into London, the profounder grew the stillness. But it was not so much the stillness of death – it was the stillness of suspense, of expectation. At any time the destruction that had already singed the north-western borders of the metropolis, and had annihilated Ealing and Kilburn, might strike among these houses and leave them smoking ruins. It was a city condemned and derelict . . .

In South Kensington the streets were clear of dead and of black powder. It was near South Kensington that I first heard the howling. It crept almost imperceptibly upon my senses. It was a sobbing alternation of two notes, 'Ulla, ulla, ulla, ulla,' keeping on perpetually. When I passed streets that ran northward it grew in volume, and houses and buildings seemed to deaden and cut it off again. It came in a full tide down Exhibition Road. I stopped, staring towards Kensington Gardens, wondering at this strange, remote wailing. It was as if that mighty desert of houses had found a voice for its fear and solitude.

'Ulla, ulla, ulla, ulla,' wailed that superhuman note – great waves of sound sweeping down the broad, sunlit roadway, between the tall buildings on each side. I turned northwards, marvelling, towards the iron gates of Hyde Park. I had half a mind to break into the Natural History Museum and find my way up to the summits of the towers, in order to see across the park. But I decided to keep to the ground, where quick hiding was possible, and so went on up the Exhibition Road. All the large mansions on each side of the road were empty and still, and my footsteps echoed against the sides of the houses. At the top, near the park gate, I came upon a strange sight – a bus overturned, and the skeleton of a horse picked clean. I puzzled over this for a time, and then went on to the bridge over the Serpentine. The voice grew stronger and stronger, though I could see nothing above the housetops on the north side of the park, save a haze of smoke to the north-west.

'Ulla, ulla, ulla, ulla,' cried the voice, coming, as it seemed to me, from the district about Regent's Park. The desolating cry worked upon my mind. The mood that had sustained me passed. The wailing took possession of me. I found I was intensely weary, footsore, and now again hungry and thirsty.

It was already past noon. Why was I wandering alone in this city of the dead? Why was I alone when all London was lying in state, and in its black shroud? I felt intolerably lonely. My mind ran on old friends that I had forgotten for years. I thought of the poisons in the chemists' shops, of the liquors the wine merchants stored; I recalled the two sodden creatures of despair, who so far as I knew, shared the city with myself . . .

I came into Oxford Street by the Marble Arch, and here again were black powder and several bodies, and an evil, ominous smell from the gratings of the cellars of some of the houses. I grew very thirsty after the heat of my long walk. With infinite trouble I managed to break into a public-house and get food and drink. I was weary after eating, and went into the parlour behind the bar, and slept on a black horsehair sofa I found there.

I awoke to find that dismal howling still in my ears, 'Ulla, ulla, ulla, ulla.' It was now dusk, and after I had routed out some biscuits and a cheese in the bar – there was a meat safe, but it contained nothing but maggots – I wandered on through the silent residential squares to Baker Street – Portman Square is the only one I can name – and so came out at last upon Regent's Park. And as I emerged from the top of Baker Street, I saw far away over the trees in the clearness of the sunset the hood of the Martian giant from which this howling proceeded. I was not terrified. I came upon him as if it were a matter of course. I watched him for some time, but he did not move. He appeared to be standing and yelling, for no reason that I could discover.

I tried to formulate a plan of action. That perpetual sound of 'Ulla, ulla, ulla, ulla,' confused my mind. Perhaps I was too tired to be very fearful. Certainly I was more curious to know the reason of this mono-tonous crying than afraid. I turned back away from the park and struck into Park Road, intending to skirt the park, went along under the shelter of the terraces, and got a view of this stationary, howling Martian from the direction of St John's Wood. A couple of hundred yards out of Baker Street I heard a yelping chorus, and saw, first a dog with a piece of putrescent red meat in his jaws coming headlong towards me, and then a pack of starving mongrels in pursuit of him. He made a wide curve to avoid me, as though he feared I might prove a fresh competitor. As the yelping died away down the silent road, the wailing sound of 'Ulla, ulla, ulla, ulla,' reasserted itself.

I came upon the wrecked handling-machine halfway to St John's Wood station. At first I thought a house had fallen across the road. It was only as I clambered among the ruins that I saw, with a start, this mechanical Samson[98] lying, with its tentacles bent and smashed and twisted, among the ruins it had made. The forepart was shattered. It seemed as if it had driven blindly straight at the house, and had been overwhelmed in its overthrow. It seemed to me then that this might have happened by a handling-machine escaping from the guidance of its Martian. I could not clamber among the ruins to see it, and the twilight was now so far advanced that the blood with which its seat was smeared, and the gnawed gristle of the Martian that the dogs had left, were invisible to me.

Wondering still more at all that I had seen, I pushed on towards Primrose Hill. Far away, through a gap in the trees, I saw a second Martian, as motionless as the first, standing in the park towards the Zoological Gardens,[99] and silent. A little beyond the ruins about the smashed handling-machine I came upon the red weed again, and found the Regent's Canal, a spongy mass of dark-red vegetation.

As I crossed the bridge, the sound of 'Ulla, ulla, ulla, ulla,' ceased. It was, as it were, cut off. The silence came like a thunderclap.

The dusky houses about me stood faint and tall and dim; the trees towards the park were growing black. All about me the red weed clambered among the ruins, writhing to get above me in the dimness. Night, the mother of fear and mystery, was coming upon me. But while that voice sounded the solitude, the desolation, had been endurable; by virtue of it London had still seemed alive, and the sense of life about me had upheld me. Then suddenly a change, the passing of something – I knew not what – and then a stillness that could be felt. Nothing but this gaunt quiet.

London about me gazed at me spectrally. The windows in the white houses were like the eye sockets of skulls. About me my imagination found a thousand noiseless enemies moving. Terror seized me, a horror of my temerity. In front of me the road became pitchy black as though it was tarred, and I saw a contorted shape lying across the pathway. I could not bring myself to go on. I turned down St John's Wood Road, and ran headlong from this unendurable stillness towards Kilburn. I hid from the night and the silence, until long after midnight, in a cabmen's shelter in Harrow Road. But before the dawn my courage returned, and while the stars were still in the sky I turned once more towards Regent's Park. I missed my way among the streets, and presently saw down a long avenue, in the half-light of the early dawn, the curve of Primrose Hill. On the summit, towering up to the fading stars, was a third Martian, erect and motionless like the others.

An insane resolve possessed me. I would die and end it. And I would save myself even the trouble of killing myself. I marched on recklessly towards this Titan, and then, as I drew nearer and the light grew, I saw that a multitude of black birds was circling and clustering about the hood. At that my heart gave a bound, and I began running along the road.

I hurried through the red weed that choked St Edmund's Terrace (I waded breast-high across a torrent of water that was rushing down from the waterworks towards the Albert Road), and emerged upon the grass before the rising of the sun. Great mounds had been heaped about the crest of the hill, making a huge redoubt of it – it was the final and largest place the Martians had made – and from behind these heaps there rose a thin smoke against the sky. Against the skyline an eager dog ran and disappeared. The thought that had flashed into my mind grew real, grew credible. I felt no fear, only a wild, trembling exultation, as I ran up the hill towards the motionless monster. Out of the hood hung lank shreds of brown, at which the hungry birds pecked and tore.

In another moment I had scrambled up the earthen rampart and stood upon its crest, and the interior of the redoubt was below me. A mighty space it was, with gigantic machines here and there within it, huge mounds of material and strange shelter places. And scattered about it, some in their overturned war-machines, some in the now rigid handling-machines, and a dozen of them stark and silent and laid in a row, were the Martians – *dead!* – slain by the putrefactive and disease bacteria against which their systems were unprepared; slain as the red weed was being slain; slain, after all man's devices had failed, by the humblest things that God, in his wisdom, has put upon this earth.

For so it had come about, as indeed I and many men might have foreseen had not terror and disaster blinded our minds. These germs of disease have taken toll of humanity since the beginning of things – taken toll of our prehuman ancestors since life began here. But by virtue of this natural selection of our kind we have developed resisting power; to no germs do we succumb without a struggle, and to many – those that cause putrefaction in dead matter, for instance – our living frames are altogether immune. But there are no bacteria in Mars, and directly these invaders arrived, directly they drank and fed, our microscopic allies began to work their overthrow. Already when I watched them they were irrevocably doomed, dying and rotting even as they went to and fro. It was inevitable. By the toll of a billion deaths man has bought his birthright of the earth, and it is his against all comers; it would still be his were the Martians ten times as mighty as they are. For neither do men live nor die in vain.

Here and there they were scattered, nearly fifty altogether, in that great gulf they had made, overtaken by a death that must have seemed to them as incomprehensible as any death could be. To me also at that time this death was incomprehensible. All I knew was that these things that had been alive and so terrible to men were dead. For a moment I believed that the destruction of Sennacherib[100] had been repeated, that God had repented, that the Angel of Death had slain them in the night.

I stood staring into the pit, and my heart lightened gloriously, even as the rising sun struck the world to fire about me with his rays. The pit was still in darkness; the mighty engines, so great and wonderful in their power and complexity, so unearthly in their tortuous forms, rose weird and vague and strange out of the shadows towards the light. A multitude of dogs, I could hear, fought over the bodies that lay darkly in the depth of the pit, far below me. Across the pit on its farther lip, flat and vast and strange, lay the great flying-machine with which they had been experimenting upon our denser atmosphere when decay and death arrested them. Death had come not a day too soon. At the sound of a cawing overhead I looked up at the huge fighting-machine that would fight no more for ever, at the tattered red shreds of flesh that dripped down upon the overturned seats on the summit of Primrose Hill.

I turned and looked down the slope of the hill to where, enhaloed now in birds, stood those other two Martians that I had seen overnight, just as death had overtaken them. The one had died, even as it had been crying to its companions; perhaps it was the last to die, and its voice had gone on perpetually until the force of its machinery was exhausted. They glittered now, harmless tripod towers of shining metal, in the brightness of the rising sun.

All about the pit, and saved as by a miracle from everlasting destruction, stretched the great Mother of Cities. Those who have only seen London veiled in her sombre robes of smoke can scarcely imagine the naked clearness and beauty of the silent wilderness of houses.

Eastward, over the blackened ruins of the Albert Terrace and the splintered spire of the church, the sun blazed dazzling in a clear sky, and here and there some facet in the great wilderness of roofs caught the light and glared with a white intensity.

Northward were Kilburn and Hampsted, blue and crowded with

houses; westward the great city was dimmed; and southward, beyond the Martians, the green waves of Regent's Park, the Langham Hotel, the dome of the Albert Hall,[101] the Imperial Institute, and the giant mansions of the Brompton Road came out clear and little in the sunrise, the jagged ruins of Westminster rising hazily beyond. Far away and blue were the Surrey hills, and the towers of the Crystal Palace glittered like two silver rods. The dome of St Paul's was dark against the sunrise, and injured, I saw for the first time, by a huge gaping cavity on its western side.

And as I looked at this wide expanse of houses and factories and churches, silent and abandoned; as I thought of the multitudinous hopes and efforts, the innumerable hosts of lives that had gone to build this human reef, and of the swift and ruthless destruction that had hung over it all; when I realised that the shadow had been rolled back, and that men might still live in the streets, and this dear vast dead city of mine be once more alive and powerful, I felt a wave of emotion that was near akin to tears.

The torment was over. Even that day the healing would begin. The survivors of the people scattered over the country – leaderless, lawless, foodless, like sheep without a shepherd – the thousands who had fled by sea, would begin to return; the pulse of life, growing stronger and stronger, would beat again in the empty streets and pour across the vacant squares. Whatever destruction was done, the hand of the destroyer was stayed. All the gaunt wrecks, the blackened skeletons of houses that stared so dismally at the sunlit grass of the hill, would presently be echoing with the hammers of the restorers and ringing with the tapping of their trowels. At the thought I extended my hands towards the sky and began thanking God. In a year, thought I – in a year. . .

With overwhelming force came the thought of myself, of my wife, and the old life of hope and tender helpfulness that had ceased for ever.

CHAPTER NINE

Wreckage

And now comes the strangest thing in my story. Yet, perhaps, it is not altogether strange. I remember, clearly and coldly and vividly, all that I did that day until the time that I stood weeping and praising God upon the summit of Primrose Hill. And then I forget.

Of the next three days I know nothing. I have learned since that, so far from my being the first discoverer of the Martian overthrow, several such wanderers as myself had already discovered this on the previous night. One man – the first – had gone to St Martin's-le-Grand, and, while I sheltered in the cabmen's hut, had contrived to telegraph to Paris. Thence the joyful news had flashed all over the world; a thousand cities, chilled by ghastly apprehensions, suddenly flashed into frantic illuminations; they knew of it in Dublin, Edinburgh, Manchester, Birmingham, at the time when I stood upon the verge of the pit. Already men, weeping with joy, as I have heard, shouting and staying their work to shake hands and shout, were making up trains, even as near as Crewe, to descend upon London. The church bells that had ceased a fortnight since suddenly caught the news, until all England was bell-ringing. Men on cycles, lean-faced, unkempt, scorched along every country lane shouting of unhoped deliverance, shouting to gaunt, staring figures of despair. And for the food! Across the Channel, across the Irish Sea, across the Atlantic, corn, bread, and meat were tearing to our relief. All the shipping in the world seemed going Londonward in those days. But of all this I have no memory. I drifted – a demented man. I found myself in a house of kindly people, who had found me on the third day wandering, weeping, and raving through the streets of St John's Wood. They have told me since that I was singing some insane doggerel about 'The Last Man Left Alive! Hurrah! The Last Man Left Alive!'[102] Troubled as they were with their own affairs, these people, whose name, much as I would like to express my gratitude to them, I may not even give here, nevertheless cumbered themselves with me, sheltered me, and protected me from myself. Apparently they had learned something of my story from me during the days of my lapse.

Very gently, when my mind was assured again, did they break to me what they had learned of the fate of Leatherhead. Two days after I was imprisoned it had been destroyed, with every soul in it, by a Martian. He had swept it out of existence, as it seemed, without any provocation, as a boy might crush an ant hill, in the mere wantonness of power.

I was a lonely man, and they were very kind to me. I was a lonely man and a sad one, and they bore with me. I remained with them four days after my recovery. All that time I felt a vague, a growing craving to look once more on whatever remained of the little life that seemed so happy and bright in my past. It was a mere hopeless desire to feast upon my misery. They dissuaded me. They did all they could to divert me from this morbidity. But at last I could resist the impulse no longer, and, promising faithfully to return to them, and parting, as I will confess, from these four-day friends with tears, I went out again into the streets that had lately been so dark and strange and empty.

Already they were busy with returning people; in places even there were shops open, and I saw a drinking fountain running water.

I remember how mockingly bright the day seemed as I went back on my melancholy pilgrimage to the little house at Woking, how busy the streets and vivid the moving life about me. So many people were abroad everywhere, busied in a thousand activities, that it seemed incredible that any great proportion of the population could have been slain. But then I noticed how yellow were the skins of the people I met, how shaggy the hair of the men, how large and bright their eyes, and that every other man still wore his dirty rags. Their faces seemed all with one of two expressions – a leaping exultation and energy or a grim resolution. Save for the expression of the faces, London seemed a city of tramps. The vestries were indiscriminately distributing bread sent us by the French government. The ribs of the few horses showed dismally. Haggard special constables with white badges stood at the corners of every street. I saw little of the mischief wrought by the Martians until I reached Wellington Street, and there I saw the red weed clambering over the buttresses of Waterloo Bridge.

At the corner of the bridge, too, I saw one of the common contrasts of that grotesque time – a sheet of paper flaunting against a thicket of the red weed, transfixed by a stick that kept it in place. It was the placard of the first newspaper to resume publication – the *Daily Mail*.[103] I bought a copy for a blackened shilling I found in my pocket. Most of it was in blank, but the solitary compositor who did the thing had amused himself by making a grotesque scheme of advertisement stereo[104] on the back page. The matter he printed was emotional; the news organisation had not as yet found its way back. I learned nothing fresh except that already in one week the examination of the Martian mechanisms had yielded astonishing results. Among other things, the article assured me what I did not believe at the time, that the 'Secret of Flying' was discovered. At Waterloo I found the free trains that were taking people to their homes. The first rush was already over. There were few people in the train, and I was in no mood for casual conversation. I got a compartment to myself, and sat with folded arms, looking greyly at the sunlit devastation that flowed past the windows. And just outside the terminus the train jolted over temporary rails, and on either side of the railway the houses were blackened ruins. To Clapham Junction the face of London was grimy with powder of the Black Smoke, in spite of two days of thunderstorms and rain, and at Clapham Junction the line had been wrecked again; there were hundreds of out-of-work clerks and shopmen working side by side with the customary navvies, and we were jolted over a hasty relaying.

All down the line from there the aspect of the country was gaunt and unfamiliar; Wimbledon particularly had suffered. Walton, by virtue of its unburned pine woods, seemed the least hurt of any place along the line. The Wandle, the Mole, every little stream, was a heaped mass of red weed, in appearance between butcher's meat and pickled cabbage. The Surrey pine woods were too dry, however, for the festoons of the red climber. Beyond Wimbledon, within sight of the line, in certain nursery grounds, were the heaped masses of earth about the sixth cylinder. A number of people were standing about it, and some sappers were busy in the midst of it. Over it flaunted a Union Jack, flapping cheerfully in the morning breeze. The nursery grounds were everywhere crimson with the weed, a wide expanse of livid colour cut with purple shadows, and very painful to the eye. One's gaze went with infinite relief from the scorched greys and sullen reds of the foreground to the blue-green softness of the eastward hills.

The line on the London side of Woking station was still undergoing repair, so I descended at Byfleet station and took the road to Maybury, past the place where I and the artilleryman had talked to the hussars, and on by the spot where the Martian had appeared to me in the thunderstorm. Here, moved by curiosity, I turned aside to find, among a tangle of red fronds, the warped and broken dog cart with the whitened bones of the horse scattered and gnawed. For a time I stood regarding these vestiges . . .

Then I returned through the pine wood, neck-high with red weed here and there, to find the landlord of the Spotted Dog had already found burial, and so came home past the College Arms. A man standing at an open cottage door greeted me by name as I passed.

I looked at my house with a quick flash of hope that faded immediately. The door had been forced; it was unfast and was opening slowly as I approached.

It slammed again. The curtains of my study fluttered out of the open window from which I and the artilleryman had watched the dawn. No one had closed it since. The smashed bushes were just as I had left them nearly four weeks ago. I stumbled into the hall, and the house felt empty. The stair carpet was ruffled and discoloured where I had crouched, soaked to the skin from the thunderstorm the night of the catastrophe. Our muddy footsteps I saw still went up the stairs.

I followed them to my study, and found lying on my writing-table still, with the selenite paperweight upon it, the sheet of work I had left on the afternoon of the opening of the cylinder. For a space I stood reading over my abandoned arguments. It was a paper on the probable development of Moral Ideas with the development of the civilising process; and the last sentence was the opening of a prophecy: 'In about two hundred years,' I had written, 'we may expect – ' The sentence ended abruptly. I remembered my inability to fix my mind that morning, scarcely a month gone by, and how I had broken off to get my *Daily Chronicle* from the newsboy. I remembered how I went down to the garden gate as he came along, and how I had listened to his odd story of 'Men from Mars'.

I came down and went into the dining room. There were the mutton and the bread, both far gone now in decay, and a beer bottle overturned, just as I and the artilleryman had left them. My home was desolate. I perceived the folly of the faint hope I had cherished so long. And then a strange thing occurred. 'It is no use,' said a voice. 'The house is deserted. No one has been here these ten days. Do not stay here to torment yourself. No one escaped but you.'

I was startled. Had I spoken my thought aloud? I turned, and the French window was open behind me. I made a step to it, and stood looking out.

And there, amazed and afraid, even as I stood amazed and afraid, were my cousin and my wife – my wife white and tearless. She gave a faint cry.

'I came,' she said. 'I knew – knew – '

She put her hand to her throat – swayed. I made a step forward, and caught her in my arms.

CHAPTER TEN

The Epilogue

I cannot but regret, now that I am concluding my story, how little I am able to contribute to the discussion of the many debatable questions which are still unsettled. In one respect I shall certainly provoke criticism. My particular province is speculative philosophy. My knowledge of comparative physiology is confined to a book or two, but it seems to me that Carver's suggestions as to the reason of the rapid death of the Martians is so probable as to be regarded almost as a proven conclusion. I have assumed that in the body of my narrative.

At any rate, in all the bodies of the Martians that were examined after the war, no bacteria except those already known as terrestrial species were found. That they did not bury any of their dead, and the reckless slaughter they perpetrated, point also to an entire ignorance of the putrefactive process. But probable as this seems, it is by no means a proven conclusion.

Neither is the composition of the Black Smoke known, which the Martians used with such deadly effect, and the generator of the Heat-Rays remains a puzzle. The terrible disasters at the Ealing and South Kensington laboratories have disinclined analysts for further investigations upon the latter. Spectrum analysis of the black powder points unmistakably to the presence of an unknown element with a brilliant group of three lines in the green, and it is possible that it combines with argon to form a compound which acts at once with deadly effect upon some constituent in the blood. But such unproven speculations will scarcely be of interest to the general reader, to whom this story is addressed. None of the brown scum that drifted down the Thames after the destruction of Shepperton was examined at the time, and now none is forthcoming.

The results of an anatomical examination of the Martians, so far as the prowling dogs had left such an examination possible, I have already given. But everyone is familiar with the magnificent and almost complete specimen in spirits at the Natural History Museum, and the countless drawings that have been made from it; and beyond that the interest of their physiology and structure is purely scientific.

A question of graver and universal interest is the possibility of another attack from the Martians. I do not think that nearly enough attention is being given to this aspect of the matter. At present the planet Mars is in conjunction, but with every return to opposition I, for one, anticipate a renewal of their adventure. In any case, we should be prepared. It seems to me that it should be possible to define the position of the gun from which the shots are discharged, to keep a sustained watch upon this part of the planet, and to anticipate the arrival of the next attack.

In that case the cylinder might be destroyed with dynamite or artillery before it was sufficiently cool for the Martians to emerge, or they might be butchered by means of guns so soon as the screw opened. It seems to me that they have lost a vast advantage in the failure of their first surprise. Possibly they see it in the same light.

Lessing has advanced excellent reasons for supposing that the Martians have actually succeeded in effecting a landing on the planet Venus. Seven months ago now, Venus and Mars were in alignment with the sun; that is to say, Mars was in opposition from the point of view of an observer on Venus. Subsequently a peculiar luminous and sinuous marking appeared on the unillumined half of the inner planet, and almost simultaneously a faint dark mark of a similar sinuous character was detected upon a photograph of the Martian disk. One needs to see the drawings of these appearances in order to appreciate fully their remarkable resemblance in character.

At any rate, whether we expect another invasion or not, our views of the human future must be greatly modified by these events. We have learned now that we cannot regard this planet as being fenced in and a secure abiding place for Man; we can never anticipate the unseen good or evil that may come upon us suddenly out of space. It may be that in the larger design of the universe this invasion from Mars is not without its ultimate benefit for men; it has robbed us of that serene confidence in the future which is the most fruitful source of decadence, the gifts to human science it has brought are enormous, and it has done much to promote the conception of the commonweal of mankind. It may be that across the immensity of space the Martians have watched the fate of these pioneers of theirs and learned their lesson, and that on the planet Venus they have found a securer settlement. Be that as it may, for many years yet there will certainly be no relaxation of the eager scrutiny of the Martian disk, and those fiery darts of the sky, the shooting stars, will bring with them as they fall an unavoidable apprehension to all the sons of men.

The broadening of men's views that has resulted can scarcely be exaggerated. Before the cylinder fell there was a general persuasion that through all the deep of space no life existed beyond the petty surface of our minute sphere. Now we see further. If the Martians can reach Venus, there is no reason to suppose that the thing is impossible for men, and when the slow cooling of the sun makes this earth uninhabitable, as at last it must do, it may be that the thread of life that has begun here will have streamed out and caught our sister planet within its toils.

Dim and wonderful is the vision I have conjured up in my mind of life spreading slowly from this little seed bed of the solar system throughout the inanimate vastness of sidereal space. But that is a remote dream. It may be, on the other hand, that the destruction of the Martians is only a reprieve. To them, and not to us, perhaps, is the future ordained.

I must confess the stress and danger of the time have left an abiding sense of doubt and insecurity in my mind. I sit in my study writing by lamplight, and suddenly I see again the healing valley below set with writhing flames, and feel the house behind and about me empty and desolate. I go out into the Byfleet Road, and vehicles pass me, a butcher boy in a cart, a cabful of visitors, a workman on a bicycle, children going to school, and suddenly they become vague and unreal, and I hurry again with the artilleryman through the hot, brooding silence. Of a night I see the black powder darkening the silent streets, and the contorted bodies shrouded in that layer; they rise upon me tattered and dog-bitten. They gibber and grow fiercer, paler, uglier, mad distortions of humanity at last, and I wake, cold and wretched, in the darkness of the night.

I go to London and see the busy multitudes in Fleet Street and the Strand, and it comes across my mind that they are but the ghosts of the past, haunting the streets that I have seen silent and wretched, going to and fro, phantasms in a dead city, the mockery of life in a galvanised body. And strange, too, it is to stand on Primrose Hill, as I did but a day before writing this last chapter, to see the great province of houses, dim and blue through the haze of the smoke and mist, vanishing at last into the vague lower sky, to see the people walking to and fro among the flower beds on the hill, to see the sight-seers about the Martian machine that stands there still, to hear the tumult of playing children, and to recall the time when I saw it all bright and clear-cut, hard and silent, under the dawn of that last great day . . .

And strangest of all is it to hold my wife's hand again, and to think that I have counted her, and that she has counted me, among the dead.

The War in the Air
and Particularly How Mr Bert Smallways
Fared While It Lasted

The War in the Air

and Particularly How Mr Bert Smallways
Fared While It lasted

———— ◆ ————

H. G. WELLS

The War in the Air was first published in Great Britain
in serial form in 1907 in the *Pall Mall Gazette*.
First published in hardback in Great Britain in 1908
by George Bell & Sons, London
and by MacMillan & Co, New York

Contents

CHAPTER ONE

Of Progress and the Smallways Family

1

'THIS HERE PROGRESS,' said Mr Tom Smallways, 'it keeps on.'
'You'd hardly think it *could* keep on,' said Mr Tom Smallways.

It was long before the War in the Air began that Mr Smallways made this remark. He was sitting on the fence at the end of his garden and surveying the great Bun Hill[105] gasworks with an eye that neither praised nor blamed. Above the clustering gasometers three unfamiliar shapes appeared, thin, wallowing bladders that flapped and rolled about, and grew bigger and bigger and rounder and rounder – balloons in course of inflation for the South of England Aero Club's[106] Saturday-afternoon ascent.

'They goes up every Saturday,' said his neighbour, Mr Stringer, the milkman. 'It's only yestiday, so to speak, when all London turned out to see a balloon go over, and now every little place in the country has its weekly outings – uppings, rather. It's been the salvation of them gas companies.'

'Larst Satiday I got three barrer-loads of gravel off my petaters,' said Mr Tom Smallways. 'Three barrer-loads! What they dropped as ballase.[107] Some of the plants was broke, and some was buried.'

'Ladies, they say, goes up!'

'I suppose we got to call 'em ladies,' said Mr Tom Smallways. 'Still, it ain't hardly my idea of a lady – flying about in the air, and throwing gravel at people. It ain't what I been accustomed to consider ladylike, whether or no.'

Mr Stringer nodded his head approvingly, and for a time they continued to regard the swelling bulks with expressions that had changed from indifference to disapproval.

Mr Tom Smallways was a greengrocer by trade and a gardener by disposition; his little wife, Jessica, saw to the shop, and Heaven had planned him for a peaceful world. Unfortunately Heaven had not planned a peaceful world for him. He lived in a world of obstinate and incessant change, and in parts where its operations were unsparingly conspicuous. Vicissitude was in the very soil he tilled; even his garden was upon a yearly tenancy, and overshadowed by a huge board that proclaimed it not so much a garden as an eligible building site. He was horticulture under notice to quit, the last patch of country in a district flooded by new and urban things. He did his best to console himself, to imagine matters near the turn of the tide.

'You'd hardly think it could keep on,' he said.

Mr Smallways' aged father could remember Bun Hill as an idyllic Kentish village. He had driven Sir Peter Bone until he was fifty, and then he took to drink a little, and driving the station bus, which lasted him until he was seventy-eight. Then he retired. He sat by the fireside, a shrivelled, very, very old coachman, full charged with reminiscences, and ready for any careless stranger. He could tell you of the vanished estate of Sir Peter Bone, long since cut up for building, and how that magnate ruled the countryside when it was countryside, of shooting and hunting, and of coaches along the high road, of how 'where the gasworks is' was a cricket-field, and of the coming of the Crystal Palace. The Crystal Palace was six miles away from Bun Hill, a great façade that glittered in the morning, and was a clear blue outline against the sky in the afternoon, and at night a source of gratuitous fireworks for all the population of Bun Hill. And then had come the railway, and then villas and villas, and then the gasworks and the waterworks, and a great, ugly sea of workmen's houses, and then drainage, and the water vanished out of the Otterbourne and left it a dreadful ditch, and then a second railway station, Bun Hill South, and more houses and more, more shops, more competition, plate-glass shops, a board-school, rates, omnibuses, tramcars – going right away into London itself – bicycles, motor cars and then more motor cars, a Carnegie library.[108]

'You'd hardly think it could keep on,' said Mr Tom Smallways, growing up among these marvels.

But it kept on. Even from the first the greengrocer's shop which he had set up in one of the smallest of the old surviving village houses in the tail of the High Street had a submerged air, an air of hiding from something that was looking for it. When they had made up the pavement of the High Street, they levelled that up so that one had to go down three steps into the shop. Tom did his best to sell only his own excellent but limited range of produce; but Progress came shoving things into his window, French artichokes and aubergines, foreign apples – apples from the State of New York, apples from California, apples from Canada, apples from New Zealand, 'pretty lookin' fruit, but not what I should call English apples', said Tom – bananas, un-familiar nuts, grapefruits, mangoes.

The motor cars that went by northward and southward grew more and more powerful and efficient, whizzed faster and smelt worse; there appeared great clangorous petrol trolleys delivering coal and parcels in the place of vanishing horse-vans; motor-omnibuses ousted the horse-omnibuses, even the Kentish strawberries going Londonward in the night took to machinery and clattered instead of creaking, and became affected in flavour by progress and petrol.

And then young Bert Smallways got a motor bicycle.

2

Bert, it is necessary to explain, was a progressive Smallways.

Nothing speaks more eloquently of the pitiless insistence of progress and expansion in our time than that it should get into the Smallways blood. But there was something advanced and enterprising about young Smallways before he was out of short frocks.[109] He was lost for a whole day before he was five, and nearly drowned in the reservoir of the new waterworks before he was seven. He had a real pistol taken away from him by a real policeman when he was ten. And he learnt to smoke, not with pipes and brown paper and cane as Tom had done, but with a penny packet of Boys of England American cigarettes.[110] His language shocked his father before he was twelve, and by that age, what with touting for parcels at the station and selling the Bun Hill *Weekly Express*, he was making three shillings a week, or more, and spending it on *Chips, Comic Cuts, Ally Sloper's Half-Holiday Illustrated*,[111] cigarettes, and all the concomitants of a life of pleasure and enlightenment. All of this without hindrance to his literary studies, which carried him up to the seventh standard[112] at an exceptionally early age. I mention these things so that you may have no doubt at all concerning the sort of stuff Bert had in him.

He was six years younger than Tom, and for a time there was an attempt to utilise him in the greengrocer's shop when Tom at twenty-one married Jessica – who was thirty, and had saved a little money in service. But it was not Bert's *forte* to be utilised. He hated digging, and when he was given a basket of stuff to deliver, a nomadic instinct arose irresistibly, it became his pack, and he did not seem to care how heavy it was nor where he took it, so long as he did not take it to its destination. Glamour filled the world, and he strayed after it, basket and all. So Tom took his goods out himself, and sought employers for Bert who did not know of this strain of poetry in his nature. Bert touched the fringe of a number of trades in succession – draper's porter, chemist's boy, doctor's page, junior assistant gas-fitter, envelope addresser, milk-cart assistant, golf caddie, and at last helper in a bicycle shop. Here, apparently, he found the progressive quality his nature had craved. His employer was a pirate-souled young man named Grubb, with a black-smeared face by day, and a music-hall side in the evening, who dreamt of a patent lever chain; and it seemed to Bert that he was the perfect model of a gentleman of spirit. He hired out quite the dirtiest and unsafest bicycles in the whole south of England, and conducted the subsequent discussions with astonishing verve. Bert and he settled down very well together. Bert lived in, became almost a trick rider[113] – he could ride bicycles for miles that would have come to pieces instantly under you or me – took to washing his face after business, and spent his surplus money upon remarkable ties and collars, cigarettes, and short-hand classes at the Bun Hill Institute.

He would go round to Tom at times, and look and talk so brilliantly that Tom and Jessie, who both had a natural tendency to be respectful to anybody or anything, looked up to him immensely.

'He's a go-ahead chap, is Bert,' said Tom. 'He knows a thing or two.'

'Let's hope he don't know too much,' said Jessica, who had a fine sense of limitations.

'It's go-ahead Times,' said Tom. 'Noo petaters, and English at that; we'll be having 'em in March if things go on as they do go. I never see such Times. See his tie last night?'

'It wasn't suited to him, Tom. It was a gentleman's tie. He wasn't up to it – not the rest of him. It wasn't becoming . . . '

Then presently Bert got a cyclist's suit, cap, badge, and all; and to see him and Grubb going down to Brighton (and back) – heads down, handlebars down, backbones curved – was a revelation in the possibilities of the Smallways blood.

Go-ahead Times!

Old Smallways would sit over the fire mumbling of the greatness of other days, of old Sir Peter, who drove his coach to Brighton and back in eight-and-twenty hours, of old Sir Peter's white top-hats, of Lady Bone, who never set foot to ground except to walk in the garden, of the great prize-fights at Crawley. He talked of pink and pigskin breeches, of foxes at Ring's Bottom, where now the County Council pauper lunatics were enclosed, of Lady Bone's chintzes and crinolines. Nobody heeded him. The world had thrown up a new type of gentleman altogether – a gentleman of most ungentlemanly energy, a gentleman in dusty oilskins and motor goggles and a wonderful cap, a stink-making gentleman, a swift, high-class badger, who fled perpetually along high roads from the dust and stink he perpetually made. And his lady, as they were able to see her at Bun Hill, was a weather-bitten goddess, as free from refinement as a gypsy – not so much dressed as packed for transit at a high velocity.

So Bert grew up, filled with ideals of speed and enterprise, and became, so far as he became anything, a kind of bicycle engineer of the let's-'ave-a-look-at-it and enamel chipping variety. Even a road-racer, geared to a hundred and twenty, failed to satisfy him, and for a time he pined in vain at twenty miles an hour along roads that were continually more dusty and more crowded with mechanical traffic. But at last his savings accumulated, and his chance came. The hire-purchase system bridged a financial gap, and one bright and memorable Sunday morning he wheeled his new possession through the shop into the road, got on to it with the advice and assistance of Grubb, and teuf-teuffed[114] off into the haze of the traffic-tortured high road, to add himself as one more voluntary public danger to the amenities of the south of England.

'Orf to Brighton!' said old Smallways, regarding his youngest son from the sitting-room window over the greengrocer's shop with something between pride and reprobation. 'When I was 'is age, I'd never been to London, never bin south of Crawley – never bin anywhere on my own where I couldn't walk. And nobody didn't go. Not unless they was gentry. Now everybody's orf everywhere; the whole dratted country sims flying to pieces. Wonder they all get back. Orf to Brighton indeed! Anybody want to buy 'orses?'

'You can't say I bin to Brighton, father,' said Tom.

'Nor don't want to go,' said Jessica sharply; 'creering about and spendin' your money.'

3

For a time the possibilities of the motor-bicycle so occupied Bert's mind that he remained regardless of the new direction in which the striving soul of man was finding exercise and refreshment. He failed to observe that the type of motor car, like the type of bicycle, was settling down and losing its adventurous quality. Indeed, it is as true as it is remarkable that Tom was the first to observe the new development. But his gardening made him attentive to the heavens, and the proximity of the Bun Hill gasworks and the Crystal Palace, from which ascents were continually being made, and presently the descent of ballast upon his potatoes, conspired to bear in upon his unwilling mind the fact that the Goddess of Change was turning her disturbing attention to the sky. The first great boom in aeronautics was beginning.

Grubb and Bert heard of it in a music-hall, then it was driven home to their minds by the cinematograph, then Bert's imagination was stimulated by a sixpenny edition of that aeronautic classic, Mr George Griffith's *Clipper of the Clouds*,[115] and so the thing really got hold of them.

At first the most obvious aspect was the multiplication of balloons. The sky of Bun Hill began to be infested by balloons. On Wednesday and Saturday afternoons particularly you could scarcely look skyward for a quarter of an hour without discovering a balloon somewhere. And then one bright day Bert, motoring towards Croydon, was arrested by the insurgence of a huge, bolster-shaped monster from the Crystal Palace grounds, and obliged to dismount and watch it. It was like a bolster with a broken nose, and below it, and comparatively small, was a stiff framework bearing a man and an engine with a screw that whizzed round in front and a sort of canvas rudder behind. The framework had an air of dragging the reluctant gas-cylinder after it like a brisk little terrier towing a shy gas-distended elephant into society. The combined monster certainly travelled and steered. It went overhead perhaps a thousand feet up (Bert heard the engine), sailed away southward, vanished over the hills, reappeared a little blue outline far off in the east, going now very fast before a gentle south-west gale, returned above the Crystal Palace towers, circled round them, chose a position for descent, and sank down out of sight.

Bert sighed deeply, and turned to his motor-bicycle again.

And that was only the beginning of a succession of strange phenomena in the heavens – cylinders, cones, pear-shaped monsters, even at last a thing of aluminium that glittered wonderfully, and that Grubb, through some confusion of ideas about armour plates, was inclined to consider a war machine.

There followed actual flight.

This, however, was not an affair that was visible from Bun Hill; it was something that occurred in private grounds or other enclosed places and under favourable conditions, and it was brought home to Grubb and Bert Smallways only by means of the magazine page of the half-penny newspapers or by cinematograph records.[116] But it was brought home very insistently, and in those days if ever one heard a man saying in a public place in a loud, reassuring, confident tone, 'It's bound to come,' the chances were ten to one he was talking of flying. And Bert got a box lid and wrote out in correct window-ticket style, and Grubb put in the window this inscription, 'Aeroplanes made and repaired'. It quite upset Tom – it seemed taking one's shop so lightly; but most of the neighbours, and all the sporting ones, approved of it as being very good indeed.

Everybody talked of flying, everybody repeated over and over again, 'Bound to come', and then you know it didn't come. There was a hitch. They flew – that was all right; they flew in machines heavier than air. But they smashed. Sometimes they smashed the engine, sometimes they smashed the aeronaut, usually they smashed both. Machines that made flights of three or four miles and came down safely, went up the next time to headlong disaster. There seemed no possible trusting to them. The breeze upset them, the eddies near the ground upset them, a passing thought in the mind of the aeronaut upset them. Also they upset – simply.

'It's this "stability" does 'em,' said Grubb, repeating his newspaper. 'They pitch and they pitch, till they pitch themselves to pieces.'

Experiments fell away after two expectant years of this sort of success, the public and then the newspapers tired of the expensive photographic reproductions, the optimistic reports, the perpetual sequence of triumph and disaster and silence. Flying slumped, even ballooning fell away to some extent, though it remained a fairly popular sport, and continued to lift gravel from the wharf of the Bun Hill gasworks and drop it upon deserving people's lawns and gardens. There were half a dozen re-assuring years for Tom – at least so far as flying was concerned. But that was the great time of monorail development, and his anxiety was only diverted from the high heavens by the most urgent threats and symptoms of change in the lower sky.

There had been talk of monorails for several years. But the real mischief began when Brennan sprang his gyroscopic monorail car[117] upon the Royal Society.[118] It was the leading sensation of the 1907 soirées; that celebrated demonstration-room was all too small for its exhibition. Brave soldiers, leading Zionists, deserving novelists, noble ladies, congested the narrow passage and thrust distinguished elbows into ribs the world would not willingly let break, deeming themselves fortunate if they could see 'just a little bit of the rail'. Inaudible, but convincing, the great inventor expounded his discovery, and sent his obedient little model of the trains of the future up gradients, round curves, and across a sagging wire. It ran along its single rail, on its single wheels, simple and sufficient; it stopped, reversed, stood still, balancing perfectly. It maintained its astounding equilibrium amidst a thunder of applause. The audience dispersed at last, discussing how far they would enjoy crossing an abyss on a wire cable. 'Suppose the gyroscope stopped!' Few of them anticipated a tithe of what the Brennan monorail would do for their railway securities and the face of the world.

In a few years they realised better. In a little while no one thought anything of crossing an abyss on a wire, and the monorail was superseding the tramlines, railways, and indeed every form of track for mechanical locomotion. Where land was cheap the rail ran along the ground, where it was dear the rail lifted up on iron standards and passed overhead; its swift, convenient cars went everywhere and did everything that had once been done along made tracks upon the ground.

When old Smallways died, Tom could think of nothing more striking to say of him than that, 'When he was a boy, there wasn't nothing higher than your chimbleys – there wasn't a wire nor a cable in the sky!'

Old Smallways went to his grave under an intricate network of wires and cables, for Bun Hill became not only a sort of minor centre of power distribution – the Home Counties Power Distribution Company[119] set up transformers and a generating station close beside the old gasworks – but also a junction on the suburban monorail system. Moreover, every tradesman in the place, and indeed nearly every house, had its own telephone.

The monorail cable standards became a striking fact in urban landscape, for the most part stout iron erections rather like tapering trestles, and painted a bright bluish green. One, it happened, bestrode Tom's house, which looked still more retiring and apologetic beneath its immensity; and another giant stood just inside the corner of his garden, which was still not built upon and unchanged, except for a couple of advertisement boards, one recommending a two-and-sixpenny watch, and one a nerve restorer. These, by the by, were placed almost horizontally to catch the eye of the passing monorail passengers above, and so served admirably to roof over a tool-shed and a mushroom-shed for Tom. All day and all night the fast cars from Brighton and Hastings went murmuring by overhead – long, broad, comfortable-looking cars, that were brightly lit after dusk. As they flew by at night, transient flares of light and a rumbling sound of passage, they kept up a perpetual summer lightning and thunderstorm in the street below.

Presently the English Channel was bridged[120] – a series of great iron Eiffel Tower pillars carrying monorail cables at a height of a hundred and fifty feet above the water, except near the middle, where they rose higher to allow the passage of the London and Antwerp shipping and the Hamburg–America liners.

Then heavy motor cars began to run about on only a couple of wheels, one behind the other, which for some reason upset Tom dreadfully, and made him gloomy for days after the first one passed the shop . . .

All this gyroscopic and monorail development naturally absorbed a vast amount of public attention, and there was also a huge excitement consequent upon the amazing gold discoveries off the coast of Anglesea made by a submarine prospector, Miss Patricia Giddy. She had taken her degree in geology and mineralogy in the University of London, and while working upon the auriferous rocks of North Wales, after a brief holiday spent in agitating for women's suffrage, she had been struck by the possibility of these reefs cropping up again under the water. She had set herself to verify this supposition by the use of the submarine crawler invented by Dr Alberto Cassini.[121] By a happy mingling of reasoning and intuition peculiar to her sex she found gold at her first descent, and emerged after three hours' submersion with about two hundredweight of ore containing gold in the unparalleled quantity of seventeen ounces to the ton. But the whole story of her submarine mining, intensely interesting as it is, must be told at some other time; suffice it now to remark simply that it was during the consequent great rise of prices, confidence, and enterprise that the revival of interest in flying occurred.

4

It is curious how the final boom of flying began. It was like the coming of a breeze on a quiet day; nothing started it, it came. People began to talk of flying with an air of never having for one moment dropped the subject. Pictures of flying and flying machines returned to the newspapers; articles and allusions increased and multiplied in the serious magazines. People asked in monorail trains, 'When are we going to fly?' A new crop of inventors sprang up in a night or so like fungi. The Aero Club announced the project of a great Flying Exhibition in a large area of ground that the removal of slums in Whitechapel had rendered available.

The advancing wave soon produced a sympathetic ripple in the Bun Hill establishment. Grubb routed out his flying-machine model again, tried it in the yard behind the shop, got a kind of flight out of it, and broke seventeen panes of glass and nine flowerpots in the greenhouse that occupied the next yard but one.

And then, springing from nowhere, sustained one knew not how, came a persistent, disturbing rumour that the problem had been solved, that the secret was known. Bert met it one early-closing afternoon as he refreshed himself in an inn near Nutfield, whither his motor-bicycle had brought him. There smoked and meditated a person in khaki, an engineer, who presently took an interest in Bert's machine. It was a sturdy piece of apparatus, and it had acquired a kind of documentary value in these quick-changing times; it was now nearly eight years old. Its points discussed, the soldier broke into a new topic with, 'My next's going to be an aeroplane, so far as I can see. I've had enough of roads and ways.'

'They *tork*,' said Bert.

'They talk – and they do,' said the soldier. 'The thing's coming – '

'It keeps *on* coming,' said Bert; 'I shall believe when I see it.'

'That won't be long,' said the soldier.

The conversation seemed degenerating into an amiable wrangle of contradiction.

'I tell you they *are* flying,' the soldier insisted. 'I see it myself.'

'We've all seen it,' said Bert.

'I don't mean flap up and smash up; I mean real, safe, steady, controlled flying, against the wind, good and right.'

'You ain't seen that!'

'I *'ave*! Aldershot.[122] They try to keep it a secret. They got it right enough. You bet – our War Office isn't going to be caught napping this time.'

Bert's incredulity was shaken. He asked questions – and the soldier expanded.

'I tell you they got nearly a square mile fenced in – a sort of valley. Fences of barbed wire ten feet high, and inside that they do things. Chaps about the camp – now and then we get a peep. It isn't only us neither. There's the Japanese; you bet they got it too – and the Germans! And I never knowed anything of this sort yet that the Frencheys didn't get ahead with – after their manner! They started ironclads, they started submarines, they started navigables, and you bet they won't be far be'ind at this.'

The soldier stood with his legs very wide apart, and filled his pipe thoughtfully. Bert sat on the low wall against which his motor-bicycle was leaning.

'Funny thing fighting'll be,' he said.

'Flying's going to break out,' said the soldier. 'When it *does* come, when the curtain does go up, I tell you you'll find everyone on the stage – busy . . . Such fighting, too! . . . I suppose you don't read the papers about this sort of thing?'

'I read 'em a bit,' said Bert.

'Well, have you noticed what one might call the remarkable case of the disappearing inventor – the inventor who turns up in a blaze of publicity, fires off a few successful experiments, and vanishes?'

'Can't say I 'ave,' said Bert.

'Well, I 'ave, anyhow. You get anybody come along who does anything striking in this line, and, you bet, he vanishes. Just goes off quietly out of sight. After a bit, you don't hear anything more of 'em at all. See? They disappear. Gone – no address. First – oh! it's an old story now – there was those Wright Brothers out in America.[123] They glided – they glided miles and miles. Finally they glided off stage. Why, it must be nineteen hundred and four, or five, *they* vanished! Then there was those people in Ireland – no, I forget their names. Everybody said they could fly. *They* went. They ain't dead that I've heard tell; but you can't say they're alive. Not a feather of 'em can you see. Then that chap who flew round Paris and upset in the Seine. De Booley,[124] was it? I forget. That was a grand fly, in spite of the accident; but where's he got to? The accident didn't hurt him. Eh? '*E*'s gone to cover.'

The soldier prepared to light his pipe.

'Looks like a secret society got hold of them,' said Bert.

'Secret society! *Naw!*'

The soldier lit his match, and drew. 'Secret society,' he repeated, with his pipe between his teeth and the match flaring, in response to his words. 'War Departments; that's more like it.' He threw his match aside, and walked to his machine. 'I tell you, sir,' he said, 'there isn't a big Power in Europe, *or* Asia, *or* America, *or* Africa, that hasn't got at least one or two flying machines hidden up its sleeve at the present time. Not one. Real, workable, flying machines. And the spying! The spying and manoeuvring to find out what the others have got. I tell you, sir, a foreigner, or, for the matter of that, an unaccredited native, can't get within four miles of Lydd[125] nowadays – not to mention our little circus at Aldershot, and the experimental camp in Galway. No!'

'Well,' said Bert, 'I'd like to see one of them, anyhow. Jest to help believing. I'll believe when I see, that I'll promise you.'

'You'll see 'em fast enough,' said the soldier, and led his machine out into the road.

He left Bert on his wall, grave and pensive, with his cap on the back of his head, and a cigarette smouldering in the corner of his mouth.

'If what he says is true,' said Bert, 'me and Grubb, we been wasting our blessed old time. Besides incurring expense with that green'ouse.'

It was while this mysterious talk with the soldier still stirred in Bert Smallways' imagination that the most astounding incident in the whole of that dramatic chapter of human history, the coming of flying, occurred. People talk glibly enough of epoch-making events; this *was* an epoch-making event. It was the unanticipated and entirely successful flight of Mr Alfred Butteridge from the Crystal Palace to Glasgow and back in a small businesslike-looking machine heavier than air – an entirely manageable and controllable machine that could fly as well as a pigeon.

It wasn't, one felt, a fresh step forward in the matter so much as a giant stride, a leap. Mr Butteridge remained in the air altogether for about nine hours, and during that time he flew with the ease and assurance of a bird. His machine was, however, neither birdlike nor butterfly-like, nor had it the wide, lateral expansion of the ordinary aeroplane. The effect upon the observer was rather something in the nature of a bee or wasp. Parts of the apparatus were spinning very rapidly, and gave one a hazy effect of transparent wings; but parts, including two peculiarly curved 'wing-cases' – if one may borrow a figure from the flying beetles – remained expanded stiffly. In the middle was a long rounded body like the body of a moth, and on this Mr Butteridge could be seen sitting astride, much as a man bestrides a horse. The wasplike resemblance was increased by the fact that the apparatus flew with a deep booming hum, exactly the sound made by a wasp at a windowpane.

Mr Butteridge took the world by surprise. He was one of those gentlemen from nowhere Fate still succeeds in producing for the stimulation of mankind. He came, it was variously said, from Australia and America and the South of France. He was also described quite incorrectly as the son of a man who had amassed a comfortable fortune in the manufacture of gold nibs and the Butteridge fountain pens. But this was an entirely different strain of Butteridges. For some years, in spite of a loud voice, a large presence, an aggressive swagger, and an implacable manner, he had been an undistinguished member of most of the existing aeronautical associations. Then one day he wrote to all the London papers to announce that he had made arrangements for an ascent from the Crystal Palace of a machine that would demonstrate satisfactorily that the outstanding difficulties in the way of flying were finally solved. Few of the papers printed his letter, still fewer were the people who believed in his claim. No one was excited even when a fracas on the steps of a leading hotel in Piccadilly, in which he tried to horse-whip a prominent German musician upon some personal account, delayed his promised ascent. The quarrel was inadequately reported, and his name spelt variously Betteridge and Betridge. Until his flight, indeed, he did not and could not contrive to exist in the public mind. There were scarcely thirty people on the look-out for him, in spite of all his clamour, when about six o'clock one summer morning the doors of the big shed in which he had been putting together his apparatus opened – it was near the big model of a megatherium in the Crystal Palace grounds – and his giant insect came droning out into a negligent and incredulous world.

But before he had made his second circuit of the Crystal Palace towers, Fame was lifting her trumpet, she drew a deep breath as the startled tramps who sleep on the seats of Trafalgar Square were roused by his buzz and awoke to discover him circling the Nelson column, and by the time he had got to Birmingham, which place he crossed about half-past ten, her deafening blast was echoing throughout the country. The despaired-of thing was done. A man was flying securely and well.

Scotland was agape for his coming. Glasgow he reached by one o'clock, and it is related that scarcely a shipyard or factory in that busy hive of industry resumed work before half-past two. The public mind was just sufficiently educated in the impossibility of flying to appreciate Mr Butteridge at his proper value. He circled the University buildings, and dropped to within shouting distance of the crowds in West End Park and on the slope of Gilmorehill. The thing flew quite steadily at a pace of about three miles an hour, in a wide circle, making a deep hum that would have drowned his full, rich voice completely had he not provided himself with a megaphone. He avoided churches, buildings, and monorail cables with consummate ease as he conversed.

'Me name's Butteridge,' he shouted; 'B-U-T-T-E-R-I-D-G-E. Got it? Me mother was Scotch.'

And having assured himself that he had been understood, he rose amidst cheers and shouting and patriotic cries, and then flew up very swiftly and easily into the south-eastern sky, rising and falling with long, easy undulations in an extraordinarily wasplike manner.

His return to London – he visited and hovered over Manchester and Liverpool and Oxford on his way, and spelt his name out to each place – was an occasion of unparalleled excitement. Everyone was staring heavenward. More people were run over in the streets upon that one day than in the previous three months, and a County Council

steamboat, the *Isaac Walton*,[126] collided with a pier of Westminster
Bridge, and narrowly escaped disaster by running ashore – it was low
water – on the mud on the south side. He returned to the Crystal Palace
grounds, that classic starting-point of aeronautical adventure, about
sunset, re-entered his shed without disaster, and had the doors locked
immediately upon the photographers and journalists who been waiting
his return.

'Look here, you chaps,' he said, as his assistant did so, 'I'm tired to
death, and saddle sore. I can't give you a word of talk. I'm too – done.
My name's Butteridge. B-U-T-T-E-R-I-D-G-E. Get that right. I'm
an Imperial Englishman. I'll talk to you all tomorrow.'

Foggy snapshots still survive to record that incident. His assistant
struggles in a sea of aggressive young men carrying notebooks or upholding cameras and wearing bowler hats and enterprising ties. He
himself towers up in the doorway, a big figure with a mouth – an
eloquent cavity beneath a vast black moustache – distorted by his shout
to those relentless agents of publicity. He towers there, the most famous
man in the country. Almost symbolically he holds and gesticulates with
a megaphone in his left hand.

6

Tom and Bert Smallways both saw that return. They watched from the
crest of Bun Hill, from which they had so often surveyed the pyro-
technics of the Crystal Palace. Bert was excited, Tom kept calm and
lumpish, but neither of them realised how their own lives were to be
invaded by the fruits of that beginning. 'P'raps old Grubb'll mind the
shop a bit now,' he said, 'and put his blessed model in the fire. Not that
that can save us, if we don't tide over with Steinhart's account.'

Bert knew enough of things and the problem of aeronautics to realise
that this gigantic imitation of a bee would, to use his own idiom, 'give
the newspapers fits'. The next day it was clear the fits had been given
even as he said: their magazine pages were black with hasty photographs,
their prose was convulsive, they foamed at the headline. The next day
they were worse. Before the week was out they were not so much
published as carried screaming into the street.

The dominant fact in the uproar was the exceptional personality of
Mr Butteridge, and the extraordinary terms he demanded for the secret
of his machine.

For it was a secret, and he kept it secret in the most elaborate fashion.

He built his apparatus himself in the safe privacy of the great Crystal Palace sheds, with the assistance of inattentive workmen, and the day next following his flight he took it to pieces single-handed, packed certain portions, and then secured unintelligent assistance in packing and dispersing the rest. Sealed packing-cases went north and east and west to various pantechnicons, and the engines were boxed with peculiar care. It became evident these precautions were not inadvisable in view of the violent demand for any sort of photograph or impressions of his machine. But Mr Butteridge, having once made his demonstration, intended to keep his secret safe from any further risk of leakage. He faced the British public now with the question whether they wanted his secret or not; he was, he said perpetually, an 'Imperial Englishman', and his first wish and his last was to see his invention the privilege and monopoly of the Empire. Only –

It was there the difficulty began.

Mr Butteridge, it became evident, was a man singularly free from any false modesty – indeed, from any modesty of any kind – singularly willing to see interviewers, answer questions upon any topic except aeronautics, volunteer opinions, criticism, and autobiography, supply portraits and photographs of himself, and generally spread his personality across the terrestrial sky. The published portraits insisted primarily upon an immense black moustache, and secondarily upon a fierceness behind the moustache. The general impression upon the public was that Butteridge was a small man. No one big, it was felt, could have so virulently aggressive an expression, though, as a matter of fact, Butteridge had a height of six feet two inches, and a weight altogether proportionate to that. Moreover, he had a love affair of large and unusual dimensions and irregular circumstances, and the still largely decorous British public learnt with reluctance and alarm that a sympathetic treatment of this affair was inseparable from the exclusive acquisition of the priceless secret of aerial stability by the British Empire. The exact particulars of the irregularity never came to light, but apparently the lady had, in a fit of high-minded inadvertence, gone through the ceremony of marriage with – one quotes the unpublished discourse of Mr Butteridge – 'a white-livered skunk', and this zoological aberration did in some legal and vexatious manner mar her social happiness. He wanted to talk about the business, to show the splendour of her nature in the light of its complications. It was really most embarrassing to a press that has always possessed a considerable turn for reticence, that wanted things personal, indeed, in the modern fashion, but not too personal. It was embarrassing, I say, to be inexorably confronted with Mr Butteridge's great heart, to see it laid open in relentless self-vivisection, and its pulsating dissepiments adorned with emphatic flag labels.

Confronted they were, and there was no getting away from it. He would make this appalling viscus beat and throb before the shrinking journalists – no uncle with a big watch and a little baby ever harped upon it so relentlessly; whatever evasion they attempted he set aside. He 'gloried in his love', he said, and compelled them to write it down.

'That's of course a private affair, Mr Butteridge,' they would object.

'The injustice, sorr, is public. I do not care whether I am up against institutions or individuals. I do not care if I am up against the Universal All. I am pleading the cause of a woman, a woman I lurve, sorr – a noble woman – misunderstood. I intend to vindicate her, sorr, to the four winds of heaven!'

'I lurve England,' he used to say – I lurve England, but Puritanism, sorr, I abhor. It fills me with loathing. It raises my gorge. Take my own case . . .'

He insisted relentlessly upon his heart, and upon seeing proofs of the interview. If they had not done justice to his erotic bellowings and gesticulations, he stuck in, in a large inky scrawl, all and more than they had omitted.

It was a strangely embarrassing thing for British journalism. Never was there a more obvious or uninteresting affair; never had the world heard the story of erratic affection with less appetite or sympathy. On the other hand it was extremely curious about Mr Butteridge's invention. But when Mr Butteridge could be deflected for a moment from the cause of the lady he championed, then he talked chiefly, and usually with tears of tenderness in his voice, about his mother and his childhood – his mother who crowned a complete encyclopaedia of maternal virtue by being 'largely Scotch'. She was not quite neat, but nearly so. 'I owe everything in me to me mother,' he asserted – 'everything. Eh!' and – 'Ask any man who's done anything. You'll hear the same story. All we have we owe to women. They are the species, sorr. Man is but a dream. He comes and goes. The woman's soul leadeth us upward and on!'[127]

He was always going on like that.

What in particular he wanted from the Government for his secret did not appear, nor what beyond a money payment could be expected from a modern state in such an affair. The general effect upon judicious observers, indeed, was not that he was treating for anything, but that he was using an unexampled opportunity to bellow and show off to an attentive world. Rumours of his real identity spread abroad. It was said that he had been the landlord of an ambiguous hotel in Cape Town, and had there given shelter to, and witnessed the experiments and finally stolen the papers and plans of, an extremely shy and friendless young inventor named Palliser, who had come to South Africa from England in an advanced stage of consumption, and died there. This, at any rate, was the allegation of the more outspoken American press. But the proof or disproof of that never reached the public.

Mr Butteridge also involved himself passionately in a tangle of disputes for the possession of a great number of valuable money prizes. Some of these had been offered so long ago as 1906 for successful mechanical flight. By the time of Mr Butteridge's success a really very considerable number of newspapers, tempted by the impunity of the pioneers in this direction, had pledged themselves to pay in some cases quite overwhelming sums to the first person to fly from Manchester to Glasgow, from London to Manchester, one hundred miles, two hundred miles in England, and the like. Most had hedged a little with ambiguous conditions, and now offered resistance; one or two paid at once, and vehemently called attention to the fact; and Mr Butteridge plunged into litigation with the more recalcitrant, while at the same time sustaining a vigorous agitation and canvass to induce the Government to purchase his invention.

One fact, however, remained permanent throughout all the developments of this affair behind Butteridge's preposterous love interest, his politics and personality, and all his shouting and boasting, and that was that, so far as the mass of people knew, he was in sole possession of the secret of the practicable aeroplane in which, for all one could tell to the contrary, the key of the future empire of the world resided. And presently, to the great consternation of innumerable people, including among others Mr Bert Smallways, it became apparent that whatever negotiations were in progress for the acquisition of this precious secret by the British Government were in danger of falling through. The London *Daily Requiem*[128] first voiced the universal alarm, and published an interview under the terrific caption of 'Mr Butteridge Speaks his Mind'.

Therein the inventor – if he was an inventor – poured out his heart.

'I came from the end of the earth,' he said, which rather seemed to confirm the Cape Town story, 'bringing me Motherland the secret that would give her the empire of the world. And what do I get?' He paused. 'I am sniffed at by elderly mandarins! . . . And the woman I love is treated like a leper!

'I am an Imperial Englishman,' he went on in a splendid outburst, subsequently written into the interview by his own hand; 'but there are limits to the human heart! There are younger nations – living nations! Nations that do not snore and gurgle helplessly in paroxysms of plethora upon beds of formality and red tape! There are nations that will not fling away the empire of earth in order to slight an unknown man and insult a noble woman whose boots they are not fitted to unlatch. There are nations not blinded to Science, not given over hand and foot to effete snobocracies and Degenerate Decadents. In short, mark my words – *there are other nations!*' . . .

This speech it was that particularly impressed Bert Smallways. 'If them Germans or them Americans get hold of this,' he said impressively to his brother, 'the British Empire's done. It's U-P. The Union Jack, so to speak, won't be worth the paper it's written on, Tom.'

'I suppose you couldn't lend us a hand this morning,' said Jessica, in his impressive pause. 'Everybody in Bun Hill seems wanting early potatoes at once. Tom can't carry half of them.'

'We're living on a volcano,' said Bert, disregarding the suggestion. 'At any moment war may come – such a war!'

He shook his head portentously.

'You'd better take this lot first, Tom,' said Jessica. She turned briskly on Bert. 'Can you spare us a morning?' she asked.

'I dessay I can,' said Bert. 'The shop's very quiet s'morning. Though all this danger to the Empire worries me something frightful.'

'Work'll take it off your mind,' said Jessica.

And presently he too was going out into a world of change and wonder, bowed beneath a load of potatoes and patriotic insecurity, that merged at last into a very definite irritation at the weight and want of style of the potatoes and a very clear conception of the entire detestableness of Jessica.

CHAPTER TWO

How Bert Smallways Got into Difficulties

1

It did not occur to either Tom or Bert Smallways that this remarkable aerial performance of Mr Butteridge was likely to affect either of their lives in any special manner, that it would in any way single them out from the millions about them; and when they had witnessed it from the crest of Bun Hill and seen the flylike mechanism, its rotating planes a golden haze in the sunset, sink humming to the harbour of its shed again, they turned back towards the sunken greengrocery beneath the great iron standard of the London to Brighton monorail, and their minds reverted to the discussion that had engaged them before Mr Butteridge's triumph had come in sight out of the London haze.

It was a difficult and unsuccessful discussion. They had to carry it on in shouts because of the moaning and roaring of the gyroscopic motor cars that traversed the High Street, and in its nature it was contentious and private. The Grubb business was in difficulties, and Grubb in a moment of financial eloquence had given a half-share in it to Bert, whose relations with his employer had been for some time unsalaried and pallish and informal.

Bert was trying to impress Tom with the idea that the reconstructed Grubb & Smallways offered unprecedented and unparalleled opportunities to the judicious small investor. It was coming home to Bert, as though it were an entirely new fact, that Tom was singularly impervious to ideas. In the end he put the financial issues on one side, and, making the thing entirely a matter of fraternal affection, succeeded in borrowing a sovereign on the security of his word of honour.

The firm of Grubb & Smallways, formerly Grubb, had indeed been persistently unlucky in the last year or so. For many years the business had struggled along with a flavour of romantic insecurity in a small, dissolute-looking shop in the High Street, adorned with brilliantly coloured advertisements of cycles, a display of bells, trouser-clips, oil-cans, pump-clips, frame-cases, wallets, and other accessories, and the announcement of 'Bicycles on Hire', 'Repairs', 'Free Inflation', 'Petrol', and similar attractions. They were agents for several obscure makes of bicycle, two samples constituted the stock, and occasionally they effected a sale; they also repaired punctures and did their best – though luck was not always on their side – with any other repairing that was brought to them. They handled a line of cheap gramophones, and did a little with musical boxes. The staple of their business was, however, the letting of bicycles on hire. It was a singular trade, obeying no known commercial or economic principles – indeed, no principles. There was a stock of ladies' and gentlemen's bicycles in a state of disrepair that passes description, and these, the hiring stock, were let to unexacting and reckless people, inexpert in the things of this world, at a nominal rate of one shilling for the first hour and sixpence per hour afterwards. But really there were no fixed prices, and insistent boys could get bicycles and the thrill of danger for an hour for so low a sum as threepence, provided they could convince Grubb that that was all they had. The saddle and handlebar were then sketchily adjusted by Grubb, a deposit exacted, except in the case of familiar boys, the machine lubricated, and the adventurer started upon his career. Usually he or she came back, but at times, when the accident was serious, Bert or Grubb had to go out and fetch the machine home. Hire was always charged up to the hour of return to the shop and deducted from the deposit. It was rare that a bicycle started out from their hands in a state of pedantic efficiency. Romantic possibilities of accident lurked in the worn thread of the screw that adjusted the saddle, in the precarious pedals, in the loose-knit chain, in the handlebars, above all in the brakes and tyres. Tappings and clankings and strange rhythmic creakings awoke as the intrepid hirer pedalled out into the country. Then perhaps the bell would jam or a brake fail to act on a hill; or the seat-pillar would get loose, and the saddle drop three or four inches with a disconcerting bump; or the loose and rattling chain would jump the cogs of the chain-wheel as the machine ran downhill, and so bring the mechanism to an abrupt and disastrous stop without at the same time arresting the forward momentum of the rider; or a tyre would bang, or sigh quietly, and give up the struggle and scrabble in the dust.

When the hirer returned, a heated pedestrian, Grubb would ignore all verbal complaints, and examine the machine gravely.

'This ain't 'ad fair usage,' he used to begin.

He became a mild embodiment of the spirit of reason. 'You can't expect a bicycle to take you up in its arms and carry you,' he used to say. 'You got to show intelligence. After all – it's machinery.'

Sometimes the process of liquidating the consequent claims bordered on violence. It was always a very rhetorical and often a trying affair, but in these progressive times you have to make a noise to get a living. It was often hard work, but nevertheless this hiring was a fairly steady source of profit, until one day all the panes in the window and door were broken and the stock on sale in the window greatly damaged and disordered by two over-critical hirers with no sense of rhetorical irrelevance. They were big, coarse stokers from Gravesend. One was annoyed because his left pedal had come off, and the other because his tyre had become deflated – small and indeed negligible accidents by Bun Hill standards, due entirely to the ungentle handling of the delicate machines entrusted to them – and they failed to see clearly how they put themselves in the wrong by this method of argument. It is a poor way of convincing a man that he has lent you a defective machine to throw his foot-pump about his shop, and take his stock of gongs outside in order to return them through the window panes. It carried no real conviction to the minds of either Grubb or Bert; it only irritated and vexed them. One quarrel makes many, and this unpleasantness led to a violent dispute between Grubb and the landlord upon the moral aspects of and legal responsibility for the consequent re-glazing. Matters came to a climax upon the eve of the Whitsuntide Holiday.

In the end Grubb and Smallways were put to the expense of a strategic nocturnal removal to another position.

It was a position they had long considered. It was a small, shed-like shop with a plate-glass window and one room behind, just at the sharp bend in the road at the bottom of Bun Hill; and here they struggled along bravely, in spite of persistent annoyance from their former land-lord, hoping for certain eventualities the peculiar situation of the shop seemed to promise. Here, too, they were doomed to disappointment.

The High Road from London to Brighton that ran through Bun Hill was like the British Empire or the British Constitution – a thing that had grown to its present importance. Unlike any other roads in Europe the British high roads have never been subjected to any organised attempts to grade or straighten them out, and to that, no doubt, their peculiar picturesqueness is to be ascribed. The old Bun Hill High Street drops at its end for perhaps eighty or a hundred feet of descent at an angle of one in five, turns at right angles to the left, runs in a curve for about thirty yards to a brick bridge over the dry ditch that had once been the Otter-bourne, and then bends sharply to the right again round a dense clump of trees and goes on, a simple, straightforward, peaceful high road. There had been one or two horse-and-van and bicycle accidents in the place before the shop Bert and Grubb took was built, and, to be frank, it was the probability of others that attracted them to it.

Its possibilities had come to them first with a humorous flavour.

'Here's one of the places where a chap might get a living by keeping hens,' said Grubb.

'You can't get a living by keeping hens,' said Bert.

'You'd keep the hen and have it spatch-cocked,' said Grubb. 'The motor chaps would pay for it.'

When they really came to take the place they remembered this conversation. Hens, however, were out of the question; there was no place for a run unless they had it in the shop. It would have been obviously out of place there. The shop was much more modern than their former one, and had a plate-glass front. 'Sooner or later,' said Bert, 'we shall get a motor car through this.'

'That's all right,' said Grubb. 'Compensation. I don't mind *when* that motor car comes along. I don't mind even if it gives me a shock to the system.'

'And meanwhile,' said Bert, with great artfulness, '*I'm* going to buy myself a dog.'

He did. He bought three in succession. He surprised the people at the Dogs' Home in Battersea[129] by demanding a deaf retriever, and rejecting every candidate that pricked up its ears. 'I want a good, deaf, slow-moving dog,' he said. 'A dog that doesn't put himself out for things.'

They displayed inconvenient curiosity; they declared a great scarcity of deaf dogs.

'You see,' they said, 'dogs aren't deaf.'

'Mine's got to be,' said Bert. 'I've *had* dogs that aren't deaf. All I want. It's like this, you see – I sell gramophones. Naturally I got to make 'em talk and tootle a bit to show 'em orf. Well, a dog that isn't deaf doesn't like it – gets excited, smells round, barks, growls. That upsets the customer. See? Then a dog that has his hearing fancies things. Makes burglars out of passing tramps. Wants to fight every motor that makes a whizz. All very well if you want livening up, but our place is lively enough. I don't want a dog of that sort. I want a quiet dog.'

In the end he got three in succession, but none of them turned out well. The first strayed off into the infinite, heeding no appeals; the second was killed in the night by a fruit motor-wagon which fled before Grubb could get down; the third got itself entangled in the front wheel of a passing cyclist, who came through the plate glass, and proved to be an actor out of work and an undischarged bankrupt. He demanded compensation for some fancied injury, would hear nothing of the valuable dog he had killed or the window he had broken, obliged Grubb by sheer physical obduracy to straighten his buckled front wheel, and pestered the struggling firm with a series of inhumanly worded solicitor's letters. Grubb answered them – stingingly, and put himself, Bert thought, in the wrong.

Affairs got more and more exasperating and strained under these pressures. The window was boarded up, and an unpleasant altercation about their delay in repairing it with the new landlord, a Bun Hill butcher – and a loud, bellowing, unreasonable person at that – served to remind them of their unsettled troubles with the old. Things were at this pitch when Bert bethought himself of creating a sort of debenture capital in the business for the benefit of Tom. But, as I have said, Tom had no enterprise in his composition. His idea of investment was the stocking; he bribed his brother not to keep the offer open.

And then ill-luck made its last lunge at their crumbling business and brought it to the ground.

2

It is a poor heart that never rejoices, and Whitsuntide had an air of coming as an agreeable break in the business complications of Grubb & Smallways. Encouraged by the practical outcome of Bert's negotiations with his brother, and by the fact that half the hiring-stock was out from Saturday to Monday, they decided to ignore the residuum of hiring-trade on Sunday and devote that day to much-needed relaxation and refreshment – to have, in fact, an unstinted good time, a beano on Whit Sunday, and return invigorated to grapple with their difficulties and the Bank Holiday repairs on the Monday. No good thing was ever done by exhausted and dispirited men. It happened that they had made the acquaintance of two young ladies in employment in Clapham, Miss Flossie Bright and Miss Edna Bunthorne, and it was resolved therefore to make a cheerful little cyclist party of four into the heart of Kent, and to picnic and spend an indolent afternoon and evening among the trees and bracken between Ashford and Maidstone.

Miss Bright could ride a bicycle, and a machine was found for her, not among the hiring-stock, but specially, in the sample held for sale. Miss Bunthorne, whom Bert particularly affected, could not ride, and so with some difficulty he hired a basketwork trailer from the big business of Wray's in the Clapham Road. To see our young men, brightly dressed and cigarettes alight, wheeling off to the rendezvous, Grubb guiding the lady's machine beside him with one skilful hand and Bert teuf-teuffing steadily, was to realise how pluck may triumph even over insolvency.

Their landlord, the butcher, said, 'Gurr!' as they passed, and shouted 'Go it!' in a loud, savage tone to their receding backs.

Much they cared.

The weather was fine, and though they were on their way southward before nine o'clock, there was already a great multitude of holiday people abroad upon the roads. There were quantities of young men and women on bicycles and motor-bicycles, and a majority of gyroscopic motor cars running bicycle-fashion on two wheels, mingled with old-fashioned four-wheeled traffic. Bank Holiday times always bring out old stored-away vehicles and odd people; one saw tricars and electric broughams and dilapidated old racing motors with huge pneumatic tyres. Once our holidaymakers saw a horse and cart, and once a youth riding a black horse amidst the badinage of the passers-by. And there were several navigable gas airships, not to mention balloons, in the air. It was all immensely interesting and refreshing after the dark anxieties of the shop. Edna wore a brown straw hat with poppies, that suited her admirably, and sat in the trailer like a queen, and the eight-year-old motor-bicycle ran like a thing of yesterday.

Little it seemed to matter to Mr Bert Smallways that a newspaper placard proclaimed:

GERMANY DENOUNCES THE MONROE DOCTRINE.[130]

AMBIGUOUS ATTITUDE OF JAPAN.

WHAT WILL BRITAIN DO?

IS IT WAR?

This sort of thing was always going on, and on holidays one disregarded it as a matter of course. Weekdays, in the slack time after the midday meal, then perhaps one might worry about the Empire and international politics; but not on a sunny Sunday, with a pretty girl trailing behind one, and envious cyclists trying to race you. Nor did our young people attach any great importance to the flitting suggestions of military activity they glimpsed ever and again. Near Maidstone they came on a string of eleven motor-guns of peculiar construction halted by the roadside, with a number of businesslike engineers grouped about them watching through field-glasses some sort of entrenchment that was going on near the crest of the downs. It signified nothing to Bert.

'What's up?' said Edna.

'Oh! – manoeuvres,' said Bert.

'Oh! I thought they did them at Easter,' said Edna, and troubled no more.

The last great British war, the Boer War,[131] was over and forgotten, and the public had lost the fashion of expert military criticism.

Our four young people picnicked cheerfully, and were happy in the manner of a happiness that was an ancient mode in Nineveh.[132] Eyes were bright, Grubb was funny and almost witty, and Bert achieved epigrams; the hedges were full of honeysuckle and dog-roses; in the woods the distant toot-toot-toot of the traffic on the dust-hazy high road might have been no more than the horns of elf-land. They laughed and gossiped and picked flowers and made love and talked, and the girls smoked cigarettes. Also they scuffled playfully. Among other things they talked aeronautics, and how they would come for a picnic together in Bert's flying-machine before ten years were out. The world seemed full of amusing possibilities that afternoon. They wondered what their great-grandparents would have thought of aeronautics. In the evening, about seven, the party turned homeward, expecting no disaster, and it was only on the crest of the downs between Wrotham and Kingsdown that disaster came.

They had come up the hill in the twilight; Bert was anxious to get as far as possible before he lit – or attempted to light, for the issue was a doubtful one – his lamps,[133] and they had scorched past a number of cyclists, and by a four-wheeled motor car of the old style lamed by a deflated tyre. Some dust had penetrated Bert's horn, and the result was a curious, amusing, wheezing sound that had got into his 'honk, honk'. For the sake of merriment and glory he was making this sound as much as possible, and Edna was in fits of laughter in the trailer. They made a sort of rushing cheerfulness along the road that affected their fellow travellers variously, according to their temperaments. She did notice a good lot of bluish, evil-smelling smoke coming from about the bearings between his feet, but she thought this was one of the natural concomitants of motor-traction, and troubled no more about it, until abruptly it burst into a little yellow-tipped flame.

'Bert!' she screamed.

But Bert had put on the brakes with such suddenness that she found herself involved with his leg as he dismounted. She got to the side of the road and hastily readjusted her hat, which had suffered.

'Gaw!' said Bert.

He stood for some fatal seconds watching the petrol drip and catch, and the flame, which was now beginning to smell of enamel as well as oil, spread and grew. His chief idea was the sorrowful one that he had not sold the machine second-hand a year ago, and that he ought to have done so – a good idea in its way, but not immediately helpful. He turned upon Edna sharply. 'Get a lot of wet sand,' he said. Then he wheeled the machine a little towards the side of the roadway, and laid it down and looked about for a supply of wet sand. The flames received this as a helpful attention, and made the most of it. They seemed to brighten and the twilight to deepen about them. The road was a flinty road in the chalk country, and ill-provided with sand.

Edna accosted a short, fat cyclist. 'We want wet sand,' she said, and added, 'our motor's on fire.' The short, fat cyclist stared blankly for a moment, then with a helpful cry began to scrabble in the road-grit. Whereupon Bert and Edna also scrabbled in the road-grit. Other cyclists arrived, dismounted and stood about, and their flame-lit faces expressed satisfaction, interest, curiosity. 'Wet sand,' said the short, fat man, scrabbling terribly – 'wet sand.' One joined him. They threw hard-earned handfuls of road-grit upon the flames, which accepted them with enthusiasm.

Grubb arrived, riding hard. He was shouting something. He sprang off and threw his bicycle into the hedge. 'Don't throw water on it!' he said – 'don't throw water on it!' He displayed commanding presence of mind. He became captain of the occasion. Others were glad to repeat the things he said and imitate his actions.

'Don't throw water on it!' they cried. Also there was no water.

'Beat it out, you fools!' he said.

He seized a rug from the trailer (it was an Austrian blanket, and Bert's winter coverlet) and began to beat at the burning petrol. For a wonderful minute he seemed to succeed. But he scattered burning pools of petrol on the road, and others, fired by his enthusiasm, imitated his action. Bert caught up a trailer-cushion and began to beat; there was another cushion and a tablecloth, and these also were seized. A young hero pulled off his jacket and joined the beating. For a moment there was less talking than hard breathing, and a tremendous flapping. Flossie, arriving on the outskirts of the crowd, cried, 'Oh, my God!' and burst loudly into tears. 'Help!' she said, and 'Fire!'

The lame motor car arrived, and stopped in consternation. A tall, goggled, grey-haired man who was driving enquired with an Oxford intonation[134] and a clear, careful enunciation, 'Can we help at all?'

It became manifest that the rug, the tablecloth, the cushions, the jacket, were getting smeared with petrol and burning. The soul seemed to go out of the cushion Bert was swaying, and the air was full of feathers, like a snowstorm in the still twilight.

Bert had got very dusty and sweaty and strenuous. It seemed to him his weapon had been wrested from him at the moment of victory. The fire lay like a dying thing, close to the ground and wicked; it gave a leap of anguish at every whack of the beaters. But now Grubb had gone off to stamp out the burning blanket; the others were slacking just at the moment of victory. One was running to the motor car. ' *'Ere!'* cried Bert; 'keep on!'

He flung the deflated burning rags of cushion aside, whipped off his jacket and sprang at the flames with a shout. He stamped into the ruin until flames ran up his boots. Edna saw him, a red-lit hero, and thought it was good to be a man.

A bystander was hit by a hot halfpenny flying out of the air. Then Bert thought of the papers in his pockets, and staggered back, trying to extinguish his burning jacket – checked, repulsed, dismayed.

Edna was struck by the benevolent appearance of an elderly spectator in a silk hat and Sabbatical garments. 'Oh!' she cried to him. 'Help this young man! How can you stand and see it?'

A cry of 'The tarpaulin!' arose.

An earnest-looking man in a very light grey cycling-suit had suddenly appeared at the side of the lame motor car and addressed the owner. 'Have you a tarpaulin?' he said.

'Yes,' said the gentlemanly man. 'Yes. We've got a tarpaulin.'

'That's it,' said the earnest-looking man, suddenly shouting. 'Let's have it, quick!'

The gentlemanly man, with feeble and deprecatory gestures, and in the manner of a hypnotised person, produced an excellent large tarpaulin.

'Here!' cried the earnest-looking man to Grubb. 'Ketch holt!'

Then everybody realised that a new method was to be tried. A number of willing hands seized upon the Oxford gentleman's tarpaulin. The others stood away with approving noises. The tarpaulin was held over the burning bicycle like a canopy, and then smothered down upon it.

'We ought to have done this before,' panted Grubb.

There was a moment of triumph. The flames vanished. Everyone who could contrive to do so touched the edge of the tarpaulin. Bert held down a corner with two hands and a foot. The tarpaulin, bulged up in the centre, seemed to be suppressing triumphant exultation. Then its self-approval became too much for it; it burst into a bright red smile in the centre. It was exactly like the opening of a mouth. It laughed with a gust of flames. They were reflected redly in the observant goggles of the gentleman who owned the tarpaulin. Everybody recoiled.

'Save the trailer!' cried someone, and that was the last round in the battle. But the trailer could not be detached; its wickerwork had caught, and it was the last thing to burn. A sort of hush fell upon the gathering. The petrol burnt low, the wickerwork trailer banged and crackled. The crowd divided itself into an outer circle of critics, advisers, and secondary characters, who had played undistinguished parts or no parts at all in the affair, and a central group of heated and distressed principals. A young man with an enquiring mind and a considerable knowledge of motor-bicycles fixed on to Grubb and wanted to argue that the thing could not have happened. Grubb was short and inattentive with him, and the young man withdrew to the back of the crowd, and there told the benevolent old gentleman in the silk hat that people who went out with machines they didn't understand had only themselves to blame if things went wrong.

The old gentleman let him talk for some time, and then remarked, in a tone of rapturous enjoyment: 'Stone deaf,' and added, 'Nasty things.'

A rosy-faced man in a straw hat claimed attention. 'I *did* save the front wheel,' he said; 'you'd have had that tyre catch, too, if I hadn't kept turning it round.' It became manifest that this was so. The front wheel had retained its tyre, was intact, was still rotating slowly among the blackened and twisted ruins of the rest of the machine. It had something of that air of conscious virtue, of unimpeachable respectability, that distinguishes a rent collector in a low neighbourhood. 'That wheel's worth a pound,' said the rosy-faced man, making a song of it. 'I kep' turning it round.'

Newcomers kept arriving from the south with the question, 'What's up?' until it got on Grubb's nerves. Londonward the crowd was constantly losing people; they would mount their various wheels with the satisfied manner of spectators who have had the best. Their voices would recede into the twilight; one would hear a laugh at the memory of this particularly salient incident or that.

'I'm afraid,' said the gentleman of the motor car, 'my tarpaulin's a bit done for.'

Grubb admitted that the owner was the best judge of that.

'Nothing else I can do for you?' said the gentleman of the motor car, it may be with a suspicion of irony.

Bert was roused to action. 'Look here,' he said. 'There's my young lady. If she ain't 'ome by ten they lock her out. See? Well, all my money was in my jacket pocket, and it's all mixed up with the burnt stuff, and that's too 'ot to touch. *Is* Clapham out of your way?'

'All in the day's work,' said the gentleman with the motor car, and turned to Edna. 'Very pleased indeed,' he said, 'if you'll come with us. We're late for dinner as it is, so it won't make much difference for us to go home by way of Clapham. We've got to get to Surbiton, anyhow. I'm afraid you'll find us a little slow.'

'But what's Bert going to do?' said Edna.

'I don't know that we can accommodate Bert,' said the motor car gentleman, 'though we're tremendously anxious to oblige.'

'You couldn't take the whole lot?' said Bert, waving his hand at the deboshed and blackened ruins on the ground.

'I'm awfully afraid I can't,' said the Oxford man. 'Awfully sorry, you know.'

'Then I'll have to stick 'ere for a bit,' said Bert. 'I got to see the thing through. You go on, Edna.'

'Don't like leavin' you, Bert.'

'You can't 'elp it, Edna . . . '

The last Edna saw of Bert was his figure, in charred and blackened shirtsleeves, standing in the dusk. He was musing deeply by the mixed ironwork and ashes of his vanished motor-bicycle, a melancholy figure. His retinue of spectators had shrunk now to half a dozen figures. Flossie and Grubb were preparing to follow her desertion.

'Cheer up, old Bert!' cried Edna, with artificial cheerfulness. 'So long.'

'So long, Edna,' said Bert.

'See you tomorrer.'

'See you tomorrer,' said Bert, though he was destined, as a matter of fact, to see much of the habitable globe before he saw her again.

Bert began to light matches from a borrowed boxful, and search for a half-crown that still eluded him among the charred remains. His face was grave and melancholy.

'I *wish* that 'adn't 'appened,' said Flossie, riding on with Grubb . . .

And at last Bert was left almost alone, a sad, blackened Promethean figure,[135] cursed by the gift of fire. He had entertained vague ideas of hiring a cart, of achieving miraculous repairs, of still snatching some residual value from his one chief possession. Now, in the darkening night, he perceived the vanity of such intentions. Truth came to him bleakly, and laid her chill conviction upon him. He took hold of the handlebar, stood the thing up, tried to push it forward. The tyreless hind-wheel was jammed hopelessly, even as he feared. For a minute or so he stood upholding his machine, a motionless despair. Then with a great effort he thrust the ruins from him into the ditch, kicked at it once, regarded it for a moment, and turned his face resolutely Londonward.

He did not once look back.

'That's the end of *that* game!' said Bert. 'No more teuf-teuf-teuf for
Bert Smallways for a year or two. Goodbye 'olidays! . . . Oh! I ought to
'ave sold the blasted thing when I had a chance three years ago.'

3

The next morning found the firm of Grubb & Smallways in a state of
profound despondency. It seemed a small matter to them that the
newspaper and cigarette shop opposite displayed such placards as this:

REPORTED AMERICAN ULTIMATUM.
BRITAIN MUST FIGHT.
OUR INFATUATED WAR OFFICE
STILL REFUSES TO LISTEN TO MR BUTTERIDGE.
GREAT MONORAIL DISASTER AT TIMBUCTOO.[136]

or this:

WAR A QUESTION OF HOURS.
NEW YORK CALM.
EXCITEMENT IN BERLIN.

or again:

WASHINGTON STILL SILENT.
WHAT WILL PARIS DO?
THE PANIC ON THE BOURSE.
THE KING'S GARDEN PARTY TO THE MASKED TWAREGS.[137]
MR BUTTERIDGE MAKES AN OFFER.
LATEST BETTING FROM TEHERAN.

or this:

WILL AMERICA FIGHT?
ANTI-GERMAN RIOT IN BAGDAD.
THE MUNICIPAL SCANDALS AT DAMASCUS.
MR BUTTERIDGE'S INVENTION FOR AMERICA.

Bert stared at these over the card of pump-clips in the pane in the
door with unseeing eyes. He wore a blackened flannel shirt, and the
jacketless ruins of the holiday suit of yesterday. The boarded-up shop
was dark and depressing beyond words, the few scandalous hiring-
machines had never looked so hopelessly disreputable. He thought of
their fellows who were 'out', and of the approaching disputations of

the afternoon. He thought of their new landlord, and of their old landlord, and of bills and claims. Life presented itself for the first time as a hopeless fight against fate . . .

'Grubb, o' man,' he said, distilling the quintessence, 'I'm fair sick of this shop.'

'So'm I,' said Grubb.

'I'm out of conceit with it. I don't seem to care ever to speak to a customer again.'

'There's that trailer,' said Grubb, after a pause.

'Blow the trailer!' said Bert. 'Anyhow, I didn't leave a deposit on it. I didn't do that. Still – '

He turned round on his friend. 'Look 'ere,' he said, 'we aren't gettin' on here. We been losing money hand over fist. We got things tied up in fifty knots.'

'What can we do?' said Grubb.

'Clear out. Sell what we can for what it will fetch, and quit. See? It's no good 'anging on to a losing concern. No sort of good. Jest foolishness.'

'That's all right,' said Grubb – 'that's all right; but it ain't your capital been sunk in it.'

'No need for us to sink after our capital,' said Bert, ignoring the point.

'I'm not going to be held responsible for that trailer, anyhow. That ain't my affair.'

'Nobody arst you to make it your affair. If you like to stick on here, well and good. I'm quitting. I'll see Bank Holiday through, and then I'm *o–r–p–h*.[138] See?'

'Leavin' me?'

'Leavin' you. If you must be left.'

Grubb looked round the shop. It certainly had become distasteful. Once upon a time it had been bright with hope and new beginnings and stock and the prospect of credit. Now – now it was failure and dust. Very likely the landlord would be round presently to go on with the row about the window . . . 'Where d'you think of going, Bert?' Grubb asked.

Bert turned round and regarded him. 'I thought it out as I was walking 'ome, and in bed. I couldn't sleep a wink.'

'What did you think out?'

'Plans.'

'What plans?'

'Oh! You're for sticking here.'

'Not if anything better was to offer.'

'It's only an ideer,' said Bert.

'Let's 'ear it.'

'You made the girls laugh yestiday, that song you sang.'

'Seems a long time ago now,' said Grubb.

'And old Edna nearly cried – over that bit of mine.'

'She got a fly in her eye,' said Grubb; 'I saw it. But what's this got to do with your plan?'

'No end,' said Bert.

' 'Ow?'

'Don't you see?'

'Not singing in the streets?'

'Streets! No fear! But 'ow about the Tour of the Waterin' Places of England, Grubb? Singing! Young men of family doing it for a lark? You ain't got a bad voice, you know, and mine's all right. I never see a chap singing on the beach yet that I couldn't 'ave sung into a cocked hat.[139] And we both know how to put on the toff a bit. Eh? Well, that's my ideer. Me and you, Grubb, with a refined song and a breakdown. Like we was doing for foolery yestiday. That was what put it into my 'ead. Easy make up a programme – easy. Six choice items, and one or two for encores and patter. I'm all right for the patter anyhow.'

Grubb remained regarding his darkened and disheartening shop; he thought of his former landlord and his present landlord, and of the general disgustingness of business in an age which re-echoes to The Bitter Cry of the Middle Class;[140] and then it seemed to him that afar off he heard the twankle, twankle of a banjo, and the voice of a stranded siren singing. He had a sense of hot sunshine upon sand, of the children of at least transiently opulent holidaymakers in a circle round about him, of the whisper, 'They are really gentlemen,' and then dollop, dollop came the coppers in the hat. Sometimes even silver. It was all income; no outgoings, no bills. 'I'm on, Bert,' he said.

'Right-o!' said Bert, and, 'Now we shan't be long.'

'We needn't start without capital neither,' said Grubb. 'If we take the best of these machines up to the Bicycle Mart in Finsbury we'd raise six or seven pounds on 'em. We could easy do that tomorrow before anybody much was about . . . '

'Nice to think of old Suet-and-Bones coming round to make his usual row with us, and finding a card up: "Closed for Repairs".'

'We'll do that,' said Grubb with zest – 'we'll do that. And we'll put up another notice, and jest arst all enquirers to go round to 'im and enquire. See? Then they'll know all about us.'

Before the day was out the whole enterprise was planned. They decided at first that they would call themselves the Naval Mr O's, a plagiarism, and not perhaps a very good one, from the title of the well-known troupe of 'Scarlet Mr E's',[141] and Bert rather clung to the idea of a uniform of bright blue serge, with a lot of gold lace and cord and ornamentation, rather like a naval officer's, but more so. But that had to be abandoned as impracticable, it would have taken too much time and money to prepare. They perceived they must wear some cheaper and more readily prepared costume, and Grubb fell back on white dominoes. They entertained the notion for a time of selecting the two worst machines from the hiring-stock, painting them over with crimson enamel paint, replacing the bells by the loudest sort of motor-horn, and doing a ride about to begin and end the entertainment. They doubted the advisability of this step.

'There's people in the world,' said Bert, 'who wouldn't recognise us, who'd know them bicycles again like a shot, and we don't want to go on with no old stories. We want a fresh start.'

'*I* do,' said Grubb, 'badly.'

'We want to forget things – and cut all these rotten old worries. They ain't doin' us good.'

Nevertheless, they decided to take the risk of these bicycles, and they decided their costumes should be brown stockings and sandals, and cheap unbleached sheets with a hole cut in the middle, and wigs and beards of tow. The rest their normal selves! 'The Desert Dervishes', they would call themselves, and their chief songs would be those popular ditties, 'In My Trailer', and 'What Price Hairpins Now?'

They decided to begin with small seaside places, and gradually, as they gained confidence, attack larger centres. To begin with they selected Littlestone in Kent, chiefly because of its unassuming name.

So they planned, and it seemed a small and unimportant thing to them that as they chattered the Governments of half the world and more were drifting into war. About midday they became aware of the first of the evening-paper placards shouting to them across the street:

THE WAR-CLOUD DARKENS.

Nothing else but that.

'Always rottin' about war now,' said Bert. 'They'll get it in the neck in real earnest one of these days, if they ain't precious careful.'

So you will understand the sudden apparition that surprised rather than delighted the quiet informality of Dymchurch sands. Dymchurch was one of the last places on the coast of England to be reached by the monorail, and so its spacious sands were still, at the time of this story, the secret and delight of quite a limited number of people. They went there to flee vulgarity and extravagances, and to bathe and sit and talk and play with their children in peace, and the Desert Dervishes did not please them at all.

The two white figures on scarlet wheels came upon them out of the infinite along the sands from Littlestone, grew nearer and larger and more audible, honk-honking and emitting weird cries, and generally threatening liveliness of the most aggressive type. 'Good heavens!' said Dymchurch, 'what's this?'

Then our young men, according to a preconcerted plan, wheeled round from file to line, dismounted and stood at attention. 'Ladies and gentlemen,' they said, 'we beg to present ourselves – the Desert Dervishes.' They bowed profoundly.

The few scattered groups upon the beach regarded them with horror for the most part, but some of the children and young people were interested and drew nearer. 'There ain't a bob on the beach,' said Grubb in an undertone, and the Desert Dervishes piled their bicycles with comic 'business', that got a laugh from one very unsophisticated little boy. Then they took a deep breath and struck into the cheerful strain of 'What Price Hairpins Now?' Grubb sang the song, Bert did his best to make the chorus a rousing one, and at the end of each verse they danced certain steps, skirts in hand, that they had carefully rehearsed.

> Ting-a-ling-a-ting-a-ling-a-ting-a-ling-a-tang.
> What Price Hairpins Now?

So they chanted and danced their steps in the sunshine on Dymchurch beach, and the children drew near these foolish young men, marvelling that they should behave in this way, and the older people looked cold and unfriendly.

All round the coasts of Europe that morning banjos were ringing, voices were bawling and singing, children were playing in the sun, pleasure-boats went to and fro; the common, abundant life of the time, unsuspicious of all the dangers that gathered darkly against it, flowed on its cheerful, aimless way. In the cities men fussed about their businesses and engagements. The newspaper placards that had cried 'wolf!' so often, cried 'wolf!' now in vain.

5

Now as Bert and Grubb bawled their chorus for the third time, they became aware of a very big, golden-brown balloon low in the sky to the north-west, and coming rapidly towards them. 'Jest as we're gettin' hold of 'em,' muttered Grubb, 'up comes a counter-attraction. Go it, Bert!'

> Ting-a-ling-a-ting-a-ling-a-ting-a-ling-a-tang
> What Price Hairpins Now?

The balloon rose and fell, went out of sight – 'Landed, thank goodness,' said Grubb – reappeared with a leap. ' '*Eng!*'[142] said Grubb. 'Step it, Bert, or they'll see it!'

They finished their dance, and then stood frankly staring.

'There's something wrong with that balloon,' said Bert.

Everybody now was looking at the balloon, drawing rapidly nearer before a brisk north-westerly breeze. The song and dance were a 'dead frost'. Nobody thought any more about it. Even Bert and Grubb forgot it, and ignored the next item on the programme altogether. The balloon was bumping as though its occupants were trying to land; it would approach, sinking slowly, touch the ground, and instantly jump fifty feet or so in the air and immediately begin to fall again. Its car touched a clump of trees, and the black figure that had been struggling in the ropes fell back, or jumped back, into the car.

In another moment it was quite close. It seemed a huge affair, as big as a house, and it floated down swiftly towards the sands; a long rope trailed behind it, and enormous shouts came from the man in the car. He seemed to be taking off his clothes, then his head came over the side of the car. 'Catch hold of the rope!' they heard, quite plain.

'Salvage, Bert!' cried Grubb, and started to head off the rope.

Bert followed him, and collided, without upsetting, with a fisherman bent upon a similar errand. A woman carrying a baby in her arms, two small boys with toy spades, and a stout gentleman in flannels all got to the trailing rope at about the same time, and began to dance over it in their attempts to secure it. Bert came up to this wriggling, elusive serpent and got his foot on it, went down on all fours and achieved a grip. In half a dozen seconds the whole diffused population of the beach had, as it were, crystallised on the rope, and was pulling against the balloon under the vehement and stimulating directions of the man in the car. 'Pull, I tell you!' said the man in the car – 'pull!'

For a second or so the balloon obeyed its momentum and the wind and tugged its human anchor seaward. It dropped, touched the water, and made a flat, silvery splash, and recoiled as one's finger recoils when one touches anything hot. 'Pull her in,' said the man in the car. '*She's fainted!*'

He occupied himself with some unseen object while the people on the rope pulled him in. Bert was nearest the balloon, and much excited and interested. He kept stumbling over the tail of the Dervish costume in his zeal. He had never imagined before what a big, light, wallowing thing a balloon was. The car was of brown coarse wickerwork, and comparatively small. The rope he tugged at was fastened to a stout-looking ring, four or five feet above the car. At each tug he drew in a yard or so of rope, and the waggling wickerwork was drawn so much nearer. Out of the car came wrathful bellowings: 'Fainted, she has!' and then: 'It's her heart – broken with all she's had to go through.'

The balloon ceased to struggle, and sank downward. Bert dropped the rope, and ran forward to catch it in a new place. In another moment he had his hand on the car. 'Lay hold of it,' said the man in the car, and his face appeared close to Bert's – a strangely familiar face, fierce eyebrows, a flattish nose, a huge black moustache. He had discarded coat and waistcoat – perhaps with some idea of presently having to swim for his life – and his black hair was extraordinarily disordered. 'Will all you people get hold round the car?' he said. 'There's a lady here fainted – or got failure of the heart. Heaven alone knows which! My name is Butteridge. Butteridge, my name is – in a balloon. Now please, all on to the edge. This is the last time I trust myself to one of these paleolithic contrivances. The ripping-cord failed, and the valve wouldn't act. If ever I meet the scoundrel who ought to have seen – '

He stuck his head out between the ropes abruptly, and said, in a note of earnest expostulation: 'Get some brandy! – some neat brandy!'

Someone went up the beach for it.

In the car, sprawling upon a sort of bed-bench, in an attitude of elaborate self-abandonment, was a large, blonde lady, wearing a fur coat and a big floriferous hat. Her head lolled back against the padded corner of the car, and her eyes were shut and her mouth open. 'Me dear!' said Mr Butteridge, in a common, loud voice, 'we're safe!'

She gave no sign.

'Me dear!' said Mr Butteridge, in a greatly intensified loud voice, 'we're safe!'

She was still quite impassive.

Then Mr Butteridge showed the fiery core of his soul. 'If she is dead,' he said, slowly lifting a fist towards the balloon above him, and speaking in an immense tremulous bellow – 'if she is dead, I will r-r-rend the heavens like a garment! I must get her out,' he cried, his nostrils dilated with emotion – 'I must get her out. I cannot have her die in a wickerwork basket nine feet square – she who was made for kings' palaces! Keep hold of this car! Is there a strong man among ye to take her if I hand her out?'

He swept the lady together by a powerful movement of his arms, and lifted her. 'Keep the car from jumping,' he said to those who clustered about him. 'Keep your weight on it. She is no light woman, and when she is out of it – it will be relieved.'

Bert leapt lightly into a sitting position on the edge of the car. The others took a firmer grip upon the ropes and ring.

'Are you ready?' said Mr Butteridge.

He stood upon the bed-bench and lifted the lady carefully. Then he sat down on the wicker edge opposite to Bert, and put one leg over to dangle outside. A rope or so seemed to incommode him. 'Will someone assist me?' he said. 'If they would take this lady?'

It was just at this moment, with Mr Butteridge and the lady balanced finely on the basket brim, that she came to. She came to suddenly and violently with a loud, heart-rending cry of 'Alfred! Save me!' And she waved her arms searchingly, and then clasped Mr Butteridge about.

It seemed to Bert that the car swayed for a moment and then buck-jumped and kicked him. Also he saw the boots of the lady and the right leg of the gentleman describing arcs through the air, preparatory to vanishing over the side of the car. His impressions were complex, but they also comprehended the fact that he had lost his balance, and was going to stand on his head inside this creaking basket. He spread out clutching arms. He did stand on his head, more or less, his tow-beard[143] came off and got in his mouth, and his cheek slid along against padding. His nose buried itself in a bag of sand. The car gave a violent lurch, and became still.

'Confound it!' he said.

He had an impression he must be stunned because of a surging in his ears, and because all the voices of the people about him had become small and remote. They were shouting like elves inside a hill.

He found it a little difficult to get on his feet. His limbs were mixed up with the garments Mr Butteridge had discarded when that gentleman had thought he must needs plunge into the sea. Bert bawled out half angry, half rueful, 'You might have said you were going to tip the basket.' Then he stood up and clutched the ropes of the car convulsively.

Below him, far below him, shining blue, were the waters of the English Channel. Far off, a little thing in the sunshine, and rushing down as if someone was bending it hollow, was the beach and the irregular cluster of houses that constituted Dymchurch. He could see the little crowd of people he had so abruptly left. Grubb, in the white wrapper of a Desert Dervish, was running along the edge of the sea. Mr Butteridge was knee-deep in the water, bawling immensely. The lady was sitting up with her floriferous hat in her lap, shockingly neglected. The beach, east and west, was dotted with little people – they seemed all heads and feet – looking up. And the balloon, released from the twenty-five stone or so of Mr Butteridge and his lady, was rushing up into the sky at the pace of a racing motor car. 'My crikey!' said Bert; 'here's a go!'

He looked down with a pinched face at the receding beach, and reflected that he wasn't giddy; then he made a superficial survey of the cords and ropes about him with a vague idea of 'doing something'. 'I'm not going to mess about with the thing,' he said at last, and sat down upon the mattress. 'I'm not going to touch it . . . I wonder what one ought to do?'

Soon he got up again and stared for a long time at the sinking world below, at white cliffs to the east and flattening marsh to the left, at a minute wide prospect of weald and downland, at dim towns and harbours and rivers and ribbon-like roads, at ships and ships' decks and foreshortened funnels upon the ever-widening sea, and at the great monorail bridge that straddled the Channel from Folkestone to Boulogne, until at length, first little wisps and then a veil of filmy cloud hid the prospect from his eyes. He wasn't at all giddy nor very much frightened, only in a state of enormous consternation.

CHAPTER THREE

The Balloon

1

Bert Smallways was a vulgar little creature, the sort of pert, limited soul that the old civilisation of the early twentieth century produced by the million in every country of the world. He had lived all his life in narrow streets, and between mean houses he could not look over, and in a narrow circle of ideas from which there was no escape. He thought the whole duty of man was to be smarter than his fellows, get his hands, as he put it, 'on the dibs',[144] and have a good time. He was, in fact, the sort of man who had made England and America what they were. The luck had been against him so far, but that was by the way. He was a mere aggressive and acquisitive individual with no sense of the State, no habitual loyalty, no devotion, no code of honour, no code even of courage. Now by a curious accident he found himself lifted out of his marvellous modern world for a time, out of all the rush and confused appeals of it, and floating like a thing dead and disembodied between sea and sky. It was as if Heaven was experimenting with him, had picked him out as a sample from the English millions, to look at him more nearly, and to see what was happening to the soul of man. But what Heaven made of him in that case I cannot profess to imagine, for I have long since abandoned all theories about the ideals and satisfactions of Heaven.

To be alone in a balloon at a height of fourteen or fifteen thousand feet – and to that height Bert Smallways presently rose – is like nothing else in human experience. It is one of the supreme things possible to man. No flying-machine can ever better it. It is to pass extraordinarily out of human things. It is to be still and alone to an unprecedented degree. It is solitude without the suggestion of intervention; it is calm without a single irrelevant murmur. It is to see the sky.

No sound reaches one of all the roar and jar of humanity, the air is clear and sweet beyond the thought of defilement. No bird, no insect comes so high. No wind blows ever in a balloon, no breeze rustles, for it moves with the wind and is itself a part of the atmosphere. Once started, it does not rock nor sway; you cannot feel whether it rises or falls. Bert felt acutely cold, but he wasn't mountain-sick; he put on the coat and overcoat and gloves Butteridge had discarded – put them over the 'Desert Dervish' sheet that covered his cheap best suit – and sat very still for a long, time, overawed by the new-found quiet of the world. Above him was the light, translucent, billowing globe of shining brown oiled silk and the blazing sunlight and the great deep blue dome of the sky. Below, far below, was a torn floor of sunlit cloud slashed by enormous rents through which he saw the sea.

If you had been watching him from below, you would have seen his head, a motionless little black knob, sticking out from the car first of all for a long time on one side, and then vanishing to reappear after a time at some other point.

He wasn't in the least degree uncomfortable nor afraid. He did think that as this uncontrollable thing had thus rushed up the sky with him it might presently rush down again, but this consideration did not trouble him very much. Essentially his state was wonder. There is no fear nor trouble in balloons – until they descend.

'Gollys!' he said at last, feeling a need for talking; 'it's better than a motorbike.'

'It's all right!'

'I suppose they're telegraphing about, about me . . .'

The second hour found him examining the equipment of the car with great particularity. Above him was the throat of the balloon bunched and tied together, but with an open lumen through which Bert could peer up into a vast, empty, quiet interior, and out of which descended two fine cords of unknown import, one white, one crimson, to pockets below the ring. The netting about the balloon ended in cords attached to the ring, a big steel-bound hoop to which the car was slung by ropes. From it depended the trail rope and grapnel, and over the sides of the car were a number of canvas bags that Bert decided must be ballast to 'chuck down' if the balloon fell. ('Not much falling just yet,' said Bert.)

There were an aneroid and another box-shaped instrument hanging from the ring. The latter had an ivory plate bearing 'statoscope' and other words in French, and a little indicator quivered and waggled, between *Montée* and *Descente*. 'That's all right,' said Bert. 'That tells if you're going up or down.' On the crimson padded seat of the balloon there lay a couple of rugs and a Kodak,[145] and in opposite corners of the bottom of the car were an empty champagne bottle and a glass. 'Refreshments,' said Bert meditatively, tilting the empty bottle. Then he had a brilliant idea. The two padded bedlike seats, each with blankets and mattress, he perceived, were boxes, and within he found

Mr Butteridge's conception of an adequate equipment for a balloon ascent: a hamper which included a game pie, a Roman pie,[146] a cold fowl, tomatoes, lettuce, ham sandwiches, shrimp sandwiches, a large cake, knives and forks and paper plates, self-heating tins of coffee and cocoa,[147] bread, butter, and marmalade, several carefully packed bottles of champagne, bottles of Perrier water, and a big jar of water for washing, a portfolio, maps, and a compass, a rucksack containing a number of conveniences, including curling-tongs and hairpins, a cap with ear-flaps, and so forth.

'A 'ome from 'ome,' said Bert, surveying this provision as he tied the ear-flaps under his chin.

He looked over the side of the car. Far below were the shining clouds. They had thickened so that the whole world was hidden. Southward they were piled in great snowy masses, so that he was half disposed to think them mountains; northward and eastward they were in wavelike levels, and blindingly sunlit.

'Wonder how long a balloon keeps up?' he said.

He imagined he was not moving, so insensibly did the monster drift with the air about it. 'No good coming down till we shift a bit,' he said.

He consulted the statoscope.

'Still Monty,' he said.

'Wonder what would happen if you pulled a cord?

'No,' he decided. 'I ain't going to mess it about.'

Afterwards he did pull both the ripping- and the valve-cords, but, as Mr Butteridge had already discovered, they had fouled a fold of silk in the throat. Nothing happened. But for that little hitch the ripping-cord would have torn the balloon open as though it had been slashed by a sword, and hurled Mr Smallways to eternity at the rate of some thousand feet a second. 'No go!' he said, giving it a final tug. Then he lunched.

He opened a bottle of champagne, which, as soon as he cut the wire, blew its cork out with incredible violence, and for the most part followed it into space. Bert, however, got about a tumblerful. 'Atmospheric pressure,' said Bert, finding a use at last for the elementary physiography of his seventh-standard days. 'I'll have to be more careful next time. No good wastin' drink.'

Then he routed about for matches to utilise Mr Butteridge's cigars; but here again luck was on his side, and he couldn't find any wherewith to set light to the gas above him. Or else he would have dropped in a flare, a splendid but transitory pyrotechnic display. ' 'Eng old Grubb!' said Bert, slapping unproductive pockets. ' 'E didn't ought to 'ave kep' my box. 'E's always sneaking matches.'

He reposed for a time. Then he got up, paddled about, rearranged the ballast bags on the floor, watched the clouds for a time, and turned over the maps on the locker. Bert liked maps, and he spent some time in trying to find one of France or the Channel; but they were all British ordnance maps[148] of English counties. That set him thinking about languages and trying to recall his seventh-standard French. 'Je suis Anglais. C'est une méprise. Je suis arrivé par accident ici,'[149] he decided upon as convenient phrases. Then it occurred to him that he would entertain himself by reading Mr Butteridge's letters and examining his pocketbook, and in this manner he wiled away the afternoon.

2

He sat upon the padded locker, wrapped about very carefully, for the air, though calm, was exhilaratingly cold and clear. He was wearing first a modest suit of blue serge and all the unpretending underwear of a suburban young man of fashion, with sandal-like cycling-shoes and brown stockings drawn over his trouser ends; then the perforated sheet proper to a Desert Dervish; then the coat and waistcoat and big fur-trimmed overcoat of Mr Butteridge; then a lady's large fur cloak, and round his knees a blanket. Over his head was a tow wig, surmounted by a large cap of Mr Butteridge's with the flaps down over his ears. And some fur sleeping-boots of Mr Butteridge's warmed his feet. The car of the balloon was small and neat, some bags of ballast the untidiest of its contents, and he had found a light folding-table and put it at his elbow, and on that was a glass with champagne. And about him, above and below, was space – such a clear emptiness and silence of space as only the aeronaut can experience.

He did not know where he might be drifting, or what might happen next. He accepted this state of affairs with a serenity creditable to the Smallways' courage, which one might reasonably have expected to be of a more degenerate and contemptible quality altogether. His impression was that he was bound to come down somewhere, and that then, if he wasn't smashed, someone, some 'society' perhaps, would probably pack him and the balloon back to England. If not, he would ask very firmly for the British Consul. 'Le Consuelo Britannique,' he decided this would be. 'Apportez moi a le Consuelo Britannique, s'il vous plaît,'[150] he would say, for he was by no means ignorant of French. In the meanwhile, he found the intimate aspects of Mr Butteridge an interesting study.

There were letters of an entirely private character addressed to Mr Butteridge, and among others several love-letters of a devouring sort in a large feminine hand. These are no business of ours, and one remarks with regret that Bert read them.

When he had read them he remarked, 'Gollys!' in an awestricken tone, and then, after a long interval, 'I wonder if that was her?

'Lord!'

He mused for a time.

He resumed his exploration of the Butteridge interior. It included a number of press cuttings of interviews and also several letters in German, then some in the same German handwriting, but in English. 'Hel–lo!' said Bert.

One of the latter, the first he took, began with an apology to Butteridge for not writing to him in English before, and for the inconvenience and delay that had been caused him by that, and went on to matter that Bert found exciting in the highest degree. 'We can understand entirely the difficulties of your position, and that you shall possibly be watched at the present juncture. But, sir, we do not believe that any serious obstacles will be put in your way if you wished to endeavour to leave the country and come to us with your plans by the customary routes – either via Dover, Ostend, Boulogne, or Dieppe. We find it difficult to think you are right in supposing yourself to be in danger of murder for your invaluable invention.'

'Funny!' said Bert, and meditated.

Then he went through the other letters.

'They seem to want him to come,' said Bert, 'but they don't seem hurting themselves to get 'im. Or else they're shamming don't care to get his prices down.

'They don't quite seem to be the gov'ment,' he reflected, after an interval. 'It's more like some firm's paper. All this printed stuff at the top. *Drachenflieger. Drachenballons. Ballonstoffe. Kugelballons.*[151] Greek to me.

'But he was trying to sell his blessed secret abroad. That's all right. No Greek about that! Gollys! Here *is* the secret!'

He tumbled off the seat, opened the locker, and had the portfolio open before him on the folding-table. It was full of drawings done in the peculiar flat style and conventional colours engineers adopt. And, in addition, there were some rather under-exposed photographs, obviously done by an amateur, at close quarters, of the actual machines Butteridge had made, in its shed near the Crystal Palace. Bert found he was trembling. 'Lord!' he said, 'here am I and the whole blessed secret of flying – lost up here on the roof of everywhere.

'Let's see!' He fell to studying the drawings and comparing them with the photographs. They puzzled him. Half of them seemed to be missing. He tried to imagine how they fitted together, and found the effort too great for his mind.

'It's tryin',' said Bert. 'I wish I'd been brought up to the engineering. If I could only make it out!'

He went to the side of the car and remained for a time staring with unseeing eyes at a huge cluster of great clouds – a cluster of slowly dissolving Monte Rosas, sunlit below. His attention was arrested by a strange black spot that moved over them. It alarmed him. It was a black spot moving slowly with him far below, following him down there, indefatigably, over the cloud mountains. Why should such a thing follow him? What could it be? . . .

He had an inspiration. 'Uv course!' he said. It was the shadow of the balloon. But he still watched it dubiously for a time.

He returned to the plans on the table.

He spent a long afternoon between his struggles to understand them and fits of meditation. He evolved a remarkable new sentence in French. 'Voici, Mossoo! – Je suis un inventeur Anglais. Mon nom est Butteridge. Beh. oo. teh. teh. eh. arr. I. deh. geh. eh. J'avais ici pour vendre le secret de le *flying-machine*. Comprenez? Vendre pour l'argent tout suite, l'argent en main. Comprenez? C'est le machine à jouer dans l'air. Comprenez? C'est le machine à faire l'oiseau. Comprenez? Balancer? Oui, exactement! Battir l'oiseau en fait, à son propre jeu. Je désire de vendre ceci à votre government national. Voulez vous me directer là?[152]

'Bit rummy, I expect, from the point of view of grammar,' said Bert, 'but they ought to get the hang of it all right.

'But then, if they arst me to explain the blessed thing?'

He returned in a worried way to the plans. 'I don't believe it's all here!' he said . . .

He got more and more perplexed up there among the clouds as to what he should do with this wonderful find of his. At any moment, so far as he could tell, he might descend among he knew not what foreign people.

'It's the chance of my life!' he said.

It became more and more manifest to him that it wasn't. 'Directly I come down they'll telegraph – put it in the papers. Butteridge'll know of it and come along – on my track.'

Butteridge would be a terrible person to be on anyone's track. Bert thought of the great black moustaches, the triangular nose, the searching bellow and the glare. His afternoon's dream of a marvellous seizure and sale of the great Butteridge secret crumpled up in his mind, dissolved, and vanished. He awoke to sanity again.

'Wouldn't do. What's the good of thinking of it?' He proceeded slowly and reluctantly to replace the Butteridge papers in pockets and portfolio as he had found them. He became aware of a splendid golden light upon the balloon above him, and of a new warmth in the blue dome of the sky. He stood up and beheld the sun, a great ball of blinding gold, setting upon a tumbled sea of gold-edged crimson and purple clouds, strange and wonderful beyond imagining. Eastward cloud-land stretched for ever, darkling blue, and it seemed to Bert the whole round hemisphere of the world was under his eyes.

Then far away over the blue he caught sight of three long, dark shapes like hurrying fish that drove one after the other, as porpoises follow one another in the water. They were very fishlike indeed – with tails. It was an unconvincing impression in that light. He blinked his eyes, stared again, and they had vanished. For a long time he scrutinised those remote blue levels and saw no more . . .

'Wonder if I ever saw anything,' he said, and then: 'There ain't such things . . .'

Down went the sun and down, not diving steeply, but passing northward as it sank, and then suddenly daylight and the expansive warmth of daylight had gone altogether, and the index of the statoscope quivered over to *Descente*.

3

'*Now* what's going to 'appen?' said Bert.

He found the cold, grey cloud wilderness rising towards him with a wide, slow steadiness. As he sank down among them the clouds ceased to seem the snowclad mountain-slopes they had resembled heretofore, became unsubstantial, confessed an immense silent drift and eddy in their substance. For a moment, when he was nearly among their twilight masses, his descent was checked. Then abruptly the sky was hidden, the last vestiges of daylight gone, and he was falling rapidly in an evening twilight through a whirl of fine snowflakes that streamed past him towards the zenith, that drifted in upon the things about him and melted, that touched his face with ghostly fingers. He shivered. His breath came smoking from his lips, and everything was instantly bedewed and wet.

He had an impression of a snowstorm pouring with unexampled and increasing fury *upward*; then he realised that he was falling faster and faster.

Imperceptibly a sound grew upon his ears. The great silence of the world was at an end.

What was this confused sound?

He craned his head over the side, concerned, perplexed.

First he seemed to see, and then not to see. Then he saw clearly little edges of foam pursuing each other, and a wide waste of weltering waters below him. Far away was a pilot boat with a big sail bearing dim black letters, and a little pinkish-yellow light, and it was rolling and pitching, rolling and pitching in a gale, while he could feel no wind at all. Soon the sound of waters was loud and near. He was dropping, dropping – into the sea!

He became convulsively active.

'Ballast!' he cried, and seized a little sack from the floor, and heaved it overboard. He did not wait for the effect of that, but sent another after it. He looked over in time to see a minute white splash in the dim waters below him, and then he was back in the snow and clouds again.

He sent out quite needlessly a third sack of ballast and a fourth, and presently had the immense satisfaction of soaring up out of the damp and chill into the clear, cold, upper air in which the day still lingered. 'Thang-God!' he said, with all his heart.

A few stars now had pierced the blue, and in the east there shone brightly a prolate moon.[153]

4

That first downward plunge filled Bert with a haunting sense of boundless waters below. It was a summer's night, but it seemed to him, nevertheless, extraordinarily long. He had a feeling of insecurity that he fancied quite irrationally the sunrise would dispel. Also he was hungry. He felt, in the dark, in the locker, put his fingers in the Roman pie, and got some sandwiches, and he also opened rather successfully a half-bottle of champagne. That warmed and restored him, he grumbled at Grubb about the matches, wrapped himself up warmly on the locker, and dozed for a time. He got up once or twice to make sure that he was still securely high above the sea. The first time the moonlit clouds were white and dense, and the shadow of the balloon ran athwart them like a dog that followed; afterwards they seemed thinner. As he lay still, staring up at the huge dark balloon above, he made a discovery. His – or rather Mr Butteridge's – waistcoat rustled as he breathed. It was lined with papers. But Bert could not see to get them out or examine them, much as he wished to do so.

He was awakened by the crowing of cocks, the barking of dogs, and a clamour of birds. He was driving slowly at a low level over a broad land lit golden by sunrise under a clear sky. He stared out upon hedgeless, well-cultivated fields intersected by roads, each lined with cable-bearing red poles. He had just passed over a compact, white-washed village with a straight church tower and steep red-tiled roofs. A number of peasants, men and women, in shiny blouses and lumpish footwear, stood regarding him, arrested on their way to work. He was so low that the end of his rope was trailing.

He stared out at these people. 'I wonder how you land,' he thought. 'S'pose I *ought* to land?'

He found himself drifting down towards a monorail line, and hastily flung out two or three handfuls of ballast to clear it.

'Lemme see! One might say just "Prenez!" Wish I knew the French for take hold of the rope! . . . I suppose they are French?'

He surveyed the country again. 'Might be Holland. Or Luxembourg. Or Lorraine's[154] far as *I* know. Wonder what those big affairs over there are? Some sort of kiln. Prosperous-looking country . . . '

The respectability of the country's appearance awakened answering chords in his nature.

'Make myself a bit shipshape first,' he said.

He resolved to rise a little and get rid of his wig (which now felt hot on his head), and so forth. He threw out a bag of ballast, and was astonished to find himself careering up through the air very rapidly.

'Blow!' said Mr Smallways. 'I've overdone the ballast trick . . . Wonder when I shall get down again? . . . Brekfus' on board, anyhow.'

He removed his cap and wig, for the air was warm, and an improvident impulse made him cast the latter object overboard. The statoscope responded with a vigorous swing to *Montée*.

'The blessed thing goes up if you only *look* overboard,' he remarked, and assailed the locker. He found among other items several tins of liquid cocoa containing explicit directions for opening that he followed with minute care. He pierced the bottom with the key provided in the holes indicated, and forthwith the can grew from cold to hotter and hotter, until at last he could scarcely touch it, and then he opened the can at the other end, and there was his cocoa smoking, without the use of match or flame of any sort. It was an old invention, but new to Bert.

There was also ham and marmalade and bread, so that he had a really very tolerable breakfast indeed.

Then he took off his overcoat, for the sunshine was now inclined to be hot, and that reminded him of the rustling he had heard in the night. He took off the waistcoat and examined it. 'Old Butteridge won't like me unpicking this.' He hesitated, and finally proceeded to unpick it. He found the missing drawings of the lateral rotating planes, on which the whole stability of the flying-machine depended.

An observant angel would have seen Bert sitting for a long time after this discovery in a state of intense meditation. Then at last he rose with an air of inspiration, took Mr Butteridge's ripped, demolished, and ransacked waistcoat, and hurled it from the balloon – whence it fluttered down slowly and eddyingly until at last it came to rest with a contented flop upon the face of a German tourist sleeping peacefully beside the Höhenweg, near Wildbad. Also this sent the balloon higher, and so into a position still more convenient for observation by our imaginary angel, who would next have seen Mr Smallways tear open his own jacket and waistcoat, remove his collar, open his shirt, thrust his hand into his bosom, and tear his heart out – or at least, if not his heart, some large bright scarlet object. If the observer, overcoming a thrill of celestial horror, had scrutinised this scarlet object more narrowly, one of Bert's most cherished secrets, one of his essential weaknesses, would have been laid bare. It was a red-flannel chest-protector, one of those large quasi-hygienic objects that with pills and medicines take the place of beneficial relics and images among the Protestant peoples of Christendom. Always Bert wore this thing; it was his cherished delusion, based on the advice of a shilling fortune-teller at Margate, that he was weak in the lungs.

He now proceeded to unbutton his fetish, to attack it with a pen-knife, and to thrust the new-found plans between the two layers of imitation Saxony flannel of which it was made. Then with the help of Mr Butteridge's small shaving-mirror and his folding canvas basin he readjusted his costume with the gravity of a man who has taken an irrevocable step in life, buttoned up his jacket, cast the white sheet of the Desert Dervish on one side, washed temperately, shaved, resumed the big cap and the fur overcoat, and, much refreshed by these exercises, surveyed the country below him.

It was indeed a spectacle of incredible magnificence. If perhaps it was not so strange and magnificent as the sunlit cloudland of the previous day, it was at any rate infinitely more interesting. The air was at its utmost clearness and except to the south and south-west there was not a cloud in the sky. The country was hilly, with occasional fir plantations and bleak upland spaces, but also with numerous farms, and the hills were deeply intersected by the gorges of several winding rivers interrupted at intervals by the banked-up ponds and weirs of electric generating wheels. It was dotted with bright-looking, steep-roofed villages, and each showed a distinctive and interesting church beside its wireless telegraph steeple; here and there were large châteaux and parks and white roads, and paths lined with red and white cable posts were extremely conspicuous in the landscape. There were walled enclosures like gardens and rickyards and great roofs of barns and many electric dairy centres. The uplands were mottled with cattle. At places he would see the track of one of the old railroads (converted now to monorails) dodging through tunnels and crossing embankments, and a rushing hum would mark the passing of a train. Everything was extraordinarily clear as well as minute. Once or twice he saw guns and soldiers, and was reminded of the stir of military preparations he had witnessed on the Bank Holiday in England; but there was nothing to tell him that these military preparations were abnormal or to explain an occasional faint irregular firing of guns that drifted up to him.

'Wish I knew how to get down,' said Bert, ten thousand feet or so above it all, and gave himself to much futile tugging at the red and white cords. Afterwards he made a sort of inventory of the provisions. Life in the high air was giving him an appalling appetite, and it seemed to him discreet at this stage to portion out his supply into rations. So far as he could see he might pass a week in the air.

At first all the vast panorama below had been as silent as a painted picture. But as the day wore on and the gas diffused slowly from the balloon, it sank earthward again, details increased, men became more visible, and he began to hear the whistle and moan of trains and cars, sounds of cattle, bugles and kettle-drums, and presently even men's voices. And at last his guide-rope was trailing again, and he found it possible to attempt a landing. Once or twice, as the rope dragged over cables, he found his hair erect with electricity, and once he had a slight shock, and sparks snapped about the car. He took these things among the chances of the voyage. He had one idea now very clear in his mind, and that was to drop the iron grapnel that hung from the ring.

From the first this attempt was unfortunate, perhaps because the place for descent was ill-chosen. A balloon should come down in an empty open space, and he chose a crowd. He made his decision suddenly, and without proper reflection. As he trailed, Bert saw ahead of him one of the most attractive little towns in the world – a cluster of steep gables surmounted by a high church tower and diversified with trees, walled, and with a fine, large gateway opening out upon a tree-lined high road. All the wires and cables of the countryside converged upon it like guests to entertainment. It had a most homelike and comfortable quality, and it was made gayer by abundant flags. Along the road a quantity of peasant folk, in big pair-wheeled carts and afoot, were coming and going, besides an occasional monorail car; and at the car-junction, under the trees outside the town, was a busy little fair of booths. It seemed a warm, human, well-rooted, and altogether delightful place to Bert. He came low over the tree-tops, with his grapnel ready to throw and so anchor him – a curious, interested, and interesting guest, so his imagination figured it, in the very middle of it all.

He thought of himself performing feats with the sign language and chance linguistics amidst a circle of admiring rustics . . .

And then the chapter of adverse accidents began.

The rope made itself unpopular long before the crowd had fully realised his advent over the trees. An elderly and apparently intoxicated peasant in a shiny black hat, and carrying a large crimson umbrella, caught sight of it first as it trailed past him, and was seized with a discreditable ambition to kill it. He pursued it briskly with unpleasant cries. It crossed the road obliquely, splashed into a pail of milk upon a stall, and slapped its milky tail athwart a motor-car load of factory girls halted outside the town gates. They screamed loudly. People looked up and saw Bert making what he meant to be genial salutations, but what they considered, in view of the feminine outcry, to be insulting gestures. Then the car hit the roof of the gatehouse smartly, snapped a flagstaff, played a tune upon some telegraph wires, and sent a broken wire like a whiplash to do its share in accumulating unpopularity. Bert, by clutching convulsively, just escaped being pitched headlong. Two young soldiers and several peasants shouted things up to him and shook fists at him and began to run in pursuit as he disappeared over the wall into the town. Admiring rustics, indeed!

The balloon leapt at once, in the manner of balloons when part of their weight is released by touching down, with a sort of flippancy, and in another moment Bert was over a street crowded with peasants and soldiers, that opened into a busy market-square. The wave of unfriendliness pursued him.

'Grapnel,' said Bert, and then with an afterthought shouted, '*Têtes* there, you!'[155] I say! I say! *Têtes*. 'Eng it!' The grapnel smashed down a steeply sloping roof, followed by an avalanche of broken tiles, jumped the street amidst shrieks and cries, and smashed into a plate-glass

window with an immense and sickening impact. The balloon rolled
nauseatingly, and the car pitched. But the grapnel had not held. It
emerged at once bearing on one fluke, with a ridiculous air of fastidious
selection, a small child's chair, and pursued by a maddened shopman.
It lifted its catch, swung about with an appearance of painful indecision
amidst a roar of wrath, and dropped it at last neatly, and as if by
inspiration, over the head of a peasant woman in charge of an
assortment of cabbages in the market-place.

Everybody now was aware of the balloon. Everybody was either trying
to dodge the grapnel or catch the trail rope. With a pendulum-like
swoop through the crowd, that sent people flying right and left, the
grapnel came to earth again, tried for and missed a stout gentleman in a
blue suit and a straw hat, smacked away a trestle from under a stall
of haberdashery, made a cyclist soldier in knickerbockers leap like a
chamois, and secured itself uncertainly among the hind-legs of a sheep –
which made convulsive, ungenerous efforts to free itself, and was dragged
into a position of rest against a stone cross in the middle of the place.
The balloon pulled up with a jerk. In another moment a score
of willing hands were tugging it earthward. At the same instant Bert
became aware for the first time of a fresh breeze blowing about him.

For some seconds he stood staggering in the car, which now swayed
sickeningly, surveying the exasperated crowd below him and trying to
collect his mind. He was extraordinarily astonished at this run of
mishaps. Were the people really so annoyed? Everybody seemed angry
with him. No one seemed interested or amused by his arrival. A dis-
proportionate amount of the outcry had the flavour of imprecation –
had, indeed, a strong flavour of riot. Several greatly uniformed officials
in cocked hats struggled in vain to control the crowd. Fists and sticks
were shaken. And when Bert saw a man on the outskirts of the crowd
run to a hay cart and get a brightly pronged pitchfork, and a blue-clad
soldier unbuckle his belt, his rising doubt whether this little town was
after all such a good place for a landing became a certainty.

He had clung to the fancy that they would make something of a hero
of him. Now he knew that he was mistaken.

He was perhaps ten feet above the people when he made his decision.
His paralysis ceased. He leapt up on the seat, and, at imminent risk of
falling headlong, released the grapnel-rope from the toggle that held
it, sprang on to the trail rope and disengaged that also. A hoarse shout
of disgust greeted the descent of the grapnel-rope and the swift leap of
the balloon, and something – he fancied afterwards it was a turnip –
whizzed by his head. The trail rope followed its fellow. The crowd

seemed to jump away from him. With an immense and horrifying rustle the balloon brushed against a telephone pole, and for a tense instant he anticipated either an electric explosion or a bursting of the oiled silk, or both. But fortune was with him.

In another second he was cowering in the bottom of the car, and, released from the weight of the grapnel and the two ropes, rushing up once more through the air. For a time he remained crouching, and when at last he looked out again the little town was very small and travelling, with the rest of lower Germany, in a circular orbit round and round the car – or at least it appeared to be doing that.

When he got used to it, he found this rotation of the balloon rather convenient; it saved moving about in the car.

5

Late in the afternoon of a pleasant summer day in the year 191-, if one may borrow a mode of phrasing that once found favour with the readers of the late G. P. R. James,[156] a solitary balloonist – replacing the solitary horseman of the classic romances – might have been observed wending his way across Franconia[157] in a north-easterly direction, and at a height of about eleven thousand feet above the sea and still spinning slowly. His head was craned over the side of the car, and he surveyed the country below with an expression of profound perplexity; ever and again his lips shaped inaudible words. 'Shootin' at a chap,' for example, and 'I'll come down right enough soon as I find out 'ow.' Over the side of the basket the robe of the Desert Dervish was hanging, an appeal for consideration, an ineffectual white flag.

He was now very distinctly aware that the world below him, so far from being the naïve countryside of his earlier imaginings that day, sleepily unconscious of him and capable of being amazed and nearly reverential at his descent, was acutely irritated by his career, and extremely impatient with the course he was taking. But indeed it was not he who took that course, but his masters, the winds of heaven.[158] Mysterious voices spoke to him in his ear, jerking the words up to him by means of megaphones, in a weird and startling manner, in a great variety of languages. Official-looking persons had signalled to him by means of flag-flapping and arm-waving. On the whole a guttural variant of English prevailed in the sentences that alighted upon the balloon; chiefly he was told to 'gome down or you will be shot'.

'All very well,' said Bert, 'but 'ow?'

Then they shot a little wide of the car. Latterly he had been shot at six or seven times, and once the bullet had gone by with a sound so persuasively like the tearing of silk that he had resigned himself to the prospect of a headlong fall. But either they were aiming near him or they had missed, and as yet nothing was torn but the air about him – and his anxious soul.

He was now enjoying a respite from these attentions, but he felt it was at best an interlude, and he was doing what he could to appreciate his position. Incidentally he was having some hot coffee and pie in an untidy inadvertent manner, with an eye fluttering nervously over the side of the car. At first he had ascribed the growing interest in his career to his ill-conceived attempt to land in the bright little upland town, but now he was beginning to realise that the military rather than the civil arm was concerned about him.

He was quite involuntarily playing that weird mysterious part – the part of an International Spy. He was seeing secret things. He had, in fact, crossed the designs of no less a power than the German Empire, he had blundered into the hot focus of Welt-Politik,[159] he was drifting helplessly towards the great Imperial secret, the immense aeronautic park that had been established at a headlong pace in Franconia to develop silently, swiftly, and on an immense scale the great discoveries of Hunstedt and Stossel, and so to give Germany before all other nations a fleet of airships, the air power and the Empire of the world.

Later, just before they shot him down altogether, Bert saw that great area of passionate work, warm lit in the evening light, a great area of upland on which the airships lay like a herd of grazing monsters at their feed. It was a vast, busy space, stretching away northward as far as he could see, methodically cut up into numbered sheds, gasometers, squad encampments, storage areas, interlaced with the omnipresent monorail lines, and altogether free from overhead wires or cables. Everywhere was the white, black and yellow of Imperial Germany, everywhere the black eagles spread their wings. Even without these indications, the large vigorous neatness of everything would have marked it German. Vast multitudes of men went to and fro, many in white and drab fatigue uniforms busy about the balloons, others drilling in sensible drab. Here and there a full uniform glittered.

The airships chiefly engaged his attention, and he knew at once it was three of these he had seen on the previous night, taking advantage of the cloud welkin to manoeuvre unobserved.

They were altogether fishlike. For the great airships with which Germany attacked New York in her last gigantic effort for world supremacy – before humanity realised that world supremacy was a dream – were the lineal descendants of the Zeppelin airship that flew over Lake Constance in 1906,[160] and of the Lebaudy navigables that made their memorable excursions over Paris in 1907 and 1908.[161]

These German airships were held together by riblike skeletons of steel and aluminium and a stout, inelastic canvas outer-skin, within which was an impervious rubber gasbag, cut up by transverse dissepiments into from fifty to a hundred compartments. These were all absolutely gas tight and filled with hydrogen, and the entire aerostat was kept at any level by means of a long internal balloonette of oiled and toughened silk canvas, into which air could be forced and from which it could be pumped. So the airship could be made either heavier or lighter than air, and losses of weight through the consumption of fuel, the casting of bombs and so forth, could also be compensated by admitting air to sections of the general gasbag. Ultimately that made a highly explosive mixture; but in all these matters risks must be taken and guarded against. There was a steel axis to the whole affair, a central backbone which terminated in the engine and propeller, and the men and magazines were forward in a series of cabins under the expanded headlike forepart. The engine, which was of the extraordinarily powerful Pforzheim type,[162] that supreme triumph of German invention, was worked by wires from this forepart, which was indeed the only really habitable part of the ship. If anything went wrong, the engineers went aft along a rope ladder beneath the frame or along a passage through the gas chambers. The tendency of the whole affair to roll was partly corrected by a horizontal lateral fin on either side, and steering was chiefly effected by two vertical fins, which normally lay back like gill-flaps on either side of the head. It was indeed a most complete adaptation of the fish form to aerial conditions, the position of swimming bladder, eyes, and brain being, however, below instead of above. A striking and unfishlike feature was the apparatus for wireless telegraphy that dangled from the forward cabin – that is to say, under the chin of the fish.

These monsters were capable of ninety miles an hour in a calm, so that they could face and make headway against nearly everything except the fiercest tornado. They varied in length from eight hundred to two thousand feet, and they had a carrying power of from seventy to two hundred tons. How many Germany possessed history does not record, but Bert counted nearly eighty great bulks receding in perspective during his brief inspection. Such were the instruments on which she chiefly relied to sustain her in her repudiation of the Monroe Doctrine and her bold bid for a share in the empire of the New World.

But not altogether did she rely on these; she had also a one-man bomb-throwing *drachenflieger* of unknown value among her resources.

But the *drachenflieger* were away in the second great aeronautic park east of Hamburg, and Bert Smallways saw nothing of them in the bird's-eye view he took of the Franconian establishment before they shot him down. For they shot him down very neatly. They used the new bullets with steel trailers that Wolffe of Engelberg had invented for aerial warfare. The bullet tore past him and made a sort of pop as its trailer pierced his balloon – a pop that was followed by a rustling sigh and a steady downward movement. And when in the confusion of the moment he dropped a bag of ballast, the Germans very politely but firmly overcame his scruples by shooting his balloon again twice.

CHAPTER FOUR

The German Air-Fleet

1

Of all the productions of the human imagination that make the world in which Mr Bert Smallways lived confusingly wonderful, there was none quite so strange, so headlong and disturbing, so noisy and persuasive and dangerous, as the modernisations of patriotism produced by imperial and international politics. In the soul of all men is a liking for kind, a pride in one's own atmosphere, a tenderness for one's mother speech and one's familiar land. Before the coming of the Scientific Age this group of gentle and noble emotions had been a fine factor in the equipment of every worthy human being, a fine factor that had its less amiable aspect in a usually harmless hostility to strange people, and a usually harmless detraction of strange lands. But with the wild rush of change in the pace, scope, materials, scale, and possibilities of human life that then occurred, the old boundaries, the old seclusions and separations were violently broken down. All the old settled mental habits and traditions of men found themselves not simply confronted by new conditions, but by constantly renewed and changing new conditions. They had no chance of adapting themselves. They were annihilated or perverted or inflamed beyond recognition.

Bert Smallways' grandfather, in the days when Bun Hill was a village under the sway of Sir Peter Bone's parent, had 'known his place' to the uttermost farthing, touched his hat to his betters, despised and condescended to his inferiors, and hadn't changed an idea from the cradle to the grave. He was Kentish and English, and that meant hops, beer, dog-roses, and the sort of sunshine that was best in the world. Newspapers and politics and visits to 'Lunnon' weren't for the likes of him. Then came the change. These earlier chapters have given an idea of what happened to Bun Hill, and how the flood of novel things had poured over its devoted rusticity. Bert Smallways was only one of countless millions in Europe and America and Asia who, instead of being born rooted in the soil, were born struggling in a torrent they never clearly understood. All the faiths of their fathers had been taken by surprise, and startled into the strangest forms and reactions. Particularly

did the fine old tradition of patriotism get perverted and distorted
in the rush of the new times. Instead of the sturdy establishment in
prejudice of Bert's grandfather, to whom the word 'Frenchified' was
the ultimate term of contempt, there flowed through Bert's brain
a squittering succession of thinly violent ideas about German competition, about the Yellow Danger, about the Black Peril,[163] about the
White Man's Burthen[164] – that is to say, Bert's preposterous right to
muddle further the naturally very muddled politics of the entirely
similar little cads to himself (except for a smear of brown) who smoked
cigarettes and rode bicycles in Buluwayo, Kingston (Jamaica), or Bom-
bay. These were Bert's 'Subject Races', and he was ready to die – by
proxy in the person of anyone who cared to enlist – to maintain his
hold upon that right. It kept him awake at nights to think that he
might lose it.

The essential fact of the politics of the age in which Bert Smallways
lived – the age that blundered at last into the catastrophe of the War in
the Air – was a very simple one, if only people had had the intelligence
to be simple about it. The development of Science had altered the scale
of human affairs. By means of rapid mechanical traction, it had brought
men nearer together, so much nearer socially, economically, physically,
that the old separations into nations and kingdoms were no longer
possible, a newer, wider synthesis was not only needed, but imperatively
demanded. Just as the once independent dukedoms of France had to
fuse into a nation, so now the nations had to adapt themselves to a
wider coalescence, they had to keep what was precious and possible,
and concede what was obsolete and dangerous. A saner world would
have perceived this patent need for a reasonable synthesis, would have
discussed it temperately, achieved and gone on to organise the great
civilisation that was manifestly possible to mankind. The world of Bert
Smallways did nothing of the sort. Its national governments, its national
interests, would not hear of anything so obvious; they were too suspicious
of each other, too wanting in generous imagination. They began to
behave like ill-bred people in a crowded public car, to squeeze against
one another, elbow, thrust, dispute and quarrel. Vain to point out to
them that they had only to rearrange themselves to be comfortable.
Everywhere, all over the world, the historian of the early twentieth
century finds the same thing, the flow and rearrangement of human
affairs inextricably entangled by the old areas, the old prejudices and a
sort of heated irascible stupidity, and everywhere congested nations in
inconvenient areas, slopping population and produce into each other,
annoying each other with tariffs and every possible commercial vexation,

and threatening each other with navies and armies that grew every year more portentous.

It is impossible now to estimate how much of the intellectual and physical energy of the world was wasted in military preparation and equipment, but it was an enormous proportion. Great Britain spent upon army and navy money and capacity that, directed into the channels of physical culture and education, would have made the British the aristo-cracy of the world. Her rulers could have kept the whole population learning and exercising up to the age of eighteen and made a broad-chested and intelligent man of every Bert Smallways in the islands, had they given the resources they spent in war material to the making of men. Instead of which they waggled flags at him until he was fourteen, incited him to cheer, and then turned him out of school to begin that career of private enterprise we have compactly recorded. France achieved similar imbecilities; Germany was, if possible, worse; Russia under the waste and stresses of militarism festered towards bankruptcy and decay. All Europe was producing big guns and countless swarms of little Smallways. The Asiatic peoples had been forced in self-defence into a like diversion of the new powers science had brought them. On the eve of the outbreak of the war there were six great powers in the world and a cluster of smaller ones, each armed to the teeth and straining every nerve to get ahead of the others in deadliness of equipment and military efficiency. The great powers were first the United States, a nation addicted to commerce, but roused to military necessities by the efforts of Germany to expand into South America, and by the natural consequences of her own unwary annexations of land in the very teeth of Japan. She maintained two immense fleets east and west, and internally she was in violent conflict between Federal and State governments upon the question of universal service in a defensive militia. Next came the great alliance of Eastern Asia, a close-knit coalescence of China and Japan, advancing with rapid strides year by year to predominance in the world's affairs. Then the German alliance still struggled to achieve its dream of imperial expansion, and its imposition of the German language upon a forcibly united Europe. These were the three most spirited and aggressive powers in the world. Far more pacific was the British Empire, perilously scattered over the globe, and distracted now by insurrectionary movements in Ireland and among all its Subject Races. It had given these Subject Races cigarettes, boots, bowler hats, cricket, race meetings, cheap revolvers, petroleum, the factory system of industry, halfpenny newspapers in both English and the vernacular, inexpensive university degrees, motor-bicycles and electric trams; it had produced a considerable literature expressing contempt for the Subject Races, and rendered it freely accessible to them, and it had been content to believe that nothing would result from these stimulants because somebody once wrote 'the immemorial east'; and also, in the inspired words of Kipling:

> East is east and west is west,
> And never the twain shall meet.[165]

Instead of which, Egypt, India, and the subject countries generally had produced new generations in a state of passionate indignation and the utmost energy, activity and modernity. The governing class in Great Britain was slowly adapting itself to a new conception of the Subject Races as waking peoples, and finding its efforts to keep the Empire together under these strains and changing ideas greatly impeded by the entirely sporting spirit with which Bert Smallways at home (by the million) cast his vote, and by the tendency of his more highly coloured equivalents to be disrespectful to irascible officials. Their impertinence was excessive; it was no mere stone-throwing and shouting. They would quote Burns at them and Mill and Darwin[166] and confute them in arguments.

Even more pacific than the British Empire were France and its allies, the Latin powers, heavily armed states indeed, but reluctant warriors, and in many ways socially and politically leading western civilisation. Russia was a pacific power perforce, divided within itself, torn between revolutionaries and reactionaries who were equally incapable of social reconstruction, and so sinking towards a tragic disorder of chronic political vendetta. Wedged in among these portentous larger bulks, swayed and threatened by them, the smaller states of the world maintained a precarious independence, each keeping itself armed as dangerously as its utmost ability could contrive.

So it came about that in every country a great and growing body of energetic and inventive men was busied either for offensive or defensive ends, in elaborating the apparatus of war, until the accumulating tensions should reach the breaking-point. Each power sought to keep its preparations secret, to hold new weapons in reserve, to anticipate and learn the preparations of its rivals. The feeling of danger from fresh discoveries affected the patriotic imagination of every people in the world. Now it was rumoured the British had an overwhelming gun, now the French an invincible rifle, now the Japanese a new explosive, now the Americans a submarine that would drive every ironclad from the seas. Each time there would be a war panic.

The strength and heart of the nations was given to the thought of war, and yet the mass of their citizens was a teeming democracy as heedless of and unfitted for fighting, mentally, morally, physically, as any population has ever been – or, one ventures to add, could ever be. That was the paradox of the time. It was a period altogether unique in the world's history. The apparatus of warfare, the art and method of fighting, changed absolutely every dozen years in a stupendous progress towards perfection, and people grew less and less warlike, and there was no war.

And then at last it came. It came as a surprise to all the world because its real causes were hidden. Relations were strained between Germany and the United States because of the intense exasperation of a tariff conflict and the ambiguous attitude of the former power towards the Monroe Doctrine, and they were strained between the United States and Japan because of the perennial citizenship question. But in both cases these were standing causes of offence. The real deciding cause, it is now known, was the perfecting of the Pforzheim engine by Germany and the consequent possibility of a rapid and entirely practicable airship. At that time Germany was by far the most efficient power in the world, better organised for swift and secret action, better equipped with the resources of modern science, and with her official and administrative classes at a higher level of education and training. These things she knew, and she exaggerated that knowledge to the pitch of contempt for the secret counsels of her neighbours. It may be that with the habit of self-confidence her spying upon them had grown less thorough. Moreover, she had a tradition of unsentimental and unscrupulous action that vitiated her international outlook profoundly. With the coming of these new weapons her collective intelligence thrilled with the sense that now her moment had come. Once again in the history of progress it seemed she held the decisive weapon. Now she might strike and conquer – before the others had anything but experiments in the air.

Particularly she must strike America, swiftly, because there, if anywhere, lay the chance of an aerial rival. It was known that America possessed a flying-machine of considerable practical value, developed out of the Wright model; but it was not supposed that the Washington War Office had made any wholesale attempts to create an aerial navy. It was necessary to strike before they could do so. France had a fleet of slow navigables, several dating from 1908, that could make no possible headway against the new type. They had been built solely for reconnoitring purposes on the eastern frontier, they were mostly too small to carry more than a couple of dozen men without arms or provisions, and not one could do forty miles an hour. Great Britain, it seemed, in an access of meanness, temporised and wrangled with the imperial-spirited Butteridge and his extraordinary invention. That also was not in play – and could not be for some months at the earliest. From Asia there came no sign. The Germans explained this by saying the yellow peoples were without invention. No other competitor was worth considering. 'Now or never,' said the Germans – 'now or never we may seize the air – as once the British seized the seas! While all the other powers are still experimenting.'

Swift and systematic and secret were their preparations, and their plan most excellent. So far as their knowledge went, America was the only dangerous possibility; America, which was also now the leading trade rival of Germany and one of the chief barriers to her Imperial expansion. So at once they would strike at America. They would fling a great force across the Atlantic heavens and bear America down unwarned and unprepared.

Altogether it was a well-imagined and most hopeful and spirited enterprise, having regard to the information in the possession of the German government. The chances of it being a successful surprise were very great. The airship and the flying-machine were very different things from ironclads, which take a couple of years to build. Given hands, given plant, they could be made innumerably in a few weeks. Once the needful parks and foundries were organised, airships and *drachenflieger* could be poured into the sky. Indeed, when the time came, they did pour into the sky like, as a bitter French writer put it, flies roused from filth.

The attack upon America was to be the first move in this tremendous game. But no sooner had it started than instantly the aeronautic parks were to proceed to put together and inflate the second fleet, which was to dominate Europe and manoeuvre significantly over London, Paris, Rome, St Petersburg, or wherever else its moral effect was required. A World Surprise it was to be – no less, a World Conquest; and it is wonderful how near the calmly adventurous minds that planned it came to succeeding in their colossal design.

Von Sternberg was the Moltke[167] of this War in the Air, but it was the curious hard romanticism of Prince Karl Albert[168] that won over the hesitating Emperor to the scheme. Prince Karl Albert was indeed the central figure of the world drama. He was the darling of the Imperialist spirit in Germany, and the ideal of the new aristocratic feeling – the new Chivalry, as it was called – that followed the overthrow of Socialism through its internal divisions and lack of discipline, and the concentration of wealth in the hands of a few great families. He was compared by obsequious flatterers to the Black Prince,[169] to Alcibiades,[170] to the young Caesar. To many he seemed Nietzsche's Over-man[171] revealed. He was big and blond and virile, and splendidly non-moral. The first great feat that startled Europe, and almost brought about a new Trojan war, was his abduction of the Princess Helena of Norway and his blank refusal to marry her. Then followed his marriage with Gretchen Krass, a Swiss girl of peerless beauty. Then came the gallant rescue, which almost cost him his life, of three drowning sailors whose boat had upset in the sea near Heligoland.[172] For that and his victory over the American yacht *Defender*, C.C.I.,[173] the Emperor forgave him and placed him in control of the new aeronautic arm of the German forces. This he developed with marvellous energy and ability, being resolved, as he said, to give to Germany land and sea and sky. The national passion for aggression found in him its supreme exponent, and achieved through him its realisation in this astounding war. But his fascination was more than national; all over the world his ruthless strength dominated minds as the Napoleonic legend had dominated minds. Englishmen turned in disgust from the slow, complex, civilised methods of their national politics to this uncompromising, forceful figure. Frenchmen believed in him. Poems were written to him in American.

He made the war.

Quite equally with the rest of the world, the general German population was taken by surprise by the swift vigour of the Imperial government. A considerable literature of military forecasts, beginning as early as 1906 with Rudolf Martin,[174] the author not merely of a brilliant book of anticipations, but of a proverb, 'The future of Germany lies in the air,' had, however, partially prepared the German imagination for some such enterprise.

2

Of all these world-forces and gigantic designs Bert Smallways knew nothing until he found himself in the very focus of it all and gaped down amazed on the spectacle of that giant herd of airships. Each one seemed as long as the Strand, and as big about as Trafalgar Square. Some must have been a third of a mile in length. He had never before seen anything so vast and disciplined as this tremendous park. For the first time in his life he really had an intimation of the extraordinary and quite important things of which a contemporary may go in ignorance. He had always clung to the illusion that Germans were fat, absurd men, who smoked china pipes, and were addicted to knowledge and horse-flesh and sauerkraut and indigestible things generally.

His bird's-eye view was quite transitory. He ducked at the first shot; and directly his balloon began to drop, his mind ran confusedly upon how he might explain himself, and whether he should pretend to be Butteridge or not. 'O Lord!' he groaned, in an agony of indecision. Then his eye caught his sandals, and he felt a spasm of self-disgust. 'They'll think I'm a bloomin' idiot,' he said, and then it was he rose up desperately and threw over the sandbag and provoked the second and third shots.

It flashed into his head, as he cowered in the bottom of the car, that he might avoid all sorts of disagreeable and complicated explanations by pretending to be mad.

That was his last idea before the airships seemed to rush up about him as if to look at him, and his car hit the ground and bounded and pitched him out on his head . . .

He awoke to find himself famous, and to hear a voice crying, 'Boot-eraidge! Ja! Ja! Herr Booteraidge! Selbst!'[175]

He was lying on a little patch of grass beside one of the main avenues of the aeronautic park. The airships receded down a great vista, an immense perspective, and the blunt prow of each was adorned with a black eagle of a hundred foot or so spread. Down the other side of the avenue ran a series of gas generators, and big hosepipes trailed everywhere across the intervening space. Close at hand was his now nearly deflated balloon and the car on its side looking minutely small, a mere broken toy, a shrivelled bubble, in contrast with the gigantic bulk of the nearer airship. This he saw almost end-on, rising like a cliff and sloping forward towards its fellow on the other side so as to overshadow the alley between them. There was a crowd of excited people about him, big men mostly in tight uniforms. Everybody was talking, and several were shouting, in German; he knew that because they splashed and aspirated sounds like startled kittens. Only one phrase, repeated again, and again could he recognise – the name of 'Herr Booteraidge'.

'Gollys!' said Bert. 'They've spotted it.'

'Besser,'[176] said someone, and some rapid German followed.

He perceived that close at hand was a field telephone, and that a tall officer in blue was talking thereat about him. Another stood close beside him with the portfolio of drawings and photographs in his hand. They looked round at him.

'Do you spik Cherman, Herr Booteraidge?'

Bert decided that he had better be dazed. He did his best to seem thoroughly dazed. 'Where *am* I?' he asked.

Volubility prevailed. 'Der Prinz' was mentioned. A bugle sounded far away, and its call was taken up by one nearer, and then by one close at hand. This seemed to increase the excitement greatly. A monorail car bumbled past. The telephone bell rang passionately, and the tall officer seemed to engage in a heated altercation. Then he approached the group about Bert, calling out something about 'mithbringen'.[177]

An earnest-faced, emaciated man with a white moustache appealed to Bert. 'Herr Booteraidge, sir, we are chust to start!'

'Where am I?' Bert repeated.

Someone shook him by the other shoulder. 'Are you Herr Booteraidge?' he asked.

'Herr Booteraidge, we are chust to start!' repeated the white moustache, and then helplessly, 'What is de goot? What can we do?'

The officer from the telephone repeated his sentence about 'Der Prinz' and 'mitbringen'. The man with the moustache stared for a moment, grasped an idea and became violently energetic, stood up and bawled directions at unseen people. Questions were asked, and the doctor at Bert's side answered, 'Ja! Ja!' several times, also something about 'Kopf'.[178] With a certain urgency he got Bert rather unwillingly to his feet. Two huge soldiers in grey advanced upon Bert and seized hold of him. ' 'Ullo!' said Bert, startled. 'What's up?'

'It is all right,' the doctor explained; 'they are to carry you.'

'Where?' asked Bert, unanswered.

'Put your arms roundt their – *hals*[179] – round them!'

'Yes! but where?'

'Hold tight!'

Before Bert could decide to say anything more he was whisked up by the two soldiers. They joined hands to seat him, and his arms were put about their necks. 'Vorwärts!'[180] Someone ran before him with the portfolio, and he was borne rapidly along the broad avenue between the gas generators and the airships, rapidly and on the whole smoothly except that once or twice his bearers stumbled over hosepipes and nearly let him down.

He was wearing Mr Butteridge's Alpine cap, and his little shoulders were in Mr Butteridge's fur-lined overcoat, and he had responded to Mr Butteridge's name. The sandals dangled helplessly. Gaw! Everybody seemed in a devil of a hurry. Why? He was carried joggling and gaping through the twilight, marvelling beyond measure.

The systematic arrangement of wide convenient spaces, the quantities of businesslike soldiers everywhere, the occasional neat piles of material, the ubiquitous monorail lines, and the towering shiplike hulls about him, reminded him a little of impressions he had got as a boy on a visit to Woolwich Dockyard.[181] The whole camp reflected the colossal power of modern science that had created it. A peculiar strangeness was produced by the lowness of the electric light, which lay upon the ground, casting all shadows upwards and making a grotesque shadow figure of himself and his bearers on the airship sides, fusing all three of them into a monstrous animal with attenuated legs and an immense fanlike humped body. The lights were on the ground because as far as possible all poles and standards had been dispensed with to prevent complications when the airships rose.

It was deep twilight now, a tranquil blue-skyed evening; everything rose out from the splashes of light upon the ground into dim, translucent, tall masses; within the cavities of the airships small inspecting lamps glowed like cloud-veiled stars, and made them seem marvellously unsubstantial. Each airship had its name in black letters on white on either flank, and forward the Imperial eagle sprawled, an overwhelming bird in the dimness. Bugles sounded, monorail cars of quiet soldiers slithered burbling by. The cabins under the heads of the airships were being lit up; doors opened in them, and revealed padded passages. Now and then a voice gave directions to workers indistinctly seen.

There was a matter of sentinels, gangways, and a long narrow passage, a scramble over a disorder of baggage, and then Bert found himself lowered to the ground and standing in the doorway of a spacious cabin – it was perhaps ten feet square and eight high, furnished with crimson padding and aluminium. A tall, birdlike young man with a small head, a long nose, and very pale hair, with his hands full of things like shaving-strops, boot-trees, hairbrushes, and toilet tidies, was saying things about Gott and thunder and Dummer[182] Booteraidge as Bert entered. He was apparently an evicted occupant. Then he vanished, and Bert was lying back on a couch in the corner with a pillow under his head and the door of the cabin shut upon him. He was alone. Everybody had hurried out again astonishingly.

'Gollys!' said Bert. 'What next?'

He stared about him at the room.

'Butteridge! Shall I try to keep it up, or shan't I?'

The room he was in puzzled him. ' 'Tisn't a prison and 'tisn't a norfis?'[183] Then the old trouble came uppermost. 'I wish to 'eaven I 'adn't these silly sandals on,' he cried querulously to the universe. 'They give the whole blessed show away.'

His door was flung open, and a compact young man in uniform appeared, carrying Mr Butteridge's portfolio, rucksack, and shaving-glass. 'I say!' he said in faultless English as he entered. He had a beaming face, and a sort of pinkish blond hair. 'Fancy you being Butteridge.'

He slapped Bert's meagre luggage down.

'We'd have started,' he said, 'in another half-hour! You didn't give yourself much time!'

He surveyed Bert curiously. His gaze rested for a fraction of a moment on the sandals. 'You ought to have come on your flying-machine, Mr Butteridge.'

He didn't wait for an answer. 'The Prince says I've got to look after you. Naturally he can't see you now, but he thinks your coming's providential. Last grace of Heaven. Like a sign. Hullo!'

He stood still and listened.

Outside there was a going to and fro of feet, a sound of distant bugles suddenly taken up and echoed close at hand, men called out in loud tones short, sharp, seemingly vital things, and were answered distantly. A bell jangled, and feet went down the corridor. Then came a stillness more distracting than sound, and then a great gurgling and rushing and splashing of water. The young man's eyebrows lifted. He hesitated, and dashed out of the room. Presently came a stupendous bang to vary the noises without, then a distant cheering. The young man reappeared.

'They're running the water out of the balloonette already.'

'What water?' asked Bert.

'The water that anchored us. Artful dodge. Eh?'

Bert tried to take it in.

'Of course!' said the compact young man. 'You don't understand.'

A gentle quivering crept upon Bert's senses.

'That's the engine,' said the compact young man approvingly. 'Now we shan't be long.'

Another long listening interval.

The cabin swayed. 'By Jove! we're starting already,' he cried. 'We're starting!'

'Starting!' cried Bert, sitting up. 'Where?'

But the young man was out of the room again. There were noises of German in the passage, and other nerve-shaking sounds.

The swaying increased. The young man reappeared. 'We're off, right enough!'

'I say!' said Bert, 'where are we starting? I wish you'd explain. What's this place? I don't understand.'

'What!' cried the young man, 'you don't understand?'

'No. I'm all dazed-like from that crack on the nob I got. Where are we? Where are we starting?'

'Don't you know where you are – what this is?'

'Not a bit of it! What's all the swaying and the row?'

'What a lark!' cried the young man. 'I say! What a thundering lark! Don't you know? We're off to America, and you haven't realised. You've just caught us by a neck. You're on the blessed old flagship with the Prince. You won't miss anything. Whatever's on, you bet the *Vaterland*[184] will be there.'

'Us! – off to America?'

'Ra-ther!'

'In an airship?'

'What do you think?'

'Me! going to America on an airship! After that balloon! 'Ere! I say – I don't want to go! I want to walk about on my legs. Let me get out! I didn't understand.'

He made a dive for the door.

The young man arrested Bert with a gesture, took hold of a strap, lifted up a panel in the padded wall, and a window appeared. 'Look!' he said. Side by side they looked out.

'Gaw!' said Bert. 'We're going up!'

'We are!' said the young man, cheerfully; 'fast!'

They were rising in the air smoothly and quietly, and moving slowly to the throb of the engine athwart the aeronautic park. Down below it stretched, dimly geometrical in the darkness, picked out at regular intervals by glowworm spangles of light. One black gap in the long line of grey, round-backed airships marked the position from which the *Vaterland* had come. Beside it a second monster now rose softly, released from its bonds and cables into the air. Then, taking a beautifully exact distance, a third ascended, and then a fourth.

'Too late, Mr Butteridge!' the young man remarked. 'We're off! I dare say it *is* a bit of a shock to you, but there you are! The Prince said you'd have to come.'

'Look 'ere,' said Bert. 'I really *am* dazed. What's this thing? Where are we going?'

'This, Mr Butteridge,' said the young man, taking pains to be explicit, 'is an airship. It's the flagship of Prince Karl Albert. This is the German air-fleet, and it is going over to America, to give that spirited people "what for". The only thing we were at all uneasy about was your invention. And here you are!'

'But! – you a German?' asked Bert.

'Lieutenant Kurt. Luft-lieutenant Kurt, at your service.'

'But you speak English!'

'Mother was English – went to school in England. Afterwards, Rhodes scholar.[185] German none the less for that. Detailed for the present, Mr Butteridge, to look after you. You're shaken by your fall. It's all right, really. They're going to buy your machine and everything. You sit down, and take it quite calmly. You'll soon get the hang of the position.'

4

Bert sat down on the locker, collecting his mind, and the young man talked to him about the airship.

He was really a very tactful young man indeed, in a natural sort of way. 'Dare say all this is new to you,' he said; 'not your sort of machine. These cabins aren't half bad.'

He got up and walked round the little apartment, showing its points.

'Here is the bed,' he said, whipping down a couch from the wall and throwing it back again with a click. 'Here are toilet things,' and he opened a neatly arranged cupboard. 'Not much washing. No water we've got; no water at all except for drinking. No baths or anything until we get to America and land. Rub over with loofah. One pint of hot for shaving. That's all. In the locker below you are rugs and blankets; you will need them presently. They say it gets cold. I don't know. Never been up before. Except a little work with gliders – which is mostly going down. Three-quarters of the chaps in the fleet haven't. Here's a folding-chair and table behind the door. Compact, eh?'

He took the chair and balanced it on his little finger. 'Pretty light, eh? Aluminium and magnesium alloy and a vacuum inside. All these cushions stuffed with hydrogen. Foxy! The whole ship's like that. And not a man in the fleet, except the Prince and one or two others, over eleven stone. Couldn't sweat the Prince, you know. We'll go all over the thing tomorrow. I'm frightfully keen on it.'

He beamed at Bert. 'You *do* look young,' he remarked. 'I always thought you'd be an old man with a beard – a sort of philosopher. I don't know why one should expect clever people always to be old. I do.'

Bert parried that compliment a little awkwardly, and then the lieutenant was struck with the riddle why Herr Butteridge had not come in his own flying-machine.

'It's a long story,' said Bert. 'Look here!' he said abruptly, 'I wish you'd lend me a pair of slippers, or something. I'm regular sick of these sandals. They're rotten things. I've been trying them for a friend.'

'Right-o!'

The ex-Rhodes scholar whisked out of the room and reappeared with a considerable choice of footwear – pumps, cloth bath-slippers, and a purple pair adorned with golden sunflowers.

But these he repented of at the last moment. 'I don't even wear them myself,' he said. 'Only brought 'em in the zeal of the moment.' He laughed confidentially. 'Had 'em worked for me – in Oxford. By a friend. Take 'em everywhere.'

So Bert chose the pumps.

The lieutenant broke into a cheerful snigger. 'Here we are trying on slippers,' he said, 'and the world going by like a panorama below. Rather a lark, eh? Look!'

Bert peeped with him out of the window, looking from the bright pettiness of the red-and-silver cabin into a dark immensity. The land below, except for a lake, was black and featureless, and the other airships were hidden. 'See more outside,' said the lieutenant. 'Let's go! There's a sort of little gallery.'

He led the way into the long passage, which was lit by one small electric light, past some notices in German, to an open balcony and a light ladder and gallery of metal lattice overhanging empty space. Bert followed his leader down to the gallery slowly and cautiously. From it he was able to watch the wonderful spectacle of the first air-fleet flying through the night. They flew in a wedge-shaped formation, the *Vaterland* highest and leading, the tail receding into the corners of the sky. They flew in long, regular undulations, great dark fishlike shapes, showing hardly any light at all, the engines making a throb-throb-throbbing sound that was very audible out on the gallery. They were going at a level of five or six thousand feet, and rising steadily. Below, the country lay silent, a clear darkness dotted and lined out with clusters of furnaces, and the lit streets of a group of big towns. The world seemed to lie in a bowl; the overhanging bulk of the airship above hid all but the lowest levels of the sky.

They watched the landscape for a space.

'Jolly it must be to invent things,' said the lieutenant suddenly. 'How did you come to think of your machine first?'

'Worked it out,' said Bert, after a pause. 'Jest ground away at it.'

'Our people are frightfully keen on you. They thought the British had got you. Weren't the British keen?'

'In a way,' said Bert. 'Still – it's a long story.'

'I think it's an immense thing – to invent. I couldn't invent a thing to save my life.'

They both fell silent, watching the darkened world and following their thoughts until a bugle summoned them to a belated dinner. Bert was suddenly alarmed. 'Don't you 'ave to dress and things?' he said. 'I've always been too hard at Science and things to go into Society and all that.'

'No fear,' said Kurt. 'Nobody's got more than the clothes they wear. We're travelling light. You might perhaps take your overcoat off. They've an electric radiator each end of the room.'

And so presently Bert found himself sitting to eat in the presence of the 'German Alexander'[186] – that great and puissant Prince, Prince Karl Albert, the War Lord, the hero of two hemispheres. He was a handsome, blond man, with deep-set eyes, a snub nose, upturned moustache, and long white hands. He sat higher than the others, under a black eagle with widespread wings and the German Imperial flags; he was, as it were, enthroned, and it struck Bert greatly that as he ate he did not look at people, but over their heads like one who sees visions. Twenty officers of various ranks stood about the table – and Bert. They all seemed extremely curious to see the famous Butteridge, and their astonishment at his appearance was ill-controlled. The Prince gave him a dignified salutation, to which, by an inspiration, he bowed. Standing next the Prince was a brown-faced, wrinkled man with silver spectacles and fluffy, dingy-grey side-whiskers, who regarded Bert with a peculiar and disconcerting attention. The company sat after ceremonies Bert could not understand. At the other end of the table was the bird-faced officer Bert had dispossessed, still looking hostile and whispering about Bert to his neighbour. Two soldiers waited. The dinner was a plain one – a soup, some fresh mutton, and cheese – and there was very little talk.

A curious solemnity indeed brooded over everyone. Partly this was reaction after the intense toil and restrained excitement of starting; partly it was the overwhelming sense of strange new experiences, of portentous adventure. The Prince was lost in thought. He roused himself to drink to the Emperor in champagne, and the company cried 'Hoch!'[187] like men repeating responses in church.

No smoking was permitted, but some of the officers went down to the little open gallery to chew tobacco. No lights whatever were safe amidst that bundle of inflammable things. Bert suddenly fell yawning and shivering. He was overwhelmed by a sense of his own insignificance amidst these great rushing monsters of the air. He felt life was too big for him – too much for him altogether.

He said something to Kurt about his head, went up the steep ladder from the swaying little gallery into the airship again, and so, as if it were a refuge, to bed.

5

Bert slept for a time, and then his sleep was broken by dreams. Mostly he was fleeing from formless terrors down an interminable passage in an airship – a passage paved at first with ravenous trap-doors, and then with openwork canvas of the most careless description.

'Gaw!' said Bert, turning over after his seventh fall through infinite space that night.

He sat up in the darkness and nursed his knees. The progress of the airship was not nearly so smooth as a balloon; he could feel a regular swaying up, up, up and then down, down, down, and the throbbing and tremulous quiver of the engines.

His mind began to teem with memories – more memories and more.

Through them, like a struggling swimmer in broken water, came the perplexing question, what am I to do tomorrow? Tomorrow, Kurt had told him, the Prince's secretary, the Graf von Winterfeld,[188] would come to him and discuss his flying-machine, and then he would see the Prince. He would have to stick it out now that he was Butteridge, and sell his invention. And then, if they found him out! He had a vision of infuriated Butteridges ... Suppose after all he owned up? Pretended it was their misunderstanding? He began to scheme devices for selling the secret and circumventing Butteridge.

What should he ask for the thing? Somehow twenty thousand pounds struck him as about the sum indicated.

He fell into that despondency that lies in wait in the small hours. He had got too big a job on – too big a job ...

Memories swamped his scheming.

'Where was I this time last night?'

He recapitulated his evenings tediously and lengthily. Last night he had been up above the clouds in Butteridge's balloon. He thought of the moment when he dropped through them and saw the cold twilight sea close below. He still remembered that disagreeable incident with a nightmare vividness. And the night before he and Grubb had been looking for cheap lodgings at Littlestone in Kent. How remote that seemed now. It might be years ago. For the first time he thought of his fellow Desert Dervish, left with the two red-painted bicycles on Dymchurch sands. ' 'E won't make much of a show of it, not without me. Any'ow 'e did 'ave the treasury – such as it was – in his pocket! . . . ' The night before that was Bank Holiday night and they had sat discussing their minstrel enterprise, drawing up a programme and rehearsing steps. And the night before was Whit Sunday.

'Lord!' cried Bert, 'what a doing that motor-bicycle give me!' He recalled the empty flapping of the eviscerated cushion, the feeling of impotence as the flames rose again.

From among the confused memories of that tragic flare one little figure emerged very bright and poignantly sweet, Edna, crying back reluctantly from the departing motor car, 'See you tomorrer, Bert?'

Other memories of Edna clustered round that impression. They led Bert's mind step by step to an agreeable state that found expression in 'I'll marry 'er if she don't look out.' And then in a flash it followed in his mind that if he sold the Butteridge secret he could! Suppose after all he did get twenty thousand pounds; such sums have been paid! With that he could buy house and garden, buy new clothes beyond dreaming, buy a motor, travel, have every delight of the civilised life as he knew it, for himself and Edna. Of course, risks were involved. 'I'll 'ave old Butteridge on my track, I expect!'

He meditated upon that. He declined again to despondency. As yet he was only in the beginning of the adventure. He had still to deliver the goods and draw the cash. And before that – Just now he was by no means on his way home. He was flying off to America to fight there. 'Not much fighting,' he considered; 'all our own way.' Still, if a shell did happen to hit the *Vaterland* on the underside! . . .

'S'pose I ought to make my will.'

He lay back for some time composing wills – chiefly in favour of Edna. He had settled now it was to be twenty thousand pounds. He left a number of minor legacies. The wills became more and more meandering and extravagant . . .

He woke from the eighth repetition of his nightmare fall through space. 'This flying gets on one's nerves,' he said.

He could feel the airship diving down, down, down, then slowly swinging to up, up, up. Throb, throb, throb, throb, quivered the engine.

He got up presently and wrapped himself about with Mr Butteridge's overcoat and all the blankets, for the air was very keen. Then he peeped out of the window to see a grey dawn breaking over clouds, then turned up his light and bolted his door, sat down to the table, and produced his chest-protector.

He smoothed the crumpled plans with his hand, and contemplated them. Then he referred to the other drawings in the portfolio. Twenty thousand pounds. If he worked it right! It was worth trying, anyhow.

Presently he opened the drawer in which Kurt had put paper and writing-materials.

Bert Smallways was by no means a stupid person, and up to a certain limit he had not been badly educated. His board school had taught him to draw up to certain limits, taught him to calculate and understand a specification. If at that point his country had tired of its efforts, and handed him over unfinished to scramble for a living in an atmosphere of advertisements and individual enterprise, that was really not his fault. He was as his State had made him, and the reader must not imagine because he was a little cockney cad,[189] that he was absolutely incapable of grasping the idea of the Butteridge flying-machine. But he found it stiff and perplexing. His motor-bicycle and Grubb's experiments and the 'mechanical drawing' he had done in standard seven all helped him out; and, moreover, the maker of these drawings, whoever he was, had been anxious to make his intentions plain. Bert copied sketches, he made notes, he made a quite tolerable and intelligent copy of the essential drawings and sketches of the others. Then he fell into a meditation upon them.

At last he rose with a sigh, folded up the originals that had formerly been in his chest-protector and put them into the breast-pocket of his jacket, and then very carefully deposited the copies he had made in the place of the originals. He had no very clear plan in his mind in doing this, except that he hated the idea of altogether parting with the secret. For a long time he meditated profoundly – nodding. Then he turned out his light and went to bed again and schemed himself to sleep.

6

The *hochgeboren*[190] Graf von Winterfeld was also a light sleeper that night, but then he was one of these people who sleep little and play chess problems in their heads to wile away the time – and that night he had a particularly difficult problem to solve.

He came in upon Bert while he was still in bed in the glow of the sunlight reflected from the North Sea below, consuming the rolls and coffee a soldier had brought him. He had a portfolio under his arm, and in the clear, early morning light his dingy grey hair and heavy, silver-rimmed spectacles made him look almost benevolent. He spoke English fluently, but with a strong German flavour. He was particularly bad with his bs, and his ths softened towards weak zeds. He called Bert explosively, 'Pooterage'.[191] He began with some indistinct civilities, bowed, took a folding-table and chair from behind the door, put the former between himself and Bert, sat down on the latter, coughed drily, and opened his portfolio. Then he put his elbows on the table, pinched his lower lip with his two forefingers, and regarded Bert disconcertingly with magnified eyes. 'You came to us, Herr Pooterage, against your will,' he said at last.

' 'Ow d'you make that out?' asked Bert, after a pause of astonishment.

'I chuge by ze maps in your car. They were all English. And your provisions. They were all picnic. Also your cords were entangled. You haf been tugging – but no good. You could not manage ze balloon, and anuzzer power than yours prought you to us. Is it not so?'

Bert thought.

'Also – where is ze laty?'

' 'Ere! – what lady?'

'You shtarted with a laty. That is evident. You shtarted for an after-noon excursion – a picnic. A man of your temperament – he would take a laty. She was not wiz you in your balloon when you came down at Dornhof. No! Only her chacket! It is your affair. Still, I am curious.'

Bert reflected. ' 'Ow d'you know that?'

'I chuge by ze nature of your farious provisions. I cannot account, Mr Pooterage, for ze laty, what you haf done with her. Nor can I tell why you should wear nature-sandals, nor why you should wear such cheap plue clothes. These are outside my instructions. Trifles, perhaps. Officially they are to be ignored. Laties come and go – I am a man of ze worldt. I haf known wise men wear sandals and efen practise vegetarian habits. I haf known men – or at any rate, I haf known chemists – who did not schmoke. You haf, no doubt, put ze laty down somewhere. Well. Let us get to – business. A higher power' – his voice changed its emotional quality, his magnified eyes seemed to dilate – 'has prought you and your secret straight to us. So!' – he bowed his head – 'so pe it. It is ze Destiny of Chermany and my Prince. I can undershtandt you always carry zat secret. You are afraidt of roppers and spies. So it comes wiz you – to us. Mr Pooterage, Chermany will puy it.'

'Will she?'

'She will,' said the secretary, looking hard at Bert's abandoned sandals in the corner of the locker. He roused himself, consulted a paper of notes for a moment, and Bert eyed his brown and wrinkled face with expectation and terror. 'Chermany, I am instructed to say,' said the secretary, with his eyes on the table and his notes spread out, 'has always been willing to puy your secret. We haf indeed peen eager to acquire it – fery eager; and it was only ze fear that you might be, on patriotic groundts, acting in collusion with your Pritish War Office zat has made us discreet in offering for your marvellous invention through inter-mediaries. We haf no hesitation whatefer now, I am instructed, in agreeing to your proposal of a hundert tousand poundts.'

'Crikey!' said Bert, overwhelmed.

'I peg your pardon?'

'Jest a twinge,' said Bert, raising his hand to his bandaged head.

'Ah! Also I am instructed to say that as for that noble, unrightly accused laty you haf championed so brafely against Pritish hypocrisy and coldness, all ze chivalry of Chermany is on her site.'

'Lady?' said Bert faintly, and then recalled the great Butteridge love story. Had the old chap also read the letters? He must think him a scorcher if he had. 'Oh! that's awright,' he said, 'about 'er. I 'adn't any doubts about that. I – '

He stopped. The secretary certainly had a most appalling stare. It seemed ages before he looked down again. 'Well, ze laty as you please. She is your affair. I haf performt my instructions. And ze title of Paron, zat also can pe done. It can all pe done, Herr Pooterage.' He drummed on the table for a second or so, and resumed. 'I haf to tell you, sir, zat you come to us at a crisis in – Welt-Politik. There can be no harm now for me to put our plans before you. Pefore you leafe this ship again they will be manifest to all ze worldt. War is perhaps already declared. We go – to America. Our fleet will descend out of ze air upon ze United States – it is a country quite unprepared for war eferywhere – efery-where. Zey have always relied on ze Atlantic. And their navy. We have selected a certain point – it is at present ze secret of our commanders – which we shall seize, and zen we shall establish a depot – a sort of inland Gibraltar. It will be – what will it be? – an eagle's nest.[192] Zere our airships will gazzer and repair, and thence they will fly to and fro ofer ze United States, terrorising cities, dominating Washington, levying what is necessary, until ze terms we dictate are accepted. You follow me?'

'Go on!' said Bert.

'We could haf done all zis wiz such *Luftschiffe*[193] and *Drachenflieger* as we possess, but ze accession of your machine renders our project complete. It not only gifs us a better *drachenflieger*, but it remofes our last uneasiness as to Great Pritain. Wizout you, sir, Great Pritain, ze land you lofed so well and zat has requited you so ill, zat land of Pharisees and reptiles, can do nozzing! – nozzing! You see, I am perfectly frank wiz you. Well, I am instructed that Chermany recognises all this. We want you to place yourself at our disposal. We want you to become our Chief Head Flight Engineer. We want you to manufacture, we want to equip a swarm of hornets unter your direction. We want you to direct this force. And it is at our depot in America we want you. So we offer you simply, and without haggling, ze full terms you demanded weeks ago – one hundert tousand poundts in cash, a salary of three tousand poundts a year, a pension of one tousand poundts a year, and ze title of Paron as you desired. These are my instructions.'

He resumed his scrutiny of Bert's face.

'That's all right, of course,' said Bert, a little short of breath, but otherwise resolute and calm; and it seemed to him that now was the time to bring his nocturnal scheming to the issue.

The secretary contemplated Bert's collar with sustained attention. Only for one moment did his gaze move to the sandals and back.

'Jes' lemme think a bit,' said Bert, finding the stare debilitating. 'Look 'ere!' he said at last, with an air of great explicitness, 'I got the secret.'

'Yes.'

'But I don't want the name of Butteridge to appear – see? I been thinking that over.'

'A little delicacy?'

'Exactly. You buy the secret – leastways, I give it you – from Bearer – see?'

His voice failed him a little, and the stare continued. 'I want to do the thing Enonymously. See?'

Still staring. Bert drifted on like a swimmer caught by a current. 'Fact is, I'm going to edop' the name of Smallways. I don't want no title of Baron; I've altered my mind. And I want the money quiet-like. I want the hundred thousand pounds paid into benks – thirty thousand into the London and County Benk Branch at Bun Hill in Kent directly I 'and over the plans; twenty thousand into the Benk of England; 'arf the rest into a good French bank, the other 'arf the German National Bank, see? I want it put there, right away. I don't want it put in the name of Butteridge. I want it put in the name of Albert Peter Smallways; that's the name I'm going to edop'. That's condition one.'

'Go on!' said the secretary.

'The nex' condition,' said Bert, 'is that you don't make any enquiries as to title. I mean what English gentlemen do when they sell or let you land. You don't arst 'ow I got it. See? 'Ere I am – I deliver you the goods – that's all right. Some people 'ave the cheek to say this isn't my invention, see? It is, you know – that's all right; but I don't want that gone into. I want a fair and square agreement saying that's all right. See?'

His 'See?' faded into a profound silence.

The secretary sighed at last, leant back in his chair and produced a toothpick, and used it to assist his meditation on Bert's case. 'What was that name?' he asked at last, putting away the toothpick; 'I must write it down.'

'Albert Peter Smallways,' said Bert, in a mild tone.

The secretary wrote it down, after a little difficulty about the spelling because of the different names of the letters of the alphabet in the two languages.

'And now, Mr Schmallvays,' he said at last, leaning back and resuming the stare, 'tell me: how did you ket hold of Mister Pooterage's balloon?'

7

When at last the Graf von Winterfeld left Bert Smallways, he left him in an extremely deflated condition, with all his little story told.

He had, as people say, made a clean breast of it. He had been pursued into details. He had had to explain the blue suit, the sandals, the Desert Dervishes – everything. For a time scientific zeal consumed the secretary, and the question of the plans remained in suspense. He even went into speculation about the previous occupants of the balloon. 'I suppose,' he said, 'the laty *was* the laty. Bot that is not our affair.

'It is fery curious and amusing, yes: but I am afraid the Prince may be annoyt. He acted wiz his usual decision – always he acts wiz wonterful decision. Like Napoleon. Directly he was tolt of your descent into the camp at Dornhof, he said, "Pring him! – pring him! It is my schtar!" His schtar of Destiny! You see? He will be dthwarted. He directed you to come as Herr Pooterage, and you haf not done so. You haf triet, of course; but it has peen a poor try. His chugments of men are fery just and right, and it is better for men to act up to them – gompletely. Especially now. Barticularly now.'

He resumed that attitude of his, with his underlip pinched between his forefingers. He spoke almost confidentially. 'It will be awkward. I triet to suggest some doubt, but I was overruled. The Prince does not listen. He is impatient in the high air. Perhaps he will think his schtar has been making a fool of him. Perhaps he will think *I* haf been making a fool of him.' He wrinkled his forehead, and drew in the corners of his mouth.

'I got the plans,' said Bert.

'Yes. There is that! Yes. But you see the Prince was interested in Herr Pooterage because of his romantic seit. Herr Pooterage was so much more – ah! – in the picture. I am afraid you are not equal to controlling the flying-machine department of our aerial park as he wished you to do. He hadt promised himself that . . .

'And der was also the prestige – the worldt prestige of Pooterage with us . . . Well, we must see what we can do.' He held out his hand. 'Gif me the plans.'

A terrible chill ran through the being of Mr Smallways. To this day he is not clear in his mind whether he wept or no, but certainly there was weeping in his voice. ' 'Ere, I say!' he protested. 'Ain't I to 'ave – nothin' for 'em?'

The secretary regarded him with benevolent eyes. 'You do not deserve anyzing!' he said.

'I might 'ave tore 'em up.'

'Zey are not yours!'

'They weren't Butteridge's!'

'No need to pay anyzing.'

Bert's being seemed to tighten towards desperate deeds.

'Gaw!' he said, clutching his coat, '*ain't* there?'

'Pe galm,' said the secretary. 'Listen! You shall haf five hundert poundts. You shall haf it on my promise. I will do that for you, and that is all I can do. Take it from me. Gif me the name of that bank. Write it down. So! I tell you the Prince – is no choke. I do not think he approffed of your appearance last night. No! I can't answer for him. He wanted Pooterage, and you haf spoilt it. The Prince – I do not understand quite, he is in a strange state. It is the excitement of the starting and this great soaring in the air. I cannot account for what he does. But if all goes well I will see to it – you shall haf five hundert poundts. Will that do? Then gif me the plans.'

'Old beggar!' said Bert, as the door clicked. 'Gaw! – what an ole beggar! – *Sharp!*'

He sat down in the folding-chair, and whistled noiselessly for a time. 'Nice old swindle for 'im if I tore 'em up! I could 'ave.'

He rubbed the bridge of his nose thoughtfully. 'I gave the whole blessed show away. If I'd jes' kep quiet about being Enonymous . . .

Gaw! . . . Too soon, Bert, my boy – too soon and too rushy. I'd like to kick my silly self.

'I couldn't 'ave kep' it up.

'After all, it ain't so very bad,' he said.

'After all, five 'undred pounds . . . It isn't *my* secret, anyhow. It's jes' a pick-up on the road. Five 'undred.

'Wonder what the fare is from America back 'ome?'

8

And later in the day an extremely shattered and disorganised Bert Smallways stood in the presence of the Prince Karl Albert.

The proceedings were in German. The Prince was in his own cabin, the end room of the airship, a charming apartment furnished in wicker-work with a long window across its entire breadth, looking forward. He was sitting at a folding-table of green baize, with Von Winterfeld and two officers sitting beside him, and littered before them was a number of American maps and Mr Butteridge's letters and his portfolio and a number of loose papers. Bert was not asked to sit down, and remained standing throughout the interview. Von Winterfeld told his story, and every now and then the words Balloon and Pooterage struck on Bert's ears. The Prince's face remained stern and ominous and the two officers watched it cautiously or glanced at Bert. There was something a little strange in their scrutiny of the Prince – a curiosity, an apprehension. Then presently he was struck by an idea, and they fell discussing the plans. The Prince asked Bert abruptly in English. 'Did you ever see this thing go op?'

Bert jumped. 'Saw it from Bun 'Ill, your Royal Highness.'

Von Winterfeld made some explanation.

'How fast did it go?'

'Couldn't say, your Royal Highness. The papers, leastways the *Daily Courier*,[194] said eighty miles an hour.'

They talked German over that for a time.

'Couldt it standt still? Op in the air? That is what I want to know.'

'It could 'ovver, your Royal Highness, like a wasp,' said Bert.

'Viel besser, nicht wahr?'[195] said the Prince to Von Winterfeld, and then went on in German for a time.

Presently they came to an end, and the two officers looked at Bert. One rang a bell, and the portfolio was handed to an attendant, who took it away.

Then they reverted to the case of Bert, and it was evident the Prince was inclined to be hard with him. Von Winterfeld protested. Apparently theological considerations came in, for there were several mentions of 'Gott!' Some conclusions emerged, and it was apparent that Von Winterfeld was instructed to convey them to Bert.

'Mr Schmallvays, you haf obtained a footing in this airship,' he said, 'by disgraceful and systematic lying.'

' 'Ardly systematic,' said Bert. 'I – '

The Prince silenced him by a gesture.

'And it is within the power of his Highness to dispose of you as a spy.'

' 'Ere! – I came to sell – '

'Ssh!' said one of the officers.

'However, in consideration of the happy chance that mate you the instrument unter Gott of this Pooterage flying-machine reaching his Highness's hand, you haf been spared. Yes – you were the pearer of goot tidings. You will be allowed to remain on this ship until it is convenient to dispose of you. Do you understandt?'

'We will bring him,' said the Prince, and added terribly with a terrible glare, '*als Ballast*.'

'You are to come with us,' said Winterfeld, 'as – pallast. Do you understandt?'

Bert opened his mouth to ask about the five hundred pounds, and then a saving gleam of wisdom silenced him. He met Von Winterfeld's eye, and it seemed to him the secretary nodded slightly.

'Go!' said the Prince, with a sweep of the great arm and hand towards the door. Bert went out like a leaf before a gale.

9

But in between the time when the Graf von Winterfeld had talked to him and this alarming conference with the Prince, Bert had explored the *Vaterland* from end to end. He had found it interesting in spite of grave preoccupations. Kurt, like the greater number of the men upon the German air-fleet, had known hardly anything of aeronautics before his appointment to the new flagship. But he was extremely keen upon this wonderful new weapon Germany had assumed so suddenly and dramatically. He showed things to Bert with a boyish eagerness and appreciation. It was as if he showed them over again to himself, like a child showing a new toy. 'Let's go all over the ship,' he said with zest. He pointed out particularly the lightness of everything, the use of exhausted aluminium tubing, of springy cushions inflated with compressed hydrogen; the partitions were hydrogen bags covered with light imitation leather, the very crockery was a light biscuit glazed in a vacuum, and weighed next to nothing. Where strength was needed there was the new Charlottenburg alloy, German steel as it was called, the toughest and most resistant metal in the world.

There was no lack of space. Space did not matter, so long as load did not grow. The habitable part of the ship was two hundred and fifty feet long, and the rooms in two tiers; above these one could go up into remarkable little white-metal turrets with big windows and airtight double doors that enabled one to inspect the vast cavity of the gas chambers. This inside view impressed Bert very much. He had never realised before that an airship was not one simple continuous gasbag containing nothing but gas. Now he saw far above him the backbone of the apparatus and its big ribs, 'like the neural and haemal canals', said Kurt, who had dabbled in biology.

'Rather!' said Bert appreciatively, though he had not the ghost of an idea what these phrases meant.

Little electric lights could be switched on up there if anything went wrong in the night. There were even ladders across the space. 'But you can't go into the gas,' protested Bert. 'You can't breve it.'

The lieutenant opened a cupboard door and displayed a diver's suit, only that it was made of oiled silk, and both its compressed-air knapsack and its helmet were of an alloy of aluminium and some light metal. 'We can go all over the inside netting and stick up bullet holes or leaks,' he explained. 'There's netting inside and out. The whole outer-case is rope ladder, so to speak.'

Aft of the habitable part of the airship was the magazine of explosives, coming near the middle of its length. They were all bombs of various types – mostly in glass – none of the German airships carried any guns at all except one small pom-pom (to use the old English nickname dating from the Boer War), which was forward in the gallery upon the shield at the heart of the eagle. From the magazine amidships a covered canvas gallery with aluminium treads on its floor and a hand-rope, ran back underneath the gas chamber to the engine-room at the tail; but along this Bert did not go, and from first to last he never saw the engines. But he went up a ladder against a gale of ventilation – a ladder that was encased in a kind of gas-tight fire escape – and ran right athwart the great forward air chamber to the little look-out gallery with a telephone, that gallery that bore the light pom-pom of German steel and its locker of shells. This gallery was all of aluminium-magnesium alloy, the tight front of the airship swelled cliff-like above and below, and the black eagle sprawled overwhelmingly gigantic, its extremities all hidden by the bulge of the gasbag.

And far down, under the soaring eagles, was England, four thousand feet below perhaps, and looking very small and defenceless indeed in the morning sunlight.

The realisation that there was England gave Bert sudden and un-expected qualms of patriotic compunction. He was struck by a quite novel idea. After all, he might have torn up those plans and thrown them away. These people could not have done so very much to him. And even if they did, ought not an Englishman to die for his country? It was an idea that had hitherto been rather smothered up by the cares of a competitive civilisation. He became violently depressed. He ought, he perceived, to have seen it in that light before. Why hadn't he seen it in that light before?

Indeed, wasn't he a sort of traitor?

He wondered how the aerial fleet must look from down there. Tremendous, no doubt, and dwarfing all the buildings.

He was passing between Manchester and Liverpool, Kurt told him; a gleaming band across the prospect was the Ship Canal,[196] and a weltering ditch of shipping far away ahead, the Mersey estuary. Bert was a southerner; he had never been north of the Midland counties, and the multitude of factories and chimneys – the latter for the most part obsolete and smokeless now, superseded by huge electric generating stations that consumed their own reek – old railway viaducts, monorail networks and goods yards, and the vast areas of dingy homes and narrow streets, spreading aimlessly, struck him as though Camberwell and Rotherhithe had run to seed. Here and there, as if caught in a net, were fields and agricultural fragments. It was a sprawl of undistinguished population. There were, no doubt, museums and town halls and even cathedrals of a sort to mark theoretical centres of municipal and religious organisation in this confusion; but Bert could not see them, they did not stand out at all in that wide disorderly vision of congested workers' houses and places to work, and shops and meanly conceived chapels and churches. And across this landscape of an industrial civilisation swept the shadows of the German airships like a hurrying shoal of fishes.

Kurt and he fell talking of aerial tactics, and presently went down to the under-gallery in order that Bert might see the *drachenflieger* that the airships of the right wing had picked up overnight and were towing behind them; each airship towing three or four. They looked like big box-kites of an exaggerated form, soaring at the ends of invisible cords. They had long, square heads and flattened tails, with lateral propellers.

'Much skill is required for those! – much skill!'

'Rather!'

Pause.

'Your machine is different from that, Mr Butteridge?'

'Quite different,' said Bert. 'More like an insect, and less like a bird. And it buzzes, and don't drive about so. What can those things do?'

Kurt was not very clear upon that himself, and was still explaining when Bert was called to the conference we have recorded with the Prince.

And after that was over, the last traces of Butteridge fell from Bert like a garment, and he became Smallways to all on board. The soldiers ceased to salute him, and the officers ceased to seem aware of his existence, except Lieutenant Kurt. He was turned out of his nice cabin, and packed in with his belongings to share that of Lieutenant Kurt, whose luck it was to be junior, and the bird-headed officer, still swearing slightly, and carrying strops and aluminium boot-trees and weightless hairbrushes and hand-mirrors and pomade in his hands, resumed possession. Bert was put in with Kurt because there was nowhere else for him to lay his bandaged head in that close-packed vessel. He was to mess, he was told, with the men.

Kurt came and stood with his legs wide apart and surveyed him for a moment as he sat despondent in his new quarters.

'What's your real name, then?' said Kurt, who was only imperfectly informed of the new state of affairs.

'Smallways.'

'I thought you were a bit of a fraud – even when I thought you were Butteridge. You're jolly lucky the Prince took it calmly. He's a pretty tidy blazer when he's roused. He wouldn't stick a moment at pitching a chap of your sort overboard if he thought fit. No! . . . . They've shoved you on to me, but it's my cabin, you know.'

'I won't forget,' said Bert.

Kurt left him, and when he came to look about him the first thing he saw pasted on the padded wall was a reproduction of the great picture by Siegfried Schmalz[197] of the War God, that terrible, trampling figure with the viking helmet and the scarlet cloak, wading through destruction, sword in hand, which had so strong a resemblance to Karl Albert, the prince it was painted to please.

CHAPTER FIVE

The Battle of the North Atlantic

1

The Prince Karl Albert had made a profound impression upon Bert. He was quite the most terrifying person Bert had ever encountered. He filled the Smallways soul with passionate dread and antipathy. For a long time Bert sat alone in Kurt's cabin, doing nothing and not venturing even to open the door lest he should be by so much nearer that appalling presence.

So it came about that he was probably the last person on board to hear the news that wireless telegraphy was bringing to the airship in throbs and fragments of a great naval battle in progress in mid-Atlantic.

He learnt it at last from Kurt.

Kurt came in with a general air of ignoring Bert, but muttering to himself in English nevertheless. 'Stupendous!' Bert heard him say. 'Here!' he said, 'get off this locker.' And he proceeded to rout out two books and a case of maps. He spread them on the folding-table, and stood regarding them. For a time his Germanic discipline struggled with his English informality and his natural kindliness and talkativeness, and at last lost.

'They're at it, Smallways,' he said.

'At what, sir?' said Bert, broken and respectful.

'Fighting! The American North Atlantic squadron and pretty nearly the whole of our fleet. Our *Eiserne Kreuz*[198] has had a gruelling and is sinking, and their *Miles Standish*[199] – she's one of their biggest – has sunk with all hands. Torpedoes, I suppose. She was a bigger ship than the *Karl der Grosse*,[200] but five or six years older . . . Gods! I wish we could see it, Smallways; a square fight in blue water, guns or nothing, and all of 'em steaming ahead!'

He spread his maps, he had to talk, and so he delivered a lecture on the naval situation to Bert.

'Here it is,' he said, 'latitude 30° 50' N., longitude 30° 50' W.[201] It's a good day off us, anyhow, and they're all going south-west by south at full pelt as hard as they can go. We shan't see a bit of it, worse luck! Not a sniff we shan't get!'

The naval situation in the North Atlantic at that time was a peculiar one. The United States was by far the stronger of the two powers upon the sea, but the bulk of the American fleet was still in the Pacific. It was in the direction of Asia that war had been most feared, for the situation between Asiatic and white had become unusually violent and dangerous, and the Japanese government had shown itself quite unprecedentedly difficult. The German attack therefore found half the American strength at Manila, and what was called the Second Fleet strung out across the Pacific in wireless contact between the Asiatic station and San Francisco. The North Atlantic Squadron was the sole American force on her eastern shore; it was returning from a friendly visit to France and Spain, and was pumping oil-fuel from tenders in mid-Atlantic – for most of its ships were steamships – when the international situation became acute. It was made up of four battleships and five armoured cruisers, ranking almost with battleships, not one of which was of a later date than 1913. The Americans had indeed grown so accustomed to the idea that Great Britain could be trusted to keep the peace of the Atlantic that a naval attack on the eastern seaboard found them unprepared even in their imaginations. But long before the declaration of war – indeed, on Whit Monday – the whole German fleet of eighteen battleships, with a flotilla of fuel tenders and converted liners containing stores to be used in support of the air-fleet, had passed through the straits of Dover and headed boldly for New York. Not only did these German battleships outnumber the Americans two to one, but they were more heavily armed and more modern in construction – seven of them having high explosive engines built of Charlottenburg steel,[202] and all carrying Charlottenburg steel guns.

The fleets came into contact on Wednesday before any actual declaration of war. The Americans had strung out in the modern fashion at distances of thirty miles or so, and were steaming to keep themselves between the Germans and either the eastern states or Panama; because, vital as it was to defend the seaboard cities and particularly New York, it was still more vital to save the canal from any attack that might prevent the return of the main fleet from the Pacific. No doubt, said Kurt, this was now making records across that ocean, 'unless the Japanese have had the same idea as the Germans'. It was obviously beyond human possibility that the American North Atlantic fleet could hope to meet and defeat the German; but, on the other hand, with luck it might fight a delaying action and inflict such damage as to greatly weaken the attack upon the coast defences. Its duty, indeed, was not victory but devotion, the severest task in the world. Meanwhile the submarine defences of New York, Panama, and the other more vital points could be put in some sort of order.

This was the naval situation, and until Wednesday in Whit week it was the only situation the American people had realised. It was then they heard for the first time of the real scale of the Dornhof aeronautic park and the possibility of an attack coming upon them not only by sea, but by the air. But it is curious that so discredited were the newspapers of that period that a large majority of New Yorkers, for example, did not believe the most copious and circumstantial accounts of the German air-fleet until it was actually in sight of New York.

Kurt's talk was half soliloquy. He stood with a map on Mercator's projection before him, swaying to the swinging of the ship and talking of guns and tonnage, of ships and their build and powers and speed, of strategic points, and bases of operation. A certain shyness that reduced him to the status of a listener at the officers' table no longer silenced him.

Bert stood by, saying very little, but watching Kurt's finger on the map. 'They've been saying things like this in the papers for a long time,' he remarked. 'Fancy it coming real!'

Kurt had a detailed knowledge of the *Miles Standish*. 'She used to be a crack ship for gunnery – held the record. I wonder if we beat her shooting, or how? I wish I was in it. I wonder which of our ships beat her. Maybe she got a shell in her engines. It's a running fight! I wonder what the *Barbarossa*[203] is doing,' he went on. 'She's my old ship. Not a first-rater, but good stuff. I bet she's got a shot or two home by now if old Schneider's up to form. Just think of it! There they are whacking away at each other, great guns going, shells exploding, magazines bursting, ironwork flying about like straw in a gale, all we've been dreaming of for years! I suppose we shall fly right away to New York – just as though it wasn't anything at all. I suppose we shall reckon we aren't wanted down there. It's no more than a covering fight on our side. All those tenders and store-ships of ours are going on south-west by west to New York to make a floating depot for us. See?' He dabbed his forefinger on the map. 'Here we are. Our train of stores goes there, our battleships elbow the Americans out of our way there.'

When Bert went down to the men's mess-room to get his evening ration, hardly anyone took notice of him except just to point him out for an instant. Everyone was talking of the battle, suggesting, contradicting – at times, until the petty officers hushed them, it rose to a great uproar. There was a news bulletin, but what it said he did not gather except that it concerned the *Barbarossa*. Some of the men stared at him, and he heard the name of 'Booteraidge' several times; but no one molested him, and there was no difficulty about his soup and bread when his turn at the end of the queue came. He had feared there might be no ration for him, and if so he did not know what he would have done.

Afterwards he ventured out upon the little hanging gallery with the solitary sentinel. The weather was still fine, but the wind was rising and the rolling swing of the airship increasing. He clutched the rail tightly and felt rather giddy. They were now out of sight of land, and over blue water rising and falling in great masses. A dingy old brigantine under the British flag rose and plunged amid the broad blue waves – the only ship in sight.

3

In the evening it began to blow and the airship to roll like a porpoise as it swung through the air. Kurt said that several of the men were seasick, but the motion did not inconvenience Bert, whose luck it was to be of that mysterious gastric disposition which constitutes a good sailor. He slept well, but in the small hours the light awoke him, and he found Kurt staggering about in search of something. He found it at last in the locker, and held it in his hand unsteadily – a compass. Then he compared his map.

'We've changed our direction,' he said, 'and come into the wind. I can't make it out. We've turned away from New York to the south. Almost as if we were going to take a hand – '

He continued talking to himself for some time.

Day came, wet and windy. The window was bedewed externally, and they could see nothing through it. It was also very cold, and Bert decided to keep rolled up in his blankets on the locker until the bugle summoned him to his morning ration. That consumed, he went out on the little gallery; but he could see nothing but eddying clouds driving headlong by, and the dim outlines of the nearer airships. Only at rare intervals could he get a glimpse of grey sea through the pouring cloud-drift.

Later in the morning the *Vaterland* changed altitude, and soared up suddenly in a high, clear sky, going, Kurt said, to a height of nearly thirteen thousand feet.

Bert was in his cabin, and chanced to see the dew vanish from the window and caught the gleam of sunlight outside. He looked out, and saw once more that sunlit cloud floor he had seen first from the balloon, and the ships of the German air-fleet rising one by one from the white, as fish might rise and become visible from deep water. He stared for a moment and then ran out to the little gallery to see this wonder better. Below was cloudland and storm, a great drift of tumbled weather going hard away to the north-east, and the air about him was clear and cold and serene save for the faintest chill breeze and a rare, drifting snow-flake. Throb, throb, throb, throb, went the engines in the stillness. That huge herd of airships rising one after another had an effect of strange, portentous monsters breaking into an altogether unfamiliar world.

Either there was no news of the naval battle that morning, or the Prince kept to himself whatever came until past midday. Then the bulletins came with a rush, bulletins that made the lieutenant wild with excitement.

'*Barbarossa* disabled and sinking,' he cried. 'Gott im Himmel! Der alte *Barbarossa*! Aber welch ein braver krieger!'

He walked about the swinging cabin, and for a time he was wholly German.

Then he became English again. 'Think of it, Smallways! The old ship we kept so clean and tidy! All smashed about, and the iron flying about in fragments, and the chaps one knew – *Gott!* – flying about too! Scalding water squirting, fire, and the smash, smash of the guns! They smash when you're near! Like everything bursting to pieces! Wool won't stop it – nothing! And me up here – so near and so far! *Der alte Barbarossa!*'

'Any other ships?' asked Smallways, presently.

'*Gott!* Yes! We've lost the *Karl der Grosse*, our best and biggest. Run down in the night by a British liner that blundered into the fighting – in trying to blunder out. They're fighting in a gale. The liner's afloat with her nose broken, sagging about! There never was such a battle! – never before! Good ships and good men on both sides – and a storm and the night and the dawn and all in the open ocean full steam ahead! No stabbing! No submarines! Guns and shooting! Half our ships we don't hear of any more, because their masts are shot away. Latitude, 30° 38' N., longitude, 40° 31' W. – where's that?'

He routed out his map again, and stared at it with eyes that did not see.

'Der alte Barbarossa! I can't get it out of my head – with shells in her engine-room, and the fires flying out of her furnaces, and the stokers and engineers scalded and dead. Men I've messed with, Smallways –

men I've talked to close! And they've had their day at last! And it wasn't all luck for them!

'Disabled and sinking! I suppose everybody can't have all the luck in a battle. Poor old Schneider! I bet he gave 'em something back!'

So it was the news of the battle came filtering through to them all that morning. The Americans had lost a second ship, name unknown; the *Hermann* had been damaged in covering the *Barbarossa* . . . Kurt fretted like an imprisoned animal about the airship, now going up to the forward gallery under the eagle, now down into the swinging gallery, now poring over his maps. He infected Smallways with a sense of the immediacy of this battle that was going on just over the curve of the earth. But when Bert went down to the gallery the world was empty and still, a clear inky-blue sky above and a rippled veil of still, thin sunlit cirrus below, through which one saw a racing drift of rain-cloud, and never a glimpse of sea. Throb, throb, throb, throb, went the engines, and the long, undulating wedge of airships hurried after the flagship like a flight of swans after their leader. Save for the quiver of the engines it was as noiseless as a dream. And down there, somewhere in the wind and rain, guns roared, shells crashed home, and, after the old manner of warfare, men toiled and died.

4

As the afternoon wore on the lower weather abated, and the sea became intermittently visible again. The air-fleet dropped slowly to the middle air, and towards sunset they had a glimpse of the disabled *Barbarossa* far away to the east. Smallways heard men hurrying along the passage, and was drawn out to the gallery, where he found nearly a dozen officers collected and scrutinising the helpless ruins of the battleship through field-glasses. Two other vessels stood by her, one an exhausted petrol tanker, very high out of the water, and the other a converted liner. Kurt was at the end of the gallery, a little apart from the others.

"Gott!' he said at last, lowering his binoculars, 'it is like seeing an old friend with his nose cut off – waiting to be finished. Der *Barbarossa*!'

With a sudden impulse he handed his glass to Bert, who had peered beneath his hands, ignored by everyone, seeing the three ships merely as three brown-black lines upon the sea.

Never had Bert seen the like of that magnified slightly hazy image before. It was not simply a battered ironclad that wallowed helpless, it was a mangled ironclad. It seemed wonderful she still floated. Her powerful engines had been her ruin. In the long chase of the night she had got out of line with her consorts, and nipped in between the *Susquehanna* [204] and the *Kansas City*. They discovered her proximity, dropped back until she was nearly broadside on to the former battleship, and signalled up the *Theodore Roosevelt* [205] and the little *Monitor*. As dawn broke she had found herself hostess of a circle. The fight had not lasted five minutes before the appearance of the *Hermann* to the east, and immediately after of the *Fürst Bismarck* [206] in the west, forced the Americans to leave her, but in that time they had smashed her iron to rags. They had vented the accumulated tensions of their hard day's retreat upon her. As Bert saw her, she seemed a mere metalworker's fantasy of frozen metal writhings. He could not tell part from part of her, except by its position.

'Gott!' murmured Kurt, taking the glasses Bert restored to him – 'Gott! Da waren Albrecht – der gute Albrecht und der alte Zimmermann – und von Rosen!' [207]

Long after the *Barbarosa* had been swallowed up in the twilight and distance he remained on the gallery peering through his glasses, and when he came back to his cabin he was unusually silent and thoughtful.

'This is a rough game, Smallways,' he said at last – 'this war is a rough game. Somehow one sees it different after a thing like that. Many men there were worked to make that *Barbarossa*, and there were men in it – one does not meet the like of them every day. Albrecht – there was a man named Albrecht – played the zither and improvised; I keep on wondering what has happened to him. He and I – we were very close friends, after the German fashion.'

5

Smallways woke the next night to discover the cabin in darkness, a draught blowing through it, and Kurt talking to himself in German. He could see him dimly by the window, which he had unscrewed and opened, peering down. That cold, clear, attenuated light which is not so much light as a going of darkness, which casts inky shadows and so often heralds the dawn in the high air, was on his face.

'What's the row?' said Bert.

'Shut up!' said the lieutenant. 'Can't you hear?'

Into the stillness came the repeated heavy thud of guns, one, two, a pause, then three in quick succession.

'Gaw!' said Bert – 'guns!' and was instantly at the lieutenant's side.

The airship was still very high and the sea below was masked by a thin veil of clouds. The wind had fallen, and Bert, following Kurt's pointing finger, saw dimly through the colourless veil first a red glow, then a quick red flash, and then at a little distance from it another. They were, it seemed for a while, silent flashes, and seconds after, when one had ceased to expect them, came the belated thuds – thud, thud. Kurt spoke in German, very quickly.

A bugle call rang through the airship.

Kurt sprang to his feet, saying something in an excited tone, still using German, and went to the door.

'I say! What's up?' cried Bert. 'What's that?'

The lieutenant stopped for an instant in the doorway, dark against the light passage. 'You stay where you are, Smallways. You keep there and do nothing. We're going into action,' he explained, and vanished.

Bert's heart began to beat rapidly. He felt himself poised over the fighting vessels far below. In a moment, were they to drop like a hawk striking a bird? 'Gaw!' he whispered at last, in awe-stricken tones.

Thud! . . . thud! He discovered far away a second ruddy flare flashing guns back at the first. He perceived some difference on the *Vaterland* for which he could not account, and then he realised that the engines had slowed to an almost inaudible beat. He stuck his head out of the window – it was a tight fit – and saw in the bleak air the other airships slowed down to a scarcely perceptible motion.

A second bugle sounded, was taken up faintly from ship to ship. Out went the lights; the fleet became dim, dark bulks against an intense blue sky that still retained an occasional star. For a long time they hung, for an interminable time it seemed to him, and then began the sound of air being pumped into the balloonette, and slowly, slowly the *Vaterland* sank down towards the clouds.

He craned his neck, but he could not see if the rest of the fleet was following them; the overhang of the gas chambers intervened. There was something that stirred his imagination deeply in that stealthy, noiseless descent.

The obscurity deepened for a time, the last fading star on the horizon vanished, and he felt the cold presence of cloud. Then suddenly the glow beneath assumed distinct outlines, became flames, and the *Vaterland* ceased to descend and hung observant, and it would seem unobserved, just beneath a drifting stratum of cloud, a thousand feet, perhaps, over the battle below.

In the night the struggling naval battle and retreat had entered upon a new phase. The Americans had drawn together the ends of the flying line skilfully and dexterously, until at last it was a column and well to the south of the lax sweeping pursuit of the Germans. Then in the darkness before the dawn they had come about and steamed northward in close order with the idea of passing through the German battle-line and falling upon the flotilla that was making for New York in support of the German air-fleet. Much had altered since the first contact of the fleets. By this time the American admiral, O'Connor, was fully informed of the existence of the airships, and he was no longer vitally concerned for Panama, since the submarine flotilla was reported arrived there from Key West, and the *Delaware* and *Abraham Lincoln*, two powerful and entirely modern ships, were already at Rio Grande, on the Pacific side of the canal. His manoeuvre was, however, delayed by a boiler explosion on board the *Susquehanna*, and dawn found this ship in sight of and indeed so close to the *Bremen* and *Weimar* that they instantly engaged. There was no alternative to her abandonment but a fleet engagement. O'Connor chose the latter course. It was by no means a hopeless fight. The Germans, though much more numerous and powerful than the Americans, were in a dispersed line measuring nearly forty-five miles from end to end, and there were many chances that before they could gather in for the fight the column of seven Americans would have ripped them from end to end.

The day broke dim and overcast, and neither the *Bremen* nor the *Weimar* realised they had to deal with more than the *Susquehanna* until the whole column drew out from behind her at a distance of a mile or less and bore down on them. This was the position of affairs when the *Vaterland* appeared in the sky. The red glow Bert had seen through the column of clouds came from the luckless *Susquehanna*; she lay almost immediately below, burning fore and aft, but still fighting two of her guns and steaming slowly southwards. The *Bremen* and the *Weimar*, both hit in several places, were going west by south and away from her. The American fleet, headed by the *Theodore Roosevelt*, was crossing behind them, pounding them in succession, steaming in between them and the big modern *Fürst Bismarck*, which was coming up from the west. To Bert, however, the names of all these ships were unknown, and for a considerable time indeed, misled by the direction in which the combatants were moving, he imagined the Germans to be Americans and the Americans Germans. He saw what appeared to him to be a column of six battleships pursuing three others who were supported by a newcomer, until the fact that the *Bremen* and *Weimar* were firing into the *Susquehanna* upset his calculations. Then for a time he was hopelessly at a loss. The noise of the guns, too, confused him, they no longer seemed to boom; they went whack, whack, whack, whack, and each faint flash made his heart jump in anticipation of the instant impact. He saw these ironclads, too, not in profile, as he was accustomed to see ironclads in pictures, but in plan and curiously foreshortened. For the most part they presented empty decks, but here and there little knots of men sheltered behind steel bulwarks. The long, agitated noses of their big guns, jetting thin transparent flashes and the broadside activity of the quick-firers, were the chief facts in this bird's-eye view. The Americans being steam-turbine ships, had from two to four blast funnels each; the Germans lay lower in the water, having explosive engines, which now for some reason made an unwonted muttering roar. Because of their steam propulsion, the American ships were larger and with a more graceful outline. He saw all these foreshortened ships rolling considerably and fighting their guns over a sea of huge low waves and under the cold, explicit light of dawn. The whole spectacle waved slowly with the long, rhythmic rising and beat of the airship.

At first only the *Vaterland* of all the flying fleet appeared upon the scene below. She hovered high, over the *Theodore Roosevelt*, keeping pace with the full speed of that ship. From that ship she must have been intermittently visible through the drifting clouds. The rest of the German fleet remained above the cloud canopy at a height of six or seven thousand feet, communicating with the flagship by wireless telegraphy, but risking no exposure to the artillery below.

It is doubtful at what particular time the unlucky Americans realised the presence of this new factor in the fight. No account now survives of their experience. We have to imagine as well as we can what it must have been to a battled-strained sailor suddenly glancing upward to discover that huge long silent shape overhead, vaster than any battleship, and trailing now from its hinder quarter a big German flag. Presently, as the sky cleared, more of such ships appeared in the blue through the dissolving clouds, and more, all disdainfully free of guns or armour, all flying fast to keep pace with the running fight below.

From first to last no gun whatever was fired at the *Vaterland*, and only a few rifle shots. It was a mere adverse stroke of chance that she had a man killed aboard her. Nor did she take any direct share in the fight until the end. She flew above the doomed American fleet while the Prince by wireless telegraphy directed the movements of her consorts. Meanwhile the *Vogelstern* and *Preussen*,[208] each with half a dozen *drachen-flieger* in tow, went full speed ahead and then dropped through the clouds, perhaps five miles ahead of the Americans. The *Theodore Roosevelt* let fly at once with the big guns in her forward barbette, but the shells burst far below the *Vogelstern*, and forthwith a dozen single-man *drachenflieger* were swooping down to make their attack.

Bert, craning his neck through the cabin porthole, saw the whole of that incident, that first encounter of aeroplane and ironclad. He saw the queer German *drachenflieger*, with their wide, flat wings and square, box-shaped heads, their wheeled bodies, and their single-man riders, soar down the air like a flight of birds. 'Gaw!' he said. One to the right pitched extravagantly, shot steeply up into the air, burst with a loud report, and flamed down into the sea; another plunged nose forward into the water and seemed to fly to pieces as it hit the waves. He saw little men on the deck of the *Theodore Roosevelt* below, men foreshortened in plan into mere heads and feet, running out preparing to shoot at the others. Then the foremost flying-machine was rushing between Bert and the American's deck, and then bang! came the thunder of its bomb flung neatly at the forward barbette, and a thin little crackling of rifle shots in reply. Whack, whack, whack, went the quick-firing guns of the Americans' battery, and smash came an answering shell from the *Fürst Bismarck*. Then a second and third flying-machine passed between Bert and the American ironclad, dropping bombs also, and a fourth, its rider hit by a bullet, reeled down and dashed itself to pieces and exploded between the shot-torn funnels, blowing them apart. Bert had a momentary glimpse of a little black creature jumping from the crumpling frame of the flying-machine, hitting the funnel, and falling limply, to be instantly caught and driven to nothingness by the blaze and rush of the explosion.

Smash! came a vast explosion in the forward part of the flagship, and a huge piece of metalwork seemed to lift out of her and dump itself into the sea, dropping men and leaving a gap into which a prompt *drachenflieger* planted a flaring bomb. And then for an instant Bert perceived only too clearly in the growing, pitiless light a number of minute, convulsively active animalculae scorched and struggling in the *Theodore Roosevelt*'s foaming wake. What were they? Not men – surely not men? Those drowning, mangled little creatures tore with their clutching fingers at Bert's soul. 'Oh, Gord!' he cried, 'Oh, Gord!' almost whimpering. He looked again and they had gone, and the black stem of the *Andrew Jackson*, a little disfigured by the sinking *Bremen*'s last shot, was parting the water that had swallowed them into two neatly symmetrical waves. For some moments sheer blank horror blinded Bert to the destruction below.

Then, with an immense rushing sound, bearing as it were a straggling volley of crashing minor explosions on its back, the *Susquehanna*, three miles and more now to the east, blew up and vanished abruptly in a boiling, steaming welter. For a moment nothing was to be seen but tumbled water, and then there came belching up from below, with immense gulping noises, eructations of steam and air and petrol and fragments of canvas and woodwork and men.

That made a distinct pause in the fight. It seemed a long pause to Bert. He found himself looking for the *drachenflieger*. The flattened ruin of one was floating abeam of the *Monitor*, the rest had passed, dropping bombs down the American column; several were in the water and apparently uninjured, and three or four were still in the air and coming round now in a wide circle to return to their mother airships. The American ironclads were no longer in column formation; the *Theodore Roosevelt*, badly damaged, had turned to the south-east, and the *Andrew Jackson*, greatly battered but uninjured in any fighting part, was passing between her and the still fresh and vigorous *Fürst Bismarck* to intercept and meet the latter's fire. Away to the west the *Hermann* and the *Germanicus* had appeared and were coming into action.

In the pause, after the *Susquehanna*'s disaster, Bert became aware of a trivial sound like the noise of an ill-greased, ill-hung door that falls ajar – the sound of the men in the *Fürst Bismarck* cheering.

And in that pause in the uproar, too, the sun rose, the dark waters became luminously blue, and a torrent of golden light irradiated the world. It came like a sudden smile in a scene of hate and terror. The cloud veil had vanished as if by magic, and the whole immensity of the German air-fleet was revealed in the sky; the air-fleet stooping now upon its prey.

'Whack-bang, whack-bang,' the guns resumed, but ironclads were not built to fight the zenith, and the only hits the Americans scored were a few lucky chances in a generally ineffectual rifle fire. Their column was now badly broken, the *Susquehanna* had gone, the *Theodore Roosevelt* had fallen astern out of the line, with her forward guns disabled, in a heap of wreckage, and the *Monitor* was in some grave trouble. These two had ceased fire altogether, and so had the *Bremen* and *Weimar*, all four ships lying within shot of each other in an involuntary truce and with their respective flags still displayed. Only four American ships now, with the *Andrew Jackson* leading, kept to the south-easterly course. And the *Fürst Bismarck*, the *Hermann*, and the *Germanicus* steamed parallel to them and drew ahead of them, fighting heavily. The *Vaterland* rose slowly in the air in preparation for the concluding act of the drama.

Then, falling into place one behind the other, a string of a dozen airships dropped with unhurrying swiftness down the air in pursuit of the American fleet. They kept at a height of two thousand feet or more until they were over and a little in advance of the rearmost ironclad, and then stooped swiftly down into a fountain of bullets, and going just a little faster than the ship below, pelted her thinly protected decks with bombs until they became sheets of detonating flame. So the airships passed one after the other along the American column as it sought to keep up its fight with the *Fürst Bismarck*, the *Hermann*, and the *Germanicus*, and each airship added to the destruction and confusion its predecessor had made. The American gunfire ceased, except for a few heroic shots, but they still steamed on, obstinately unsubdued, bloody, battered, and wrathfully resistant, spitting bullets at the airships and unmercifully pounded by the German ironclads. But now Bert had but intermittent glimpses of them between the nearer bulks of the airships that assailed them . . .

It struck Bert suddenly that the whole battle was receding and growing small and less thunderously noisy. The *Vaterland* was rising in the air, steadily and silently, until the impact of the guns no longer smote upon the heart but came to the ear dulled by distance, until the four silenced ships to the eastward were little distant things: but were there four? Bert now could see only three of those floating, blackened, and smoking rafts of ruin against the sun. But the *Bremen* had two boats out; the *Theodore Roosevelt* was also dropping boats to where the drift of minute objects struggled, rising and falling on the big, broad Atlantic waves . . . The *Vaterland* was no longer following the fight. The whole of that hurrying tumult drove away to the south-eastward, growing smaller and less audible as it passed. One of the airships lay on the water burning, a remote monstrous fount of flames, and far in the south-west appeared first one and then three other German iron-clads hurrying in support of their consorts . . .

6

Steadily the *Vaterland* soared, and the air-fleet soared with her and came round to head for New York, and the battle became a little thing far away, an incident before breakfast. It dwindled to a string of dark shapes and one smoking yellow flare that presently became a mere indistinct smear upon the vast horizon and the bright new day, that was at last altogether lost to sight . . .

So it was that Bert Smallways saw the first fight of the airship and the last fight of those strangest things in the whole history of war: the ironclad battleships, which began their career with the floating batteries of the Emperor Napoleon III in the Crimean War[209] and lasted, with an enormous expenditure of human energy and resources, for seventy years. In that space of time the world produced over twelve thousand five hundred of these strange monsters, in schools, in types, in series, each larger and heavier and more deadly than its predecessors. Each in its turn was hailed as the last birth of time, most in their turn were sold for old iron. Only about five per cent of them ever fought in a battle. Some foundered, some went ashore, and broke up, several rammed one another by accident and sank. The lives of countless men were spent in their service, the splendid genius and patience of thousands of engineers and inventors, wealth and material beyond estimating; to their account we must put stunted and starved lives on land, millions of children sent to toil unduly, innumerable opportunities of fine living undeveloped and lost. Money had to be found for them at any cost – that was the law of a nation's existence during that strange time. Surely they were the weirdest, most destructive and wasteful megatheria in the whole history of mechanical invention.

And then cheap things of gas and basketwork made an end of them altogether, smiting out of the sky! . . .

Never before had Bert Smallways seen pure destruction, never had he realised the mischief and waste of war. His startled mind rose to the conception; this also is in life. Out of all this fierce torrent of sensation one impression rose and became cardinal – the impression of the men of the *Theodore Roosevelt* who had struggled in the water after the explosion of the first bomb. 'Gaw!' he said at the memory; 'it might 'ave been me and Grubb! . . . I suppose you kick about and get the water in your mouf. I don't suppose it lasts long.'

He became anxious to see how Kurt was affected by these things. Also he perceived he was hungry. He hesitated towards the door of the cabin and peeped out into the passage. Down forward, near the gangway to the men's mess, stood a little group of air sailors looking at something that was hidden from him in a recess. One of them was in the light diver's costume Bert had already seen in the gas chamber turret, and he was moved to walk along and look at this person more closely and examine the helmet he carried under his arm. But he forgot about the helmet when he got to the recess, because there he found lying on the floor the dead body of the boy who had been killed by a bullet from the *Theodore Roosevelt*.

Bert had not observed that any bullets at all had reached the *Vaterland* or, indeed, imagined himself under fire. He could not understand for a time what had killed the lad, and no one explained to him.

The boy lay just as he had fallen and died, with his jacket torn and scorched, his shoulder-blade smashed and burst away from his body and all the left side of his body ripped and rent. There was much blood. The sailors stood listening to the man with the helmet, who made explanations and pointed to the round bullet hole in the floor and the smash in the panel of the passage upon which the still vicious missile had spent the residue of its energy. All the faces were grave and earnest: they were the faces of sober, blond, blue-eyed men accustomed to obedience and an orderly life, to whom this waste, wet, painful thing that had been a comrade came almost as strangely as it did to Bert.

A peal of wild laughter sounded down the passage in the direction of the little gallery and something spoke – almost shouted – in German, in tones of exultation.

Other voices at a lower, more respectful pitch replied.

'*Der Prinz*,' said a voice, and all the men became stiffer and less natural. Down the passage appeared a group of figures, Lieutenant Kurt walking in front carrying a packet of papers.

He stopped point blank when he saw the thing in the recess, and his ruddy face went white. 'So!' said he in surprise.

The Prince was following him, talking over his shoulder to Von Winterfeld and the Kapitän. 'Eh?' he said to Kurt, stopping in mid-sentence, and followed the gesture of Kurt's hand. He glared at the crumpled object in the recess and seemed to think for a moment.

He made a slight, careless gesture towards the boy's body and turned to the Kapitän.

'Dispose of that,' he said in German, and passed on, finishing his sentence to Von Winterfeld in the same cheerful tone in which it had begun.

7

The deep impression of helplessly drowning men that Bert had brought from the actual fight in the Atlantic mixed itself up inextricably with that of the lordly figure of Prince Karl Albert gesturing aside the dead body of the *Vaterland* sailor. Hitherto he had rather liked the idea of war as being a jolly, smashing, exciting affair, something like a Bank Holiday rag on a large scale, and on the whole agreeable and exhilarating. Now he knew it a little better.

The next day there was added to his growing disillusionment a third ugly impression, trivial indeed to describe, a mere necessary everyday incident of a state of war, but very distressing to his urbanised imagination. One writes 'urbanised' to express the distinctive gentleness of the period. It was quite peculiar to the crowded townsmen of that time, and different altogether from the normal experience of any preceding age, that they never saw anything killed, never encountered, save through the mitigating media of book or picture, the fact of lethal violence that underlies all life. Three times in his existence, and three times only, had Bert seen a dead human being, and he had never assisted at the killing of anything bigger than a new-born kitten.

The incident that gave him his third shock was the execution of one of the men on the *Adler*[210] for carrying a box of matches. The case was a flagrant one. The man had forgotten he had it upon him when coming aboard. Ample notice had been given to everyone of the gravity of this offence, and notices appeared at numerous points all over the airships. The man's defence was that he had grown so used to the notices and had been so preoccupied with his work that he hadn't applied them to himself; he pleaded, in his defence, what is indeed in military affairs another serious crime, inadvertency. He was tried by his captain, and the sentence confirmed by wireless telegraphy by the Prince, and it was decided to make his death an example to the whole fleet. 'The Germans,' the Prince declared, 'hadn't crossed the Atlantic to go wool gathering.' And in order that this lesson in discipline and obedience might be visible to everyone, it was determined not to electrocute or drown but hang the offender.

Accordingly the air-fleet came clustering round the flagship like carp in a pond at feeding time. The *Adler* hung at the zenith immediately alongside the flagship. The whole crew of the *Vaterland* assembled upon the hanging gallery; the crews of the other airships manned the air chambers, that is to say, clambered up the outer netting to the upper sides. The officers appeared upon the machine-gun platforms. Bert thought it an altogether stupendous sight, looking down, as he was, upon the entire fleet. Far off below two steamers on the rippled blue water, one British and the other flying the American flag, seemed the minutest objects, and marked the scale. They were immensely distant. Bert stood on the gallery, curious to see the execution, but uncomfortable, because that terrible blond Prince was within a dozen feet of him, glaring terribly, with his arms folded, and his heels together in military fashion.

They hung the man from the *Adler*. They gave him sixty feet of rope, so that he should hang and dangle in the sight of all evil-doers who might be hiding matches or contemplating any kindred disobedience. Bert saw the man standing, a living, reluctant man, no doubt scared and rebellious enough in his heart, but outwardly erect and obedient, on the lower gallery of the *Adler* about a hundred yards away. Then they had thrust him overboard.

Down he fell, hands and feet extending, until with a jerk he was at the end of the rope. Then he ought to have died and swung edifyingly, but instead a more terrible thing happened; his head came right off, and down the body went spinning to the sea, feeble, grotesque, fantastic, with the head racing it in its fall.

'Ugh!' said Bert, clutching the rail before him, and a sympathetic grunt came from several of the men beside him.

'So!' said the Prince, stiffer and sterner, glared for some seconds, then turned to the gangway up into the airship.

For a long time Bert remained clinging to the railing of the gallery. He was almost physically sick with the horror of this trifling incident. He found it far more dreadful than the battle. He was indeed a very degenerate, latter-day, civilised person.

Late that afternoon Kurt came into the cabin and found him curled up on his locker, and looking very white and miserable. Kurt had also lost something of his pristine freshness.

'Seasick?' he asked.

'No!'

'We ought to reach New York this evening. There's a good breeze coming up under our tails. Then we shall see things.'

Bert did not answer.

Kurt opened out folding-chair and table, and rustled for a time with his maps. Then he fell thinking darkly. He roused himself presently, and looked at his companion. 'What's the matter?' he said.

'Nothing!'

Kurt stared threateningly. 'What's the matter?'

'I saw them kill that chap. I saw that flying-machine man hit the funnels of the big ironclad. I saw that dead chap in the passage. I seen too much smashing and killing lately. That's the matter. I don't like it. I didn't know war was this sort of thing. I'm a civilian. I don't like it.'

'*I* don't like it,' said Kurt. 'By Jove, no!'

'I've read about war, and all that, but when you see it it's different. And I'm gettin' giddy. I'm gettin' giddy. I didn't mind a bit being up in that balloon at first, but all this looking down and floating over things and smashing up people, it's getting on my nerves. See?'

'It'll have to get off again . . . '

Kurt thought. 'You're not the only one. The men are all getting strung up. The flying – that's just flying. Naturally it makes one a little swimmy in the head at first. As for the killing, we've got to be blooded; that's all. We're tame, civilised men. And we've got to get blooded. I suppose there's not a dozen men on the ship who've really seen bloodshed. Nice, quiet, law-abiding Germans they've been so far . . . Here they are – in for it. They're a bit squeamy now, but you wait till they've got their hands in.'

He reflected. 'Everybody's getting a bit strung up,' he said.

He turned again to his maps. Bert sat crumpled up in the corner, apparently heedless of him. For some time both kept silence.

'What did the Prince want to go and 'ang that chap for?' asked Bert, suddenly.

'That was all right,' said Kurt, 'that was all right. *Quite* right. Here were the orders, plain as the nose on your face, and here was that fool going about with matches – '

'Gaw! I shan't forget that bit in a 'urry,' said Bert irrelevantly.

Kurt did not answer him. He was measuring their distance from New York and speculating. 'Wonder what the American aeroplanes are like?' he said. 'Something like our *drachenflieger* . . . We shall know by this time tomorrow . . . I wonder what we shall know? I wonder. Suppose, after all, they put up a fight . . . Rum sort of fight!'

He whistled softly and mused. Presently he fretted out of the cabin, and later Bert found him in the twilight upon the swinging platform, staring ahead, and speculating about the things that might happen on the morrow. Clouds veiled the sea again, and the long straggling wedge of airships rising and falling as they flew seemed like a flock of strange new births in a Chaos that had neither earth nor water but only mist and sky.

CHAPTER SIX

How War Came to New York

1

The City of New York was in the year of the German attack the largest, richest, in many respects the most splendid, and in some, the wickedest city the world had ever seen. She was the supreme type of the City of the Scientific Commercial Age; she displayed its greatness, its power, its ruthless anarchic enterprise, and its social disorganisation most strikingly and completely. She had long ousted London from her pride of place as the modern Babylon, she was the centre of the world's finance, the world's trade, and the world's pleasure; and men likened her to the apocalyptic cities of the ancient prophets. She sat drinking up the wealth of a continent as Rome once drank the wealth of the Mediterranean and Babylon the wealth of the east. In her streets one found the extremes of magnificence and misery, of civilisation and disorder. In one quarter, palaces of marble, laced and crowned with light and flame and flowers, towered up into her marvellous twilights beautiful beyond description; in another, a black and sinister polyglot population sweltered in indescribable congestion in warrens, and excavations beyond the power and knowledge of government. Her vice, her crime, her law alike were inspired by a fierce and terrible energy, and like the great cities of mediaeval Italy, her ways were dark and adventurous with private war.

It was the peculiar shape of Manhattan Island, pressed in by arms of the sea on either side, and incapable of comfortable expansion, except along a narrow northward belt, that first gave the New York architects their bias for extreme vertical dimensions. Every need was lavishly supplied them – money, material, labour; only space was restricted. To begin, therefore, they built high perforce. But to do so was to discover a whole new world of architectural beauty, of exquisite ascendant lines, and long after the central congestion had been relieved by tunnels under the sea, four colossal bridges over the east river, and a dozen monorail cables east and west, the upward growth went on. In many ways New York and her gorgeous plutocracy repeated Venice; in the magnificence of her architecture, painting, metalwork and sculpture, for example, in the grim intensity of her political method, in her maritime and commercial ascendancy. But she repeated no previous state at all in the lax disorder of her internal administration, a laxity that made vast sections of her area lawless beyond precedent, so that it was possible for whole districts to be impassable, while civil war raged between street and street, and for Alsatias to exist in her midst in which the official police never set foot. She was an ethnic whirlpool. The flags of all nations flew in her harbour, and at the climax, the yearly coming and going overseas numbered together upwards of two million human beings. To Europe she was America, to America she was the gateway of the world. But to tell the story of New York would be to write a social history of the world; saints and martyrs, dreamers and scoundrels, the traditions of a thousand races and a thousand religions, went to her making and throbbed and jostled in her streets. And over all that torrential confusion of men and purposes fluttered that strange flag, the stars and stripes, that meant at once the noblest thing in life, and the least noble, that is to say, Liberty on the one hand, and on the other the base jealousy the individual self-seeker feels towards the common purpose of the State.

For many generations New York had taken no heed of war, save as a thing that happened far away, that affected prices and supplied the newspapers with exciting headlines and pictures. The New Yorkers felt perhaps even more certainly than the English had done that war in their own land was an impossible thing. In that they shared the delusion of all North America. They felt as secure as spectators at a bullfight; they risked their money perhaps on the result, but that was all. And such ideas of war as the common Americans possessed were derived from the limited, picturesque, adventurous war of the past. They saw war as they saw history, through an iridescent mist, deodorised, scented indeed, with all its essential cruelties tactfully hidden away. They were inclined to regret it as something ennobling, to sigh that it could no longer come into their own private experience. They read with interest, if not with avidity, of their new guns, of their immense and still more immense ironclads, of their incredible and still more incredible explosives, but just what these tremendous engines of destruction might mean for their personal lives never entered their heads. They did not, so far as one can judge from their contemporary literature, think that they meant anything to their personal lives at all. They thought America was safe amidst all this piling up of explosives. They cheered the flag by habit and tradition, they despised other nations, and whenever there was an international difficulty they were intensely patriotic, that is to say, they were ardently against any native politician who did not say, threaten, and do harsh and uncompromising things to the antagonist people. They were spirited to Asia, spirited to Germany, so spirited to Great Britain that the international attitude of the mother country to her great daughter was constantly compared in contemporary caricature to that between a hen-pecked husband and a vicious young wife. And for the rest, they all went about their business and pleasure as if war had died out with the megatherium . . .

And then suddenly, into a world peacefully busied for the most part upon armaments and the perfection of explosives, war came; came the shock of realising that the guns were going off, that the masses of inflammable material all over the world were at last ablaze.

2

The immediate effect upon New York of the sudden onset of war was merely to intensify her normal vehemence.

The newspapers and magazines that fed the American mind – for books upon this impatient continent had become simply material for the energy of collectors – were instantly a coruscation of war pictures and of headlines that rose like rockets and burst like shells. To the normal high-strung energy of New York streets was added a touch of war-fever. Great crowds assembled, more especially in the dinner hour, in Madison Square about the Farragut monument,[211] to listen to and cheer patriotic speeches, and a veritable epidemic of little flags and buttons swept through these great torrents of swiftly moving young people, who poured into New York of a morning by car and monorail and subway and train, to toil, and ebb home again between the hours of five and seven. It was dangerous not to wear a war button. The splendid music-halls of the time sank every topic in patriotism and evolved scenes of wild enthusiasm, strong men wept at the sight of the national banner sustained by the whole strength of the ballet, and special searchlights and illuminations amazed the watching angels. The churches re-echoed the national enthusiasm in graver key and slower measure, and the aerial and naval preparations on the East River were greatly incommoded by the multitude of excursion steamers which thronged, helpfully cheering, about them. The trade in small-arms was enormously stimulated, and many overwrought citizens found an immediate relief for their emotions in letting off fireworks of a more or less heroic, dangerous, and national character in the public streets.

Small children's air-balloons of the latest model attached to string became a serious check to the pedestrian in Central Park. And amidst scenes of indescribable emotion the Albany legislature[212] in permanent session, and with a generous suspension of rules and precedents, passed through both Houses the long-disputed Bill for universal military service in New York State.

Critics of the American character are disposed to consider that up to the actual impact of the German attack the people of New York dealt altogether too much with the war as if it were a political demonstration. Little or no damage, they urge, was done to either the German or Japanese forces by the wearing of buttons, the waving of small flags, the fireworks, or the songs. They forgot that, under the conditions of warfare a century of science had brought about, the non-military section of the population could do no serious damage in any form to their enemies, and that there was no reason, therefore, why they should not do as they did. The balance of military efficiency was shifting back from the many to the few, from the common to the specialised. The days when the emotional infantryman decided battles had passed by for ever. War had become a matter of apparatus of special training and skill of the most intricate kind. It had become undemocratic. And whatever the value of the popular excitement, there can be no denying that the small regular establishment of the United States Government, confronted by this totally unexpected emergency of an armed invasion from Europe, acted with vigour, science, and imagination. They were taken by surprise so far as the diplomatic situation was concerned, and their equipment for building either navigables or aeroplanes was contemptible in comparison with the huge German parks. Still they set to work at once to prove to the world that the spirit that had created the *Monitor* and the Southern submarines of 1864[213] was not dead. The chief of the aeronautic establishment near West Point was Cabot Sinclair,[214] and he allowed himself but one single moment of the posturing that was so universal in that democratic time. 'We have chosen our epitaphs,' he said to a reporter, 'and we are going to have, "They did all they could". Now run away!'

The curious thing is that they did all do all they could; there is no exception known. Their only defect indeed was a defect of style. One of the most striking facts historically about this war, and the one that makes the complete separation that had arisen between the methods of warfare and the necessity of democratic support, is the effectual secrecy of the Washington authorities about their airships. They did not bother to confide a single fact of their preparations to the public. They did not even condescend to talk to Congress. They burked and suppressed every enquiry. The war was fought by the President and the Secretaries of State in an entirely autocratic manner. Such publicity as they sought was merely to anticipate and prevent inconvenient agitation to defend particular points. They realised that the chief danger in aerial warfare from an excitable and intelligent public would be a clamour for local airships and aeroplanes to defend local interests. This, with such resources as they possessed, might lead to a fatal division and distribution of the national forces. Particularly they feared that they might be forced into a premature action to defend New York. They realised with prophetic insight that this would be the particular advantage the Germans would seek. So they took great pains to direct the popular mind towards defensive artillery, and to divert it from any thought of aerial battle. Their real preparations they masked beneath ostensible ones. There was at Washington a large reserve of naval guns, and these were distributed rapidly, conspicuously, and with much press attention, among the eastern cities. They were mounted for the most part upon hills and prominent crests around the threatened centres of population. They were mounted upon rough adaptations of the Doan swivel, which at that time gave the maximum vertical range to a heavy gun. Much of this artillery was still unmounted, and nearly all of it was unprotected when the German air-fleet reached New York. And down in the crowded streets, when that occurred, the readers of the New York papers were regaling themselves with wonderful and wonderfully illustrated accounts of such matters as:

THE SECRET OF THE THUNDERBOLT

AGED SCIENTIST PERFECTS ELECTRIC GUN
TO ELECTROCUTE AIRSHIP CREWS BY UPWARD LIGHTNING

WASHINGTON ORDERS FIVE HUNDRED

WAR SECRETARY LODGE DELIGHTED
SAYS THEY WILL SUIT THE GERMANS
DOWN TO THE GROUND

PRESIDENT PUBLICLY APPLAUDS THIS MERRY QUIP

The German fleet reached New York in advance of the news of the American naval disaster. It reached New York in the late afternoon and was first seen by watchers at Ocean Grove and Long Branch coming swiftly out of the southward sea and going away to the north-west. The flagship passed almost vertically over the Sandy Hook observation station,[215] rising rapidly as it did so, and in a few minutes all New York was vibrating to the Staten Island guns.

Several of these guns, and especially that at Giffords and the one on Beacon Hill above Matawan,[216] were remarkably well handled. The former, at a distance of five miles, and with an elevation of six thousand feet, sent a shell to burst so close to the *Vaterland* that a pane of the Prince's forward window was smashed by a fragment. This sudden explosion made Bert tuck in his head with the celerity of a startled tortoise. The whole air-fleet immediately went up steeply to a height of about twelve thousand feet and at that level passed unscathed over the ineffectual guns. The airships lined out as they moved forward into the form of a flattened V, with its apex towards the city, and with the flagship going highest at the apex. The two ends of the V passed over Plumfield and Jamaica Bay, respectively, and the Prince directed his course a little to the east of the Narrows, soared over Upper Bay, and came to rest over Jersey City in a position that dominated lower New York. There the monsters hung, large and wonderful in the evening light, serenely regardless of the occasional rocket explosions and flashing shell-bursts in the lower air.

It was a pause of mutual inspection. For a time naïve humanity swamped the conventions of warfare altogether; the interest of the millions below and of the thousands above alike was spectacular. The evening was unexpectedly fine – only a few thin level bands of clouds at seven or eight thousand feet broke its luminous clarity. The wind had dropped; it was an evening infinitely peaceful and still. The heavy concussions of the distant guns and those incidental harmless pyro-technics at the level of the clouds seemed to have as little to do with killing and force, terror and submission, as a salute at a naval review. Below, every point of vantage bristled with spectators, the roofs of the towering buildings, the public squares, the active ferry boats, and every favourable street intersection had its crowds: all the river piers were dense with people, the Battery Park was solid black with east-side population, and every position of advantage in Central Park and along

Riverside Drive had its peculiar and characteristic assembly from the adjacent streets. The footways of the great bridges over the East River were also closely packed and blocked. Everywhere shopkeepers had left their shops, men their work, and women and children their homes, to come out and see the marvel.

'It beat,' they declared, 'the newspapers.'

And from above, many of the occupants of the airships stared with an equal curiosity. No city in the world was ever so finely placed as New York, so magnificently cut up by sea and bluff and river, so admirably disposed to display the tall effects of buildings, the complex immensities of bridges and mono-railways and feats of engineering. London, Paris, Berlin, were shapeless, low agglomerations beside it. Its port reached to its heart like Venice, and, like Venice, it was obvious, dramatic, and proud. Seen from above it was alive with crawling trains and cars, and at a thousand points it was already breaking into quivering light. New York was altogether at its best that evening, its splendid best.

'Gaw! *What* a place!' said Bert.

It was so great, and in its collective effect so pacifically magnificent, that to make war upon it seemed incongruous beyond measure, like laying siege to the National Gallery or attacking respectable people in an hotel dining-room with battle-axe and mail. It was in its entirety so large, so complex, so delicately immense, that to bring it to the issue of warfare was like driving a crowbar into the mechanism of a clock. And the fishlike shoal of great airships hovering light and sunlit above, filling the sky, seemed equally remote from the ugly forcefulness of war. To Kurt, to Smallways, to I know not how many more of the people in the air-fleet came the distinctest apprehension of these incompatibilities. But in the head of the Prince Karl Albert were the vapours of romance: he was a conqueror, and this was the enemy's city. The greater the city, the greater the triumph. No doubt he had a time of tremendous exultation and sensed beyond all precedent the sense of power that night.

There came an end at last to that pause. Some wireless communications had failed of a satisfactory ending, and fleet and city remembered they were hostile powers. 'Look!' cried the multitude; 'look!'

'What are they doing?'

'What?' . . . Down through the twilight sank five attacking airships, one to the Navy Yard on East River, one to City Hall, two over the great business buildings of Wall Street and Lower Broadway, one to the Brooklyn Bridge, dropping from among their fellows through the danger zone from the distant guns smoothly and rapidly to a safe proximity to the city masses. At that descent all the cars in the streets stopped with dramatic suddenness, and all the lights that had been coming on in the streets and houses went out again. For the City Hall had awakened and was conferring by telephone with the Federal command and taking measures for defence. The City Hall was asking for airships, refusing to surrender as Washington advised, and developing into a centre of intense emotion, of hectic activity. Everywhere and hastily the police began to clear the assembled crowds. 'Go to your homes,' they said; and the word was passed from mouth to mouth, 'There's going to be trouble.' A chill of apprehension ran through the city, and men hurrying in the unwonted darkness across City Hall Park and Union Square came upon the dim forms of soldiers and guns, and were challenged and sent back. In half an hour New York had passed from serene sunset and gaping admiration to a troubled and threatening twilight.

The first loss of life occurred in the panic rush from Brooklyn Bridge as the airship approached it.

With the cessation of the traffic an unusual stillness came upon New York, and the disturbing concussions of the futile defending guns on the hills about grew more and more audible. At last these ceased also. A pause of further negotiation followed. People sat in darkness, sought counsel from telephones that were dumb. Then into the expectant hush came a great crash and uproar, the breaking down of the Brooklyn Bridge, the rifle fire from the Navy Yard, and the bursting of bombs in Wall Street and the City Hall. New York as a whole could do nothing, could understand nothing. New York in the darkness peered and listened to these distant sounds until presently they died away as suddenly as they had begun. 'What could be happening?' They asked it in vain.

A long, vague period intervened, and people looking out of the windows of upper rooms discovered the dark hulls of German airships, gliding slowly and noiselessly, quite close at hand. Then quietly the electric lights came on again, and an uproar of nocturnal news vendors began in the streets.

The units of that vast and varied population bought and learnt what had happened; there had been a fight and New York had hoisted the white flag . . .

The lamentable incidents that followed the surrender of New York seem now in the retrospect to be but the necessary and inevitable consequence of the clash of modern appliances and social conditions produced by the scientific century on the one hand, and the tradition of a crude, romantic patriotism on the other. At first people received the fact with an irresponsible detachment, much as they would have received the slowing down of the train in which they were travelling or the erection of a public monument by the city to which they belonged.

'We have surrendered. Dear me! *Have* we?' was rather the manner in which the first news was met. They took it in the same spectacular spirit they had displayed at the first apparition of the air-fleet. Only slowly was this realisation of a capitulation suffused with the flush of passion, only with reflection did they make any personal application. '*We* have surrendered!' came later; 'in us America is defeated.' Then they began to burn and tingle.

The newspapers which were issued about one in the morning contained no particulars of the terms upon which New York had yielded – nor did they give any intimation of the quality of the brief conflict that had preceded the capitulation. The later issues remedied these deficiencies. There came the explicit statement of the agreement to victual the German airships, to supply the complement of explosives to replace those employed in the fight and in the destruction of the North Atlantic fleet, to pay the enormous ransom of forty million dollars, and to surrender the flotilla in the East River. There came, too, longer and longer descriptions of the smashing up of the City Hall and the Navy Yard, and people began to realise faintly what those brief minutes of uproar had meant. They read the tale of men blown to bits, of futile soldiers in that localised battle fighting against hope amidst an indescribable wreckage, of flags hauled down by weeping men. And these strange nocturnal editions contained also the first brief cables from Europe of the fleet disaster, the North Atlantic fleet for which New York had always felt an especial pride and solicitude. Slowly, hour by hour, the collective consciousness woke up, the tide of patriotic astonishment and humiliation came floating in. America had come upon disaster; suddenly New York discovered herself with amazement giving place to wrath unspeakable, a conquered city under the hand of her conqueror.

As that fact shaped itself in the public mind, there sprang up, as flames spring up, an angry repudiation. 'No!' cried New York, waking in the dawn. 'No! I am not defeated. This is a dream.' Before day broke the swift American anger was running through all the city, through every soul in those contagious millions. Before it took action, before it took shape, the men in the airships could feel the gigantic insurgence of emotion, as cattle and natural creatures feel, it is said, the coming of an earthquake. The newspapers of the Knype group first gave the thing words and a formula. 'We do not agree,' they said simply. 'We have been betrayed!' Men took that up everywhere, it passed from mouth to mouth, at every street corner under the paling lights of dawn orators stood unchecked, calling upon the spirit of America to arise, making the shame a personal reality to everyone who heard. To Bert, listening five hundred feet above, it seemed that the city, which had at first produced only confused noises, was now humming like a hive of bees – of very angry bees.

After the smashing of the City Hall and Post Office, the white flag had been hoisted from a tower of the old Park Row Building, and thither had gone Mayor O'Hagen,[217] urged thither indeed by the terror-stricken property owners of lower New York, to negotiate the capitulation with Von Winterfeld. The *Vaterland*, having dropped the secretary by a rope ladder, remained hovering, circling very slowly above the great buildings, old and new, that clustered round City Hall Park, while the *Helmholz*, which had done the fighting there, rose overhead to a height of perhaps two thousand feet. So Bert had a near view of all that occurred in that central place. The City Hall and Court House, the Post Office and a mass of buildings on the west side of Broadway, had been badly damaged, and the three former were a heap of blackened ruins. In the case of the first two the loss of life had not been considerable, but a great multitude of workers, including many girls and women, had been caught in the destruction of the Post Office, and a little army of volunteers with white badges entered behind the firemen, bringing out the often still living bodies, for the most part frightfully charred, and carrying them into the big Monson Building[218] close at hand. Everywhere the busy firemen were directing their bright streams of water upon the smouldering masses; their hose lay about the square, and long cordons of police held back the gathering black masses of people, chiefly from the east side, from these central activities.

In violent and extraordinary contrast with this scene of destruction, close at hand were the huge newspaper establishments of Park Row. They were all alight and working; they had not been abandoned even while the actual bomb throwing was going on, and now staff and presses were vehemently active, getting out the story, the immense and dreadful story of the night, developing comment and, in most cases, spreading the idea of resistance under the very noses of the airships. For a long time Bert could not imagine what these callously active offices could be, then he detected the noise of the presses and emitted his 'Gaw!'

Beyond these newspaper buildings again, and partially hidden by the arches of the old Elevated Railway of New York[219] (long since converted into a monorail), there was another cordon of police and a sort of encampment of ambulances and doctors, busy with the dead and wounded who had been killed early in the night by the panic upon Brooklyn Bridge. All this he saw in the perspectives of a bird's-eye view, as things happening in a big, irregular-shaped pit below him, between cliffs of high building. Northward he looked along the steep canyon of Broadway, down whose length at intervals crowds were assembling about excited speakers; and when he lifted his eyes he saw the chimneys and cable-stacks and roof spaces of New York, and everywhere now over these the watching, debating people clustered, except where the fires raged and the jets of water flew. Everywhere, too, were flagstaffs devoid of flags; one white sheet drooped and flapped and drooped again over the Park Row buildings. And upon the lurid lights, the festering movement and intense shadows of this strange scene, there was breaking now the cold, impartial dawn.

For Bert Smallways all this was framed in the frame of the open porthole. It was a pale, dim world outside that dark and tangible rim. All night he had clutched at that rim, jumped and quivered at explosions, and watched phantom events. Now he had been high and now low; now almost beyond hearing, now flying close to crashings and shouts and outcries. He had seen airships flying low and swift over darkened and groaning streets; watched great buildings, suddenly red-lit amidst the shadows, crumple at the smashing impact of bombs; witnessed for the first time in his life the grotesque, swift onset of insatiable conflagrations. From it all he felt detached, disembodied. The *Vaterland* did not even fling a bomb; she watched and ruled. Then down they had come at last to hover over City Hall Park, and it had crept in upon his mind, chillingly, terrifyingly, that these illuminated black masses were great offices afire, and that the going to and fro of minute, dim spectres of lantern-lit grey and white was a harvesting of the wounded and the dead. As the light grew clearer he began to understand more and more what these crumpled black things signified . . .

He had watched hour after hour since first New York had risen out of the blue indistinctness of the landfall. With the daylight he experienced an intolerable fatigue.

He lifted weary eyes to the pink flush in the sky, yawned immensely, and crawled back whispering to himself across the cabin to the locker. He did not so much lie down upon that as fall upon it and instantly become asleep.

There, hours after, sprawling undignified and sleeping profoundly, Kurt found him, a very image of the democratic mind confronted with the problems of a time too complex for its apprehension. His face was pale and indifferent, his mouth wide open, and he snored. He snored disagreeably.

Kurt regarded him for a moment with a mild distaste. Then he kicked his ankle.

'Wake up,' he said to Smallways' stare, 'and lie down decent.'

Bert sat up and rubbed his eyes.

'Any more fightin' yet?' he asked.

'No,' said Kurt, and sat down, a tired man.

'Gott!' he cried presently, rubbing his hands over his face, 'but I'd like a cold bath! I've been looking for stray bullet holes in the air chambers all night until now.' He yawned. 'I must sleep. You'd better clear out, Smallways. I can't stand you here this morning. You're so infernally ugly and useless. Have you had your rations? No! Well, go in and get 'em, and don't come back. Stick in the gallery . . . '

5

So Bert, slightly refreshed by coffee and sleep, resumed his helpless co-operation in the War in the Air. He went down into the little gallery as the lieutenant had directed, and clung to the rail at the extreme end beyond the look-out man, trying to seem as inconspicuous and harmless a fragment of life as possible.

A wind was rising rather strongly from the south-east. It obliged the *Vaterland* to come about in that direction, and made her roll a great deal as she went to and fro over Manhattan Island. Away in the north-west clouds gathered. The throb, throb of her slow screw working against the breeze was much more perceptible than when she was going full speed ahead; and the friction of the wind against the underside of the gas chamber drove a series of shallow ripples along it and made a faint flapping sound like, but fainter than, the beating of ripples under the stem of a boat. She was stationed over the temporary City Hall in the

Park Row building, and every now and then she would descend to resume communication with the mayor and with Washington. But the restlessness of the Prince would not suffer him to remain for long in any one place. Now he would circle over the Hudson and East River; now he would go up high, as if to peer away into the blue distances; once he ascended so swiftly and so far that mountain sickness overtook him and the crew and forced him down again; and Bert shared the dizziness and nausea.

The swaying view varied with these changes of altitude. Now they would be low and close, and he would distinguish in that steep, unusual perspective, windows, doors, street and sky signs, people and the minutest details, and watch the enigmatical behaviour of crowds and clusters upon the roofs and in the streets; then as they soared the details would shrink, the sides of streets draw together, the view widen, the people cease to be significant. At the highest the effect was that of a concave relief map; Bert saw the dark and crowded land everywhere intersected by shining waters, saw the Hudson River like a spear of silver, and Lower Island Sound like a shield. Even to Bert's unphilosophical mind the contrast of city below and fleet above pointed an opposition, the opposition of the adventurous American's tradition and character with German order and discipline. Below, the immense buildings, tremendous and fine as they were, seemed like the giant trees of a jungle fighting for life; their picturesque magnificence was as planless as the chances of crag and gorge, their casualty enhanced by the smoke and confusion of still unsubdued and spreading conflagrations. In the sky soared the German airships like beings in a different, entirely more orderly world, all oriented to the same angle of the horizon, uniform in build and appearance, moving accurately with one purpose as a pack of wolves will move, distributed with the most precise and effectual co-operation.

It dawned upon Bert that hardly a third of the fleet was visible. The others had gone upon errands he could not imagine, beyond the compass of that great circle of earth and sky. He wondered, but there was no one to ask. As the day wore on, about a dozen reappeared in the east with their stores replenished from the flotilla and towing a number of *drachenflieger*. Towards afternoon the weather thickened, driving clouds appeared in the south-west and ran together and seemed to engender more clouds, and the wind came round into that quarter and blew stronger. Towards the evening the wind became a gale into which the now tossing airships had to beat.

All that day the Prince was negotiating with Washington, while his

detached scouts sought far and wide over the Eastern States looking for
anything resembling an aeronautic park. A squadron of twenty airships
detached overnight had dropped out of the air upon Niagara and was
holding the town and power works.

Meanwhile the insurrectionary movement in the giant city grew
uncontrollable. In spite of five great fires already involving many acres,
and spreading steadily, New York was still not satisfied that she was
beaten.

At first the rebellious spirit below found vent only in isolated shouts,
street-crowd speeches, and newspaper suggestions; then it found much
more definite expression in the appearance in the morning sunlight of
American flags at point after point above the architectural cliffs of the
city. It is quite possible that in many cases this spirited display of
bunting by a city already surrendered was the outcome of the innocent
informality of the American mind, but it is also undeniable that in
many it was a deliberate indication that the people 'felt wicked'.

The German sense of correctitude was deeply shocked by this outbreak. The Graf von Winterfeld immediately communicated with the
mayor, and pointed out the irregularity, and the fire look-out stations
were instructed in the matter. The New York police was speedily hard
at work, and a foolish contest in full swing between impassioned citizens
resolved to keep the flag flying, and irritated and worried officers
instructed to pull it down.

The trouble became acute at last in the streets above Columbia
University. The captain of the airship watching this quarter seems to
have stooped to lasso and drag from its staff a flag hoisted upon Morgan
Hall. As he did so a volley of rifle and revolver shots was fired from the
upper windows of the huge apartment building that stands between
the University and Riverside Drive.

Most of these were ineffectual, but two or three perforated gas
chambers, and one smashed the hand and arm of a man upon the
forward platform. The sentinel on the lower gallery immediately replied,
and the machine gun on the shield of the eagle let fly and promptly
stopped any further shots. The airship rose and signalled the flagship
and City Hall, police and militiamen were directed at once to the spot,
and this particular incident closed.

But hard upon that came the desperate attempt of a party of young
clubmen from New York, who, inspired by patriotic and adventurous
imaginations, slipped off in half a dozen motor cars to Beacon Hill, and
set to work with remarkable vigour to improvise a fort about the Doan
swivel gun that had been placed there. They found it still in the hands

of the disgusted gunners, who had been ordered to cease fire at the capitulation, and it was easy to infect these men with their own spirit. They declared their gun hadn't had half a chance, and were burning to show what it could do. Directed by the newcomers, they made a trench and bank about the mounting of the piece, and constructed flimsy shelter-pits of corrugated iron.

They were actually loading the gun when they were observed by the airship *Preussen* and the shell they succeeded in firing before the bombs of the latter smashed them and their crude defences to fragments, burst over the middle gas chambers of the *Bingen*, and brought her to earth, disabled, upon Staten Island. She was badly deflated, and dropped among trees, over which her empty central gasbags spread in canopies and festoons. Nothing, however, had caught fire, and her men were speedily at work upon her repair. They behaved with a confidence that verged upon indiscretion. While most of them commenced patching the tears of the membrane, half a dozen of them started off for the nearest road in search of a gas main, and presently found themselves prisoners in the hands of a hostile crowd. Close at hand was a number of villa residences, whose occupants speedily developed from an un-friendly curiosity to aggression. At that time the police control of the large polyglot population of Staten Island had become very lax, and scarcely a household but had its rifle or pistols and ammunition. These were presently produced, and after two or three misses, one of the men at work was hit in the foot. Thereupon the Germans left their sewing and mending, took cover among the trees, and replied.

The crackling of shots speedily brought the *Preussen* and *Kiel* on the scene, and with a few hand grenades they made short work of every villa within a mile. A number of non-combatant American men, women, and children were killed and the actual assailants driven off. For a time the repairs went on in peace under the immediate protection of these two airships. Then when they returned to their quarters, an intermittent sniping and fighting round the stranded *Bingen* was resumed, and went on all the afternoon, and merged at last in the general combat of the evening . . .

About eight the *Bingen* was rushed by an armed mob, and all its defenders killed after a fierce, disorderly struggle.

The difficulty of the Germans in both these cases came from the impossibility of landing any efficient force or, indeed, any force at all from the air-fleet. The airships were quite unequal to the transport of any adequate landing parties; their complement of men was just sufficient to manoeuvre and fight them in the air. From above they could inflict immense damage; they could reduce any organised Government to a capitulation in the briefest space, but they could not disarm, much less could they occupy, the surrendered areas below. They had to trust to the pressure upon the authorities below of a threat to renew the bombardment. It was their sole resource. No doubt, with a highly organised and undamaged Government and a homogeneous and well-disciplined people that would have sufficed to keep the peace. But this was not the American case. Not only was the New York Government a weak one and insufficiently provided with police, but the destruction of the City Hall and Post Office and other central ganglia had hopelessly disorganised the co-operation of part with part. The street cars and railways had ceased; the telephone service was out of gear and only worked intermittently. The Germans had struck at the head, and the head was conquered and stunned – only to release the body from its rule. New York had become a headless monster, no longer capable of collective submission. Everywhere it lifted itself rebelliously; everywhere authorities and officials left to their own initiative were joining in the arming and flag-hoisting and excitement of that afternoon.

6

The disintegrating truce gave place to a definite general breach with the assassination of the *Wetterhorn* – for that is the only possible word for the act – above Union Square, and not a mile away from the exemplary ruins of City Hall. This occurred late in the afternoon, between five and six. By that time the weather had changed very much for the worse, and the operations of the airships were embarrassed by the necessity they were under of keeping head-on to the gusts. A series of squalls, with hail and thunder, followed one another from the south by south-east, and in order to avoid these as much as possible, the air-fleet came low over the houses, diminishing its range of observation and exposing itself to a rifle attack.

Overnight there had been a gun placed in Union Square. It had never been mounted, much less fired, and in the darkness after the surrender it was taken with its supplies and put out of the way under the arches of the great Dexter building.[220] Here late in the morning it was remarked by a number of patriotic spirits. They set to work to hoist and mount it inside the upper floors of the place. They made, in fact, a masked battery behind the decorous office blinds, and there lay in wait as simply excited as children until at last the stem of the luckless *Wetterhorn* appeared, beating and rolling at quarter speed over the recently reconstructed pinnacles of Tiffany's.[221] Promptly that one-gun battery unmasked. The airship's look-out man must have seen the whole of the tenth storey of the Dexter building crumble out and smash in the street below to discover the black muzzle looking out from the shadows behind. Then, perhaps, the shell hit him.

The gun fired two shells before the frame of the Dexter building collapsed, and each shell raked the *Wetterhorn* from stem to stern. They smashed her exhaustively. She crumpled up like a can that has been kicked by a heavy boot, her forepart came down in the square, and the rest of her length, with a great snapping and twisting of shafts and stays, descended, collapsing athwart Tammany Hall[222] and the streets towards Second Avenue. Her gas escaped to mix with air, and the air of her rent balloonette poured into her deflating gas chambers. Then with an immense impact she exploded . . .

The *Vaterland* at that time was beating up to the south of City Hall from over the ruins of the Brooklyn Bridge, and the reports of the gun, followed by the first crashes of the collapsing Dexter building, brought Kurt and Smallways to the cabin porthole. They were in time to see the flash of the exploding gun, and then they were first flattened against the window and then rolled head over heels across the floor of the cabin by the air wave of the explosion. The *Vaterland* bounded like a football someone has kicked and when they looked out again, Union Square was small and remote and shattered, as though some cosmically vast giant had rolled over it. The buildings to the east of it were ablaze at a dozen points, under the flaming tatters and warping skeleton of the airship, and all the roofs and walls were ridiculously askew and crumbling as one looked. 'Gaw!' said Bert. 'What's happened? Look at the people!'

But before Kurt could produce an explanation, the shrill bells of the airship were ringing to quarters, and he had to go. Bert hesitated and stepped thoughtfully into the passage, looking back at the window as he did so. He was knocked off his feet at once by the Prince, who was rushing headlong from his cabin to the central magazine.

Bert had a momentary impression of the great figure of the Prince, white with rage, bristling with gigantic anger, his huge fist swinging. 'Blut und Eisen!'[223] cried the Prince, as one who swears. 'Oh! Blut und Eisen!'

Someone fell over Bert – something in the manner of falling suggested Von Winterfeld – and someone else paused and kicked him spitefully and hard. Then he was sitting up in the passage, rubbing a freshly bruised cheek and readjusting the bandage he still wore on his head. 'Dem that Prince,' said Bert, indignant beyond measure. ' 'E 'asn't the menners of a 'og!'

He stood up, collected his wits for a minute, and then went slowly towards the gangway of the little gallery. As he did so he heard noises suggestive of the return of the Prince. The lot of them were coming back again. He shot into his cabin like a rabbit into its burrow, just in time to escape that shouting terror.

He shut the door, waited until the passage was still, then went across to the window and looked out. A drift of cloud made the prospect of the streets and squares hazy, and the rolling of the airship swung the picture up and down. A few people were running to and fro, but for the most part the aspect of the district was desertion. The streets seemed to broaden out, they became clearer, and the little dots that were people larger as the *Vaterland* came down again. Presently she was swaying along above the lower end of Broadway. The dots below, Bert saw, were not running now, but standing and looking up. Then suddenly they were all running again.

Something had dropped from the aeroplane, something that looked small and flimsy. It hit the pavement near a big archway just underneath Bert. A little man was sprinting along the sidewalk within half a dozen yards, and two or three others and one woman were bolting across the roadway. They were odd little figures, so very small were they about the heads, so very active about the elbows and legs. It was really funny to see their legs going. Foreshortened, humanity has no dignity. The little man on the pavement jumped comically – no doubt with terror – as the bomb fell beside him.

Then blinding flames squirted out in all directions from the point of impact, and the little man who had jumped became, for an instant, a flash of fire and vanished – vanished absolutely. The people running out into the road took preposterous clumsy leaps, then flopped down and lay still, with their torn clothes smouldering into flame. Then pieces of the archway began to drop, and the lower masonry of the building to fall in with the rumbling sound of coals being shot into a cellar. A faint screaming reached Bert, and then a crowd of people ran out into the street, one man limping and gesticulating awkwardly. He halted, and went back towards the building. A falling mass of brick-work hit him and sent him sprawling to lie still and crumpled where he fell. Dust and black smoke came pouring into the street, and were presently shot with red flame . . .

In this manner the massacre of New York began. She was the first of the great cities of the Scientific Age to suffer by the enormous powers and grotesque limitations of aerial warfare. She was wrecked as in the previous century endless barbaric cities had been bombarded, because she was at once too strong to be occupied and too undisciplined and proud to surrender in order to escape destruction. Given the circumstances, the thing had to be done. It was impossible for the Prince to desist, and own himself defeated, and it was impossible to subdue the city except by largely destroying it. The catastrophe was the logical outcome of the situation, created by the application of science to warfare. It was unavoidable that great cities should be destroyed. In spite of his intense exasperation with his dilemma, the Prince sought to be moderate even in massacre. He tried to give a memorable lesson with the minimum waste of life and the minimum expenditure of explosives. For that night he proposed only the wrecking of Broadway. He directed the air-fleet to move in column over the route of this thoroughfare, dropping bombs, the *Vaterland* leading. And so our Bert Smallways became a participant in one of the most cold-blooded slaughters in the world's history, in which men who were neither excited nor, except for the remotest chance of a bullet, in any danger, poured death and destruction upon homes and crowds below.

He clung to the frame of the porthole as the airship tossed and swayed, and stared down through the light rain that now drove before the wind, into the twilight streets, watching people running out of the houses, watching buildings collapse and fires begin. As the airships sailed along they smashed up the city as a child will shatter its cities of brick and card. Below, they left ruins and blazing conflagrations and heaped and scattered dead; men, women, and children mixed together as though they had been no more than Moors, or Zulus, or Chinese. Lower New York was soon a furnace of crimson flames, from which there was no escape. Cars, railways, ferries, all had ceased, and never a light lit the way of the distracted fugitives in that dusky confusion but the light of burning. He had glimpses of what it must mean to be down there – glimpses. And it came to him suddenly as an incredible discovery, that such disasters were not only possible now in this strange, gigantic, foreign New York, but also in London – in Bun Hill! that the little island in the silver seas was at the end of its immunity, that nowhere in the world any more was there a place left where a Smallways might lift his head proudly and vote for war and a spirited foreign policy, and go secure from such horrible things.

CHAPTER SEVEN

The Vaterland *is Disabled*

1

And then above the flames of Manhattan Island came a battle, the first battle in the air. The Americans had realised the price their waiting game must cost, and struck with all the strength they had, if haply they might still save New York from this mad Prince of Blood and Iron, and from fire and death.

They came down upon the Germans on the wings of a great gale in the twilight, amidst thunder and rain. They came from the yards of Washington and Philadelphia, full tilt in two squadrons, and but for one sentinel airship hard by Trenton, the surprise would have been complete.

The Germans, sick and weary with destruction, and half empty of ammunition, were facing up into the weather when the news of this onset reached them. New York they had left behind to the south-eastward, a darkened city with one hideous red scar of flames. All the airships rolled and staggered, bursts of hailstorm bore them down and forced them to fight their way up again; the air had become bitterly cold. The Prince was on the point of issuing orders to drop earthward and trail copper lightning chains when the news of the aeroplane attack came to him. He faced his fleet in line abreast south, had the *drachen-flieger* manned and held ready to cast loose, and ordered a general ascent into the freezing clearness above the wet and darkness.

The news of what was imminent came slowly to Bert's perceptions. He was standing in the mess room at the time and the evening rations were being served out. He had resumed Butteridge's coat and gloves, and in addition he had wrapped his blanket about him. He was dipping his bread into his soup and was biting off big mouthfuls. His legs were wide apart, and he leant against the partition in order to steady himself amidst the pitching and oscillation of the airship. The men about him looked tired and depressed; a few talked, but most were sullen and thoughtful, and one or two were airsick. They all seemed to share the peculiarly outcast feeling that had followed the murders of the evening, a sense of a land beneath them, and an outraged humanity grown more hostile than the sea.

Then the news hit them. A red-faced sturdy man, a man with light eyelashes and a scar, appeared in the doorway and shouted something in German that manifestly startled everyone. Bert felt the shock of the altered tone, though he could not understand a word that was said. The announcement was followed by a pause, and then a great outcry of questions and suggestions. Even the airsick men flushed and spoke. For some minutes the mess room was Bedlam, and then, as if it were a confirmation of the news, came the shrill ringing of the bells that called the men to their posts.

Bert with pantomime suddenness found himself alone.

'What's up?' he said, though he partly guessed.

He stayed only to gulp down the remainder of his soup, and then ran along the swaying passage and, clutching tightly, down the ladder to the little gallery. The weather hit him like cold water squirted from a hose. The airship engaged in some new feat of atmospheric Jiu-Jitsu. He drew his blanket closer about him, clutching with one straining hand. He found himself tossing in a wet twilight, with nothing to be seen but mist pouring past him. Above him the airship was warm with lights and busy with the movements of men going to their quarters. Then abruptly the lights went out, and the *Vaterland* with bounds and twists and strange writhings was fighting her way up the air.

He had a glimpse, as the *Vaterland* rolled over, of some large buildings burning close below them, a quivering acanthus of flames, and then he saw indistinctly through the driving weather another airship wallowing along like a porpoise, and also working up. Presently the clouds swallowed her again for a time, and then she came back to sight as a dark and whale-like monster, amidst streaming weather. The air was full of flappings and pipings, of void, gusty shouts and noises; it buffeted him and confused him; ever and again his attention became rigid – a blind and deaf balancing and clutching.

'Wow!'

Something fell past him out of the vast darknesses above and vanished into the tumults below, going obliquely downward. It was a German *drachenflieger*. The thing was going so fast he had but an instant apprehension of the dark figure of the aeronaut crouched together clutching at his wheel. It might be a manoeuvre, but it looked like a catastrophe.

'Gaw!' said Bert.

'Pup-pup-pup' went a gun somewhere in the murk ahead and suddenly and quite horribly the *Vaterland* lurched, and Bert and the sentinel were clinging to the rail for dear life. 'Bang!' came a vast impact out of the zenith, followed by another huge roll, and all about him the tumbled clouds flashed red and lurid in response to flashes unseen, revealing immense gulfs. The rail went right overhead, and he was hanging loose in the air holding on to it.

For a time Bert's whole mind and being was given to clutching. 'I'm going into the cabin,' he said, as the airship righted again and brought back the gallery floor to his feet. He began to make his way cautiously towards the ladder. 'Whee-wow!' he cried as the whole gallery reared itself up forward, and then plunged down like a desperate horse.

Crack! Bang! Bang! Bang! And then hard upon this little rattle of shots and bombs came, all about him, enveloping him, engulfing him, immense and overwhelming, a quivering white blaze of lightning and a thunderclap that was like the bursting of a world.

Just for the instant before that explosion the universe seemed to be standing still in a shadowless glare.

It was then he saw the American aeroplane. He saw it in the light of the flash as a thing altogether motionless. Even its screw appeared still, and its men were rigid dolls. (For it was so near he could see the men upon it quite distinctly.) Its stern was tilting down, and the whole machine was heeling over. It was of the Colt-Coburn-Langley pattern,[224] with double up-tilted wings and the screw ahead, and the men were in a boatlike body netted over. From this very light long body, magazine guns projected on either side. One thing that was strikingly odd and wonderful in that moment of revelation was that the left upper wing was burning downward with a reddish, smoky flame. But this was not the most wonderful thing about this apparition. The most wonderful thing was that it and a German airship five hundred yards below were threaded as it were on the lightning flash, which turned out of its path as if to take them, and, that out from the corners and projecting points of its huge wings everywhere, little branching thorn trees of lightning were streaming.

Like a picture Bert saw these things, a picture a little blurred by a thin veil of wind-torn mist.

The crash of the thunderclap followed the flash and seemed a part of it, so that it is hard to say whether Bert was the rather deafened or blinded in that instant.

And then darkness, utter darkness, and a heavy report and a thin small sound of voices that went wailing downward into the abyss below.

There followed upon these things a long, deep swaying of the airship, and then Bert began a struggle to get back to his cabin. He was drenched and cold and terrified beyond measure, and now more than a little airsick. It seemed to him that the strength had gone out of his knees and hands, and that his feet had become icily slippery over the metal they trod upon. But that was because a thin film of ice had frozen upon the gallery.

He never knew how long his ascent of the ladder back into the airship took him, but in his dreams afterwards, when he recalled it, that experience seemed to last for hours. Below, above, around him were gulfs, monstrous gulfs of howling wind and eddies of dark, whirling snowflakes, and he was protected from it all by a little metal grating and a rail, a grating and rail that seemed madly infuriated with him, passionately eager to wrench him off and throw him into the tumult of space.

Once he had a fancy that a bullet tore by his ear, and that the clouds and snowflakes were lit by a flash, but he never even turned his head to see what new assailant whirled past them in the void. He wanted to get into the passage! He wanted to get into the passage! He wanted to get into the passage! Would the arm by which he was clinging hold out, or would it give way and snap? A handful of hail smacked him in the face, so that for a time he was breathless and nearly insensible. Hold tight, Bert! He renewed his efforts.

He found himself, with an enormous sense of relief and warmth, in the passage. The passage was behaving like a dice-box, its disposition was evidently to rattle him about and then throw him out again. He hung on with the convulsive clutch of instinct until the passage lurched down ahead. Then he would make a short run cabin-ward, and clutch again as the fore-end rose.

Behold! He was in the cabin!

He snapped-to the door, and for a time he was not a human being, he was a case of airsickness. He wanted to get somewhere that would fix him, that he needn't clutch. He opened the locker and got inside among the loose articles, and sprawled there helplessly, with his head sometimes bumping one side and sometimes the other. The lid shut upon him with a click. He did not care then what was happening any more. He did not care who fought who, or what bullets were fired or explosions occurred. He did not care if presently he was shot or smashed to pieces. He was full of feeble, inarticulate rage and despair. 'Foolery!' he said, his one exhaustive comment on human enterprise, adventure, war, and the chapter of accidents that had entangled him. 'Foolery! Ugh!' He included the order of the universe in that comprehensive condemnation. He wished he was dead.

He saw nothing of the stars, as presently the *Vaterland* cleared the rush and confusion of the lower weather, nor of the duel she fought with two circling aeroplanes, how they shot her rearmost chambers through, and how she fought them off with explosive bullets and turned to run as she did so.

The rush and swoop of these wonderful night birds was all lost upon him; their heroic dash and self-sacrifice. The *Vaterland* was rammed, and for some moments she hung on the verge of destruction, and sinking swiftly, with the American aeroplane entangled with her smashed propeller, and the Americans trying to scramble aboard. It signified nothing to Bert. To him it conveyed itself simply as vehement swaying. Foolery! When the American airship dropped off at last, with most of its crew shot or fallen, Bert in his locker appreciated nothing but that the *Vaterland* had taken a hideous upward leap.

But then came infinite relief, incredibly blissful relief. The rolling, the pitching, the struggle ceased, ceased instantly and absolutely. The *Vaterland* was no longer fighting the gale; her smashed and exploded engines throbbed no more; she was disabled and driving before the wind as smoothly as a balloon, a huge, wind-spread, tattered cloud of aerial wreckage.

To Bert it was no more than the end of a series of disagreeable sensations. He was not curious to know what had happened to the airship, nor what had happened to the battle. For a long time he lay waiting apprehensively for the pitching and tossing and his qualms to return, and so, lying, boxed up in the locker, he presently fell asleep.

3

He awoke tranquil but very stuffy, and at the same time very cold, and quite unable to recollect where he could be. His head ached, and his breath was suffocated. He had been dreaming confusedly of Edna, and Desert Dervishes, and of riding bicycles in an extremely perilous manner through the upper air amidst a pyrotechnic display of crackers and Bengal lights – to the great annoyance of a sort of composite person made up of the Prince and Mr Butteridge. Then for some reason Edna and he had begun to cry pitifully for each other, and he woke up with wet eyelashes into this ill-ventilated darkness of the locker. He would never see Edna any more, never see Edna any more.

He thought he must be back in the bedroom behind the cycle shop at the bottom of Bun Hill, and he was sure the vision he had had of the destruction of a magnificent city, a city quite incredibly great and splendid, by means of bombs, was no more than a particularly vivid dream.

'Grubb!' he called, anxious to tell him.

The answering silence, and the dull resonance of the locker to his voice, supplementing the stifling quality of the air, set going a new train of ideas. He lifted up his hands and feet, and met an inflexible resistance. He was in a coffin, he thought! He had been buried alive! He gave way at once to wild panic. ' 'Elp!' he screamed. ' 'Elp!' and drummed with his feet, and kicked and struggled. 'Let me out! Let me out!'

For some seconds he struggled with this intolerable horror, and then the side of his imagined coffin gave way, and he was flying out into daylight. Then he was rolling about on what seemed to be a padded floor with Kurt, and being punched and sworn at lustily.

He sat up. His head bandage had become loose and got over one eye, and he whipped the whole thing off. Kurt was also sitting up, a yard away from him, pink as ever, wrapped in blankets, and with an aluminium diver's helmet over his knee, staring at him with a severe expression, and rubbing his downy unshaven chin. They were both on a slanting floor of crimson padding, and above them was an opening like a long, low cellar flap that Bert by an effort perceived to be the cabin door in a half-inverted condition. The whole cabin had in fact turned on its side.

'What the deuce do you mean by it, Smallways?' said Kurt, 'jumping out of that locker when I was certain you had gone overboard with the rest of them? Where have you been?'

'What's up?' asked Bert.

'This end of the airship is up. Most other things are down.'

'Was there a battle?'

'There was.'

'Who won?'

'I haven't seen the papers, Smallways. We left before the finish. We got disabled and unmanageable, and our colleagues – consorts I mean – were too busy most of them to trouble about us, and the wind blew us – Heaven knows where the wind *is* blowing us. It blew us right out of action at the rate of eighty miles an hour or so. *Gott!* what a wind that was! What a fight! And here we are!'

'Where?'

'In the air, Smallways – in the air! When we get down on the earth again we shan't know what to do with our legs.'

'But what's below us?'

'Canada, to the best of my knowledge – and a jolly bleak, empty, inhospitable country it looks.'

'But why ain't we right ways up?'

Kurt made no answer for a space.

'Last I remember was seeing a sort of flying-machine in a lightning flash,' said Bert. 'Gaw! that was 'orrible. Guns going off! Things explodin'! Clouds and 'ail. Pitching and tossing. I got so scared and desperate – and sick. You don't know how the fight came off?'

'Not a bit of it. I was up with my squad in those divers' dresses, inside the gas chambers, with sheets of silk for caulking. We couldn't see a thing outside except the lightning flashes. I never saw one of those American aeroplanes. Just saw the shots flicker through the chambers and sent off men for the tears. We caught fire a bit – not much, you know. We were too wet, so the fires spluttered out before we banged. And then one of their infernal things dropped out of the air on us and rammed. Didn't you feel it?'

'I felt everything,' said Bert. 'I didn't notice any particular smash – '

'They must have been pretty desperate if they meant it. They slashed down on us like a knife; simply ripped the after gas chambers like gutting herrings, crumpled up the engines and screw. Most of the engines dropped off as they fell off us – or we'd have grounded – but the rest is sort of dangling. We just turned up our nose to the heavens and stayed there. Eleven men rolled off us from various points, and poor old Winterfeld fell through the door of the Prince's cabin into the chart-room and broke his ankle. Also we got our electric gear shot or carried away – no one knows how. That's the position, Smallways. We're driving through the air like a common aerostat, at the mercy of the elements, almost due north – probably to the North Pole.[225] We don't know what aeroplanes the Americans have, or anything at all about it. Very likely we have finished 'em up. One fouled us, one was struck by lightning, some of the men saw a third upset, apparently just for fun. They were going cheap anyhow. Also we've lost most of our *drachen-flieger*. They just skated off into the night. No stability in 'em. That's all. We don't know if we've won or lost. We don't know if we're at war with the British Empire yet or at peace. Consequently, we daren't get down. We don't know what we are up to or what we are going to do. Our Napoleon is alone, forward, and I suppose he's rearranging his plans. Whether New York was our Moscow[226] or not remains to be seen. We've had a high old time and murdered no end of people! War! Noble war! I'm sick of it this morning. I like sitting in rooms right way up and not on slippery partitions. I'm a civilised man. I keep thinking of old Albrecht and the *Barbarossa* . . . I feel I want a wash and kind words and a quiet home. When I look at you, I *know* I want a wash. *Gott!*' – he stifled a vehement yawn – 'What a cockney tadpole of a ruffian you look!'

'Can we get any grub?' asked Bert.

'Heaven knows!' said Kurt.

He meditated upon Bert for a time. 'So far as I can judge, Smallways,' he said, 'the Prince will probably want to throw you overboard – next time he thinks of you. He certainly will if he sees you . . . After all, you know, you came *als Ballast* . . . And we shall have to lighten ship extensively pretty soon. Unless I'm mistaken, the Prince will wake up presently and start doing things with tremendous vigour . . . I've taken a fancy to you. It's the English strain in me. You're a rum little chap. I shan't like seeing you whizz down the air . . . You'd better make yourself useful, Smallways. I think I shall requisition you for my squad. You'll have to work, you know, and be infernally intelligent and all that. And you'll have to hang about upside down a bit. Still, it's the best chance you have. We shan't carry passengers much farther this trip, I fancy. Ballast goes overboard – if we don't want to ground precious soon and be taken prisoners of war. The Prince won't do that anyhow. He'll be game to the last.'

4

By means of a folding-chair, which was still in its place behind the door, they got to the window and looked out in turn and contemplated a sparsely wooded country below, with no railways nor roads, and only occasional signs of habitation. Then a bugle sounded, and Kurt interpreted it as a summons to food. They got through the door and clambered with some difficulty up the nearly vertical passage, holding on desperately with toes and fingertips, to the ventilating perforations in its floor. The mess stewards had found their fireless heating arrangements intact, and there was hot cocoa for the officers and hot soup for the men.

Bert's sense of the queerness of this experience was so keen that it blotted out any fear he might have felt. Indeed, he was far more

interested now than afraid. He seemed to have touched down to
the bottom of fear and abandonment overnight. He was growing
accustomed to the idea that he would probably be killed presently, that
this strange voyage in the air was in all probability his death journey.
No human being can keep permanently afraid: fear goes at last to the
back of one's mind, accepted, and shelved, and done with. He squatted
over his soup, sopping it up with his bread, and contemplated his
comrades. They were all rather yellow and dirty, with four-day beards,
and they grouped themselves in the tired, unpremeditated manner of
men on a wreck. They talked little. The situation perplexed them
beyond any suggestion of ideas. Three had been hurt in the pitching
up of the ship during the fight, and one had a bandaged bullet wound.
It was incredible that this little band of men had committed murder
and massacre on a scale beyond precedent. None of them who squatted
on the sloping gas-padded partition, soup mug in hand, seemed really
guilty of anything of the sort, seemed really capable of hurting a dog
wantonly. They were all so manifestly built for homely chalets on
the solid earth and carefully tilled fields and blonde wives and cheery
merrymaking. The red-faced, sturdy man with light eyelashes who had
brought the first news of the air battle to the men's mess had finished
his soup, and with an expression of maternal solicitude was readjusting
the bandages of a youngster whose arm had been sprained.

Bert was crumbling the last of his bread into the last of his soup, eking
it out as long as possible, when suddenly he became aware that every one
was looking at a pair of feet that were dangling across the downturned
open doorway. Kurt appeared and squatted across the hinge. In some
mysterious way he had shaved his face and smoothed down his light
golden hair. He looked extraordinarily cherubic. 'Der Prinz,' he said.

A second pair of boots followed, making wide and magnificent
gestures in their attempts to feel the door frame. Kurt guided them to
a foothold, and the Prince, shaved and brushed and beeswaxed and
clean and big and terrible, slid down into position astride of the door.
All the men and Bert also stood up and saluted.

The Prince surveyed them with the gesture of a man who sits a steed.
The head of the Kapitän appeared beside him.

Then Bert had a terrible moment. The blue blaze of the Prince's eye
fell upon him, the great finger pointed, a question was asked. Kurt
intervened with explanations.

'*So*,' said the Prince, and Bert was disposed of.

Then the Prince addressed the men in short, heroic sentences,
steadying himself on the hinge with one hand and waving the other in

a fine variety of gesture. What he said Bert could not tell, but he perceived that their demeanour changed, their backs stiffened. They began to punctuate the Prince's discourse with cries of approval. At the end their leader burst into song and all the men with him. 'Ein feste Burg ist unser Gott,'[227] they chanted in deep, strong tones, with an immense moral uplifting. It was glaringly inappropriate in a damaged, half-overturned and sinking airship, which had been disabled and blown out of action after inflicting the cruellest bombardment in the world's history; but it was immensely stirring nevertheless. Bert was deeply moved. He could not sing any of the words of Luther's great hymn, but he opened his mouth and emitted loud, deep, and partially harmonious notes . . .

Far below, this deep chanting struck on the ears of a little camp of Christianised half-breeds who were lumbering. They were breakfasting, but they rushed out cheerfully, quite prepared for the Second Advent. They stared at the shattered and twisted *Vaterland* driving before the gale, amazed beyond words. In so many respects it was like their idea of the Second Advent, and then again in so many respects it wasn't. They stared at its passage, awe-stricken and perplexed beyond their power of words. The hymn ceased. Then after a long interval a voice came out of heaven. 'Vat id diss blace here galled itself; vat?'

They made no answer. Indeed they did not understand, though the question repeated itself.

And at last the monster drove away northward over a crest of pine woods and was no more seen. They fell into a hot and long disputation . . .

The hymn ended. The Prince's legs dangled up the passage again, and everyone was briskly prepared for heroic exertion and triumphant acts. 'Smallways!' cried Kurt, 'come here!'

5

Then Bert, under Kurt's direction, had his first experience of the work of an air-sailor.

The immediate task before the captain of the *Vaterland* was a very simple one. He had to keep afloat. The wind, though it had fallen from its earlier violence, was still blowing strongly enough to render the grounding of so clumsy a mass extremely dangerous, even if it had been desirable for the Prince to land in inhabited country, and so risk capture. It was necessary to keep the airship up until the wind fell and then, if possible, to descend in some lonely district of the Territory where there would be a chance of repair or rescue by some searching consort. In order to do this weight had to be dropped, and Kurt was detailed with a dozen men to climb down among the wreckage of the deflated air chambers and cut the stuff clear, portion by portion, as the airship sank. So Bert, armed with a sharp cutlass, found himself clambering about upon netting four thousand feet up in the air, trying to understand Kurt when he spoke in English and to divine him when he used German.

It was giddy work, but not nearly so giddy as a rather over-nourished reader sitting in a warm room might imagine. Bert found it quite possible to look down and contemplate the wild sub-arctic landscape below, now devoid of any sign of habitation, a land of rocky cliffs and cascades and broad swirling desolate rivers, and of trees and thickets that grew more stunted and scrubby as the day wore on. Here and there on the hills were patches and pockets of snow. And over all this he worked, hacking away at the tough and slippery oiled silk and clinging stoutly to the netting. Presently they cleared and dropped a tangle of bent steel rods and wires from the frame, and a big chunk of silk bladder. That was trying. The airship flew up at once as this loose hamper parted. It seemed almost as though they were dropping all Canada. The stuff spread out in the air and floated down and hit and twisted up in a nasty fashion on the lip of a gorge. Bert clung like a frozen monkey to his ropes and did not move a muscle for five minutes.

But there was something very exhilarating, he found, in this dangerous work, and above everything else, there was the sense of fellowship. He was no longer an isolated and distrustful stranger among these others, he had now a common object with them, he worked with a friendly rivalry to get through with his share before them. And he developed a great respect and affection for Kurt, which had hitherto been only latent in him. Kurt with a job to direct was altogether admirable; he was resourceful, helpful, considerate, swift. He seemed to be everywhere. One forgot his pinkness, his light cheerfulness of manner. Directly one had trouble he was at hand with sound and confident advice. He was like an elder brother to his men.

All together they cleared three considerable chunks of wreckage, and then Bert was glad to clamber up into the cabins again and give place to a second squad. He and his companions were given hot coffee, and indeed, even gloved as they were, the job had been a cold one. They sat drinking it and regarding each other with satisfaction. One man spoke to Bert amiably in German, and Bert nodded and smiled. Through

Kurt, Bert, whose ankles were almost frozen, succeeded in getting a pair of top-boots from one of the disabled men.

In the afternoon the wind abated greatly, and small, infrequent snow-flakes came drifting by. Snow also spread more abundantly below, and the only trees were clumps of pine and spruce in the lower valleys. Kurt went with three men into the still intact gas chambers, let out a certain quantity of gas from them, and prepared a series of ripping panels for the descent. Also the residue of the bombs and explosives in the magazine were thrown overboard and fell, detonating loudly, in the wilderness below. And about four o'clock in the afternoon upon a wide and rocky plain within sight of snow-crested cliffs, the *Vaterland* ripped and grounded.

It was necessarily a difficult and violent affair, for the *Vaterland* had not been planned for the necessities of a balloon. The captain got one panel ripped too soon and the others not soon enough. She dropped heavily, bounced clumsily, and smashed the hanging gallery into the forepart, mortally injuring Von Winterfeld, and then came down in a collapsing heap after dragging for some moments. The forward shield and its machine gun tumbled in upon the things below. Two men were hurt badly – one got a broken leg and one was internally injured – by flying rods and wires, and Bert was pinned for a time under the side. When at last he got clear and could take a view of the situation, the great black eagle that had started so splendidly from Franconia six evenings ago, sprawled deflated over the cabins of the airship and the frostbitten rocks of this desolate place and looked a most unfortunate bird – as though someone had caught it and wrung its neck and cast it aside. Several of the crew of the airship were standing about in silence, contemplating the wreckage and the empty wilderness into which they had fallen. Others were busy under the impromptu tent made by the empty gas chambers. The Prince had gone a little way off and was scrutinising the distant heights through his field-glass. They had the appearance of old sea cliffs; here and there were small clumps of conifers, and in two places tall cascades. The nearer ground was strewn with glaciated boulders and supported nothing but a stunted Alpine vegetation of compact clustering stems and stalkless flowers. No river was visible, but the air was full of the rush and babble of a torrent close at hand. A bleak and biting wind was blowing. Ever and again a snowflake drifted past. The springless frozen earth under Bert's feet felt strangely dead and heavy after the buoyant airship.

So it came about that that great and powerful Prince Karl Albert was for a time thrust out of the stupendous conflict he chiefly had been instrumental in provoking. The chances of battle and the weather conspired to maroon him in Labrador, and there he raged for six long days, while war and wonder swept the world. Nation rose against nation and air-fleet grappled air-fleet, cities blazed and men died in multitudes; but in Labrador one might have dreamt that, except for a little noise of hammering, the world was at peace.

There the encampment lay; from a distance the cabins, covered over with the silk of the balloon part, looked like a gipsy's tent on a rather exceptional scale, and all the available hands were busy in building out of the steel of the framework a mast from which the *Vaterland*'s electricians might hang the long conductors of the apparatus for wireless telegraphy that was to link the Prince to the world again. There were times when it seemed they would never rig that mast. From the outset the party suffered hardship. They were not too abundantly provisioned, and they were put on short rations, and for all the thick garments they had, they were but ill-equipped against the piercing wind and inhospitable violence of this wilderness.

The first night was spent in darkness and without fires. The engines that had supplied power were smashed and dropped far away to the south, and there was never a match among the company. It had been death to carry matches. All the explosives had been thrown out of the magazine, and it was only towards morning that the bird-faced man whose cabin Bert had taken in the beginning confessed to a brace of duelling pistols and cartridges, with which a fire could be started. Afterwards the lockers of the machine gun were found to contain a supply of unused ammunition.

The night was a distressing one and seemed almost interminable. Hardly anyone slept. There were seven wounded men aboard, and Von Winterfeld's head had been injured, and he was shivering and in delirium, struggling with his attendant and shouting strange things about the burning of New York. The men crept together in the mess room in the darkling, wrapped in what they could find, and drank cocoa from the fireless heaters and listened to his cries. In the morning the Prince made them a speech about Destiny, and the God of his Fathers and the pleasure and glory of giving one's life for his dynasty, and a number of similar considerations that might otherwise have been neglected in that bleak wilderness. The men cheered without enthusiasm, and far away a wolf howled.

Then they set to work, and for a week they toiled to put up a mast of steel, and hang from it a gridiron of copper wires two hundred feet by twelve. The theme of all that time was work, work continually, straining and toilsome work, and all the rest was grim hardship and evil chances, save for a certain wild splendour in the sunset and sunrise in the torrents and drifting weather, in the wilderness about them. They built and tended a ring of perpetual fires, gangs roamed for brushwood and met with wolves, and the wounded men and their beds were brought out from the airship cabins, and put in shelters about the fires. There old Von Winterfeld raved and became quiet and presently died, and three of the other wounded sickened for want of good food, while their fellows mended. These things happened, as it were, in the wings; the central facts before Bert's consciousness were always firstly the perpetual toil, the holding and lifting, and lugging at heavy and clumsy masses, the tedious filing and winding of wires, and secondly, the Prince, urgent and threatening whenever a man relaxed. He would stand over them, and point over their heads, southward into the empty sky. 'The world there,' he said in German, 'is waiting for us! Fifty centuries come to their Consummation.'[228] Bert did not understand the words, but he read the gesture. Several times the Prince grew angry; once with a man who was working slowly, once with a man who stole a comrade's ration. The first he scolded and set to a more tedious task; the second he struck in the face and ill-used. He did no work himself. There was a clear space near the fires in which he would walk up and down, sometimes for two hours together, with arms folded, muttering to himself of Patience and his destiny. At times these mutterings broke out into rhetoric, into shouts and gestures that would arrest the workers; they would stare at him until they perceived that his blue eyes glared and his waving hand addressed itself always to the southward hills. On Sunday the work ceased for half an hour, and the Prince preached on faith and God's friendship for David, and afterwards they all sang: 'Ein feste Burg ist unser Gott.'

In an improvised hovel lay Von Winterfeld, and all one morning he raved of the greatness of Germany. 'Blut und Eisen!' he shouted, and then, as if in derision, 'Welt-Politik – ha, ha!' Then he would explain complicated questions of polity to imaginary hearers, in low, wily tones. The other sick men kept still, listening to him. Bert's distracted attention would be recalled by Kurt. 'Smallways, take that end. So!'

Slowly, tediously, the great mast was rigged and hoisted foot by foot into place. The electricians had contrived a catchment pool and a wheel in the torrent close at hand – for the little Mulhausen dynamo with its turbinal volute used by the telegraphists was quite adaptable to water driving, and on the sixth day in the evening the apparatus was in working order and the Prince was calling – weakly, indeed, but calling – to his air-fleet across the empty spaces of the world. For a time he called unheeded.

The effect of that evening was to linger long in Bert's memory. A red fire spluttered and blazed close by the electricians at their work, and red gleams ran up the vertical steel mast and threads of copper wire towards the zenith. The Prince sat on a rock close by, with his chin on his hand, waiting. Beyond and to the northward was the cairn that covered Von Winterfeld, surmounted by a cross of steel, and from among the tumbled rocks in the distance the eyes of a wolf gleamed redly. On the other hand was the wreckage of the great airship and the men bivouacked about a second ruddy flare. They were all keeping very still, as if waiting to hear what news might presently be given them. Far away, across many hundreds of miles of desolation, other wireless masts would be clicking, and snapping, and waking into responsive vibration. Perhaps they were not. Perhaps those throbs upon the ether wasted themselves upon a regardless world. When the men spoke, they spoke in low tones. Now and then a bird shrieked remotely, and once a wolf howled. All these things were set in the immense cold spaciousness of the wild.

7

Bert got the news last, and chiefly in broken English, from a linguist among his mates. It was only far on in the night that the weary telegraphist got an answer to his calls, but then the messages came clear and strong. And such news it was!

'I say,' said Bert at his breakfast, amidst a great clamour, 'tell us a bit.'

'All de vorlt is at vor!' said the linguist, waving his cocoa in an illustrative manner, 'all de vorlt is at vor!'

Bert stared southward into the dawn. It did not seem so.

'All de vorlt is at vor! They haf burn' Berlin; they haf burn' London; they haf burn' Hamburg and Paris. Chapan hass burn San Francisco. We haf mate a camp at Niagara. Dat is whad they are telling us. China has cot *drachenflieger* and *luftschiffe* beyont counting. All de vorlt is at vor!'

'Gaw!' said Bert.

'Yess,' said the linguist, drinking his cocoa.

'Burnt up London, 'ave they? Like we did New York?'

'It was a bombardment.'

'They don't say anything about a place called Clapham, or Bun Hill, do they?'

'I haf heard noding,' said the linguist.

That was all Bert could get for a time. But the excitement of all the men about him was contagious, and presently he saw Kurt standing alone, hands behind him, and looking at one of the distant waterfalls very steadfastly. He went up and saluted, soldier-fashion. 'Beg pardon, lieutenant,' he said.

Kurt turned his face. It was unusually grave that morning. 'I was just thinking I would like to see that waterfall closer,' he said. 'It reminds me – what do you want?'

'I can't make 'ead or tail of what they're saying, sir. Would you mind telling me the news?'

'Damn the news,' said Kurt. 'You'll get news enough before the day's out. It's the end of the world. They're sending the *Graf Zeppelin* for us. She'll be here by the morning, and we ought to be at Niagara – or eternal smash – within eight and forty hours . . . I want to look at that waterfall. You'd better come with me. Have you had your rations?'

'Yessir.'

'Very well. Come.'

And musing profoundly, Kurt led the way across the rocks towards the distant waterfall. For a time Bert walked behind him in the character of an escort; then as they passed out of the atmosphere of the encampment, Kurt lagged for him to come alongside.

'We shall be back in it all in two days' time,' he said. 'And it's a devil of a war to go back to. That's the news. The world's gone mad. Our fleet beat the Americans the night we got disabled, that's clear. We lost eleven – eleven airships certain, and all their aeroplanes got smashed. God knows how much we smashed or how many we killed. But that was only the beginning. Our start's been like firing a magazine. Every country was hiding flying-machines. They're fighting in the air all over Europe – all over the world. The Japanese and Chinese have joined in. That's the great fact. That's the supreme fact. They've pounced into our little quarrels . . . The Yellow Peril was a peril after all! They've got thousands of airships. They're all over the world. We bombarded London and Paris, and now the French and English have smashed up Berlin. And now Asia is at us all, and on the top of us all . . . It's mania.

China on the top. And they don't know where to stop. It's limitless. It's the last confusion. They're bombarding capitals, smashing up dock-yards and factories, mines and fleets.'

'Did they do much to London, sir?' asked Bert.

'Heaven knows . . .'

He said no more for a time.

'This Labrador seems a quiet place,' he resumed at last. 'I've half a mind to stay here. Can't do that. No! I've got to see it through. I've got to see it through. You've got to, too. Every one . . . But why? . . . I tell you – our world's gone to pieces. There's no way out of it, no way back. Here we are! We're like mice caught in a house on fire, we're like cattle overtaken by a flood. Presently we shall be picked up, and back we shall go into the fighting. We shall kill and smash again – perhaps. It's a Chino-Japanese air-fleet this time, and the odds are against us. Our turn will come. What will happen to you I don't know, but for myself, I know quite well; I shall be killed.'

'You'll be all right,' said Bert, after a queer pause.

'No!' said Kurt, 'I'm going to be killed. I didn't know it before, but this morning, at dawn, I knew it – as though I'd been told.'

' 'Ow?'

'I tell you I know.'

'But 'ow *could* you know?'

'I know.'

'Like being told?'

'Like being certain.

'I know,' he repeated, and for a time they walked in silence towards the waterfall.

Kurt, wrapped in his thoughts, walked heedlessly, and at last broke out again. 'I've always felt young before, Smallways, but this morning I feel old – old. So old! Nearer to death than old men feel. And I've always thought life was a lark. It isn't . . . This sort of thing has always been happening, I suppose – these things, wars and earthquakes, that sweep across all the decency of life. It's just as though I had woke up to it all for the first time. Every night since we were at New York I've dreamt of it . . . And it's always been so – it's the way of life. People are torn away from the people they care for; homes are smashed, creatures full of life, and memories, and little peculiar gifts are scalded and smashed, and torn to pieces, and starved, and spoilt. London! Berlin! San Francisco! Think of all the human histories we ended in New York! . . . And the others go on again as though such things weren't possible. As I went on! Like animals! Just like animals.'

He said nothing for a long time, and then he dropped out, 'The Prince is a lunatic!'

They came to a place where they had to climb, and then to a long peat level beside a rivulet. There a quantity of delicate little pink flowers caught Bert's eye. 'Gaw!' he said, and stooped to pick one. 'In a place like this.'

Kurt stopped and half turned. His face winced.

'I never see such a flower,' said Bert. 'It's so delicate.'

'Pick some more if you want to,' said Kurt.

Bert did so, while Kurt stood and watched him.

'Funny 'ow one always wants to pick flowers,' said Bert.

Kurt had nothing to add to that.

They went on again, without talking, for a long time.

At last they came to a rocky hummock, from which the view of the waterfall opened out. There Kurt stopped and seated himself on a rock. 'That's as much as I wanted to see,' he explained. 'It isn't very like, but it's like enough.'

'Like what?'

'Another waterfall I knew.'

He asked a question abruptly. 'Got a girl, Smallways?'

'Funny thing,' said Bert, 'those flowers, I suppose – I was jes' thinking of 'er.'

'So was I.'

'*What!* Edna?'

'No. I was thinking of *my* Edna. We've all got Ednas, I suppose, for our imaginations to play about. This was a girl. But all that's past for ever. It's hard to think I can't see her just for a minute – just let her know I'm thinking of her.'

'Very likely,' said Bert, 'you'll see 'er all right.'

'No,' said Kurt with decision, 'I *know*.

'I met her,' he went on, 'in a place like this – in the Alps – Engstlen Alp. There's a waterfall rather like this one – a broad waterfall down towards Innertkirchen. That's why I came here this morning. We slipped away and had half a day together beside it. And we picked flowers. Just such flowers as you picked. The same for all I know. And gentian.'

'I know,' said Bert, 'me and Edna – we done things like that. Flowers. And all that. Seems years off now.'

'She was beautiful and daring and shy, *Mein Gott*! I can hardly hold myself for the desire to see her and hear her voice again before I die. Where is she? . . . Look here, Smallways, I shall write a sort of letter – And there's her portrait.' He touched his breast pocket.

'You'll see 'er again all right,' said Bert.

'No! I shall never see her again . . . I don't understand why people should meet just to be torn apart. But I know she and I will never meet again. That I know as surely as that the sun will rise, and that cascade come shining over the rocks after I am dead and done . . . Oh! It's all foolishness and haste and violence and cruel folly, stupidity and blundering hate and selfish ambition – all the things that men have done – all the things they will ever do. *Gott!* Smallways, what a muddle and confusion life has always been – the battles and massacres and disasters, the hates and harsh acts, the murders and sweatings, the lynchings and cheatings. This morning I am tired of it all, as though I'd just found it out for the first time. I *have* found it out. When a man is tired of life, I suppose it is time for him to die. I've lost heart, and death is over me. Death is close to me, and I know I have got to end. But think of all the hopes I had only a little time ago, the sense of fine beginnings! . . . It was all a sham. There were no beginnings . . . We're just ants in ant-hill cities, in a world that doesn't matter; that goes on and rambles into nothingness. New York – New York doesn't even strike me as horrible. New York was nothing but an ant-hill kicked to pieces by a fool!

'Think of it, Smallways: there's war everywhere! They're smashing up their civilisation before they have made it. The sort of thing the English did at Alexandria, the Japanese at Port Arthur, the French at Casablanca,[229] is going on everywhere. Everywhere! Down in South America even they are fighting among themselves![230] No place is safe – no place is at peace. There is no place where a woman and her daughter can hide and be at peace. The war comes through the air, bombs drop in the night. Quiet people go out in the morning, and see air-fleets passing overhead – dripping death – dripping death!'

CHAPTER EIGHT

A World at War

1

It was only very slowly that Bert got hold of this idea that the whole world was at war, that he formed any image at all of the crowded countries south of these Arctic solitudes stricken with terror and dismay as these new-born aerial navies swept across their skies. He was not used to thinking of the world as a whole, but as a limitless hinterland of happenings beyond the range of his immediate vision. War in his imagination was something, a source of news and emotion, that happened in a restricted area, called the Seat of War. But now the whole atmosphere was the Seat of War, and every land a cockpit. So closely had the nations raced along the path of research and invention, so secret and yet so parallel had been their plans and acquisitions, that it was within a few hours of the launching of the first fleet in Franconia that an Asiatic Armada beat its westward way across, high above the marvelling millions in the plain of the Ganges. But the preparations of the Confederation of Eastern Asia had been on an altogether more colossal scale than the German. 'With this step,' said Tan Ting-siang,[231] 'we overtake and pass the West. We recover the peace of the world that these barbarians have destroyed.'

Their secrecy and swiftness and inventions had far surpassed those of the Germans, and where the Germans had had a hundred men at work the Asiatics had ten thousand. There came to their great aeronautic parks at Chinsi-fu and Tsingyen, by the monorails that now laced the whole surface of China, a limitless supply of skilled and able workmen, workmen far above the average European in industrial efficiency. The news of the German World Surprise simply quickened their efforts. At the time of the bombardment of New York it is doubtful if the Germans had three hundred airships altogether in the world; the score of Asiatic fleets flying east and west and south must have numbered several thousand. Moreover the Asiatics had a real fighting flying-machine, the *Niaio*[232] as they were called, a light but quite efficient weapon, infinitely superior to the German *drachenflieger*. Like that, it was a one-man machine, but it was built very lightly of steel and cane and chemical silk, with a transverse engine, and a flapping side wing. The aeronaut carried a gun firing explosive bullets loaded with oxygen, and in addition, and true to the best tradition of Japan, a sword. Mostly they were Japanese, and it is characteristic that from the first it was contemplated that the aeronaut should be a swordsman. The wings of these flyers had batlike hooks forward, by which they were to cling to their antagonist's gas chambers while boarding him. These light flying-machines were carried with the fleets, and also sent overland or by sea to the front with the men. They were capable of flights of from two to five hundred miles according to the wind.

So, hard upon the uprush of the first German air-fleet, these Asiatic swarms took to the atmosphere. Instantly every organised Government in the world was frantically and vehemently building airships and whatever approach to a flying-machine its inventors' had discovered. There was no time for diplomacy. Warnings and ultimatums were telegraphed to and fro, and in a few hours all the panic-fierce world was openly at war, and at war in the most complicated way. For Britain and France and Italy had declared war upon Germany and outraged Swiss neutrality; India, at the sight of Asiatic airships, had broken into a Hindu insurrection in Bengal and a Mohammedan revolt hostile to this in the North West Province – the latter spreading like wildfire from Gobi to the Gold Coast – and the Confederation of Eastern Asia had seized the oil wells of Burma and was impartially attacking America and Germany. In a week they were building airships in Damascus and Cairo and Johannesburg; Australia and New Zealand were frantically equipping themselves. One unique and terrifying aspect of this development was the swiftness with which these monsters could be produced. To build an ironclad took from two to four years; an airship could be put together in as many weeks. Moreover, compared with even a torpedo boat, the airship was remarkably simple to construct; given the air-chamber material, the engines, the gas plant, and the design, it was really not more complicated and far easier than an ordinary wooden boat had been a hundred years before. And now from Cape Horn to Nova Zembla, and from Canton round to Canton again,[233] there were factories and workshops and industrial resources.

And the German airships were barely in sight of the Atlantic waters, the first Asiatic fleet was scarcely reported from Upper Burma, before the fantastic fabric of credit and finance that had held the world together economically for a hundred years strained and snapped. A tornado of realisation swept through every stock exchange in the world; banks stopped payment, business shrank and ceased, factories ran on for a day or so by a sort of inertia, completing the orders of bankrupt and extinguished customers, then stopped. The New York Bert Smallways saw, for all its glare of light and traffic, was in the pit of an economic and financial collapse unparalleled in history. The flow of the food supply was already a little checked. And before the world war had lasted two weeks – by the time, that is, that mast was rigged in Labrador – there was not a city or town in the world outside China, however far from the actual centres of destruction, where police and government were not adopting special emergency methods to deal with a want of food and a glut of unemployed people.

The special peculiarities of aerial warfare were of such a nature as to trend, once it had begun, almost inevitably towards social disorganisation. The first of these peculiarities was brought home to the Germans in their attack upon New York; the immense power of destruction an airship has over the thing below, and its relative inability to occupy or police or guard or garrison a surrendered position. Necessarily, in the face of urban populations in a state of economic disorganisation and infuriated and starving, this led to violent and destructive collisions, and even where the air-fleet floated inactive above, there would be civil conflict and passionate disorder below. Nothing comparable to this state of affairs had been known in the previous history of warfare, unless we take such a case as that of a nineteenth-century warship attacking some large savage or barbaric settlement, or one of those naval bombardments that disfigure the history of Great Britain in the late eighteenth century. Then, indeed, there had been cruelties and destruction that faintly foreshadowed the horrors of the aerial war. Moreover, before the twentieth century the world had had but one experience, and that a comparatively light one, in the Communist insurrection of Paris, 1871,[234] of the possibilities of a modern urban population under warlike stresses.

A second peculiarity of airship war as it first came to the world that also made for social collapse, was the ineffectiveness of the early airships against each other. Upon anything below they could rain explosives in the most deadly fashion, forts and ships and cities lay at their mercy, but unless they were prepared for a suicidal grapple they could do remarkably little mischief to each other. The armament of the huge German airships, big as the biggest mammoth liners afloat, was one machine gun that could easily have been packed up on a couple of mules. In addition, when it became evident that the air must be fought for, the air-sailors were provided with rifles with explosive bullets of oxygen or inflammable substance, but no airship at any time ever carried as much in the way of guns and armour as the smallest gunboat on the navy list had been accustomed to do. Consequently, when these monsters met in battle, they manoeuvred for the upper place, or grappled and fought like junks, throwing grenades, fighting hand to hand in an entirely mediaeval fashion. The risks of a collapse and fall on either side came near to balancing in every case the chances of victory. As a consequence, and after their first experiences of battle, one finds a growing tendency on the part of the air-fleet admirals to evade joining battle, and to seek rather the moral advantage of a destructive counter-attack.

And if the airships were too ineffective, the early *drachenflieger* were either too unstable, like the German, or too light, like the Japanese, to produce immediately decisive results. Later, it is true, the Brazilians launched a flying-machine of a type and scale that was capable of dealing with an airship, but they built only three or four, they operated only in South America, and they vanished from history untraceably in the time when world-bankruptcy put a stop to all further engineering production on any considerable scale.

The third peculiarity of aerial warfare was that it was at once enormously destructive and entirely indecisive. It had this unique feature, that both sides lay open to punitive attack. In all previous forms of war, both by land and sea, the losing side was speedily unable to raid its antagonist's territory and the communications. One fought on a 'front', and behind that front the winner's supplies and resources, his towns and factories and capital, the peace of his country, were secure. If the war was a naval one, you destroyed your enemy's battle fleet and then blockaded his ports, secured his coaling stations, and hunted down any stray cruisers that threatened your ports of commerce. But to blockade and watch a coastline is one thing, to blockade and watch the whole surface of a country is another, and cruisers and privateers are things that take long to make, that cannot be packed up and hidden and carried unostentatiously from point to point. In aerial war the stronger side, even supposing it destroyed the main battle fleet of the weaker, had then either to patrol and watch or destroy every possible point at which he might produce another and perhaps a novel and more deadly form of flyer. It meant darkening his air with airships. It meant building them by the thousand and making aeronauts by the hundred thousand. A small uninflated airship could be hidden in a railway shed, in a village street, in a wood; a flying-machine is even less conspicuous.

And in the air are no streets, no channels, no point where one can say

of an antagonist, 'If he wants to reach my capital he must come by here.'
In the air all directions lead everywhere.

Consequently it was impossible to end a war by any of the established
methods. A, having outnumbered and overwhelmed B, hovers, a
thousand airships strong, over his capital, threatening to bombard it
unless B submits. B replies by wireless telegraphy that he is now in the
act of bombarding the chief manufacturing city of A by means of three
raider airships. A denounces B's raiders as pirates and so forth, bombards
B's capital, and sets off to hunt down B's airships, while B, in a state of
passionate emotion and heroic unconquerableness, sets to work amidst
his ruins, making fresh airships and explosives for the benefit of A.
The war became perforce a universal guerilla war, a war inextricably
involving civilians and homes and all the apparatus of social life.

These aspects of aerial fighting took the world by surprise. There had
been no foresight to deduce these consequences. If there had been, the
world would have arranged for a Universal Peace Conference in 1900.[235]
But mechanical invention had gone faster than intellectual and social
organisation, and the world, with its silly old flags, its silly unmeaning
tradition of nationality, its cheap newspapers and cheaper passions and
imperialisms, its base commercial motives and habitual insincerities and
vulgarities, its race lies and conflicts, was taken by surprise. Once the
war began there was no stopping it. The flimsy fabric of credit that had
grown with no man foreseeing, and that had held those hundreds of
millions in an economic interdependence that no man clearly understood, dissolved in panic. Everywhere went the airships dropping
bombs, destroying any hope of a rally, and everywhere below were
economic catastrophe, starving workless people, rioting, and social
disorder. Whatever constructive guiding intelligence there had been
among the nations vanished in the passionate stresses of the time.
Such newspapers and documents and histories as survive from this
period all tell one universal story of towns and cities with the food
supply interrupted and their streets congested with starving unemployed; of crises in administration and states of siege, of provisional
Governments and Councils of Defence, and, in the cases of India and
Egypt, insurrectionary committees taking charge of the rearming of the
population, of the making of batteries and gun-pits, of the vehement
manufacture of airships and flying-machines.

One sees these things in glimpses, in illuminated moments, as if
through a driving reek of clouds, going on all over the world. It was
the dissolution of an age; it was the collapse of the civilisation that had
trusted to machinery, and the instruments of its destruction were

machines. But while the collapse of the previous great civilisation, that of Rome, had been a matter of centuries, had been a thing of phase and phase, like the ageing and dying of a man, this, like his killing by railway or motor car, was one swift, conclusive smashing and an end.

2

The early battles of the aerial war were no doubt determined by attempts to realise the old naval maxim, to ascertain the position of the enemy's fleet and to destroy it. There was first the battle of the Bernese Oberland, in which the Italian and French navigables in their flank raid upon the Franconian Park were assailed by the Swiss experimental squadron, supported as the day wore on by German airships, and then the encounter of the British Winterhouse-Dunne aeroplanes[236] with three unfortunate Germans.

Then came the Battle of North India, in which the entire Anglo-Indian aeronautic settlement establishment fought for three days against overwhelming odds, and was dispersed and destroyed in detail.

And simultaneously with the beginning of that, commenced the momentous struggle of the Germans and Asiatics that is usually known as the Battle of Niagara because of the objective of the Asiatic attack. But it passed gradually into a sporadic conflict over half a continent. Such German airships as escaped destruction in battle descended and surrendered to the Americans, and were remanned, and in the end it became a series of pitiless and heroic encounters between the Americans, savagely resolved to exterminate their enemies, and a continually reinforced army of invasion from Asia quartered upon the Pacific slope and supported by an immense fleet. From the first the war in America was fought with implacable bitterness; no quarter was asked, no prisoners were taken. With ferocious and magnificent energy the Americans constructed and launched ship after ship to battle and perish against the Asiatic multitudes. All other affairs were subordinate to this war, the whole population was presently living or dying for it. Presently, as I shall tell, the white men found in the Butteridge machine a weapon that could meet and fight the flying-machines of the Asiatic swordsman.

The Asiatic invasion of America completely effaced the German–American conflict. It vanishes from history. At first it had seemed to promise quite sufficient tragedy in itself – beginning as it did in un-forgettable massacre. After the destruction of central New York all America had risen like one man, resolved to die a thousand deaths rather than submit to Germany. The Germans grimly resolved upon beating the Americans into submission and, following out the plans developed by the Prince, had seized Niagara – in order to avail themselves of its enormous power-works; expelled all its inhabitants and made a desert of its environs as far as Buffalo. They had also, directly Great Britain and France declared war, wrecked the country upon the Canadian side for nearly ten miles inland. They began to bring up men and material from the fleet off the east coast, stringing out to and fro like bees getting honey. It was then that the Asiatic forces appeared, and it was in their attack upon this German base at Niagara that the airfleets of East and West first met and the greater issue became clear.

One conspicuous peculiarity of the early aerial fighting arose from the profound secrecy with which the airships had been prepared. Each power had had but the dimmest inkling of the schemes of its rivals, and even experiments with its own devices were limited by the needs of secrecy. None of the designers of airships and aeroplanes had known clearly what their inventions might have to fight; many had not imagined they would have to fight anything whatever in the air; and had planned them only for the dropping of explosives. Such had been the German idea. The only weapon for fighting another airship with which the Franconian fleet had been provided was the machine gun forward. Only after the fight over New York were the men given short rifles with detonating bullets. Theoretically, the *drachenflieger* were to have been the fighting weapon. They were declared to be aerial torpedoboats, and the aeronaut was supposed to swoop close to his antagonist and cast his bombs as he whirled past. But indeed these contrivances were hopelessly unstable; not one-third in any engagement succeeded in getting back to the mother airship. The rest were either smashed up or grounded.

The allied Chino-Japanese fleet made the same distinction as the Germans between airships and fighting machines heavier than air, but the type in both cases was entirely different from the Occidental models, and – it is eloquent of the vigour with which these great peoples took up and bettered the European methods of scientific research – in almost every particular the invention of Asiatic engineers. Chief among these, it is worth remarking, was Mohini K. Chatterjee,[237] a political exile who had formerly served in the British-Indian aeronautic park at Lahore.

The German airship was fish-shaped, with a blunted head; the Asiatic airship was also fish-shaped, but not so much on the lines of a cod or goby as of a ray or sole. It had a wide, flat underside, unbroken by windows or any opening except along the middle line. Its cabins occupied its axis, with a sort of bridge deck above, and the gas chambers gave the whole affair the shape of a gipsy's hooped tent, except that it was much flatter. The German airship was essentially a navigable balloon very much lighter than air; the Asiatic airship was very little lighter than air and skimmed through it with much greater velocity if with considerably less stability. They carried fore and aft guns, the latter much the larger, throwing inflammatory shells, and in addition they had nests for riflemen on both the upper and the under side. Light as this armament was in comparison with the smallest gunboat that ever sailed, it was sufficient for them to out-fight as well as out-fly the German monster airships. In action they flew to get behind or over the Germans: they even dashed underneath, avoiding only passing immediately beneath the magazine, and then as soon as they had crossed let fly with their rear gun, and sent flares or oxygen shells into the antagonist's gas chambers.

It was not in their airships, but, as I have said, in their flying-machines proper, that the strength of the Asiatics lay. Next only to the Butteridge machine, these were certainly the most efficient heavier-than-air fliers that had ever appeared. They were the invention of a Japanese artist, and they differed in type extremely from the box-kite quality of the German *drachenflieger*. They had curiously curved, flexible side wings, more like *bent* butterfly's wings than anything else, and made of a substance like celluloid and of brightly painted silk, and they had a long hummingbird tail. At the forward corner of the wings were hooks, rather like the claws of a bat, by which the machine could catch and hang and tear at the walls of an airship's gas chamber. The solitary rider sat between the wings above a transverse explosive engine, an explosive engine that differed in no essential particular from those in use in the light motor bicycles of the period. Below was a single large wheel. The rider sat astride of a saddle, as in the Butteridge machine, and he carried a large double-edged two-handed sword, in addition to his explosive-bullet-firing rifle.

3

One sets down these particulars and compares the points of the American and German pattern of aeroplane and navigable, but none of these facts were clearly known to any of those who fought in this monstrously confused battle above the American great lakes.

Each side went into action against it knew not what, under novel conditions and with apparatus that even without hostile attacks was capable of producing the most disconcerting surprises. Schemes of action, attempts at collective manoeuvring necessarily went to pieces directly the fight began, just as they did in almost all the early ironclad battles of the previous century. Each captain then had to fall back upon individual action and his own devices; one would see triumph in what another read as a cue for flight and despair. It is as true of the Battle of Niagara[238] as of the Battle of Lissa[239] that it was not a battle but a bundle of 'battlettes'!

To such a spectator as Bert it presented itself as a series of incidents, some immense, some trivial, but collectively incoherent. He never had a sense of any plain issue joined, of any point struggled for and won or lost. He saw tremendous things happen and in the end his world darkened to disaster and ruin.

He saw the battle from the ground, from Prospect Park and from Goat Island, whither he fled.

But the manner in which he came to be on the ground needs explaining.

The Prince had resumed command of his fleet through wireless telegraphy long before the *Zeppelin* had located his encampment in Labrador. By his direction the German air-fleet, whose advance scouts had been in contact with the Japanese over the Rocky Mountains, had concentrated upon Niagara and awaited his arrival. He had rejoined his command early in the morning of the twelfth, and Bert had his first prospect of the Gorge of Niagara while he was doing net drill outside the middle gas chamber at sunrise. The *Zeppelin* was flying very high at the time, and far below he saw the water in the gorge marbled with froth and then away to the west the great crescent of the Canadian Fall shining, flickering and foaming in the level sunlight and sending up a deep, incessant thudding rumble to the sky. The air-fleet was keeping station in an enormous crescent, with its horns pointing south-westward, a long array of shining monsters with tails rotating slowly and German ensigns now trailing from their bellies aft of their Marconi pendants.[240]

Niagara City was still largely standing then, albeit its streets were empty of all life. Its bridges were intact; its hotels and restaurants still flying flags and inviting sky signs; its power-stations running. But about it the country on both sides of the gorge might have been swept by a colossal broom. Everything that could possibly give cover to an attack upon the German position at Niagara had been levelled as ruthlessly as machinery and explosives could contrive; houses blown up and burnt, woods burnt, fences and crops destroyed. The monorails had been torn up, and the roads in particular cleared of all possibility of concealment or shelter. Seen from above, the effect of this wreckage was grotesque. Young woods had been destroyed wholesale by dragging wires, and the spoilt saplings, smashed or uprooted, lay in swathes like corn after the sickle. Houses had an appearance of being flattened down by the pressure of a gigantic finger. Much burning was still going on, and large areas had been reduced to patches of smouldering and sometimes still glowing blackness. Here and there lay the debris of belated fugitives, carts, and dead bodies of horses and men; and where houses had had water-supplies there were pools of water and running springs from the ruptured pipes. In unscorched fields horses and cattle still fed peacefully. Beyond this desolated area the countryside was still standing, but almost all the people had fled. Buffalo was on fire to an enormous extent, and there were no signs of any efforts to grapple with the flames.

Niagara City itself was being rapidly converted to the needs of a military depot. A large number of skilled engineers had already been brought from the fleet and were busily at work adapting the exterior industrial apparatus of the place to the purposes of an aeronautic park. They had made a gas recharging station at the corner of the American Fall above the funicular railway, and they were opening up a much larger area to the south for the same purpose. Over the power houses and hotels and suchlike prominent or important points the German flag was flying.

The *Zeppelin* circled slowly over this scene twice while the Prince surveyed it from the swinging gallery; it then rose towards the centre of the crescent and transferred the Prince and his suite, Kurt included, to the *Hohenzollern*,[241] which had been chosen as the flagship during the impending battle. They were swung up on a small cable from the forward gallery, and the men of the *Zeppelin* manned the outer netting as the Prince and his staff left them. The *Zeppelin* then came about, circled down and grounded in Prospect Park, in order to land the wounded and take aboard explosives; for she had come to Labrador with her magazines empty, it being uncertain what weight she might need to carry. She also replenished the hydrogen in one of her forward chambers which had leaked.

Bert was detailed as a bearer and helped carry the wounded one by one into the nearest of the large hotels that faced the Canadian shore. The hotel was quite empty except that there were two trained American nurses and a porter, and three or four Germans awaiting them. Bert went with the *Zeppelin*'s doctor into the main street of the place, and they broke into a drug shop and obtained various things of which they stood in need. As they returned they found an officer and two men making a rough inventory of the available material in the various stores. Except for them the wide, main street of the town was quite deserted, the people had been given three hours to clear out, and everybody, it seemed, had done so. At one corner a dead man lay against the wall – shot. Two or three dogs were visible up the empty vista, but towards its river end the passage of a string of monorail cars broke the stillness and the silence. They were loaded with hose, and were passing to the trainful of workers who were converting Prospect Park into an airship dock.

Bert pushed a case of medicine balanced on a bicycle taken from an adjacent shop, to the hotel, and then he was sent to load bombs into the *Zeppelin* magazine, a duty that called for elaborate care. From this job he was presently called off by the captain of the *Zeppelin*, who sent him with a note to the officer in charge of the Anglo-American Power Company, for the field telephone had still to be adjusted. Bert received his instructions in German, whose meaning he guessed, and saluted and took the note, not caring to betray his ignorance of the language. He started off with a bright air of knowing his way and turned a corner or so, and was only beginning to suspect that he did not know where he was going when his attention was recalled to the sky by the report of a gun from the *Hohenzollern* and celestial cheering.

He looked up and found the view obstructed by the houses on either side of the street. He hesitated, and then curiosity took him back towards the bank of the river. Here his view was inconvenienced by trees, and it was with a start that he discovered the *Zeppelin*, which he knew had still a quarter of her magazines to fill, was rising over Goat Island. She had not waited for her complement of ammunition. It occurred to him that he was left behind. He ducked back among the trees and bushes until he felt secure from any afterthought on the part of the *Zeppelin*'s captain. Then his curiosity to see what the German air-fleet faced overcame him, and drew him at last halfway across the bridge to Goat Island. From that point he had nearly a hemisphere of sky and got his first glimpse of the Asiatic airships low in the sky above the glittering tumults of the Upper Rapids.

They were far less impressive than the German ships. He could not judge the distance, and they flew edgeways to him, so as to conceal the broader aspect of their bulk.

Bert stood there in the middle of the bridge, in a place that most people who knew it remembered as a place populous with sightseers and excursionists, and he was the only human being in sight there. Above him, very high in the heavens, the contending air-fleets manoeuvred; below him the river seethed like a sluice towards the American Fall. He was curiously dressed. His cheap blue serge trousers were thrust into German airship rubber boots, and on his head he wore an aeronaut's white cap that was a trifle too large for him. He thrust that back to reveal his staring little cockney face, still scarred upon the brow. 'Gaw!' he whispered.

He stared. He gesticulated. Once or twice he shouted and applauded.

Then at a certain point terror seized him and he took to his heels in the direction of Goat Island.

4

For a time after they were in sight of each other, neither fleet attempted to engage. The Germans numbered sixty-seven great airships and they maintained the crescent formation at a height of nearly four thousand feet. They kept a distance of about one and a half lengths, so that the horns of the crescent were nearly thirty miles apart. Closely in tow of the airships of the extreme squadrons on either wing were about thirty *drachenflieger* ready manned, but these were too small and distant for Bert to distinguish.

At first, only what was called the Southern fleet of the Asiatics was visible to him. It consisted of forty airships, carrying altogether nearly four hundred one-man flying-machines upon their flanks, and for some time it flew slowly and at a minimum distance of perhaps a dozen miles from the Germans, eastward across their front. At first Bert could distinguish only the greater bulks, then he perceived the one-man machines as a multitude of very small objects drifting like motes in the sunshine about and beneath the larger shapes.

Bert saw nothing then of the second fleet of the Asiatics, though probably that was coming into sight of the Germans at the time, in the north-west.

The air was very still, the sky almost without a cloud, and the German fleet had risen to an immense height, so that the airships seemed no longer of any considerable size. Both ends of their crescent showed plainly. As they beat southward they passed slowly between Bert and the sunlight, and became black outlines of themselves. The *drachenflieger* appeared as little flecks of black on either wing of this aerial Armada.

The two fleets seemed in no hurry to engage. The Asiatics went far away into the east, quickening their pace and rising as they did so, and then tailed out into a long column and came flying back, rising towards the German left. The squadrons of the latter came about, facing this oblique advance, and suddenly little flickerings and a faint crepitating sound told that they had opened fire. For a time no effect was visible to the watcher on the bridge. Then, like a handful of snowflakes, the *drachenflieger* swooped to the attack, and a multitude of red specks whirled up to meet them. It was to Bert's sense not only enormously remote but singularly inhuman. Not four hours since he had been on one of those very airships, and yet they seemed to him now not gasbags carrying men, but strange sentient creatures that moved about and did things with a purpose of their own. The flight of the Asiatic and German flying-machines joined and dropped earthward, became like a handful of white and red rose petals flung from a distant window, grew larger, until Bert could see the overturned ones spinning through the air, and were hidden by great volumes of dark smoke that were rising in the direction of Buffalo. For a time they all were hidden, then two or three white and a number of red ones rose again into the sky, like a swarm of big butterflies, and circled fighting and drove away out of sight again towards the east.

A heavy report recalled Bert's eyes to the zenith, and behold, the great crescent had lost its dressing and burst into a disorderly long cloud of airships! One had dropped halfway down the sky. It was flaming fore and aft, and even as Bert looked it turned over and fell, spinning over and over itself and vanished into the smoke of Buffalo.

Bert's mouth opened and shut, and he clutched tighter on the rail of the bridge. For some moments – they seemed long moments – the two fleets remained without any further change flying obliquely towards each other, and making what came to Bert's ears as a midget uproar. Then suddenly from either side airships began dropping out of alignment, smitten by missiles he could neither see nor trace. The string of Asiatic ships swung round and either charged into or over (it was difficult to say from below) the shattered line of the Germans, who seemed to open out to give way to them. Some sort of manoeuvring began, but Bert could not grasp its import. The left of the battle became a confused dance of airships. For some minutes up there the two crossing lines of ships looked so close it seemed like a hand-to-hand scuffle in the sky. Then they broke up into groups and duels. The descent of German airships towards the lower sky increased. One of them flared down and vanished far away in the north; two dropped with something twisted and crippled in their movements; then a group of antagonists came down from the zenith in an eddying conflict, two Asiatics against one German, and were presently joined by another, and drove away eastward altogether with others dropping out of the German line to join them. One Asiatic either rammed or collided with a still more gigantic German, and the two went spinning to destruction together. The northern squadron of Asiatics came into the battle unnoted by Bert, except that the multitude of ships above seemed presently increased. In a little while the fight was utter confusion, drifting on the whole to the south-west against the wind. It became more and more a series of group encounters. Here a huge German airship flamed earthward with a dozen flat Asiatic craft about her, crushing her every attempt to recover. Here another hung with its screw fighting off the swordsmen from a swarm of flying-machines. Here, again, an Asiatic aflame at either end swooped out of the battle. His attention went from incident to incident in the vast clearness overhead; these conspicuous cases of destruction caught and held his mind; it was only very slowly that any sort of scheme manifested itself between those nearer, more striking episodes.

The mass of the airships that eddied remotely above was, however, neither destroying nor destroyed. The majority of them seemed to be going at full speed and circling upward for position, exchanging ineffectual shots as they did so. Very little ramming was essayed after the first tragic downfall of rammer and rammed, and whatever attempts at boarding were made were invisible to Bert. There seemed, however, a steady attempt to isolate antagonists, to cut them off from their fellows and bear them down, causing a perpetual sailing back and interlacing of these shoaling bulks. The greater numbers of the Asiatics and their swifter heeling movements gave them the effect of persistently attacking the Germans. Overhead, and evidently endeavouring to keep itself in touch with the works of Niagara, a body of German airships drew itself together into a compact phalanx, and the Asiatics became more and more intent upon breaking this up. He was grotesquely reminded of fish in a fishpond struggling for crumbs. He could see puny puffs of smoke and the flash of bombs, but never a sound came down to him . . .

A flapping shadow passed for a moment between Bert and the sun and was followed by another. A whirring of engines, click, clock, clitter clock, smote upon his ears. Instantly he forgot the zenith.

Perhaps a hundred yards above the water, out of the south, riding like Valkyries swiftly through the air on the strange steeds the engineering of Europe had begotten upon the artistic inspiration of Japan, came a long string of Asiatic swordsmen. The wings flapped jerkily, click, clock, clitter clock, and the machines drove up; they spread and ceased, and the apparatus came soaring through the air. So they rose and fell and rose again. They passed so closely overhead that Bert could hear their voices calling to one another. They swooped towards Niagara City and landed one after another in a long line in a clear space before the hotel. But he did not stay to watch them land. One yellow face had craned over and looked at him, and for one enigmatical instant met his eyes . . .

It was then the idea came to Bert that he was altogether too conspicuous in the middle of the bridge, and that he took to his heels towards Goat Island. Thence, dodging about among the trees, with perhaps an excessive self-consciousness, he watched the rest of the struggle.

5

When Bert's sense of security was sufficiently restored for him to watch the battle again, he perceived that a brisk little fight was in progress between the Asiatic aeronauts and the German engineers for the possession of Niagara City. It was the first time in the whole course of the war that he had seen anything resembling fighting as he had studied it in the illustrated papers of his youth. It seemed to him almost as though things were coming right. He saw men carrying rifles and taking cover and running briskly from point to point in a loose attacking formation. The first batch of aeronauts had probably been under the impression that the city was deserted. They had grounded in the open near Prospect Park and approached the houses towards the power-works before they were disillusioned by a sudden fire. They had scattered back to the cover of a bank near the water – it was too far for them to reach their machines again; they were lying and firing at the men in the hotels and frame-houses about their power-works.

Then to their support came a second string of red flying-machines driving up from the east. They rose up out of the haze above the houses and came round in a long curve as if surveying the position below. The fire of the Germans rose to a roar, and one of those soaring shapes gave an abrupt jerk backwards and fell among the houses. The others swooped down exactly like great birds upon the roof of the power house. They caught upon it, and from each sprang a nimble little figure and ran towards the parapet.

Other flapping bird-shapes came into this affair, but Bert had not seen their coming. A staccato of shots came over to him, reminding him of army manoeuvres, of newspaper descriptions of fights, of all that was entirely correct in his conception of warfare. He saw quite a number of Germans running from the outlying houses towards the power house. Two fell. One lay still, but the other wriggled and made efforts for a time. The hotel that was used as a hospital, and to which he had helped carry the wounded men from the *Zeppelin* earlier in the day, suddenly ran up the Geneva flag. The town that had seemed so quiet had evidently been concealing a considerable number of Germans, and they were now concentrating to hold the central power house. He wondered what ammunition they might have. More and more of the Asiatic flying-machines came into the conflict. They had disposed of the unfortunate German *drachenflieger* and were now aiming at the incipient aeronautic park, the electric gas generators and repair stations which formed the German base. Some landed, and their aeronauts took cover and became energetic infantry soldiers. Others hovered above the fight, their men ever and again firing shots down at some chance exposure below. The firing came in paroxysms; now there would be a watchful lull and now a rapid tattoo of shots, rising to a roar. Once or twice flying-machines, as they circled warily, came right overhead, and for a time Bert gave himself body and soul to cowering.

Ever and again a large thunder mingled with the rattle and reminded him of the grapple of airships far above, but the nearer fight held his attention.

Abruptly something dropped from the zenith; something like a barrel or a huge football.

Crash! It smashed with an immense report. It had fallen among the grounded Asiatic aeroplanes that lay among the turf and flower-beds near the river. They flew in scraps and fragments, turf, trees, and gravel leapt and fell; the aeronauts still lying along the canal bank were thrown about like sacks, catspaws flew across the foaming water. All the windows of the hotel hospital that had been shiningly reflecting blue sky and airships the moment before became vast black stars. Bang! – a second followed. Bert looked up and was filled with a sense of a number of monstrous bodies swooping down, coming down on the whole affair like a flight of bellying blankets, like a string of vast dish-covers. The central tangle of the battle above was circling down as if to come into touch with the power house fight. He got a new effect of airships altogether, as vast things coming down upon him, growing swiftly larger and larger and more overwhelming, until the houses over the way seemed small, the American rapids narrow, the bridge flimsy, the combatants infinitesimal. As they came down they became audible as a complex of shootings and vast creakings and groanings and beatings and throbbings and shouts and shots. The foreshortened black eagles at the fore-ends of the Germans had an effect of actual combat of flying feathers.

Some of these fighting airships came within five hundred feet of the ground. Bert could see men on the lower galleries of the Germans firing rifles; could see Asiatics clinging to the ropes; saw one man in aluminium diver's gear fall flashing headlong into the waters above Goat Island. For the first time he saw the Asiatic airships closely. From this aspect they reminded him more than anything else of colossal snowshoes; they had a curious patterning in black and white, in forms that reminded him of the engine-turned cover of a watch. They had no hanging galleries, but from little openings on the middle line peeped out men and the muzzles of guns. So, driving in long, descending and ascending curves, these monsters wrestled and fought. It was like clouds fighting, like puddings trying to assassinate each other. They whirled and circled about each other, and for a time threw Goat Island and Niagara into a smoky twilight, through which the sunlight smote in shafts and beams. They spread and closed and spread and grappled and drove round over the rapids, and two miles away or more into Canada, and back over the Falls again. A German caught fire, and the whole crowd broke away from her flare and rose about her dispersing, leaving her to drop towards Canada and blow up as she dropped. Then with renewed uproar the others closed again. Once from the men in Niagara City came a sound like an ant-hill cheering. Another German burnt, and one, badly deflated by the prow of an antagonist, flopped out of action southward.

It became more and more evident that the Germans were getting the worst of the unequal fight. More and more obviously were they being persecuted. Less and less did they seem to fight with any object other than escape. The Asiatics swept by them and above them, ripped their bladders, set them alight, picked off their dimly seen men in diving clothes, who struggled against fire and tear with fire extinguishers and silk ribbons in the inner netting. They answered only with ineffectual shots. Thence the battle circled back over Niagara, and then suddenly the Germans, as if at a preconcerted signal, broke and dispersed, going east, west, north, and south, in open and confused flight. The Asiatics, as they realised this, rose to fly above them and after them. Only one little knot of four Germans and perhaps a dozen Asiatics remained fighting about the *Hohenzollern* and the Prince as he circled in a last attempt to save Niagara.

Round they swooped once again over the Canadian Fall, over the waste of waters eastward, until they were distant and small, and then round and back, hurrying, bounding, swooping towards the one gaping spectator.

The whole struggling mass approached very swiftly, growing rapidly larger, and coming out black and featureless against the afternoon sun and above the blinding welter of the Upper Rapids. It grew like a storm cloud until once more it darkened the sky. The flat Asiatic airships kept high above the Germans and behind them, and fired unanswered bullets into their gas chambers and upon their flanks – the one-man flying-machines hovered and alighted like a swarm of attacking bees. Nearer they came, and nearer, filling the lower heaven. Two of the Germans swooped and rose again, but the *Hohenzollern* had suffered too much for that. She lifted weakly, turned sharply as if to get out of the battle, burst into flames fore and aft, swept down to the water, splashed into it obliquely, and rolled over and over and came downstream rolling and smashing and writhing like a thing alive, halting and then coming on again, with her torn and bent propeller still beating the air. The bursting flames spluttered out again in clouds of steam. It was a disaster gigantic in its dimensions. She lay across the rapids like an island, like tall cliffs, tall cliffs that came rolling, smoking, and crumpling, and collapsing, advancing with a sort of fluctuating rapidity upon Bert. One Asiatic airship – it looked to Bert from below like three hundred yards of pavement – whirled back and circled two or three times over that great overthrow, and half a dozen crimson flying-machines danced for a moment like great midges in the sunlight before they swept on after their fellows. The rest of the fight had already gone over the island, a wild crescendo of shots and yells and smashing uproar. It was hidden from Bert now by the trees of the island, and forgotten by him in the nearer spectacle of the huge advance of the defeated German airship. Something fell with a mighty smashing and splintering of boughs unheeded behind him.

It seemed for a time that the *Hohenzollern* must needs break her back upon the Parting of the Waters, and then for a time her propeller flopped and frothed in the river and thrust the mass of buckling, crumpled wreckage towards the American shore. Then the sweep of the torrent that foamed down to the American Fall caught her, and in another minute the immense mass of deflating wreckage, with flames spurting out in three new places, had crashed against the bridge that joined Goat Island and Niagara City, and forced a long arm, as it were, in a heaving tangle under the central span. Then the middle

338 THE WAR IN THE AIR

chambers blew up with a loud report, and in another moment the bridge had given way and the main bulk of the airship, like some grotesque cripple in rags, staggered, flapping and waving flambeaux to the crest of the Fall and hesitated there and vanished in a desperate suicidal leap.

Its detached fore-end remained jammed against that little island, Green Island it used to be called, which forms the stepping-stone between the mainland and Goat Island's patch of trees.

Bert followed this disaster from the Parting of the Waters to the bridge head. Then, regardless of cover, regardless of the Asiatic airship hovering like a huge house roof without walls above the Suspension Bridge, he sprinted along towards the north and came out for the first time upon that rocky point by Luna Island that looks sheer down upon the American Fall. There he stood breathless amidst that eternal rush of sound, breathless and staring.

Far below, and travelling rapidly down the gorge, whirled something like a huge empty sack. For him it meant – what did it not mean? – the German air-fleet, Kurt, the Prince, Europe, all things stable and familiar, the forces that had brought him, the forces that had seemed indisputably victorious. And it went down the rapids like an empty sack and left the visible world to Asia, to yellow people beyond Christendom, to all that was terrible and strange!

Remote over Canada receded the rest of that conflict and vanished beyond the range of his vision . . .

CHAPTER NINE

On Goat Island

1

The whack of a bullet on the rocks beside him reminded him that he was a visible object and wearing at least portions of a German uniform. It drove him into the trees again, and for a time he dodged and dropped and sought cover like a chick hiding among reeds from imaginary hawks. 'Beaten,' he whispered. 'Beaten and done for . . . Chinese! Yellow chaps chasing 'em!'

At last he came to rest in a clump of bushes near a locked-up and deserted refreshment shed within view of the American side. They made a sort of hole and harbour for him; they met completely overhead. He looked across the rapids, but the firing had ceased now altogether and everything seemed quiet. The Asiatic aeroplane had moved from its former position above the Suspension Bridge, was motionless now above Niagara City, shadowing all that district about the power house which had been the scene of the land fight. The monster had an air of quiet and assured predominance, and from its stern it trailed, serene and ornamental, a long streaming flag, the red, black, and yellow of the great alliance, the Sunrise and the Dragon. Beyond, to the east, at a much higher level, hung a second consort, and Bert, presently gathering courage, wriggled out and craned his neck to find another still airship against the sunset in the south.

'Gaw!' he said. 'Beaten and chased! My Gawd!'

The fighting, it seemed at first, was quite over in Niagara City, though a German flag was still flying from one shattered house. A white sheet was hoisted above the power house, and this remained flying all through the events that followed. But presently came a sound of shots and then German soldiers running. They disappeared among the houses, and then came two engineers in blue shirts and trousers hotly pursued by three Japanese swordsmen. The foremost of the two fugitives was a shapely man, and ran lightly and well; the second was a sturdy little man, and rather fat. He ran comically in leaps and bounds, with his plump arms bent up by his side and his head thrown back. The pursuers ran with uniforms and dark thin metal and leather headdresses. The little man stumbled, and Bert gasped, realising a new horror in war.

The foremost swordsman won three strides on him and was near enough to slash at him and miss as he spurted.

A dozen yards they ran, and then the swordsman slashed again, and Bert could hear across the waters a little sound like the moo of an elfin cow as the fat little man fell forward. Slash went the swordsman and slash at something on the ground that tried to save itself with ineffectual hands. 'Oh, I carn't!' cried Bert, near blubbering, and staring with starting eyes.

The swordsman slashed a fourth time and went on as his fellows came up after the better runner. The hindmost swordsman stopped and turned back. He had perceived some movement perhaps; but at any rate he stood, and ever and again slashed at the fallen body.

'Oo-oo!' groaned Bert at every slash, and shrank closer into the bushes and became very still. Presently came a sound of shots from the town, and then everything was quiet, everything, even the hospital.

He saw presently little figures sheathing swords come out from the houses and walk to the debris of the flying-machines the bomb had destroyed. Others appeared wheeling undamaged aeroplanes upon their wheels as men might wheel bicycles, and sprang into the saddles and flapped into the air. A string of three airships appeared far away in the east and flew towards the zenith. The one that hung low above Niagara City came still lower and dropped a rope ladder to pick up men from the power house.

For a long time he watched the further happenings in Niagara City as a rabbit might watch a meet. He saw men going from building to building, to set fire to them, as he presently realised, and he heard a series of dull detonations from the wheel pit of the power house. Some similar business went on among the works on the Canadian side. Meanwhile more and more airships appeared, and many more flying-machines, until at last it seemed to him nearly a third of the Asiatic fleet had reassembled. He watched them from his bush, cramped but immovable, watched them gather and range themselves and signal and pick up men, until at last they sailed away towards the glowing sunset, going to the great Asiatic rendez vous, above the oil wells of Cleveland. They dwindled and passed away, leaving him alone, so far as he could tell, the only living man in a world of ruin and strange loneliness almost beyond describing. He watched them recede and vanish. He stood gaping after them.

'Gaw!' he said at last, like one who rouses himself from a trance.

It was far more than any personal desolation extremity that flooded his soul. It seemed to him indeed that this must be the sunset of his race.

He did not at first envisage his own plight in definite and comprehensible terms. Things had happened to him so much of late, his own efforts had counted for so little, that he had become passive and planless. His last scheme had been to go round the coast of England as a Desert Dervish giving refined entertainment to his fellow-creatures. Fate had quashed that. Fate had seen fit to direct him to other destinies, had hurried him from point to point, and dropped him at last upon this little wedge of rock between the cataracts. It did not instantly occur to him that now it was his turn to play. He had a singular feeling that all must end as a dream ends, that presently surely he would be back in the world of Grubb and Edna and Bun Hill, that this roar, this glittering presence of incessant water, would be drawn aside as a curtain is drawn aside after a holiday lantern show, and old familiar, customary things reassume their sway. It would be interesting to tell people how he had seen Niagara. And then Kurt's words came into his head: 'People torn away from the people they care for; homes smashed, creatures full of life and memories and peculiar little gifts – torn to pieces, starved, and spoilt . . .'

He wondered, half incredulous, if that was indeed true. It was so hard to realise it. Out beyond there was it possible that Tom and Jessica were also in some dire extremity? That the little greengrocer's shop was no longer standing open, with Jessica serving respectfully, warming Tom's ear in sharp asides, or punctually sending out the goods?

He tried to think what day of the week it was, and found he had lost his reckoning. Perhaps it was Sunday. If so, were they going to church or were they hiding, perhaps in bushes? What had happened to the landlord, the butcher, and to Butteridge and all those people on Dymchurch beach? Something, he knew, had happened to London – a bombardment. But who had bombarded? Were Tom and Jessica too being chased by strange brown men with long bare swords and evil eyes? He thought of various possible aspects of affliction, but presently one phase ousted all the others. Were they getting much to eat? The question haunted him, obsessed him.

If one was very hungry would one eat rats?

It dawned upon him that a peculiar misery that oppressed him was not so much anxiety and patriotic sorrow as hunger. Of course he was hungry!

He reflected and turned his steps towards the little refreshment shed that stood near the end of the ruined bridge. 'Ought to be somethin' – '

He strolled round it once or twice, and then attacked the shutters with his pocket-knife, reinforced presently by a wooden stake he found conveniently near. At last he got a shutter to give, and tore it back and stuck in his head.

'Grub,' he remarked, 'anyhow. Leastways – '

He got at the inside fastening of the shutter and had presently this establishment open for his exploration. He found several sealed bottles of sterilised milk, much mineral water, two tins of biscuits and a crock of very stale cakes, cigarettes in great quantity but very dry, some rather dry oranges, nuts, some tins of canned meat and fruit, and plates and knives and forks and glasses sufficient for several score of people. There was also a zinc locker, but he was unable to negotiate the padlock of this.

'Shan't starve,' said Bert, 'for a bit, anyhow.' He sat on the vendor's seat and regaled himself with biscuits and milk, and felt for a moment quite contented.

'Quite restful,' he muttered, munching and glancing about him restlessly, 'after what I been through.

'Crikey! *Wot* a day! Oh! *Wot* a day!'

Wonder took possession of him. 'Gaw!' he cried: 'Wot a fight it's been! Smashing up the poor fellers! 'Eadlong! The airships – the fliers and all. I wonder what happened to the *Zeppelin*? . . . And that chap Kurt – I wonder what happened to 'im? 'E was a good sort of chap, was Kurt.'

Some phantom of imperial solicitude floated through his mind. 'Injia,' he said . . .

A more practical interest arose.

'I wonder if there's anything to open one of these tins of corned beef?'

3

After he had feasted, Bert lit a cigarette and sat meditative for a time. 'Wonder where Grubb is?' he said; 'I do wonder that! Wonder if any of 'em wonder about me?'

He reverted to his own circumstances. 'Dessay I shall 'ave to stop on this island for some time.'

He tried to feel at his ease and secure, but presently the indefinable restlessness of the social animal in solitude distressed him. He began to want to look over his shoulder, and, as a corrective, roused himself to explore the rest of the island.

It was only very slowly that he began to realise the peculiarities of his position, to perceive that the breaking down of the arch between Green Island and the mainland had cut him off completely from the world. Indeed it was only when he came back to where the fore-end of the *Hohenzollern* lay like a stranded ship, and was contemplating the shattered bridge, that this dawned upon him. Even then it came with no sort of shock to his mind, a fact among a number of other extraordinary and unmanageable facts. He stared at the shattered cabins of the *Hohenzollern* and its widow's garment of dishevelled silk for a time, but without any idea of its containing any living thing; it was all so twisted and smashed and entirely upside down. Then for a while he gazed at the evening sky. A cloud haze was now appearing and not an airship was in sight. A swallow flew by and snapped some invisible victim. 'Like a dream,' he repeated.

Then for a time the rapids held his mind. 'Roaring. It keeps on roaring and splashin' always and always. Keeps on . . . '

At last his interests became personal. 'Wonder what I ought to do now?'

He reflected. 'Not an idea,' he said.

He was chiefly conscious that a fortnight ago he had been in Bun Hill with no idea of travel in his mind, and that now he was between the Falls of Niagara amidst the devastation and ruins of the greatest air fight in the world, and that in the interval he had been across France, Belgium, Germany, England, Ireland, and a number of other countries. It was an interesting thought and suitable for conversation, but of no great practical utility. 'Wonder 'ow I can get orf this?' he said. 'Wonder if there is a way out? If not . . . rummy!'

Further reflection decided, 'I believe I got myself in a bit of a 'ole coming over that bridge . . .

'Any'ow – got me out of the way of them Japanesy chaps. Wouldn't 'ave taken 'em long to cut *my* froat. No. Still – '

He resolved to return to the point of Luna Island. For a long time he stood without stirring, scrutinising the Canadian shore and the wreckage of hotels and houses and the fallen trees of the Victoria Park, pink now in the light of sundown. Not a human being was perceptible in that scene of headlong destruction. Then he came back to the American side of the island, crossed close to the crumpled aluminium wreckage of the *Hohenzollern* to Green Islet, and scrutinised the hopeless breach in the further bridge and the water that boiled beneath it. Towards Buffalo there was still much smoke, and near the position of the Niagara railway station the houses were burning vigorously. Everything was deserted now, everything was still. One little abandoned thing lay on a transverse path between town and road, a crumpled heap of clothes with sprawling limbs . . .

' 'Ave a look round,' said Bert, and taking a path that ran through the middle of the island he presently discovered the wreckage of the two Asiatic aeroplanes that had fallen out of the struggle that ended the *Hohenzollern*.

With the first he found the wreckage of an aeronaut too.

The machine had evidently dropped vertically and was badly knocked about amidst a lot of smashed branches in a clump of trees. Its bent and broken wings and shattered stays sprawled amidst new splintered wood, and its forepeak stuck into the ground. The aeronaut dangled weirdly head downward among the leaves and branches some yards away, and Bert only discovered him as he turned from the aeroplane. In the dusky evening light and stillness – for the sun had gone now and the wind had altogether fallen – this inverted yellow face was anything but a tranquillising object to discover suddenly a couple of yards away. A broken branch had run clean through the man's thorax, and he hung, so stabbed, looking limp and absurd. In his hand he still clutched, with the grip of death, a short, light rifle.

For some time Bert stood very still, inspecting this thing.

Then he began to walk away from it, looking constantly back at it.

Presently in an open glade he came to a stop.

'Gaw!' he whispered, 'I don' like dead bodies some'ow! I'd almost rather that chap was alive.'

He would not go along the path athwart which the Chinaman hung. He felt he would rather not have trees round him any more, and that it would be more comfortable to be quite close to the sociable splash and uproar of the rapids.

He came upon the second aeroplane in a clear grassy space by the side of the streaming water, and it seemed scarcely damaged at all. It looked as though it had floated down into a position of rest. It lay on its side with one wing in the air. There was no aeronaut near it, dead or alive. There it lay abandoned, with the water lapping about its long tail.

Bert remained a little aloof from it for a long time, looking into the gathering shadows among the trees, in the expectation of another Chinaman alive or dead. Then very cautiously he approached the machine and stood regarding its widespread vans, its big steering wheel and empty saddle. He did not venture to touch it.

'I wish that other chap wasn't there,' he said. 'I do wish 'e wasn't there!'

He saw, a few yards away, something bobbing about in an eddy that spun within a projecting head of rock. As it went round it seemed to draw him unwillingly towards it . . .

What could it be?

'Blow!' said Bert. 'It's another of 'em.'

It held him. He told himself that it was the other aeronaut that had been shot in the fight and fallen out of the saddle as he strove to land. He tried to go away, and then it occurred to him that he might get a branch or something and push this rotating object out into the stream. That would leave him with only one dead body to worry about. Perhaps he might get along with one. He hesitated, and then with a certain emotion forced himself to do this. He went towards the bushes and cut himself a wand and returned to the rocks and clambered out to a corner between the eddy and the stream. By that time the sunset was over and the bats were abroad – and he was wet with perspiration.

He prodded the floating blue-clad thing with his wand, failed, tried again successfully as it came round, and as it went out into the stream it turned over, the light gleamed on golden hair and – it was Kurt.

It was Kurt, white and dead and very calm. There was no mistaking him. There was still plenty of light for that. The stream took him and he seemed to compose himself in its swift grip as one who stretches himself to rest. White-faced he was now, and all the colour gone out of him.

A feeling of infinite distress swept over Bert as the body swept out of sight towards the fall. 'Kurt!' he cried. 'Kurt! I didn't mean to! Kurt! don' leave me 'ere! Don' leave me!'

Loneliness and desolation overwhelmed him. He gave way. He stood on the rock in the evening light, weeping and wailing passionately like a child. It was as though some link that had held him to all these things had broken and gone. He was afraid like a child in a lonely room, shamelessly afraid.

The twilight was closing about him. The trees were full now of strange shadows. All the things about him became strange and unfamiliar with that subtle queerness one feels oftenest in dreams. 'O God! I carn' stand this,' he said, and crept back from the rocks to the grass and crouched down, and suddenly wild sorrow for the death of Kurt, Kurt the brave, Kurt the kindly, came to his help and he broke from whimpering to weeping. He ceased to crouch; he sprawled upon the grass and clenched an impotent fist.

'This war,' he cried, 'this blarsted foolery of a war.

'O Kurt! Lieutenant Kurt!

'I done,' he said, 'I done. I've 'ad all I want, and more than I want. The world's all rot, and there ain't no sense in it. The night's coming . . . If 'E comes after me – 'E can't come after me – 'E can't! . . .

'If 'E comes after me, I'll fro' myself into the water . . . '

Presently he was talking again in a low undertone.

'There ain't nothing to be afraid of reely. It's jest imagination. Poor old Kurt – he thought it would happen. Prevision like. 'E never gave me that letter or tole me who the lady was. It's like what 'e said – people tore away from everything they belonged to – everywhere. Exactly like what 'e said . . . 'Ere I am cast away – thousands of miles from Edna or Grubb or any of my lot – like a plant tore up by the roots . . . And every war's been like this, only I 'adn't the sense to understand it. Always. All sorts of 'oles and corners chaps 'ave died in. And people 'adn't the sense to understand, 'adn't the sense to feel it and stop it. Thought war was fine. My Gawd! . . .

'Dear old Edna. She was a fair bit of all right – she was. That time we 'ad a boat at Kingston . . .

'I bet – I'll see 'er again yet. Won't be my fault if I don't . . . '

4

Suddenly, on the very verge of this heroic resolution, Bert became rigid with terror. Something was creeping towards him through the grass. Something was creeping and halting and creeping again towards him through the dim dark grass. The night was electrical with horror. For a time everything was still. Bert ceased to breathe. It could not be. No, it was too small!

It advanced suddenly upon him with a rush, with a little mewling cry and tail erect. It rubbed its head against him and purred. It was a tiny, skinny little kitten.

'Gaw, Pussy! 'ow you frightened me!' said Bert, with drops of perspiration on his brow.

He sat with his back to a tree stump all that night, holding the kitten in his arms. His mind was tired, and he talked or thought coherently no longer. Towards dawn he dozed.

When he awoke, he was stiff but in better heart, and the kitten slept warmly and reassuringly inside his jacket. And fear, he found, had gone from amidst the trees.

He stroked the kitten, and the little creature woke up to excessive fondness and purring. 'You want some milk,' said Bert. 'That's what you want. And I could do with a bit of brekker too.'

He yawned and stood up, with the kitten on his shoulder, and stared about him, recalling the circumstances of the previous day, the grey, immense happenings.

'Mus' do something,' he said.

He turned towards the trees, and was presently contemplating the dead aeronaut again. The kitten he held companionably against his neck. The body was horrible, but not nearly so horrible as it had been at twilight, and now the limbs were limper and the gun had slipped to the ground and lay half hidden in the grass.

'I suppose we ought to bury 'im, Kitty,' said Bert, and looked helplessly at the rocky soil about him. 'We got to stay on the island with 'im.'

It was some time before he could turn away and go on towards that provision shed. 'Brekker first,' he said, 'anyhow,' stroking the kitten on his shoulder. She rubbed his cheek affectionately with her furry little face and presently nibbled at his ear. 'Wan' some milk, eh?' he said, and turned his back on the dead man as though he mattered nothing.

He was puzzled to find the door of the shed open, though he had closed and latched it very carefully overnight, and he found also some dirty plates he had not noticed before on the bench. He discovered that the hinges of the tin locker were unscrewed and that it could be opened. He had not observed this overnight.

'Silly of me!' said Bert. ' 'Ere I was puzzlin' and whackin' away at the padlock, never noticing.' It had been used apparently as an ice-chest, but it contained nothing now but the remains of half a dozen boiled chickens, some ambiguous substance that might once have been butter, and a singularly unappetising smell. He closed the lid again carefully.

He gave the kitten some milk in a dirty plate and sat watching its busy little tongue for a time. Then he was moved to make an inventory of the provisions. There were six bottles of milk unopened and one opened, sixty bottles of mineral water and a large stock of syrups, about two thousand cigarettes and upwards of a hundred cigars, nine oranges, two unopened tins of corned beef and one opened, and five large tins California peaches. He jotted it down on a piece of paper. ' 'Ain't much solid food,' he said. 'Still – A fortnight, say!

'Anything might happen in a fortnight.'

He gave the kitten a small second helping and a scrap of beef and then went down with the little creature running after him, tail erect and in high spirits, to look at the remains of the *Hohenzollern*. It had shifted in the night and seemed on the whole more firmly grounded on Green Island than before. From it his eye went to the shattered bridge and then across to the still desolation of Niagara City. Nothing moved over there but a number of crows. They were busy with the engineer he had seen cut down on the previous day. He saw no dogs, but he heard one howling.

'We got to get out of this some'ow, Kitty,' he said. 'That milk won't last for ever – not at the rate you lap it.'

He regarded the sluice-like flood before him.

'Plenty of water,' he said. 'Won't be drink we shall want.'

He decided to make a careful exploration of the island. Presently he came to a locked gate labelled 'Biddle Stairs', and clambered over to discover a steep old wooden staircase leading down the face of the cliff amidst a vast and increasing uproar of waters. He left the kitten above and descended these, and discovered with a thrill of hope a path leading among the rocks at the foot of the roaring downrush of the Centre Fall. Perhaps this was a sort of way!

It led him only to the choking and deafening experience of the Cave of the Winds, and after he had spent a quarter of an hour in a partially stupefied condition flattened between solid rock and nearly as solid waterfall, he decided that this was after all no practicable route to Canada and retraced his steps. As he reascended the Biddle Stairs, he heard what he decided at last must be a sort of echo, a sound of someone walking about on the gravel paths above. When he got to the top, the place was as solitary as before.

Thence he made his way, with the kitten skirmishing along beside him in the grass, to a staircase that led to a lump of projecting rock that enfiladed the huge green majesty of the Horseshoe Fall. He stood there for some time in silence.

'You wouldn't think,' he said at last, 'there was so much water . . . This roarin' and splashin', it gets on one's nerves at last . . . Sounds like people talking . . . Sounds like people going about . . . Sounds like anything you fancy.'

He retired up the staircase again. 'I s'pose I shall keep on goin' round this blessed island,' he said drearily. 'Round and round and round.'

He found himself presently beside the less damaged Asiatic aeroplane again. He stared at it and the kitten smelt it. 'Broke!' he said.

He looked up with a convulsive start.

Advancing slowly towards him out from among the trees were two tall, gaunt figures. They were blackened and tattered and bandaged; the hindmost one limped and had his head swathed in white, but the foremost one still carried himself as a Prince should do, for all that his left arm was in a sling and one side of his face scalded a livid crimson. He was the Prince Karl Albert, the War Lord, the 'German Alexander', and the man behind him was the bird-faced man whose cabin had once been taken from him and given to Bert.

6

With that apparition began a new phase of Goat Island in Bert's experience. He ceased to be a solitary representative of humanity in a vast and violent and incomprehensible universe, and became once more a social creature, a man in a world of other men. For an instant these two were terrible, then they seemed sweet and desirable as brothers. They, too, were in this scrape with him, marooned and puzzled. He wanted extremely to hear exactly what had happened to them. What mattered it if one was a Prince and both were foreign soldiers, if neither perhaps had adequate English? His native cockney freedom flowed too generously for him to think of that, and surely the Asiatic fleets had purged all such trivial differences. 'Ul–lo!' he said; ' 'ow did you get 'ere?'

'It is the Englishman who brought us the Butteridge machine,' said the bird-faced officer in German, and then in a tone of horror, as Bert advanced, 'Salute!' and again louder, '*Salute!*'

'Gaw!' said Bert, and stopped with a second comment under his breath. He stared and saluted awkwardly and became at once a masked defensive thing with whom co-operation was impossible.

For a time these two perfected modern aristocrats stood regarding the difficult problem of the Anglo-Saxon citizen, that ambiguous citizen who, obeying some mysterious law in his blood, would neither drill nor be a democrat. Bert was by no means a beautiful object, but in some inexplicable way he looked resistant. He wore his cheap suit of serge, now showing many signs of wear, and its loose fit made him seem sturdier than he was; above his disengaging face was a white German cap that was altogether too big for him, and his trousers were crumpled up his legs and their ends tucked into the rubber highlows of a deceased German aeronaut. He looked an inferior, though by no means an easy inferior, and instinctively they hated him.

The Prince pointed to the flying-machine and said something in broken English that Bert took for German and failed to understand. He intimated as much.

'Dummer Kerl!'[242] said the bird-faced officer from among his bandages.

The Prince pointed again with his undamaged hand. 'You verstehen dis drachenflieger?'

Bert began to comprehend the situation. He regarded the Asiatic machine. The habits of Bun Hill returned to him. 'It's a foreign make,' he said ambiguously.

The two Germans consulted. 'You are an expert?' said the Prince.

'We reckon to repair,' said Bert, in the exact manner of Grubb.

The Prince sought in his vocabulary. 'Is dat,' he said, 'goot to fly?'

Bert reflected and scratched his cheek slowly. 'I got to look at it,' he replied . . . 'It's 'ad rough usage!'

He made a sound with his teeth he had also acquired from Grubb, put his hands in his trouser pockets, and strolled back to the machine. Typically Grubb chewed something, but Bert could chew only imaginatively. 'Three days' work in this,' he said, teething. For the first time it dawned on him that there were possibilities in this machine. It was evident that the wing that lay on the ground was badly damaged. The three stays that held it rigid had snapped across a ridge of rock and there was also a strong possibility of the engine being badly damaged. The wing hook on that side was also askew, but probably that would not affect the flight. Beyond that there probably wasn't much the matter. Bert scratched his cheek again and contemplated the broad sunlit waste of the Upper Rapids. 'We might make a job of this . . . You leave it to me.'

He surveyed it intently again, and the Prince and his officer watched him. In Bun Hill Bert and Grubb had developed to a very high pitch among the hiring-stock a method of repair by substituting; they substituted bits of other machines. A machine that was too utterly and obviously done for even to proffer for hire, had nevertheless still capital value. It became a sort of quarry for nuts and screws and wheels, bars and spokes, chain-links and the like; a mine of ill-fitting 'parts' to replace the defects of machines still current. And back among the trees was a second Asiatic aeroplane . . .

The kitten caressed Bert's airship boots unheeded.

'Mend dat *drachenflieger*,' said the Prince.

'If I do mend it,' said Bert, struck by a new thought, 'none of us ain't to be trusted to fly it.'

'*I* vill fly it,' said the Prince.

'Very likely break your neck,' said Bert, after a pause.

The Prince did not understand him and disregarded what he said. He pointed his gloved finger to the machine and turned to the bird-faced officer with some remark in German. The officer answered and the Prince responded with a sweeping gesture towards the sky. Then he spoke – it seemed eloquently. Bert watched him and guessed his meaning. 'Much more likely to break your neck,' he said. ' 'Owever. 'Ere goes.'

He began to pry about the saddle and engine of the *drachenflieger* in a search for tools. Also he wanted some black oily stuff for his hands and face. For the first rule in the art of repairing, as it was known to the firm of Grubb & Smallways, was to get your hands and face thoroughly and conclusively blackened. Also he took off his jacket and waistcoat and put his cap carefully to the back of his head in order to facilitate scratching.

The Prince and the officer seemed disposed to watch him, but he succeeded in making it clear to them that this would inconvenience him and that he had to 'puzzle out a bit' before he could get to work. They thought him over, but his shop experience had given him something of the authoritative way of the expert with common men. And at last they went away. Thereupon he went straight to the second aeroplane, got the aeronaut's gun and ammunition and hid them in a clump of nettles close at hand. 'That's all right,' said Bert, and then proceeded to a careful inspection of the debris of the wings in the trees. Then he went back to the first aeroplane to compare the two. The Bun Hill method was quite possibly practicable if there was nothing hopeless or incomprehensible in the engine.

The Germans returned presently to find him already generously smutty and touching and testing knobs and screws and levers with an expression of profound sagacity. When the bird-faced officer addressed a remark to him, he waved him aside with, 'Nong comprong. Shut it! It's no good.'

Then he had an idea. 'Dead chap back there wants burying,' he said, jerking a thumb over his shoulder.

With the appearance of these two men Bert's whole universe had changed again. A curtain fell before the immense and terrible desolation that had overwhelmed him. He was in a world of three people, a minute human world that nevertheless filled his brain with eager speculations and schemes and cunning ideas. What were they thinking of? What did they think of him? What did they mean to do? A hundred busy threads interlaced in his mind as he pottered studiously over the Asiatic aeroplane. New ideas came up like bubbles in soda water.

'Gaw!' he said suddenly. He had just appreciated as a special aspect of this irrational injustice of fate that these two men were alive and that Kurt was dead. All the crew of the *Hohenzollern* were shot or burnt or smashed or drowned, and these two lurking in the padded forward cabin had escaped.

'I suppose 'e thinks it's 'is bloomin' Star,' he muttered, and found himself uncontrollably exasperated.

He stood up, facing round to the two men. They were standing side by side regarding him. 'It's no good,' he said, 'starin' at me. You only put me out.' And then, seeing they did not understand, he advanced towards them, wrench in hand. It occurred to him as he did so that the Prince was really a very big and powerful and serene-looking person. But he said, nevertheless, pointing through the trees, 'dead man!'

The bird-faced man intervened with a reply in German.

'Dead man!' said Bert to him. 'There.'

He had great difficulty in inducing them to inspect the dead China-man, and at last led them to him. Then they made it evident that they proposed that he, as a common person below the rank of officer, should have the sole and undivided privilege of disposing of the body by dragging it to the water's edge. There was some heated gesticulation, and at last the bird-faced officer abased himself to help. Together they dragged the limp and now swollen Asiatic through the trees, and after a rest or so – for he trailed very heavily – dumped him into the westward rapid. Bert returned to his expert investigation of the flying-machine at last with aching arms and in a state of gloomy rebellion. 'Brasted cheek!' he said. 'One'd think I was one of 'is beastly German slaves!

'Prancing beggar!'

And then he fell speculating what would happen when the flying-machine was repaired – if it could be repaired.

The two Germans went away again, and after some reflection Bert removed several nuts, resumed his jacket and vest, pocketed those nuts and his tools and hid the set of tools from the second aeroplane in the fork of a tree. 'Right-o,' he said, as he jumped down after the last of these precautions. The Prince and his companion reappeared as he returned to the machine by the water's edge. The Prince surveyed his progress for a time, and then went towards the Parting of the Waters and stood with folded arms gazing upstream in profound thought. The bird-faced officer came up to Bert, heavy with a sentence in English.

'Go,' he said with a helping gesture, 'und eat.'

When Bert got to the refreshment shed, he found all the food had vanished except one measured ration of corned beef and three biscuits.

He regarded this with open eyes and mouth.

The kitten appeared from under the vendor's seat with an ingratiating purr. 'Of course!' said Bert. 'Why! where's your milk?'

He accumulated wrath for a moment or so, then seized the plate in one hand, and the biscuits in another, and went in search of the Prince, breathing vile words anent 'grub' and his intimate interior. He approached without saluting.

' 'Ere!' he said fiercely. 'Whad the devil's this?'

An entirely unsatisfactory altercation followed. Bert expounded the Bun Hill theory of the relations of grub to efficiency in English, the bird-faced man replied with points about nations and discipline in German. The Prince, having made an estimate of Bert's quality and physique, suddenly hectored. He gripped Bert by the shoulder and shook him, making his pockets rattle, shouted something to him, and flung him struggling back. He hit him as though he was a German private. Bert went back, white and scared, but resolved by all his cockney standards upon one thing. He was bound in honour to 'go for' the Prince. 'Gaw!' he gasped, buttoning his jacket.

'Now,' cried the Prince, 'vill you go?' and then catching the heroic gleam in Bert's eye, drew his sword.

The bird-faced officer intervened, saying something in German and pointing skyward.

Far away in the south-west appeared a Japanese airship coming fast towards them. Their conflict ended at that. The Prince was first to grasp the situation and lead the retreat. All three scuttled like rabbits for the trees, and ran to and fro for cover until they found a hollow in which the grass grew rank. There they all squatted within six yards of one another. They sat in this place for a long time, up to their necks in the grass and watching through the branches for the airship. Bert had dropped some of his corned beef, but he found the biscuits in his hand

and ate them quietly. The monster came nearly overhead and then went away to Niagara and dropped beyond the power-works. When it was near, they all kept silence, and then presently they fell into an argument that was robbed perhaps of immediate explosive effect only by their failure to understand one another.

It was Bert began the talking and he talked on regardless of what they understood or failed to understand. But his voice must have conveyed his cantankerous intentions.

'You want that machine done,' he said first, 'you better keep your 'ands off me!'

They disregarded that and he repeated it.

Then he expanded his idea and the spirit of speech took hold of him. 'You think you got 'old of a chap you can kick and 'it like you do your private soldiers – you're jolly well mistaken. See? I've 'ad about enough of you and your antics. I been thinking you over, you and your war and your Empire and all the rot of it. Rot it is! It's you Germans made all the trouble in Europe first and last. And all for nothin'. Jest silly prancing! Jest because you've got the uniforms and flags! 'Ere I was – I didn't want to 'ave anything to do with you. I jest didn't care a 'eng at all about you. Then you get 'old of me – steal me practically – and 'ere I am, thousands of miles away from 'ome and everything, and all your silly fleet smashed up to rags. And you want to go on prancin' *now*! Not if I know it!

'Look at the mischief you done! Look at the way you smashed up New York – the people you killed, the stuff you wasted. Can't you learn?'

'Dummer Kerl!' said the bird-faced man suddenly in a tone of concentrated malignancy, glaring under his bandages. 'Esel!'[243]

'That's German for silly ass! I know. But who's the silly ass – 'im or me? When I was a kid, I used to read penny-dreadfuls about 'aving adventures and bein' a great c'mander and all that rot. I stowed it. But what's 'e got in 'is head? Rot about Napoleon, rot about Alexander, rot about 'is blessed family and 'im and Gawd and David and all that. Anyone who wasn't a dressed-up silly fool of a Prince could 'ave told all this was goin' to 'appen. There was us in Europe all at sixes and sevens with our silly flags and our silly newspapers raggin' us up against each other and keepin' us apart, and there was China, solid as a cheese, with millions and millions of men only wantin' a bit of science and a bit of enterprise to be as good as all of us. You thought they couldn't get at you. And then they got flying-machines. And bif! – 'ere we are. Why, when they didn't go on making guns and armies in China, we went and poked 'em up until they did. They '*ad* to give us this lickin' they've give us. We wouldn't be happy until they did, and as I say, 'ere we are!'

The bird-faced officer shouted to him to be quiet, and then began a conversation with the Prince.

'British citizen,' said Bert. 'You ain't obliged to listen, but I ain't obliged to shut up.' And for some time he continued his dissertation upon Imperialism, militarism, and international politics. But their talking put him out, and for a time he was certainly merely repeating abusive terms, 'prancin' nincompoops' and the like, old terms and new.

Then suddenly he remembered his essential grievance. ' 'Owever, look 'ere – 'ere! – the thing I started this talk about is where's that food there was in that shed? That's what I want to know. Where you put it?'

He paused. They went on talking in German. He repeated his question. They disregarded him. He asked a third time in a manner insupportably aggressive.

There fell a tense silence. For some seconds the three regarded one another. The Prince eyed Bert steadfastly, and Bert quailed under his eye. Slowly the Prince rose to his feet and the bird-faced officer jerked up beside him. Bert remained squatting.

'Be quaiat,' said the Prince.

Bert perceived this was no moment for eloquence.

The two Germans regarded him as he crouched there. Death for a moment seemed near.

Then the Prince turned away and the two of them went towards the flying-machine.

'Gaw!' whispered Bert, and then uttered under his breath one single word of abuse. He sat crouched together for perhaps three minutes, then he sprang to his feet and went off towards the Chinese aeronaut's gun hidden among the weeds.

8

There was no pretence after that moment that Bert was under the orders of the Prince or that he was going on with the repairing of the flying-machine. The two Germans took possession of that and set to work upon it. Bert, with his new weapon, went off to the neighbourhood of Terrapin Rock, and there sat down to examine it. It was a short rifle with a big cartridge, and a nearly full magazine. He took out the cartridges carefully and then tried the trigger and fittings until he felt sure he had the use of it. He reloaded carefully. Then he remembered he was hungry and went off, gun under his arm, to hunt in and about the refreshment shed. He had the sense to perceive that he must not show himself with the gun to the Prince and his companion. So long as they thought him unarmed they would leave him alone, but there was no knowing what the Napoleonic person might do if he saw Bert's weapon. Also he did not go near them because he knew that within himself boiled a reservoir of rage and fear, that he wanted to shoot these two men. He wanted to shoot them, and he thought that to shoot them would be a quite horrible thing to do. The two sides of his inconsistent civilisation warred within him.

Near the shed the kitten turned up again, obviously keen for milk. This greatly enhanced his own angry sense of hunger. He began to talk as he hunted about, and presently stood still, shouting insults. He talked of war and pride and Imperialism. 'Any other Prince but you would have died with his men and his ship!' he cried.

The two Germans at the machine heard his voice going ever and again, amidst the clamour of the waters. Their eyes met and they smiled slightly.

He was disposed for a time to sit in the refreshment shed waiting for them, but then it occurred to him that so he might get them both at close quarters. He strolled off presently to the point of Luna Island to think the situation out.

It had seemed a comparatively simple one at first, but as he turned it over in his mind its possibilities increased and multiplied. Both these men had swords – had either a revolver?

Also, if he shot them both, he might never find the food!

So far he had been going about with this gun under his arm, and a sense of lordly security in his mind, but what if they saw the gun and decided to ambush him? Goat Island is nearly all cover, trees, rocks, thickets, and irregularities.

Why not go and murder them both now?

'I carn't,' said Bert, dismissing that. 'I got to be worked up.'

But it was a mistake to get right away from them. That suddenly became clear. He ought to keep them under observation, ought to 'scout' them. Then he would be able to see what they were doing, whether either of them had a revolver, where they had hidden the food. He would be better able to determine what they meant to do to him. If he didn't 'scout' them, presently they would begin to 'scout' him. This seemed so eminently reasonable that he acted upon it forthwith. He thought over his costume and threw his collar and the tell-tale aeronaut's white cap into the water far below. He turned his coat collar up to hide any gleam of his dirty shirt. The tools and nuts in his pockets were disposed to clank, but he rearranged them and wrapped some letters and his pocket-handkerchief about them. He started off circumspectly and noiselessly, listening and peering at every step. As he drew near his antagonists, much grunting and creaking served to locate them. He discovered them engaged in what looked like a wrestling match with the Asiatic flying-machine. Their coats were off, their swords laid aside, they were working magnificently. Apparently they were turning it round and were having a good deal of difficulty with the long tail among the trees. He dropped flat at the sight of them and wriggled into a little hollow, and so lay watching their exertions. Ever and again, to pass the time, he would cover one or other of them with his gun.

He found them quite interesting to watch, so interesting that at times he came near shouting to advise them. He perceived that when they had the machine turned round, they would then be in immediate want of the nuts and tools he carried. Then they would come after him. They would certainly conclude he had them or had hidden them. Should he hide his gun and do a deal for food with these tools? He felt he would not be able to part with the gun again now he had once felt its reassuring company. The kitten turned up again and made a great fuss with him and licked and bit his ear.

The sun clambered to midday, and once that morning he saw, though the Germans did not, an Asiatic airship very far to the south, going swiftly eastward.

At last the flying-machine was turned and stood poised on its wheel, with its hooks pointing up the Rapids. The two Germans wiped their faces, resumed jackets and swords, spoke and bore themselves like men who congratulated themselves on a good laborious morning. Then they went off briskly towards the refreshment shed, the Prince leading. Bert became active in pursuit; but he found it impossible to stalk them quickly enough and silently enough to discover the hiding-place of the food. He found them, when he came into sight of them again, seated with their backs against the shed, plates on knee, and a tin of corned beef and a plateful of biscuits between them. They seemed in fairly good spirits, and once the Prince laughed. At this vision of eating Bert's plans gave way. Fierce hunger carried him. He appeared before them suddenly at a distance of perhaps twenty yards, gun in hand. ' 'Ands up!' he said in a hard, ferocious voice.

The Prince hesitated, and then up went two pairs of hands. The gun had surprised them both completely.

'Stand up,' said Bert . . . 'Drop that fork!'

They obeyed again.

'What nex'?' said Bert to himself. ' 'Orf stage, I suppose. That way,' he said. 'Go!'

The Prince obeyed with remarkable alacrity. When he reached the head of the clearing, he said something quickly to the bird-faced man and they both, with an entire lack of dignity, *ran*!

Bert was struck with an exasperating afterthought.

'Gord!' he cried with infinite vexation. 'Why! I ought to 'ave took their swords! 'Ere!'

But the Germans were already out of sight, and no doubt taking cover among the trees. Bert fell back upon imprecations, then he went up to the shed, cursorily examined the possibility of a flank attack, put his gun handy, and set to work, with a convulsive listening pause before each mouthful, on the Prince's plate of corned beef. He had finished that up and handed its gleanings to the kitten and he was falling-to on the second plateful, when the plate broke in his hand! He stared, with the fact slowly creeping upon him that an instant before he had heard a crack among the thickets. Then he sprang to his feet, snatched up his gun in one hand and the tin of corned beef in the other, and fled round the shed to the other side of the clearing. As he did so came a second crack from the thickets, and something went *phwit*! by his ear.

He didn't stop running until he was in what seemed to him a strongly defensible position near Luna Island. Then he took cover, panting, and crouched expectant.

'They got a revolver after all!' he panted . . . 'Wonder if they got two? If they 'ave – Gord! I'm done!

'Where's the kitten? Finishin' up that corned beef, I suppose. Little beggar!'

9

So it was that war began upon Goat Island. It lasted a day and a night, the longest day and the longest night in Bert's life. He had to lie close and listen and watch. Also he had to scheme what he should do. It was clear now that he had to kill these two men if he could, and that if they could, they would kill him. The prize was first food and then the flying-machine and the doubtful privilege of trying to ride it. If one failed, one would certainly be killed; if one succeeded, one would get away somewhere over there. For a time Bert tried to imagine what it was like over there. His mind ran over possibilities, deserts, angry

Americans, Japanese, Chinese – perhaps Red Indians! (Were there still Red Indians?)

'Got to take what comes,' said Bert. 'No way out of it that I can see!'

Was that voices? He realised that his attention was wandering. For a time all his senses were very alert. The uproar of the Falls was very confusing, and it mixed in all sorts of sounds, like feet walking, like voices talking, like shouts and cries.

'Silly great catarac',' said Bert. 'There ain't no sense in it, fallin' and fallin'.'

Never mind that, now! What were the Germans doing?

Would they go back to the flying-machine? They couldn't do anything with it, because he had those nuts and screws and the wrench and other tools. But suppose they found the second set of tools he had hidden in a tree! He had hidden the things well, of course, but they *might* find them. One wasn't sure, of course – one wasn't sure. He tried to remember just exactly how he had hidden those tools. He tried to persuade himself they were certainly and surely hidden, but his memory began to play antics. Had he really left the handle of the wrench sticking out, shining out at the fork of the branch?

Ssh! What was that? Someone stirring in those bushes? Up went an expectant muzzle. No! Where was the kitten? No! It was just imagination, not even the kitten.

The Germans would certainly miss and hunt about for the tools and nuts and screws he carried in his pockets; that was clear. Then they would decide he had them and come for him. He had only to remain still under cover, therefore, and he would get them. Was there any flaw in that? Would they take off more removable parts of the flying-machine and then lie up for him? No, they wouldn't do that, because they were two to one; they would have no apprehension of his getting off in the flying-machine, and no sound reason for supposing he would approach it, and so they would do nothing to damage or disable it. That he decided was clear. But suppose they lay up for him by the food. Well, that they wouldn't do, because they would know he had this corned beef; there was enough in this can to last, with moderation, several days. Of course they might try to tire him out instead of attacking him –

He roused himself with a start. He had just grasped the real weakness of his position. He might go to sleep!

It needed but ten minutes under the suggestion of that idea, before he realised that he was going to sleep!

He rubbed his eyes and handled his gun. He had never before realised the intensely soporific effect of the American sun, of the American air, the drowsy, sleep-compelling uproar of Niagara. Hitherto these things had on the whole seemed stimulating . . .

If he had not eaten so much and eaten it so fast, he would not be so heavy. Are vegetarians always bright? . . .

He roused himself with a jerk again.

If he didn't do something, he would fall asleep, and if he fell asleep, it was ten to one they would find him snoring, and finish him forthwith. If he sat motionless and noiseless, he would inevitably sleep. It was better, he told himself, to take even the risks of attacking than that. This sleep trouble, he felt, was going to beat him, must beat him in the end. They were all right; one could sleep and the other could watch. That, come to think of it, was what they would always do; one would do anything they wanted done, the other would lie under cover near at hand, ready to shoot. They might even trap him like that. One might act as a decoy.

That set him thinking of decoys. What a fool he had been to throw his cap away. It would have been invaluable on a stick – especially at night.

He found himself wishing for a drink. He settled that for a time by putting a pebble in his mouth. And then the sleep craving returned.

It became clear to him he must attack.

Like many great generals before him, he found his baggage, that is to say his tin of corned beef, a serious impediment to mobility. At last he decided to put the beef loose in his pocket and abandon the tin. It was not perhaps an ideal arrangement, but one must make sacrifices when one is campaigning. He crawled perhaps ten yards, and then for a time the possibilities of the situation paralysed him.

The afternoon was still. The roar of the cataract simply threw up that immense stillness in relief. He was doing his best to contrive the death of two better men than himself. Also they were doing their best to contrive his. What, behind this silence, were they doing?

Suppose he came upon them suddenly and fired, and missed?

He crawled, and halted listening, and crawled again until nightfall, and no doubt the German Alexander and his lieutenant did the same. A large-scale map of Goat Island marked with red and blue lines to show these strategic movements would no doubt have displayed much inter-lacing, but as a matter of fact neither side saw anything of the other throughout that age-long day of tedious alertness. Bert never knew how near he got to them nor how far he kept from them. Night found him no longer sleepy, but athirst, and near the American Fall. He was inspired by the idea that his antagonists might be in the wreckage of the *Hohenzollern* cabins that was jammed against Green Island. He became enterprising, broke from any attempt to conceal himself, and went across the little bridge at the double. He found nobody. It was his first visit to these huge fragments of airships, and for a time he explored them curiously in the dim light. He discovered the forward cabin was nearly intact, with its door slanting downward and a corner under water. He crept in, drank, and then was struck by the brilliant idea of shutting the door and sleeping on it.

But now he could not sleep at all.

He nodded towards morning and woke up to find it fully day. He breakfasted on corned beef and water, and sat for a long time appreciative of the security of his position. At last he became enterprising and bold. He would, he decided, settle this business forthwith, one way or the other. He was tired of all this crawling. He set out in the morning sunshine, gun in hand, scarcely troubling to walk softly. He went round the refreshment shed without finding anyone, and then through the trees towards the flying-machine. He came upon the bird-faced man sitting on the ground with his back against a tree, bent up over his folded arms, sleeping, his bandage very much over one eye.

Bert stopped abruptly and stood perhaps fifteen yards away, gun in hand ready. Where was the Prince? Then, sticking out at the side of the tree beyond, he saw a shoulder. Bert took five deliberate paces to the left. The great man became visible, leaning up against the trunk, pistol in one hand and sword in the other, and yawning – yawning. You can't shoot a yawning man, Bert found. He advanced upon his antagonist with his gun levelled, some foolish fancy of 'hands up' in his mind. The Prince became aware of him, the yawning mouth shut like a trap and he stood stiffly up. Bert stopped, silent. For a moment the two regarded one another.

Had the Prince been a wise man he would, I suppose, have dodged behind the tree. Instead, he gave vent to a shout, and raised pistol and sword. At that, like an automaton, Bert pulled his trigger.

It was his first experience of an oxygen-containing bullet. A great flame spurted from the middle of the Prince, a blinding flare, and there came a thud like the firing of a gun. Something hot and wet struck Bert's face. Then through a whirl of blinding smoke and steam he saw limbs and a collapsing, burst body fling themselves to earth.

Bert was so astonished that he stood agape, and the bird-faced officer might have cut him to the earth without a struggle. But instead the bird-faced officer was running away through the undergrowth, dodging as he went. Bert roused himself to a brief ineffectual pursuit, but he had no stomach for further killing. He returned to the mangled, scattered thing that had so recently been the great Prince Karl Albert. He surveyed the scorched and splashed vegetation about it. He made some speculative identifications. He advanced gingerly and picked up the hot revolver, to find all its chambers strained and burst. He became aware of a cheerful and friendly presence. He was greatly shocked that one so young should see so frightful a scene.

' 'Ere, Kitty,' he said, 'this ain't no place for you.'

He made three strides across the devastated area, captured the kitten neatly, and went his way towards the shed, with her purring loudly on his shoulder.

'*You* don't seem to mind,' he said.

For a time he fussed about the shed, and at last discovered the rest of the provisions hidden in the roof. 'Seems 'ard,' he said, as he administered a saucerful of milk, 'when you get three men in a 'ole like this, they can't work together. But 'im and 'is prancing was jest a bit too thick!'

'Gaw!' he reflected, sitting on the counter and eating, 'what a thing life is! 'Ere am I; I seen 'is picture, 'eard 'is name since I was a kid in frocks. Prince Karl Albert! And if anyone 'ad tole me I was going to blow 'im to smithereens – there! I shouldn't 'ave believed it, Kitty.

'That chap at Margit ought to 'ave tole me about it. All 'e tole me was that I got a weak chess.

'That other chap, 'e ain't going to do much. Wonder what I ought to do about 'im?'

He surveyed the trees with a keen blue eye and fingered the gun on his knee. 'I don't like this killing, Kitty,' he said. 'It's like Kurt said about being blooded. Seems to me you got to be blooded young . . . If that Prince 'ad come up to me and said, "Shake 'ands!" I'd 'ave shook 'ands . . . Now 'ere's that other chap, dodging about! 'E's got 'is 'ead 'urt already, and there's something wrong with his leg. And burns. Golly! it isn't three weeks ago I first set eyes on 'im, and then 'e was smart and set up – 'ands full of 'airbrushes and things, and swearin' at me. A regular gentleman! Now 'e's 'arfway to a wild man. What am I to do with 'im? What the 'ell am I to do with 'im? I can't leave 'im 'ave that flying-machine; that's a bit too good, and if I don't kill 'im, 'e'll jest 'ang about this island and starve . . .

' 'E's got a sword, of course . . . '

He resumed his philosophising after he had lit a cigarette.

'War's a silly gaim, Kitty. It's a silly gaim! We common people – we were fools. We thought those big people knew what they were up to – and they didn't. Look at that chap! 'E 'ad all Germany be'ind 'im, and what 'as 'e made of it? Smeshin' and blunderin' and destroyin', and there 'e is! Jest a mess of blood and boots and things! Jest an 'orrid splash! Prince Karl Albert! And all the men 'e led and the ships 'e 'ad, the airships, and the dragon-fliers – all scattered like a paper-chase between this 'ole and Germany. And fightin' going on and burnin' and killin' that 'e started, war without end all over the world!

'I suppose I shall 'ave to kill that other chap. I suppose I must. But it ain't at all the sort of job I fancy, Kitty!'

For a time he hunted about the island amidst the uproar of the waterfall, looking for the wounded officer, and at last he started him out of some bushes near the head of Biddle Stairs. But as he saw the bent and bandaged figure in limping flight before him, he found his cockney softness too much for him again; he could neither shoot nor pursue. 'I carn't,' he said, 'that's flat. I 'aven't the guts for it! 'E'll 'ave to go.'

He turned his steps towards the flying-machine . . .

He never saw the bird-faced officer again, nor any further evidence of his presence. Towards evening he grew fearful of ambushes and hunted vigorously for an hour or so, but in vain. He slept in a good defensible position at the extremity of the rocky point that runs out to the Canadian Fall, and in the night he woke in panic terror and fired his gun. But it was nothing. He slept no more that night. In the morning he became curiously concerned for the vanished man, and hunted for him as one might for an erring brother. 'If I knew some German,' he said, 'I'd 'oller. It's jest not knowing German does it. You can't explain.'

He discovered, later, traces of an attempt to cross the gap in the broken bridge. A rope with a bolt attached had been flung across and had caught in a fenestration of a projecting fragment of railing. The end of the rope trailed in the seething water towards the fall.

But the bird-faced officer was already rubbing shoulders with certain inert matter that had once been Lieutenant Kurt and the Chinese aeronaut and a dead cow, and much other uncongenial company, in the huge circle of the whirlpool two and a quarter miles away. Never had that great gathering place, that incessant, aimless, unprogressive hurry of waste and battered things, been so crowded with strange and melancholy derelicts. Round they went and round, and every day brought its new contributions, luckless brutes, shattered fragments of boat and flying-machine, endless citizens from the cities upon the shores of the great lakes above. Much came from Cleveland. It all gathered here, and whirled about indefinitely, and over it all gathered daily a greater abundance of birds.

CHAPTER TEN

The World Under the War

1

Bert spent two more days upon Goat Island, and finished all his provisions except the cigarettes and mineral water, before he brought himself to try the Asiatic flying-machine.

Even at last he did not so much go off upon it as get carried off. It had taken only an hour or so to substitute wing stays from the second flying-machine and to replace the nuts he had himself removed. The engine was in working order, and differed only very simply and obviously from that of a contemporary motor-bicycle. The rest of the time was taken up by a vast musing and delaying and hesitation. Chiefly he saw himself splashing into the rapids and whirling down them to the Fall, clutching and drowning, but also he had a vision of being hopelessly in the air, going fast and unable to ground. His mind was too concentrated upon the business of flying for him to think very much of what might happen to an indefinite-spirited cockney without credential who arrived on an Asiatic flying-machine amidst the war-infuriated population beyond.

He still had a lingering solicitude for the bird-faced officer. He had a haunting fancy he might be lying disabled or badly smashed in some way in some nook or cranny of the island; and it was only after a most exhaustive search that he abandoned that distressing idea. 'If I found 'im,' he reasoned the while, 'what could I do wiv 'im? You can't blow a chap's brains out when 'e's down. And I don' see 'ow else I can 'elp 'im.'

Then the kitten bothered his highly developed sense of social responsibility. 'If I leave 'er, she'll starve . . . Ought to catch mice for 'erself . . . *Are* there mice? . . . Birds? . . . She's too young . . . She's like me; she's a bit too civilised.'

Finally he stuck her in his side pocket, and she became greatly interested in the memories of corned beef she found there.

With her in his pocket, he seated himself in the saddle of the flying-machine. Big, clumsy thing it was – and not a bit like a bicycle. Still the working of it was fairly plain. You set the engine going – *so*; kicked yourself up until the wheel was vertical, *so*; engaged the gyroscope, *so*, and then – then – you just pulled up this lever.

Rather stiff it was, but suddenly it came over –

The big curved wings on either side flapped disconcertingly, flapped again click, clock, click, clock, clitter-clock!

Stop! The thing was heading for the water; its wheel was in the water. Bert groaned from his heart and struggled to restore the lever to its first position. Click, clock, clitter-clock, he was rising! The machine was lifting its dripping wheel out of the eddies, and he was going up! There was no stopping now, no good in stopping now. In another moment Bert, clutching and convulsive and rigid, with staring eyes and a face pale as death, was flapping up above the Rapids, jerking to every jerk of the wings, and rising, rising.

There was no comparison in dignity and comfort between a flying-machine and a balloon. Except in its moments of descent, the balloon was a vehicle of faultless urbanity; this was a buck-jumping mule, a mule that jumped up and never came down again. Click, clock, click, clock; with each beat of the strangely shaped wings it jumped Bert upward and caught him neatly again half a second later on the saddle. And while in ballooning there is no wind, since the balloon is a part of the wind, flying is a wild perpetual creation of, and plunging into, wind. It was a wind that above all things sought to blind him, to force him to close his eyes. It occurred to him presently to twist his knees and legs inward and grip with them, or surely he would have been bumped into two clumsy halves. And he was going up, a hundred yards high, two hundred, three hundred, over the streaming, frothing wilderness of water below – up, up, up. That was all right, but how presently would one go horizontally? He tried to think if these things did go horizontally. No! They flapped up and then they soared down. For a time he would keep on flapping up. Tears streamed from his eyes. He wiped them with one temerariously disengaged hand.

Was it better to risk a fall over land or over water – such water?

He was flapping up above the Upper Rapids towards Buffalo. It was at any rate a comfort that the Falls and the wild swirl of waters below them were behind him. He was flying up straight. That he could see. How did one turn?

He was presently almost cool, and his eyes got more used to the rush of air, but he was getting very high, very high. He tilted his head forwards and surveyed the country, blinking. He could see all over Buffalo, a place with three great blackened scars of ruin, and hills and stretches beyond. He wondered if he was half a mile high, or more. There were some people among some houses near a railway station between Niagara and Buffalo, and then more people. They went like ants busily in and out of the houses. He saw two motor cars gliding along the road towards Niagara City. Then far away in the south he saw a great Asiatic airship going eastward. 'Oh, Gord!' he said, and became earnest in his ineffectual attempts to alter his direction. But that airship took no notice of him, and he continued to ascend convulsively. The world got more and more extensive and maplike. Click, clock, clitter-clock. Above him and very near to him now was a hazy stratum of cloud.

He determined to disengage the wing clutch. He did so. The lever resisted his strength for a time, then over it came, and instantly the tail of the machine cocked up and the wings became rigidly spread. Instantly everything was swift and smooth and silent. He was gliding rapidly down the air against a wild gale of wind, his eyes three-quarters shut.

A little lever that had hitherto been obdurate now confessed itself mobile. He turned it over gently to the right, and whiroo! – the left wing had in some mysterious way given at its edge and he was sweeping round and downward in an immense right-handed spiral. For some moments he experienced all the helpless sensations of catastrophe. He restored the lever to its middle position with some difficulty, and the wings were equalised again.

He turned it to the left and had a sensation of being spun round backwards. 'Too much!' he gasped.

He discovered that he was rushing down at a headlong pace towards a railway line and some factory buildings. They appeared to be tearing up to him to devour him. He must have dropped all that height. For a moment he had the ineffectual sensations of one whose bicycle bolts downhill. The ground had almost taken him by surprise. ' 'Ere!' he cried; and then with a violent effort of all his being he got the beating engine at work again and set the wings flapping. He swooped down and up and resumed his quivering and pulsating ascent of the air.

He went high again, until he had a wide view of the pleasant upland country of western New York State, and then made a long coast down, and so up again, and then a coast. Then as he came swooping a quarter of a mile above a village he saw people running about, running away – evidently in relation to his hawklike passage. He got an idea that he had been shot at.

'Up!' he said, and attacked that lever again. It came over with remarkable docility, and suddenly the wings seemed to give way in the middle. But the engine was still! It had stopped. He flung the lever back rather by instinct than design. What to do?

Much happened in a few seconds, but also his mind was quick, he thought very quickly. He couldn't get up again, he was gliding down the air; he would have to hit something.

He was travelling at the rate of perhaps thirty miles an hour down, down.

That plantation of larches looked the softest thing – mossy almost!

Could he get it? He gave himself to the steering. Round to the right – left!

Swirroo! Crackle! He was gliding over the tops of the trees, ploughing through them, tumbling into a cloud of green, sharp leaves and black twigs. There was a sudden snapping, and he fell off the saddle forward, a thud and a crashing of branches. Some twigs hit him smartly in the face . . .

He was between a tree-stem and the saddle, with his leg over the steering lever and, so far as he could realise, not hurt. He tried to alter his position and free his leg, and found himself slipping and dropping through branches with everything giving way beneath him. He clutched and found himself in the lower branches of a tree beneath the flying-machine. The air was full of a pleasant resinous smell. He stared for a moment motionless, and then very carefully clambered down branch by branch to the soft needle-covered ground below.

'Good business,' he said, looking up at the bent and tilted kite-wings above.

'I dropped soft!'

He rubbed his chin with his hand and meditated. 'Blowed if I don't think I'm a rather lucky fellow!' he said, surveying the pleasant sun-bespattered ground under the trees. Then he became aware of a violent tumult at his side. 'Lord!' he said, 'You must be 'arf smothered,' and extracted the kitten from his pocket-handkerchief and pocket. She was twisted and crumpled and extremely glad to see the light again. Her little tongue peeped between her teeth. He put her down, and she ran a dozen paces and shook herself and stretched and sat up and began to wash.

'Nex'?' he said, looking about him, and then with a gesture of vexation, 'Desh it! I ought to 'ave brought that gun!'

He had rested it against a tree when he had seated himself in the flying-machine saddle.

He was puzzled for a time by the immense peacefulness in the quality of the world, and then he perceived that the roar of the cataract was no longer in his ears.

He had no very clear idea of what sort of people he might come upon in this country. It was, he knew, America. Americans, he had always understood, were the citizens of a great and powerful nation, dry and humorous in their manner, addicted to the use of the bowie-knife and revolver, and in the habit of talking through the nose like Norfolk, and saying 'allow' and 'reckon' and 'calculate', after the manner of the people who live on the New Forest side of Hampshire. Also they were very rich, had rocking-chairs, and put their feet at unusual altitudes, and they chewed tobacco, gum, and other substances, with untiring industry. Commingled with them were cowboys, Red Indians, and comic, respectful niggers.[244] This he had learnt from the fiction in his public library. Beyond that he had learnt very little. He was not surprised, therefore, when he met armed men.

He decided to abandon the shattered flying-machine. He wandered through the trees for some time, and then struck a road that seemed to his urban English eyes to be remarkably wide but not properly 'made'. Neither hedge nor ditch nor curbed distinctive footpath separated it from the woods, and it went in that long easy curve which distinguishes the tracks of an open continent. Ahead he saw a man carrying a gun under his arm, a man in a soft black hat, a blue blouse, and black trousers, and with a round, fat face quite innocent of goatee. This person regarded him askance and heard him speak with a start.

'Can you tell me whereabouts I am at all?' asked Bert.

The man regarded him, and more particularly his rubber boots, with sinister suspicion. Then he replied in a strange outlandish tongue that was, as a matter of fact, Czech. He ended suddenly at the sight of Bert's blank face with 'Don't spik English.'

'Oh!' said Bert. He reflected gravely for a moment, and then went his way.

'Thenks,' he said as an afterthought. The man regarded his back for a moment, was struck with an idea, began an abortive gesture, sighed, gave it up, and went on also with a depressed countenance.

Presently Bert came to a big wooden house standing casually among the trees. It looked a bleak, bare box of a house to him, no creeper grew on it, no hedge nor wall nor fence parted it off from the woods about it. He stopped before the steps that led up to the door, perhaps thirty yards away. The place seemed deserted. He would have gone up to the door and rapped, but suddenly a big black dog appeared at the side and regarded him. It was a huge heavy-jawed dog of some unfamiliar breed, and it wore a spike-studded collar. It did not bark nor approach him, it just bristled quietly and emitted a single sound like a short, deep cough.

Bert hesitated and went on.

He stopped thirty paces away and stood peering about him among the trees. 'If I 'aven't been and lef' that kitten,' he said.

Acute sorrow wrenched him for a time. The black dog came through the trees to get a better look at him and coughed that well-bred cough again. Bert resumed the road.

'She'll do all right,' he said. 'She'll catch things . . .

'She'll do all right,' he said presently, without conviction. But if it had not been for the black dog, he would have gone back.

When he was out of sight of the house and the black dog, he went into the woods on the other side of the way and emerged after an interval trimming a very tolerable cudgel with his pocket-knife. Presently he saw an attractive-looking rock by the track and picked it up and put it in his pocket. Then he came to three or four houses, wooden like the last, each with an ill-painted white verandah (that was his name for it) and all standing in the same casual way upon the ground. Behind, through the woods, he saw pigsties and a rooting black sow leading a brisk, adventurous family. A wild-looking woman with sloe-black eyes and dishevelled black hair sat upon the steps of one of the houses nursing a baby, but at the sight of Bert she got up and went inside, and he heard her bolting the door. Then a boy appeared among the pigsties, but he would not understand Bert's hail.

'I suppose it is America!' said Bert.

The houses became more frequent down the road, and he passed two other extremely wild and dirty-looking men without addressing them. One carried a gun and the other a hatchet, and they scrutinised him and his cudgel scornfully. Then he struck a cross-road with a monorail at its side, and there was a notice board at the corner with 'Wait here for the cars.' 'That's all right, any'ow,' said Bert. 'Wonder 'ow long I should 'ave to wait?' It occurred to him that in the present disturbed state of the country the service might be interrupted, and as there seemed more houses to the right than the left he turned to the right. He passed an old negro. ' 'Ullo!' said Bert. 'Goo'-morning!'

'Good-day, sah!' said the old negro, in a voice of almost incredible richness.

'What's the name of this place?' asked Bert.

'Tanooda,[245] sah!' said the negro.

'Thenks!' said Bert.

'Thank *you*, sah!' said the negro, overwhelmingly.

Bert came to houses of the same detached, unwalled, wooden type, but adorned now with enamelled advertisements partly in English and partly in Esperanto.[246] Then he came to what he concluded was a grocer's shop. It was the first house that professed the hospitality of an open door, and from within came a strangely familiar sound. 'Gaw!' he said, searching in his pockets. 'Why! I 'aven't wanted money for free weeks! I wonder if I – Grubb 'ad most of it. Ah!' He produced a handful of coins and regarded it; three pennies, sixpence, and a shilling. 'That's all right,' he said, forgetting a very obvious consideration.

He approached the door, and as he did so a compactly built, grey-faced man in shirt sleeves appeared in it and scrutinised him and his cudgel. 'Mornin',' said Bert. 'Can I get anything to eat 'r drink in this shop?'

The man in the door replied, thank Heaven, in clear, good American. 'This, sir, is not A shop, it is A store.'[247]

'Oh!' said Bert, and then, 'Well, can I get anything to eat?'

'You can,' said the American in a tone of confident encouragement, and led the way inside.

The shop seemed to him by his Bun Hill standards extremely roomy, well lit, and unencumbered. There was a long counter to the left of him, with drawers and miscellaneous commodities ranged behind it, a number of chairs, several tables, and two spittoons to the right, various barrels, cheeses, and bacon up the vista, and beyond, a large archway leading to more space. A little group of men was assembled round one of the tables, and a woman of perhaps five-and-thirty leant with her elbows on the counter. All the men were armed with rifles, and the barrel of a gun peeped above the counter. They were all listening idly, inattentively, to a cheap, metallic-toned gramophone that occupied a table near at hand. From its brazen throat came words that gave Bert a qualm of homesickness, that brought back in his memory a sunlit beach, a group of children, red-painted bicycles, Grubb, and an approaching balloon:

> Ting-a-ling-a-ting-a-ling-a-ting-a-ling-a-tang
> What Price Hairpins Now?

A heavy-necked man in a straw hat, who was chewing something, stopped the machine with a touch, and they all turned their eyes on Bert. And all their eyes were tired eyes.

'Can we give this gentleman anything to eat, mother, or can we not?' said the proprietor.

'He kin have what he likes,' said the woman at the counter, without moving, 'right up from a cracker to a square meal.' She struggled with a yawn, after the manner of one who has been up all night.

'I want a meal,' said Bert, 'but I 'aven't very much money. I don' want to give mor'n a shillin'.'[248]

'Mor'n a *what*?' said the proprietor, sharply.

'Mor'n a shillin',' said Bert, with a sudden disagreeable realisation coming into his mind.

'Yes,' said the proprietor, startled for a moment from his courtly bearing. 'But what in hell *is* a shilling?'

'He means a quarter,' said a wise-looking, lank young man in riding gaiters.

Bert, trying to conceal his consternation, produced a coin. 'That's a shilling,' he said.

'He calls A store A shop,' said the proprietor, 'and he wants A meal for A shilling. May I ask you, sir, what part of America you hail from?'

Bert replaced the shilling in his pocket as he spoke. 'Niagara,' he said.

'And when did you leave Niagara?'

' 'Bout an hour ago.'

'Well,' said the proprietor, and turned with a puzzled smile to the others. 'Well!'

They asked various questions simultaneously.

Bert selected one or two for reply. 'You see,' he said, 'I been with the German air-fleet. I got caught up by them, sort of by accident, and brought over here.'

'From England?'

'Yes – from England. Way of Germany. I was in a great battle with them Asiatics, and I got lef' on a little island between the Falls.'

'Goat Island?'

'I don' know what it was called. But any'ow I found a flying-machine and made a sort of fly with it and got here.'

Two men stood up with incredulous eyes on him. 'Where's the flying-machine?' they asked; 'outside?'

'It's back in the woods here – 'bout arf a mile away.'

'Is it good?' said a thick-lipped man with a scar.

'I come down rather a smash – '

Everybody got up and stood about him and talked confusingly. They wanted him to take them to the flying-machine at once.

'Look 'ere,' said Bert, 'I'll show you – only I 'aven't 'ad anything to eat since yestiday – except mineral water.'

A gaunt, soldierly-looking young man with long lean legs in riding gaiters and a bandolier, who had hitherto not spoken, intervened now on his behalf in a note of confident authority. 'That's aw right,' he said. 'Give him a feed, Mr Logan – from me. I want to hear more of that story of his. We'll see his machine afterwards. If you ask me, I should say it's a remarkably interesting accident had dropped this gentleman here. I guess we requisition that flying-machine – if we find it – for local defence.'

3

So Bert fell on his feet again, and sat eating cold meat and good bread and mustard and drinking very good beer, and telling in the roughest outline and with the omissions and inaccuracies of statement natural to his type of mind, the simple story of his adventures. He told how he and a 'gentleman friend' had been visiting the seaside for their health, how a 'chep' came along in a balloon and fell out as he fell in, how he had drifted to Franconia, how the Germans had seemed to mistake him for someone and had 'took him prisoner' and brought him to New York, how he had been to Labrador and back, how he had got to Goat Island and found himself there alone. He omitted the matter of the Prince and the Butteridge aspect of the affair, not out of any deep deceitfulness, but because he felt the inadequacy of his narrative powers. He wanted everything to seem easy and natural and correct, to present himself as a trustworthy and understandable Englishman in a sound mediocre position, to whom refreshment and accommodation might be given with freedom and confidence.

When his fragmentary story came to New York and the battle of Niagara, they suddenly produced newspapers which had been lying about on the table, and began to check him and question him by these vehement accounts. It became evident to him that his descent had revived and roused to flames again a discussion, a topic, that had been burning continuously, that had smouldered only through sheer exhaustion of material during the temporary diversion of the gramophone, a discussion that had drawn these men together, rifle in hand, the one supreme topic of the whole world, the War and the methods of the War. He found any question of his personality and his personal adventures falling into the background, found himself taken for granted, and no more than a source of information. The ordinary affairs of life, the buying and selling of everyday necessities, the cultivation of the ground, the tending of beasts, was going on as it were by force of routine, as the common duties of life go on in a house whose master lies under the knife of some supreme operation. The overruling interest was furnished by those great Asiatic airships that went upon incalculable missions across the sky, the crimson-clad swordsmen who might come fluttering down demanding petrol, or food, or news. These men were asking, all the continent was asking, 'What are we to do? What can we try? How can we get at them?' Bert fell into his place as an item, ceased even in his own thoughts to be a central and independent thing.

After he had eaten and drunken his fill and sighed and stretched and told them how good the food seemed to him, he lit a cigarette they gave him and led the way, with some doubts and trouble, to the flying-machine amidst the larches. It became manifest that the gaunt young man, whose name, it seemed, was Laurier, was a leader both by position and natural aptitude. He knew the names and characters and capabilities of all the men who were with him, and he set them to work at once with vigour and effect to secure this precious instrument of war. They got the thing down to the ground deliberately and carefully, felling a couple of trees in the process, and they built a wide flat roof of timbers and tree boughs to guard their precious find against its chance discovery by any passing Asiatics. Long before evening they had an engineer from the next township at work upon it, and they were casting lots among the seventeen picked men who wanted to take it for its first flight. And Bert found his kitten and carried it back to Logan's store and handed it with earnest admonition to Mrs Logan. And it was reassuringly clear to him that in Mrs Logan both he and the kitten had found a congenial soul.

Laurier was not only a masterful person and a wealthy property owner and employer – he was president, Bert learnt with awe, of the Tanooda Canning Corporation – but he was popular and skilful in the arts of popularity. In the evening quite a crowd of men gathered in the store and talked of the flying-machine and of the war that was tearing the world to pieces. And presently came a man on a bicycle with an ill-printed newspaper of a single sheet which acted like fuel in a blazing furnace of talk. It was nearly all American news; the old-fashioned cables had fallen into disuse for some years, and the Marconi stations across the ocean and along the Atlantic coastline seemed to have furnished particularly tempting points of attack.

But such news it was.

Bert sat in the background – for by this time they had gauged his personal quality pretty completely – listening. Before his staggering mind passed strange, vast images as they talked, of great issues at a crisis, of nations in tumultuous march, of continents overthrown, of famine and destruction beyond measure. Ever and again, in spite of his efforts to suppress them, certain personal impressions would scamper across the weltering confusion, the horrible mess of the exploded Prince, the Chinese aeronaut upside down, the limping and bandaged bird-faced officer blundering along in miserable and hopeless flight . . .

They spoke of fire and massacre, of cruelties and counter cruelties, of things that had been done to harmless Asiatics by race-mad men, of the wholesale burning and smashing up of towns, railway junctions, bridges, of whole populations in hiding and exodus. 'Every ship they've got is in the Pacific,' he heard one man exclaim. 'Since the fighting began they can't have landed on the Pacific slope less than a million men. They've come to stay in these States, and they will – living or dead.'

Slowly, broadly, invincibly, there grew upon Bert's mind realisation of the immense tragedy of humanity into which his life was flowing; the appalling and universal nature of the epoch that had arrived; the conception of an end to security and order and habit. The whole world was at war and it could not get back to peace, it might never recover peace.

He had thought the things he had seen had been exceptional, conclusive things, that the besieging of New York and the battle of the Atlantic were epoch-making events between long years of security. And they had been but the first warning impacts of universal cataclysm. Each day destruction and hate and disaster grew, the fissures widened between man and man, new regions of the fabric of civilisation crumbled and gave way. Below, the armies grew and the people perished; above, the airships and aeroplanes fought and fled, raining destruction.

It is difficult, perhaps, for the broad-minded and long-perspectived reader to understand how incredible the breaking down of the scientific civilisation seemed to those who actually lived at this time, who in their own persons went down in that débâcle. Progress had marched as it seemed invincible about the earth, never now to rest again. For three hundred years and more the long steadily accelerated diastole of Europeanised civilisation had been in progress: towns had been multiplying, populations increasing, values rising, new countries developing; thought, literature, knowledge unfolding and spreading. It seemed but a part of the process that every year the instruments of war were vaster and more powerful, and that armies and explosives outgrew all other growing things . . .

Three hundred years of diastole, and then came the swift and unexpected systole, like the closing of a fist. They could not understand it was a systole. They could not think of it as anything but a jolt, a hitch, a mere oscillatory indication of the swiftness of their progress. Collapse, though it happened all about them, remained incredible. Presently some falling mass smote them down, or the ground opened beneath their feet. They died incredulous . . .

These men in the store made a minute, remote group under this immense canopy of disaster. They turned from one little aspect to another. What chiefly concerned them was defence against Asiatic raiders swooping for petrol or to destroy weapons or communications. Everywhere levies were being formed at that time to defend the plant of the railroads day and night in the hope that communication would speedily be restored. The land war was still far away. A man with a flat voice distinguished himself by a display of knowledge and cunning. He told them all with confidence just what had been wrong with the German *drachenflieger* and the American aeroplanes, just what advantage the Japanese flyers possessed. He launched out into a romantic description of the Butteridge machine and riveted Bert's attention. 'I *see* that,' said Bert, and was smitten silent by a thought. The man with the flat voice talked on, without heeding him, of the strange irony of Butteridge's death. At that Bert had a little twinge of relief – he would never meet Butteridge again. It appeared Butteridge had died suddenly, very suddenly.

'And his secret, sir, perished with him! When they came to look for the parts – none could find them. He had hidden them all too well.'

'But couldn't he tell?' asked the man in the straw hat. 'Did he die so suddenly as that?'

'Struck down, sir. Rage and apoplexy. At a place called Dymchurch in England.'

'That's right,' said Laurier. 'I remember a page about it in the *Sunday American*. At the time they said it was a German spy had stolen his balloon.'

'Well, sir,' said the flat-voiced man, 'that fit of apoplexy at Dymchurch was the worst thing – ab-so-lutely the worst thing that ever happened to the world. For if it had not been for the death of Mr Butteridge – '

'No one knows his secret?'

'Not a soul. It's gone. His balloon, it appears, was lost at sea, with all the plans. Down it went, and they went with it.'

Pause.

'With machines such as he made we could fight these Asiatic fliers on more than equal terms. We could out-fly and beat down those scarlet hummingbirds wherever they appeared. But it's gone, it's gone, and there's no time to reinvent it now. We got to fight with what we got –

and the odds are against us. *That* won't stop us fightin'. No! but just think of it!'

Bert was trembling violently. He cleared his throat hoarsely.

'I say,' he said, 'look here, I – '

Nobody regarded him. The man with the flat voice was opening a new branch of the subject. 'I allow – ' he began.

Bert became violently excited. He stood up. He made clawing motions with his hands. 'I say!' he exclaimed, 'Mr Laurier. Look 'ere – I want – about that Butteridge machine – .'

Mr Laurier, sitting on an adjacent table, with a magnificent gesture, arrested the discourse of the flat-voiced man. 'What's *he* saying?' said he.

Then the whole company realised that something was happening to Bert; either he was suffocating or going mad. He was spluttering. 'Look 'ere! I say! 'Old on a bit!' and trembling and eagerly unbuttoning himself.

He tore open his collar and opened vest and shirt. He plunged into his interior and for an instant it seemed he was plucking forth his liver. Then as he struggled with buttons on his shoulder they perceived this flattened horror was in fact a terribly dirty flannel chest-protector. In another moment Bert, in a state of irregular décolletage, was standing over the table displaying a sheaf of papers.

'These!' he gasped. 'These are the plans! . . . You know! Mr Butteridge – his machine! What died! I was the chap that went off in that balloon!'

For some seconds everyone was silent. They stared from these papers to Bert's white face and blazing eyes, and back to the papers on the table. Nobody moved. Then the man with the flat voice spoke.

'Irony!' he said, with a note of satisfaction. 'Real right-down Irony! *When it's too late to think of making 'em any more!*'

4

They would all no doubt have been eager to hear Bert's story over again, but it was at this point that Laurier showed his quality. 'No, *sir*,' he said, and slid from off his table.

He impounded the dispersing Butteridge plans with one comprehensive sweep of his arm, rescuing them even from the expository finger-marks of the man with the flat voice, and handed them to Bert. 'Put those back,' he said, 'where you had 'em. We have a journey before us.'

Bert took them.

'Whar?' said the man in the straw hat.

'Why, sir, we are going to find the President of these States and give these plans over to him. I decline to believe, sir, we are too late.'

'Where is the President?' asked Bert weakly in that pause that followed.

'Logan,' said Laurier, disregarding that feeble enquiry, 'you must help us in this.'

It seemed only a matter of a few minutes before Bert and Laurier and the storekeeper were examining a number of bicycles that were stowed in the hinder room of the store. Bert didn't like any of them very much. They had wood rims, and an experience of wood rims in the English climate had taught him to hate them. That, however, and one or two other objections to an immediate start were overruled by Laurier. 'But where *is* the President?' Bert repeated as they stood behind Logan while he pumped up a deflated tyre.

Laurier looked down on him. 'He is reported in the neighbourhood of Albany – out towards the Berkshire Hills. He is moving from place to place and, as far as he can, organising the defence by telegraph and telephone. The Asiatic air-fleet is trying to locate him. When they think they have located the seat of government, they throw bombs. This inconveniences him, but so far they have not come within ten miles of him. The Asiatic air-fleet is at present scattered all over the Eastern States, seeking out and destroying gasworks and whatever seems conducive to the building of airships or the transport of troops. Our retaliatory measures are slight in the extreme. But with these machines – Sir, this ride of ours will count among the historical rides of the world!'

He came near to striking an attitude.

'We shan't get to him tonight?' asked Bert.

'No, sir!' said Laurier. 'We shall have to ride some days, sure!'

'I suppose we can't get a lift on a train – or anything?'

'No, sir! There's been no transit by Tanooda for three days. It is no good waiting. We shall have to get on as well as we can.'

'Startin' now?'

'Starting now!'

'But 'ow about – We shan't be able to do much tonight.'

'May as well ride till we're fagged and sleep then. So much clear gain. Our road is eastward.'

'Of course – ' began Bert, with memories of the dawn upon Goat Island, and left his sentence unfinished.

He gave his attention to the more scientific packing of the chest-protector, for several of the plans flapped beyond his vest.

For a week Bert led a life of mixed sensations. Amidst these fatigue in the legs predominated. Mostly he rode, rode with Laurier's back inexorably ahead, through a land like a larger England, with bigger hills and wider valleys, larger fields, wider roads, fewer hedges, and wooden houses with commodious piazzas. He rode. Laurier made enquiries, Laurier chose the turnings, Laurier doubted, Laurier decided. Now it seemed they were in telephonic touch with the President; now something had happened and he was lost again. But always they had to go on, and always Bert rode. A tyre was deflated. Still he rode. He grew saddle sore. Laurier declared that unimportant. Asiatic flying ships passed overhead, the two cyclists made a dash for cover until the sky was clear. Once a red Asiatic flying-machine came fluttering after them, so low they could distinguish the aeronaut's head. He followed them for a mile. Now they came to regions of panic, now to regions of destruction; here people were fighting for food, here they seemed hardly stirred from the countryside routine. They spent a day in a deserted and damaged Albany. The Asiatics had descended and cut every wire and made a cinder-heap of the Junction, and our travellers pushed on eastward. They passed a hundred half-heeded incidents, and always Bert was toiling after Laurier's indefatigable back . . .

Things struck upon Bert's attention and perplexed him, and then he passed on with unanswered questionings fading from his mind.

He saw a large house on fire on a hillside to the right, and no man heeding it . . .

They came to a narrow railroad bridge and presently to a monorail train standing in the track on its safety feet. It was a remarkably sumptuous train, the Last Word Trans-Continental Express,[249] and the passengers were all playing cards or sleeping or preparing a picnic meal on a grassy slope near at hand. They had been there six days . . .

At one point ten dark-complexioned men were hanging in a string from the trees along the roadside. Bert wondered why . . .

At one peaceful-looking village where they stopped off to get Bert's tyre mended and found beer and biscuits, they were approached by an extremely dirty little boy without boots, who spoke as follows:

'Deyse[250] been hanging a Chink in dose woods!'

'Hanging a Chinaman?' said Laurier.

'Sure. Der sleuths got him rubberin' der railroad sheds!'

'Oh!'

'Dose guys done wase cartridges. Deyse hung him and dey pulled his legs. Deyse doin' all der Chinks dey can fine dat weh! Dey ain't takin' no risks. All der Chinks dey can fine.'

Neither Bert nor Laurier made any reply, and presently, after a little skilful expectoration, the young gentleman was attracted by the appearance of two of his friends down the road and shuffled off, whooping weirdly . . .

That afternoon they almost ran over a man shot through the body and partly decomposed, lying near the middle of the road, just outside Albany. He must have been lying there for some days . . .

Beyond Albany they came upon a motor car with a tyre burst and a young woman sitting absolutely passive beside the driver's seat. An old man was under the car trying to effect some impossible repairs. Beyond, sitting with a rifle across his knees, with his back to the car, and staring into the woods, was a young man. The old man crawled out at their approach and still on all-fours accosted Bert and Laurier. The car had broken down overnight. The old man said he could not understand what was wrong, but he was trying to puzzle it out. Neither he nor his son-in-law had any mechanical aptitude. They had been assured this was a foolproof car. It was dangerous to have to stop in this place. The party had been attacked by tramps and had had to fight. It was known they had provisions. He mentioned a great name in the world of finance. Would Laurier and Bert stop and help him? He proposed it first hopefully, then urgently, at last in tears and terror.

'No!' said Laurier inexorably. 'We must go on! We have something more than a woman to save. We have to save America!'

The girl never stirred . . .

And once they passed a madman singing . . .

At last they found the President hiding in a small saloon upon the outskirts of a place called Pinkerville on the Hudson, and gave the plans of the Butteridge machine into his hands.

CHAPTER ELEVEN

The Great Collapse

1

And now the whole fabric of civilisation was bending and giving, and dropping to pieces and melting in the furnace of the war. The stages of the swift and universal collapse of the financial and scientific civilisation with which the twentieth century opened followed each other very swiftly, so swiftly that upon the foreshortened page of history they seem altogether to overlap. To begin with, one sees the world nearly at a maximum of wealth and prosperity. To its inhabitants indeed it seemed also at a maximum of security. When now in retrospect the thoughtful observer surveys the intellectual history of this time, when one reads its surviving fragments of literature, its scraps of political oratory, the few small voices that chance has selected out of a thousand million utterances to speak to later days, the most striking thing of all this web of wisdom and error is surely that hallucination of security. To men living in our present world state, orderly, scientific and secured, nothing seems so precarious, so giddily dangerous, as the fabric of the social order with which the men of the opening of the twentieth century were content. To us it seems that every institution and relationship was the fruit of haphazard and tradition and the manifest sport of chance, their laws each made for some separate occasion and having no relation to any future needs, their customs illogical, their education aimless and wasteful. Their method of economic exploitation indeed impresses a trained and informed mind as the most frantic and destructive scramble it is possible to conceive; their credit and monetary system resting on an unsubstantial tradition of the worthiness of gold, seems a thing almost fantastically unstable. And they lived in planless cities, for the most part dangerously congested; their rails and roads and population were distributed over the earth in the wanton confusion ten thousand irrelevant considerations had made. Yet they thought confidently that this was a secure and permanent progressive system, and on the strength of some three hundred years of change and irregular improvement answered the doubter with, 'Things always *have* gone well. We'll worry through!'

But when we contrast the state of man in the opening of the twentieth century with the condition of any previous period in his history, then perhaps we may begin to understand something of that blind confidence. It was not so much a reasoned confidence as the inevitable consequence of sustained good fortune. By such standards as they possessed, things *had* gone amazingly well for them. It is scarcely an exaggeration to say that for the first time in history whole populations found themselves regularly supplied with more than enough to eat, and the vital statistics of the time witness to an amelioration of hygienic conditions rapid beyond all precedent, and to a vast development of intelligence and ability in all the arts that make life wholesome. The level and quality of the average education had risen tremendously; and at the dawn of the twentieth century comparatively few people in Western Europe or America were unable to read or write. Never before had there been such reading masses. There was wide social security. A common man might travel safely over three-quarters of the habitable globe, could go round the earth at a cost of less than the annual earnings of a skilled artisan. Compared with the liberality and comfort of the ordinary life of the time, the order of the Roman Empire under the Antonines[251] was local and limited. And every year, every month, came some new increment to human achievement, a new country opened up, new mines, new scientific discoveries, a new machine!

For those three hundred years, indeed, the movement of the world seemed wholly beneficial to mankind. Men said, indeed, that moral organisation was not keeping pace with physical progress, but few attached any meaning to these phrases, the understanding of which lies at the basis of our present safety. Sustaining and constructive forces did indeed for a time more than balance the malign drift of chance and the natural ignorance, prejudice, blind passion, and wasteful self-seeking of mankind.

The accidental balance on the side of Progress was far slighter and infinitely more complex and delicate in its adjustments than the people of that time suspected; but that did not alter the fact that it was an effective balance. They did not realise that this age of relative good fortune was an age of immense but temporary opportunity for their kind. They complacently assumed a necessary progress towards which they had no moral responsibility. They did not realise that this security of progress was a thing still to be won or lost, and that the time to win it was a time that passed. They went about their affairs energetically enough and yet with a curious idleness towards those threatening things. No one troubled over the real dangers of mankind. They saw their armies and navies grow larger and more portentous; some of their ironclads at the last cost as much as the whole annual expenditure upon advanced education; they accumulated explosives and the machinery of destruction; they allowed their national traditions and jealousies to accumulate; they contemplated a steady enhancement of race hostility as the races drew closer without concern or understanding, and they permitted the growth in their midst of an evil-spirited press, mercenary and unscrupulous, incapable of good, and powerful for evil. Their State had practically no control over the press at all. Quite heedlessly they allowed this torch-paper to lie at the door of their war magazine for any spark to fire. The precedents of history were all one tale of the collapse of civilisations, the dangers of the time were manifest. One is incredulous now to believe they could not see.

Could mankind have prevented this disaster of the War in the Air? An idle question that, as idle as to ask could mankind have prevented the decay that turned Assyria and Babylon to empty deserts or the slow decline and fall, the gradual social disorganisation, phase by phase, that closed the chapter of the Empire of the West! They could not, because they did not, they had not the will to arrest it. What mankind could achieve with a different will is a speculation as idle as it is magnificent. And this was no slow decadence that came to the Europeanised world; those other civilisations rotted and crumbled down, the Europeanised civilisation was, as it were, blown up. Within the space of five years it was altogether disintegrated and destroyed. Up to the very eve of the War in the Air one sees a spacious spectacle of incessant advance, a worldwide security, enormous areas with highly organised industry and settled populations, gigantic cities spreading gigantically, the seas and oceans dotted with shipping, the land netted with rails and open ways. Then suddenly the German air-fleets sweep across the scene, and we are in the beginning of the end.

2

This story has already told of the swift rush upon New York of the first German air-fleet and of the wild, inevitable orgy of inconclusive destruction that ensued. Behind it a second air-fleet was already swelling at its gasometers when England and France and Spain and Italy showed their hands. None of these countries had prepared for aeronautic warfare on the magnificent scale of the Germans, but each guarded secrets, each in a measure was making ready, and a common dread of German vigour and that aggressive spirit Prince Karl Albert embodied, had long been drawing these powers together in secret anticipation of some such attack. This rendered their prompt co-operation possible, and they certainly co-operated promptly. The second aerial power in Europe at this time was France; the British, nervous for their Asiatic empire, and sensible of the immense moral effect of the airship upon half-educated populations, had placed their aeronautic parks in North India, and were able to play but a sub-ordinate part in the European conflict. Still, even in England they had nine or ten big navigables, twenty or thirty smaller ones, and a variety of experimental aeroplanes. Before the fleet of Prince Karl Albert had crossed England, while Bert was still surveying Manchester in bird's-eye view, the diplomatic exchanges were going on that led to an attack upon Germany. A heterogeneous collection of navigable balloons of all sizes and types gathered over the Bernese Oberland, crushed and burnt the twenty-five Swiss airships that unexpectedly resisted this concentration in the battle of the Alps, and then, leaving the Alpine glaciers and valleys strewn with strange wreckage, divided into two fleets and set itself to terrorise Berlin and destroy the Franconian Park, seeking to do this before the second air-fleet could be inflated.

Both over Berlin and Franconia the assailants with their modern explosives effected great damage before they were driven off. In Fran-conia twelve fully distended and five partially filled and manned giants were able to make headway against, and at last, with the help of a squadron of *drachenflieger* from Hamburg, defeat and pursue the attack and to relieve Berlin, and the Germans were straining every nerve to get an overwhelming fleet in the air, and were already raiding London and Paris when the advance fleets from the Asiatic air-parks, the first intimation of a new factor in the conflict, were reported from Burma and Armenia.

Already the whole financial fabric of the world was staggering when that occurred. With the destruction of the American fleet in the North Atlantic, and the smashing conflict that ended the naval existence of Germany in the North Sea, with the burning and wrecking of billions of pounds' worth of property in the four cardinal cities of the world, the fact of the hopeless costliness of war came home for the first time, came, like a blow in the face, to the consciousness of mankind. Credit went down in a wild whirl of selling. Everywhere appeared a phenomenon that had already in a mild degree manifested itself in preceding periods of panic; a desire to *secure and hoard gold* before prices reached bottom. But now it spread like wildfire, it became universal. Above was visible conflict and destruction; below something was happening far more deadly and incurable to the flimsy fabric of finance and commercialism in which men had so blindly put their trust. As the airships fought above, the visible gold supply of the world vanished below. An epidemic of private cornering and universal distrust swept the world. In a few weeks, money, except for depreciated paper, vanished into vaults, into holes, into the walls of houses, into ten million hiding-places. Money vanished, and at its disappearance trade and industry came to an end. The economic world staggered and fell dead. It was like the stroke of some disease; it was like the water vanishing out of the blood of a living creature; it was a sudden, universal coagulation of intercourse . . .

And as the credit system, that had been the living fortress of the scientific civilisation, reeled and fell upon the millions it had held together in economic relationship, as these people, perplexed and helpless, faced this marvel of credit utterly destroyed, the airships of Asia, countless and relentless, poured across the heavens, swooped eastward to America and westward to Europe. The page of history becomes a long crescendo of battle. The main body of the British-Indian air-fleet perished upon a pyre of blazing antagonists in Burma; the Germans were scattered in the great battle of the Carpathians; the vast peninsula of India burst into insurrection and civil war from end to end, and from Gobi to Morocco rose the standards of the 'Jehad'.[252] For some weeks of warfare and destruction it seemed as though the Confederation of Eastern Asia must needs conquer the world, and then the jerry-built 'modern' civilisation of China too gave way under the strain. The teeming and peaceful population of China had been 'westernised' during the opening years of the twentieth century with the deepest resentment and reluctance; they had been dragooned and disciplined under Japanese and European influence into an acquiescence with sanitary methods, police controls, military service, and a wholesale process of exploitation against which their whole tradition rebelled. Under the stresses of the war their endurance reached the breaking point, the whole of China rose in incoherent revolt, and the practical destruction of the central government at Peking by a handful of British and German airships that had escaped from the main battles rendered that revolt invincible. In Yokohama appeared barricades, the black flag and the social revolution. With that the whole world became a welter of conflict.

So that a universal social collapse followed, as it were a logical consequence, upon worldwide war. Wherever there were great populations, great masses of people found themselves without work, without money, and unable to get food. Famine was in every working-class quarter in the world within three weeks of the beginning of the war. Within a month there was not a city anywhere in which the ordinary law and social procedure had not been replaced by some form of emergency control, in which firearms and military executions were not being used to keep order and prevent violence. And still in the poorer quarters, and in the populous districts, and even here and there already among those who had been wealthy, famine spread.

3

So what historians have come to call the Phase of the Emergency Committees sprang from the opening phase and from the phase of social collapse. Then followed a period of vehement and passionate conflict against disintegration; everywhere the struggle to keep order and to keep fighting went on. And at the same time the character of the war altered through the replacement of the huge gas-filled airships by flying-machines as the instruments of war. So soon as the big fleet engagements were over, the Asiatics endeavoured to establish in close proximity to the more vulnerable points of the countries against which they were acting, fortified centres from which flying-machine raids could be made. For a time they had everything their own way in this, and then, as this story has told, the lost secret of the Butteridge machine came to light, and the conflict became equalised and less conclusive than ever. For these small flying-machines, ineffectual for any large expedition or conclusive attack, were horribly convenient for guerilla warfare, rapidly and cheaply made, easily used, easily hidden. The design of them was hastily copied and printed in Pinkerville and scattered broadcast over the United States, and copies were sent to Europe, and there reproduced. Every man, every town, every parish that could, was exhorted to make and use them. In a little while they were being constructed not only by governments and local authorities, but by robber bands, by insurgent committees, by every type of private person. The peculiar social destructiveness of the Butteridge machine lay in its complete simplicity. It was nearly as simple as a motor-bicycle. The broad outlines of the earlier stages of the war disappeared under its influence, the spacious antagonism of nations and empires and races vanished in a seething mass of detailed conflict. The world passed at a stride from a unity and simplicity broader than that of the Roman Empire at its best, to a social fragmentation as complete as the robber-baron period of the Middle Ages. But this time, for a long descent down gradual slopes of disintegration, comes a fall like a fall over a cliff. Everywhere were men and women perceiving this and struggling desperately to keep, as it were, a hold upon the edge of the cliff.

A fourth phase follows. Through the struggle against Chaos, in the wake of the Famine, came now another old enemy of humanity – the Pestilence, the Purple Death.[253] But the war does not pause. The flags still fly. Fresh air-fleets rise, new forms of airship, and beneath their swooping struggles the world darkens – scarcely heeded by history.

It is not within the design of this book to tell that further story, to tell how the War in the Air kept on through the sheer inability of any authorities to meet and agree and end it, until every organised government in the world was as shattered and broken as a heap of china beaten with a stick. With every week of those terrible years history becomes more detailed and confused, more crowded and uncertain. Not without great and heroic resistance was civilisation borne down. Out of the bitter social conflict below rose patriotic associations, brother-hoods of order, city mayors, princes, provisional committees, trying to establish an order below and to keep the sky above. The double effort destroyed them. And as the exhaustion of the mechanical resources of civilisation clears the heavens of airships at last altogether, Anarchy, Famine and Pestilence are discovered triumphant below. The great nations and empires have become but names in the mouths of men. Everywhere there are ruins and unburied dead, and shrunken, yellow-faced survivors in a mortal apathy. Here there are robbers, here vigilance committees, and here guerilla bands ruling patches of exhausted territory, strange federations and brotherhoods form and dissolve, and religious fanaticisms begotten of despair gleam in famine-bright eyes. It is a universal dissolution. The fine order and welfare of the earth have crumpled like an exploded bladder. In five short years the world and the scope of human life have undergone a retrogressive change as great as that between the age of the Antonines and the Europe of the ninth century . . .

4

Across this sombre spectacle of disaster goes a minute and insignificant person for whom perhaps the readers of this story have now some slight solicitude. Of him there remains to be told just one single and miraculous thing. Through a world darkened and lost, through a civilisation in its death agony, our little cockney errant went and found his Edna! He found his Edna!

He got back across the Atlantic partly by means of an order from the President and partly through his own good luck. He contrived to get himself aboard a British brig in the timber trade that put out from Boston without cargo, chiefly, it would seem, because its captain had a vague idea of 'getting home' to South Shields. Bert was able to ship himself upon her mainly because of the seamanlike appearance of his rubber boots. They had a long, eventful voyage; they were chased, or imagined themselves to be chased, for some hours by an Asiatic ironclad, which was presently engaged by a British cruiser. The two ships fought for three hours, circling and driving southward as they fought, until the twilight and the cloud-drift of a rising gale swallowed them up. A few days later Bert's ship lost her rudder and mainmast in a gale. The crew ran out of food and subsisted on fish. They saw strange airships going eastward near the Azores and landed to get provisions and repair the rudder at Tenerife. There they found the town destroyed and two big liners, with dead still aboard, sunken in the harbour. From there they got canned food and material for repairs, but their operations were greatly impeded by the hostility of a band of men amidst the ruins of the town, who sniped them and tried to drive them away.

At Mogador,[254] they stayed and sent a boat ashore for water, and were nearly captured by an Arab ruse. Here too they got the Purple Death aboard, and sailed with it incubating in their blood. The cook sickened first, and then the mate, and presently everyone was down and three in the forecastle were dead. It chanced to be calm weather, and they drifted helplessly and indeed careless of their fate backwards towards the Equator. The captain doctored them all with rum. Nine died altogether, and of the four survivors none understood navigation; when at last they took heart again and could handle a sail, they made a course by the stars roughly northward and were already short of food once more when they fell in with a petrol-driven ship from Rio to Cardiff, short-handed by reason of the Purple Death and glad to take them aboard. So at last, after a year of wandering, Bert reached England. He landed in bright June weather, and found the Purple Death was there just beginning its ravages.

The people were in a state of panic in Cardiff and many had fled to the hills, and directly the steamer came to the harbour she was boarded and her residue of food impounded by some unauthenticated Provisional Committee. Bert tramped through a country disorganised by pestilence, foodless, and shaken to the very base of its immemorial order. He came near death and starvation many times, and once he was drawn into scenes of violence that might have ended his career. But the Bert Smallways who tramped from Cardiff to London vaguely 'going home', vaguely seeking something of his own that had no tangible form but Edna, was a very different person from the Desert Dervish who was swept out of England in Mr Butteridge's balloon a year before. He was brown and lean and enduring, steady-eyed and pestilence-salted, and his mouth, which had once hung open, shut now like a steel trap. Across his brow ran a white scar that he had got in a fight on the brig. In Cardiff he had felt the need of new clothes and a weapon, and had, by means that would have shocked him a year ago, secured a flannel shirt, a corduroy suit, and a revolver and fifty cartridges from an abandoned pawnbroker's. He also got some soap and had his first real wash for thirteen months in a stream outside the town. The Vigilance bands that had at first shot plunderers very freely were now either entirely dispersed by the plague, or busy between town and cemetery in a vain attempt to keep pace with it. He prowled on the outskirts of the town for three or four days, starving, and then went back to join the Hospital Corps for a week, and so fortified himself with a few square meals before he started eastward.

The Welsh and English countryside at that time presented the strangest mingling of the assurance and wealth of the opening twentieth century with a sort of Düreresque[255] mediaevalism. All the gear, the houses and monorails, the farm hedges and power cables, the roads and pavements, the signposts and advertisements of the former order were still for the most part intact. Bankruptcy, social collapse, famine, and pestilence had done nothing to damage these, and it was only to the great capitals and ganglionic centres, as it were, of this State, that positive destruction had come. Anyone dropped suddenly into the country would have noticed very little difference. He would have remarked first, perhaps, that all the hedges needed clipping, that the roadside grass grew rank, that the road-tracks were unusually rain-worn, and that the cottages by the wayside seemed in many cases shut up, that a telephone wire had dropped here, and that a cart stood abandoned by the wayside. But he would still find his hunger whetted by the bright assurance that Wilder's Canned Peaches were excellent, or that there was nothing so good for the breakfast table as Gobble's Sausages. And then suddenly would come the Düreresque element; the skeleton of a horse, or some crumpled mass of rags in the ditch, with gaunt extended feet and a yellow, purple-blotched skin and face, or what had been a face, gaunt and glaring and devastated. Then here would be a field that had been ploughed and not sown, and here a field of corn carelessly trampled by beasts, and here a hoarding torn down across the road to make a fire.

Then presently he would meet a man or a woman, yellow-faced and probably negligently dressed and armed – prowling for food. These people would have the complexions and eyes and expressions of tramps or criminals, and often the clothing of prosperous middle-class or upper-class people. Many of these would be eager for news, and willing to give help and even scraps of queer meat, or crusts of grey and doughy bread, in return for it. They would listen to Bert's story with avidity, and attempt to keep him with them for a day or so. The virtual cessation of postal distribution and the collapse of all newspaper enterprise had left an immense and aching gap in the mental life of this time. Men had suddenly lost sight of the ends of the earth and had still to recover the rumour-spreading habits of the Middle Ages. In their eyes, in their bearing, in their talk, was the quality of lost and deoriented souls.

As Bert travelled from parish to parish, and from district to district, avoiding as far as possible those festering centres of violence and despair, the larger towns, he found the condition of affairs varying widely. In one parish he would find the large house burnt, the vicarage wrecked, evidently in violent conflict for some suspected and perhaps imaginary store of food, unburied dead everywhere, and the whole mechanism of the community at a standstill. In another he would find organising forces stoutly at work, newly-painted notice boards warning off vagrants, the roads and still cultivated fields policed by armed men, the pestilence under control, even nursing going on, a store of food husbanded, the cattle and sheep well guarded, and a group of two or three justices, the village doctor or a farmer, dominating the whole place; a reversion, in fact, to the autonomous community of the fifteenth century. But at any time such a village would be liable to a raid of Asiatics or Africans or suchlike air-pirates, demanding petrol and alcohol or provisions. The price of its order was an almost intolerable watchfulness and tension. Then the approach to the confused problems of some larger centre of population and the presence of a more intricate conflict would be marked by roughly smeared notices of 'Quarantine' or 'Strangers Shot', or by a string of decaying plunderers dangling from the telephone poles at the roadside. About Oxford big boards were put on the roofs warning all air wanderers off with the single word, 'Guns'.

Taking their risks amidst these things, cyclists still kept abroad, and once or twice during Bert's long tramp powerful motor cars containing masked and goggled figures went tearing past him. There were few police in evidence, but ever and again squads of gaunt and tattered soldier-cyclists would come drifting along, and such encounters became more frequent as he got out of Wales into England. Amidst all this wreckage they were still campaigning. He had had some idea of resorting to the workhouses for the night if hunger pressed him too closely, but some of these were closed and others converted into temporary hospitals, and one he came up to at twilight near a village in Gloucestershire stood with all its doors and windows open, silent as the grave, and, as he found to his horror by stumbling along evil-smelling corridors, full of unburied dead.

From Gloucestershire Bert went northward to the British aeronautic park outside Birmingham, in the hope that he might be taken on and given food, for there the Government, or at any rate the War Office, still existed as an energetic fact, concentrated amidst collapse and social disaster upon the effort to keep the British flag still flying in the air, and trying to brisk up mayor and mayor and magistrate and magistrate in a new effort of organisation. They had brought together all the best of the surviving artisans from that region, they had provisioned the park for a siege, and they were urgently building a larger type of Butteridge machine. Bert could get no footing at this work: he was not sufficiently skilled, and he had drifted to Oxford when the great fight occurred in which these works were finally wrecked. He saw something, but not very much, of the battle from a place called Boar Hill. He saw the Asiatic squadron coming up across the hills to the south-west, and he saw one of their airships circling southward again chased by two aero-planes, the one that was ultimately overtaken, wrecked and burnt at Edge Hill. But he never learnt the issue of the combat as a whole.

He crossed the Thames from Eton to Windsor and made his way round the south of London to Bun Hill, and there he found his brother Tom, looking like some dark, defensive animal in the old shop, just recovering from the Purple Death, and Jessica upstairs delirious, and, as it seemed to him, dying grimly. She raved of sending out orders to customers, and scolded Tom perpetually lest he should be late with Mrs Thompson's potatoes and Mrs Hopkins' cauliflower, though all business had long since ceased and Tom had developed a quite uncanny skill in the snaring of rats and sparrows and the concealment of certain stores of cereals and biscuits from plundered grocers' shops. Tom received his brother with a sort of guarded warmth.

'Lor!' he said, 'it's Bert. I thought you'd be coming back some day, and I'm glad to see you. But I carn't arst you to eat anything, because I 'aven't got anything to eat . . . Where you been, Bert, all this time?'

Bert reassured his brother by a glimpse of a partly eaten swede, and was still telling his story in fragments and parentheses, when he discovered behind the counter a yellow and forgotten note addressed to himself. 'What's this?' he said, and found it was a year-old note from Edna. 'She came 'ere,' said Tom, like one who recalls a trivial thing, 'arstin' for you and arstin' us to take 'er in. That was after the battle and settin' Clapham Rise afire. I was for takin' 'er in, but Jessica wouldn't 'ave it – and so she borrowed five shillings of me quiet like and went on. I dessay she's tole you – '

She had, Bert found. She had gone on, she said in her note, to an aunt and uncle who had a brickfield near Horsham. And there at last, after another fortnight of adventurous journeying, Bert found her.

5

When Bert and Edna set eyes on one another, they stared and laughed foolishly, so changed they were, and so ragged and surprised. And then they both fell weeping.

'Oh! Bertie, boy!' she cried. 'You've come – you've come!' and put out her arms and staggered. 'I told 'im. He said he'd kill me if I didn't marry him.'

But Edna was not married, and when presently Bert could get talk from her, she explained the task before him. That little patch of lonely agricultural country had fallen under the power of a band of bullies led by a chief called Bill Gore, who had begun life as a butcher boy and developed into a prizefighter and a professional 'sport'. They had been organised by a local nobleman of former eminence upon the turf, but after a time he had disappeared, no one quite knew how, and Bill had succeeded to the leadership of the countryside, and had developed his teacher's methods with considerable vigour. There had been a strain of advanced philosophy about the local nobleman, and his mind ran to 'improving the race' and producing the Over-Man, which in practice took the form of himself especially and his little band in moderation marrying with some frequency. Bill followed up the idea with an enthusiasm that even trenched upon his popularity with his followers. One day he had happened upon Edna tending her pigs, and had at once fallen a-wooing with great urgency among the troughs of slush. Edna had made a gallant resistance, but he was still vigorously about and extraordinarily impatient. He might, she said, come at any time, and she looked Bert in the eyes. They were back already in the barbaric stage when a man must fight for his love.

And here one deplores the conflicts of truth with the chivalrous tradition. One would like to tell of Bert sallying forth to challenge his rival, of a ring formed and a spirited encounter, and Bert by some miracle of pluck and love and good fortune winning. But indeed nothing of the sort occurred. Instead, he reloaded his revolver very carefully, and then sat in the best room of the cottage by the derelict brickfield, looking anxious and perplexed, and listening to talk about Bill and his ways, and thinking, thinking. Then suddenly Edna's aunt, with a thrill in her voice, announced the appearance of that individual. He was coming with two others of his gang through the garden gate. Bert got up, put the woman aside, and looked out. They presented remarkable figures. They wore a sort of uniform of red golfing jackets and white sweaters, football singlets and stockings and boots, and each had let his fancy play about his head-dress. Bill had a woman's hat full of cock's feathers, and all had wild, slouching cowboy brims.

Bert sighed and stood up, deeply thoughtful, and Edna watched him, marvelling. The women stood quite still. He left the window, and went out into the passage rather slowly, and with the careworn expression of a man who gives his mind to a complex and uncertain business. 'Edna!' he called, and when she came he opened the front door.

He asked very simply, and pointing to the foremost of the three, 'That 'im? . . . Sure? . . . ' and being told that it was, shot his rival instantly and very accurately through the chest. He then shot Bill's best man much less tidily in the head, and then shot at and winged the third man as he fled. The third gentleman yelped, and continued running with a comical end-on twist.

Then Bert stood still meditating with the pistol in his hand, and quite regardless of the women behind him.

So far things had gone well.

It became evident to him that if he did not go into politics at once, he would be hanged as an assassin, and accordingly, and without a word to the women, he went down to the village public-house he had passed an hour before on his way to Edna, entered it from the rear, and confronted the little band of ambiguous roughs, who were drinking in the tap-room[256] and discussing matrimony and Bill's affection in a facetious but envious manner, with a casually held but carefully reloaded revolver, and an invitation to join what he called, I regret to say, a 'Vigilance Committee'[257] under his direction. 'It's wanted about 'ere, and some of us are gettin' it up.' He presented himself as one having friends outside, though indeed he had no friends at all in the world but Edna and her aunt and two female cousins.

There was a quick but entirely respectful discussion of the situation. They thought him a lunatic who had tramped into, this neighbourhood ignorant of Bill. They desired to temporise until their leader came. Bill would settle him. Someone spoke of Bill.

'Bill's dead, I jest shot 'im,' said Bert. 'We don't need reckon with '*im*. 'E's shot, and a red-'aired chap with a squint, '*e's* shot. We've settled up all that. There ain't going to be no more Bill, ever. 'E'd got wrong ideas about marriage and things. It's 'is sort of chap we're after.'

That carried the meeting.

Bill was perfunctorily buried, and Bert's Vigilance Committee (for so it continued to be called) reigned in his stead.

That is the end of this story so far as Bert Smallways is concerned. We leave him with his Edna to become squatters among the clay and oak thickets of the Weald, far away from the stream of events. From that time forth life became a succession of peasant encounters, an affair of pigs and hens and small needs and little economies and children, until Clapham and Bun Hill and all the life of the Scientific Age became to Bert no more than the fading memory of a dream. He never knew how the War in the Air went on, nor whether it still went on. There were rumours of airships going and coming, and of happenings Londonward. Once or twice their shadows fell on him as he worked, but whence they came or whither they went he could not tell. Even his desire to tell died out for want of food. At times came robbers and thieves, at times came diseases among the beasts and shortness of food, once the country was worried by a pack of boar-hounds he helped to kill; he went through many inconsecutive, irrelevant adventures. He survived them all.

Accident and death came near them both ever and again, and passed them by; and they loved and suffered and were happy, and she bore him many children – eleven children – one after the other, of whom only four succumbed to the necessary hardships of their simple life. They lived and did well, as well was understood in those days. They went the way of all flesh, year by year.

The Epilogue

It happened that one bright summer's morning exactly thirty years after the launching of the first German air-fleet, an old man took a small boy to look for a missing hen through the ruins of Bun Hill and out towards the splintered pinnacles of the Crystal Palace. He was not a very old man; he was, as a matter of fact, still within a few weeks of sixty-three, but constant stooping over spades and forks and the carrying of roots and manure, and exposure to the damps of life in the open air without a change of clothing, had bent him into the form of a sickle. Moreover, he had lost most of his teeth and that had affected his digestion and through that his skin and temper. In face and expression he was curiously like that old Thomas Smallways who had once been coachman to Sir Peter Bone, and this was just as it should be, for he was Tom Smallways the son, who formerly kept the little greengrocer's shop under the straddle of the monorail viaduct in the High Street of Bun Hill. But now there were no greengrocer's shops, and Tom was living in one of the derelict villas hard by that unoccupied building site that had been and was still the scene of his daily horticulture. He and his wife lived upstairs, and in the drawing and dining rooms, which had each French windows opening on the lawn, and all about the ground floor generally, Jessica, who was now a lean and lined and baldish but still very efficient and energetic old woman, kept her three cows and a multitude of gawky hens.

These two were part of a little community of stragglers and returned fugitives, perhaps a hundred and fifty souls of them altogether, that had settled down to the new conditions of things after the Panic and Famine and Pestilence that followed in the wake of the War. They had come back from strange refuges and hiding-places and had squatted down among the familiar houses and begun that hard struggle against nature for food which was now the chief interest of their lives. They were by sheer preoccupation with that a peaceful people, more particularly after Wilkes, the house agent, driven by some obsolete dream of acquisition, had been drowned in the pool by the ruined gasworks for making enquiries into title and displaying a litigious turn of mind. (He had not been murdered, you understand, but the people had carried an exemplary ducking ten minutes or so beyond its healthy limits.)

This little community had returned from its original habits of suburban parasitism to what no doubt had been the normal life of humanity for nearly immemorial years, a life of homely economies in the most intimate contact with cows and hens and patches of ground, a life that breathes and exhales the scent of cows and finds the need for stimulants satisfied by the activity of the bacteria and vermin it engenders. Such had been the life of the European peasant from the dawn of history to the beginning of the Scientific Era, so it was the large majority of the people of Asia and Africa had always been wont to live. For a time it had seemed that, by virtue of machines, and scientific civilisation, Europe was to be lifted out of this perpetual round of animal drudgery, and that America was to evade it very largely from the outset. And with the smash of the high and dangerous and splendid edifice of mechanical civilisation that had arisen so marvellously, back to the land came the common man, back to the manure.

The little communities, still haunted by ten thousand memories of a greater state, gathered and developed almost tacitly a customary law and fell under the guidance of a medicine man or a priest. The world rediscovered religion and the need of something to hold its communities together. At Bun Hill this function was entrusted to an old Baptist minister. He taught a simple but adequate faith. In his teaching a good principle called the Word[258] fought perpetually against a diabolical female influence called the Scarlet Woman[259] and an evil being called Alcohol. This Alcohol had long since become a purely spiritualised conception deprived of any element of material application; it had no relation to the occasional finds of whisky and wine in Londoners' cellars that gave Bun Hill its only holidays. He taught this doctrine on Sundays, and on weekdays he was an amiable and kindly old man, distinguished by his quaint disposition to wash his hands, and if possible his face, daily, and with a wonderful genius for cutting up pigs. He held his Sunday services in the old church in the Beckenham Road, and then the countryside came out in a curious reminiscence of the urban dress of Edwardian times. All the men without exception wore frock coats, top hats, and white shirts, though many had no boots. Tom was particularly distinguished on these occasions because he wore a top hat with gold lace about it and a green coat and trousers that he had found upon a skeleton in the basement of the Urban and District Bank. The women, even Jessica, came in jackets and immense hats extravagantly trimmed with artificial flowers and exotic birds' feathers – of which there were abundant supplies in the shops to the north – and the children (there were not many children, because a large proportion of the babies born in Bun Hill died in a few days' time of inexplicable maladies) had similar clothes cut down to accommodate them; even Stringer's little grandson of four wore a large top hat.

That was the Sunday costume of the Bun Hill district, a curious and interesting survival of the genteel traditions of the Scientific Age. On a weekday the folk were dingily and curiously hung about with dirty rags of housecloth and scarlet flannel, sacking, curtain serge, and patches of old carpet, and went either barefooted or on rude wooden sandals. These people, the reader must understand, were an urban population sunken back to the state of a barbaric peasantry, and so without any of the simple arts a barbaric peasantry would possess. In many ways they were curiously degenerate and incompetent. They had lost any idea of making textiles, they could hardly make up clothes when they had material, and they were forced to plunder the continually dwindling supplies of the ruins about them for cover. All the simple arts they had ever known they had lost, and with the breakdown of modern drainage, modern water supply, shopping, and the like, their civilised methods were useless. Their cooking was worse than primitive. It was a feeble muddling with food over wood fires in rusty drawing-room fireplaces; for the kitcheners burnt too much. Among them all no sense of baking or brewing or metal-working was to be found.

Their employment of sacking and suchlike coarse material for workaday clothing, and their habit of tying it on with string and of thrusting wadding and straw inside it for warmth, gave these people an odd, 'packed' appearance, and as it was a weekday when Tom took his little nephew for the hen-seeking excursion, so it was they were attired.

'So you've really got to Bun Hill at last, Teddy,' said old Tom, beginning to talk and slackening his pace so soon as they were out of range of old Jessica. 'You're the last of Bert's boys for me to see. Wat I've seen, young Bert I've seen, Sissie and Matt, Tom what's called after me, and Peter. The traveller people brought you along all right, eh?'

'I managed,' said Teddy, who was a dry little boy.

'Didn't want to eat you on the way?'

'They was all right,' said Teddy, 'and on the way near Leatherhead we saw a man riding on a bicycle.'

'My word!' said Tom, 'there ain't many of those about nowadays. Where was he going?'

'Said 'e was going to Dorking if the High Road was good enough. But I doubt if he got there. All about Burford it was flooded. We came over the hill, uncle – what they call the Roman Road. That's high and safe.'

'Don't know it,' said old Tom. 'But a bicycle! You're sure it was a bicycle? Had two wheels?'

'It was a bicycle right enough.'

'Why! I remember a time, Teddy, where there was bicycles no end, when you could stand just here – the road was as smooth as a board then – and see twenty or thirty coming and going at the same time, bicycles and moty-bicycles; moty cars, all sorts of whirly things.'

'No!' said Teddy.

'I do. They'd keep on going by all day, – 'undreds and 'undreds.'

'But where was they all going?' asked Teddy.

'Tearin' off to Brighton – you never seen Brighton, I expect – it's down by the sea, used to be a moce 'mazing place – and coming and going from London.'

'Why?'

'They did.'

'But why?'

'Lord knows why, Teddy. They did. Then you see that great thing there like a great big rusty nail sticking up higher than all the houses, and that one yonder, and that, and how something's fell in between 'em among the houses. They was parts of the monorail. They went down to Brighton too and all day and night there was people going, great cars as big as 'ouses full of people.'

The little boy regarded the rusty evidences across the narrow, muddy ditch of cow-droppings that had once been a High Street. He was clearly disposed to be sceptical, and yet there the ruins were! He grappled with ideas beyond the strength of his imagination.

'What did they go for?' he asked, 'all of 'em?'

'They *'ad* to. Everything was on the go those days – everything.'

'Yes, but where did they come from?'

'All round 'ere, Teddy, there was people living in those 'ouses, and up the road more 'ouses and more people. You'd 'ardly believe me, Teddy, but it's Bible truth. You can go on that way for ever and ever, and keep on coming on 'ouses, more 'ouses, and more. There's no end to 'em. No end. They get bigger and bigger.' His voice dropped as though he named strange names. 'It's *London*,' he said.

'And it's all empty now and left alone. All day it's left alone. You don't find 'ardly a man, you won't find nothing but dogs and cats after the rats until you get round by Bromley and Beckenham, and there you find the Kentish men[260] herding swine. (Nice rough lot they are, too!) I tell you that so long as the sun is up it's as still as the grave. I been about by day – orfen and orfen.' He paused.

'And all those 'ouses and streets and ways used to be full of people before the War in the Air and the Famine and the Purple Death. They used to be full of people, Teddy, and then came a time when they was full of corpses, when you couldn't go a mile that way before the stink of 'em drove you back. It was the Purple Death 'ad killed 'em every one. The cats and dogs and 'ens and vermin caught it. Everything and everyone 'ad it. Jest a few of us 'appened to live. I pulled through, and your aunt, though it made 'er lose 'er 'air. Why, you find the skeletons in the 'ouses now. This way we been into all the 'ouses and took what we wanted and buried moce of the people, but up that way, Norwood way, there's 'ouses with the glass in the windows still, and the furniture not touched – all dusty and falling to pieces – and the bones of the people lying, some in bed, some about the 'ouse, jest as the Purple Death left 'em five-and-twenty years ago. I went into one – me and old Higgins las' year – and there was a room with books, Teddy – you know what I mean by books, Teddy?'

'I seen 'em. I seen 'em with pictures.'

'Well, books all round, Teddy, 'undreds of books, beyond rhyme or reason, as the saying goes, green-mouldy and dry. I was for leaven' 'em alone – I was never much for reading – but ole Higgins he must touch 'em. "I believe I could read one of 'em *now*," 'e says.

' "Not it," I says.

' "I could," 'e says, laughing, and takes one out and opens it.

'I looked, and there, Teddy, was a cullud picture, oh, so lovely! It was a picture of women and serpents in a garden. I never see anything like it.

' "This suits me," said old Higgins, "to rights."

'And then kind of friendly he gave the book a pat – '

Old Tom Smallways paused impressively.

'And then?' said Teddy.

'It all fell to dus'. White dus'!' He became still more impressive. 'We didn't touch no more of them books that day. Not after that.'

For a long time both were silent. Then Tom, playing with a subject that attracted him with a fatal fascination, repeated, 'All day long they lie – still as the grave.'

Teddy took the point at last. 'Don't they lie o' nights?' he asked.

Old Tom shook his head. 'Nobody knows, boy, nobody knows.'

'But what could they do?'

'Nobody knows. Nobody ain't seen to tell not nobody.'

'Nobody?'

'They tell tales,' said old Tom. 'They tell tales, but there ain't no believing 'em. I gets 'ome about sundown, and keeps indoors, so I can't say nothing, can I? But there's them that thinks some things and them as thinks others. I've 'eard it's unlucky to take clo'es off of 'em unless they got white bones. There's stories – '

The boy watched his uncle sharply. '*Wot* stories?' he said.

'Stories of moonlight nights and things walking about. But I take no stock in 'em. I keeps in bed. If you listen to stories – Lord! You'll get afraid of yourself in a field at midday.'

The little boy looked round and ceased his questions for a space.

'They say there's a 'og man in Beck'n'am what was lost in London three days and three nights. 'E went up after whisky to Cheapside, and lorst 'is way among the ruins and wandered. Three days and three nights 'e wandered about and the streets kep' changing so's he couldn't get 'ome. If 'e 'adn't remembered some words out of the Bible 'e might 'ave been there now. All day 'e went and all night – and all day long it was still. It was as still as death all day long, until the sunset came and the twilight thickened, and then it began to rustle and whisper and go pit-a-pat with a sound like 'urrying feet.'

He paused.

'Yes,' said the little boy breathlessly. 'Go on. What then?'

'A sound of carts and 'orses there was, and a sound of cabs and omnibuses, and then a lot of whistling, shrill whistles, whistles that froze 'is marrer. And directly the whistles began things begun to show, people in the streets 'urrying, people in the 'ouses and shops busying themselves, moty cars in the streets, a sort of moonlight in all the lamps and winders. People, I say, Teddy, but they wasn't people. They was the ghosts of them that was overtook, the ghosts of them that used to crowd those streets. And they went past 'im and through 'im and never 'eeded 'im, went by like fogs and vapours, Teddy. And sometimes they was cheerful and sometimes they was 'orrible, 'orrible beyond words. And once 'e come to a place called Piccadilly, Teddy, and there was lights blazing like daylight and ladies and gentlemen in splendid clo'es crowding the pavement, and taxicabs follering along the road. And as 'e looked, they all went evil – evil in the face, Teddy. And it seemed to 'im suddenly *they saw 'im*, and the women began to look at 'im and say things to 'im – 'orrible – wicked things. One come very near 'im, Teddy, right up to 'im, and looked into 'is face – close. And she 'adn't got a face to look with, only a painted skull, and then 'e see; they was all painted skulls. And one after another they crowded on 'im saying 'orrible things, and catchin' at 'im and threatenin' and coaxing 'im, so that 'is 'eart near left 'is body for fear . . . '

'Yes,' gasped Teddy in an unendurable pause.

'Then it was he remembered the words of Scripture and saved himself alive. "The Lord is my 'Elper," 'e says, "therefore I will fear nothing," and straight away there came a cock-crowing and the street was empty from end to end. And after that the Lord was good to 'im and guided 'im 'ome.'

Teddy stared and caught at another question. 'But who was the people,' he asked, 'who lived in all these 'ouses? What was they?'

'Gent'men in business, people with money – leastways we thought it was money till everything smashed up, and then seemingly it was jes' paper – all sorts. Why, there was 'undreds of thousands of them. There was millions. I've seen that 'I Street there regular so's you couldn't walk along the pavements, shoppin' time, with women and people shoppin'.'

'But where'd they get their food and things?'

'Bort 'em in shops like I used to 'ave. I'll show you the place, Teddy, if we go back. People nowadays 'aven't no idee of a shop – no idee. Plate-glass winders – it's all Greek to them. Why, I've 'ad as much as a ton and a 'arf of petaties to 'andle all at one time. You'd open your eyes till they dropped out to see jes' what I used to 'ave in my shop. Baskets of pears 'eaped up, marrers, apples and pears, d'licious great nuts.' His voice became luscious – 'Benanas, oranges.'

'What's benanas?' asked the boy, 'and oranges?'

'Fruits they was. Sweet, juicy, d'licious fruits. Foreign fruits. They brought 'em from Spain and N' York and places. In ships and things. They brought 'em to me from all over the world, and I sold 'em in my shop. *I* sold 'em, Teddy! me what goes about now with you, dressed up in old sacks and looking for lost 'ens. People used to come into my shop, great beautiful ladies like you'd 'ardly dream of now, dressed up to the nines, and say, "Well, Mr Smallways, what you got 'smorning?" and I'd say, "Well, I got some very nice C'nadian apples," or p'raps I got custed marrers.[261] See? And they'd buy 'em. Right off they'd say, "Send me some up." Lord! what a life that was. The business of it, the bussel, the smart things you saw, moty cars going by, kerridges,[262] people, organ-grinders, German bands. Always something going past – always. If it wasn't for those empty 'ouses, I'd think it all a dream.'

'But what killed all the people, uncle?' asked Teddy.

'It was a smash-up,' said old Tom. 'Everything was going right until they started that War. Everything was going like clockwork. Everybody was busy and everybody was 'appy and everybody got a good square meal every day.' He met incredulous eyes. 'Everybody,' he said firmly. 'If you couldn't get it anywhere else, you could get it in the workhuss, a nice 'ot bowl of soup called skilly, and bread better'n anyone knows 'ow to make now, reg'lar *white* bread, gov'ment bread.'

Teddy marvelled, but said nothing. It made him feel deep longings that he found it wisest to fight down.

For a time the old man resigned himself to the pleasures of gustatory reminiscence. His lips moved. 'Pickled sammin!'[263] he whispered, 'an' vinegar . . . Dutch cheese, *beer*! A pipe of terbakker.'

'But '*ow* did the people get killed?' asked Teddy presently.

'There was the War. The War was the beginning of it. The War banged and flummocked about, but it didn't really *kill* many people. But it upset things. They came and set fire to London and burnt and sank all the ships there used to be in the Thames – we could see the smoke and steam for weeks – and they threw a bomb into the Crystal Palace and made a bust-up, and broke down the rail lines and things like that. But as for killin' people, it was just accidental if they did. They killed each other more. There was a great fight all hereabout one day, Teddy – up in the air. Great things bigger than fifty 'ouses, bigger than the Crystal Palace – bigger, bigger than anything, flying about up in the air and whacking at each other and dead men fallin' off 'em. T'riffic! But it wasn't so much the people they killed as the business they stopped. There wasn't any business doin', Teddy, there wasn't any money about, and nothin' to buy if you 'ad it.'

'But 'ow did the people get *killed*?' said the little boy in the pause.

'I'm tellin' you, Teddy,' said the old man. 'It was the stoppin' of business come next. Suddenly there didn't seem to be any money. There was cheques – they was a bit of paper written on, and they was jes' as good as money – jes' as good if they come from customers you knew. Then all of a sudden they wasn't. I was left with three of 'em and two I'd given change. Then it got about that five-pun' notes were no good, and then the silver sort of went off. Gold you couldn't get for love or – anything. The banks in London 'ad got it, and the banks was all smashed up. Everybody went bankrup'. Everybody was thrown out of work. Everybody!'

He paused, and scrutinised his hearer. The small boy's intelligent face expressed hopeless perplexity.

'That's 'ow it 'appened,' said old Tom. He sought for some means of expression. 'It was like stoppin' a clock,' he said. 'Things were quiet for a bit, deadly quiet, except for the airships fighting about in the sky, and then people begun to get excited. I remember my lars' customer, the very lars' customer that ever I 'ad. He was a Mr Moses Gluckstein, a city gent, and very pleasant and fond of sparrowgrass and chokes,[264] and 'e cut in – there 'adn't been no customers for days – and began to talk very fast, offerin' me for anything I 'ad, anything, petaties or anything, its weight in gold. 'E said it was a little speculation 'e wanted to try. 'E said it was a sort of bet reely, and very likely 'e'd lose; but never mind that, 'e wanted to try. 'E always 'ad been a gambler, 'e said. 'E said I'd only got to weigh it out and 'e'd give me 'is cheque right away. Well, that led to a bit of a argument, perfectly respectful it was, but a argument about whether a cheque was still good, and while 'e was explaining there come by a lot of these here unemployed with a great banner they 'ad for everyone to read – everyone could read those days – "We want Food." Three or four of 'em suddenly turns and comes into my shop.

' "Got any food?" says one.

' "No," I says, "not to sell. I wish I 'ad. But if I 'ad, I'm afraid I couldn't let you have it. This gent, 'e's been offerin' me – "

'Mr Gluckstein 'e tried to stop me, but it was too late.

' "What's 'e been offerin' you?" says a great big chap with a 'atchet; "what's 'e been offerin you?" I 'ad to tell.

' "Boys," 'e said, " 'ere's another feenancier!" and they took 'im out there and then, and 'ung 'im on a lam'pose down the street. 'E never lifted a finger to resist. After I tole on 'im 'e never said a word . . . '

Tom meditated for a space. 'First chap I ever sin 'ung!' he said.

' 'Ow old was you?' asked Teddy.

' 'Bout thirty,' said old Tom.

'Why! I saw free pig-stealers 'ung before I was six,' said Teddy. 'Father took me because of my birfday being near. Said I ought to be blooded . . . '

'Well, you never saw no one killed by a moty car, any'ow,' said old Tom after a moment of chagrin. 'And you never saw no dead men carried into a chemis' shop.'

Teddy's momentary triumph faded. 'No,' he said, 'I 'aven't.'

'Nor won't. Nor won't. You'll never see the things I've seen, never. Not if you live to be a 'undred . . . Well, as I was saying, that's how the Famine and Riotin' began. Then there was strikes and Socialism, things I never did 'old with, worse and worse. There was fightin' and shootin' down, and burnin' and plunderin'. They broke up the banks up in London and got the gold, but they couldn't make food out of gold. 'Ow did *we* get on? Well, we kep' quiet. We didn't interfere with no one and no one didn't interfere with us. We 'ad some old 'tatoes about, but mocely we lived on rats. Ours was a old 'ouse, full of rats, and the famine never seemed to bother 'em. Orfen we got a rat. Orfen. But moce of the people who lived hereabouts was too tender stummicked for rats. Didn't seem to fancy 'em. They'd been used to all sorts of fallals, and they didn't take to 'onest feeding, not till it was too late. Died rather.

'It was the famine began to kill people. Even before the Purple Death came along they was dying like flies at the end of the summer. 'Ow I remember it all! I was one of the first to 'ave it. I was out, seein' if I mightn't get 'old of a cat or somethin', and then I went round to my bit of ground to see whether I couldn't get up some young turnips I'd forgot, and I was took something awful. You've no idee the pain, Teddy – it doubled me up pretty near. I jes' lay down by that there corner, and your aunt come along to look for me and dragged me 'ome like a sack.

'I'd never 'ave got better if it 'adn't been for your aunt. "Tom," she says to me, "you got to get well," and I *ad* to. Then *she* sickened. She sickened but there ain't much dyin' about your aunt. "Lor!" she says, "as if I'd leave you to go muddlin' along alone!" That's what she says. She's got a tongue, 'as your aunt. But it took 'er 'air off – and arst though I might, she's never cared for the wig I got 'er – orf the old lady what was in the vicarage garden.

'Well, this 'ere Purple Death, – it jes' wiped people out, Teddy. You couldn't bury 'em. And it took the dogs and the cats too, and the rats and 'orses. At last every 'ouse and garden was full of dead bodies. London way, you couldn't go for the smell of them, and we 'ad to move out of the 'I street into that villa we got. And all the water run short that way. The drains and underground tunnels took it. Gor' knows where the Purple Death come from; some say one thing and some another. Some said it come from eatin' rats and some from eatin' nothin'. Some say the Asiatics brought it from some 'I place, Tibet, I think, where it never did nobody much 'arm. All I know is it come after the Famine. And the Famine come after the Penic and the Penic come after the War.'

Teddy thought. 'What made the Purple Death?' he asked.

' 'Aven't I tole you!'

'But why did they 'ave a Penic?'

'They 'ad it.'

'But why did they start the War?'

'They couldn't stop theirselves. 'Aving them airships made 'em.'

'And 'ow did the War end?'

'Lord knows if it's ended, boy,' said old Tom. 'Lord knows if it's ended. There's been travellers through 'ere – there was a chap only two summers ago – say it's goin' on still. They say there's bands of people up north who keep on with it and people in Germany and China and 'Merica and places. 'E said they still got flying-machines and gas and things. But we 'aven't seen nothin' in the air now for seven years, and nobody 'asn't come nigh of us. Last we saw was a crumpled sort of airship going away – over there. It was a littleish-sized thing and lop-sided, as though it 'ad something the matter with it.'

He pointed, and came to a stop at a gap in the fence, the vestiges of the old fence from which, in the company of his neighbour Mr Stringer the milkman, he had once watched the South of England Aero Club's Saturday-afternoon ascents. Dim memories, it may be, of that particular afternoon returned to him.

'There, down there, where all that rus' looks so red and bright, that's the gasworks.'

'What's gas?' asked the little boy.

'Oh, a hairy sort of nothin' what you put in balloons to make 'em go up. And you used to burn it till the 'lectricity come.'

The little boy tried vainly to imagine gas on the basis of these particulars. Then his thoughts reverted to a previous topic.

'But why didn't they end the War?'

'Obstinacy. Everybody was getting 'urt, but everybody was 'urtin' and everybody was 'igh-spirited and patriotic, and so they smeshed up things instead. They jes' went on smeshin'. And afterwards they jes' got desp'rite and savige.'

'It ought to 'ave ended,' said the little boy.

'It didn't ought to 'ave begun,' said old Tom, 'But people was proud. People was la-dy-da-ish and uppish and proud. Too much meat and drink they 'ad. Give in – not them! And after a bit nobody arst 'em to give in. Nobody arst 'em . . . '

He sucked his old gums thoughtfully, and his gaze strayed away across the valley to where the shattered glass of the Crystal Palace glittered in the sun. A dim large sense of waste and irrevocable lost opportunities pervaded his mind. He repeated his ultimate judgement upon all these things, obstinately, slowly, and conclusively, his final saying upon the matter.

'You can say what you like,' he said. 'It didn't ought ever to 'ave begun.'

He said it simply – somebody somewhere ought to have stopped something, but who or how or why were all beyond his ken.

ENDNOTES

Places are noted only where there is a particular resonance or they are no longer known by the same name; Wells's geography is generally realist.

THE WAR OF THE WORLDS

1 (p. 29 – Epigraph) Johannes Kepler (1571–1630), who was a German mathematician and astronomer, is quoted by the English cleric and mathematician Robert Burton (1577–1640) in his classic *The Anatomy of Melancholy* (1621). Wells misquotes slightly and elides; Burton's quotation actually reads: 'But who shall dwell in these vast bodies, earths, worlds, if they be inhabited? rational creatures? or have they souls to be saved? or do they inhabit a better part of the world than we do? are we or they lords of the world? and how are all things made for man?'

2 (p. 37) *the beasts that perish* Psalm 49:20: 'Man that is in honour, and understandeth not, is like the beasts that perish.' All quotations are from the King James Bible.

3 (p. 37) *planet Mars* Mars, the planet next farther away from the sun than the earth, also evokes the Roman god of war.

4 (p. 37) *nebular hypothesis* the theory that the solar system derives from nebulous material, developed by the German philosopher Immanuel Kant (1724–1804) in *Universal Natural History and Theory of the Heavens* (1755), following earlier work by the Swedish polymath Emanuel Swedenborg (1688–1772)

5 (p. 38) *secular cooling* Secular is used here in the obscure scientific sense of 'over several centuries': he is talking about entropy. Max Planck solidified the second law of thermodynamics in the late nineteenth century, and his *Treatise on Thermodynamics* (1897) was translated into English in 1903.

6 (p. 38) *vanished bison and the dodo* The dodo became extinct in the latter part of the seventeenth century; the last sighting was in 1662. The bison was not extinct but was known to be in extreme danger in the late nineteenth century.

7 (p. 38) *Tasmanians, in spite of their human likeness* British colonists practically eradicated Aboriginal Tasmanians between 1803 and 1833, and those who survived were moved off the island.

8 (p. 38) *Schiaparelli* The Italian astronomer Giovanni Schiaparelli (1835–1910) was notable for his observations of Mars from the Brera Observatory, naming the 'seas', 'continents', and 'channels' of Mars (an optical illusion). The latter term was mistranslated from the Italian (*canali*) into English as 'canals'.

9 (p. 39) *Opposition of 1894* Opposition is when the earth is situated directly between Mars and the sun, and conditions are particularly good for observation by telescope.

10 (p. 39) *Lick Observatory* on the summit of Mount Hamilton, near San Jose, the observatory of the University of California. It was opened in 1888.

11 (p. 39) *Perrotin of Nice* Henri Joseph Anastase Perrotin (1845–1904), a French astronomer who was director of the Nice Observatory from 1884 until his death

12 (p. 39) *issue of Nature dated August 2nd* the unsigned article 'A Strange Light on Mars' in *Nature* on 2 August 1894 describes an observation by the French astronomer Stéphane Javelle (1864–1917), who worked with Perrotin at the Nice Observatory. The report offers the tongue-in-cheek suggestion that the light is a signal from Martians. 'Lavelle of Java' in the following paragraph plays on that name.

13 (p. 39) *Daily Telegraph* conservative British newspaper, founded in 1855

14 (p. 39) *Ogilvy, the well-known astronomer, at Ottershaw* a fictional astronomer, who features in the same context in Wells's 'The Star' (1897)

15 (p. 41) *the serio-comic periodical Punch* prominent British humorous and satirical magazine (1841–1992; 1996–2002), noted for its cartoons

16 (p. 42) *Denning, our greatest authority on meteorites* noted amateur British astronomer William Frederick Denning (1848–1931)

17 (p. 44) *Daily Chronicle* British left-wing newspaper (1872–1930) that supported radical Liberalism

18 (p. 45) *gas float* unmanned boat-shaped beacon

19 (p. 46) *wire to the Astronomical Exchange* The Central Bureau for Astronomical Telegrams was founded in 1882 at Kiel in Germany to collect and distribute news about new discoveries of astronomical objects.

20 (p. 46) *the three kingdoms*   England, Scotland and Ireland. Wales is a principality; the Prince of Wales is the British monarchy's heir apparent.

21 (p. 46) *flys*   single-horse-drawn covered carriages, usually hired

22 (p. 46) *basket-chaise*   horse-drawn wicker carriage, usually for one or two people

23 (p. 46) *Stent, the Astronomer Royal*   The Astronomer Royal is a post within the British Royal Household. Started by King Charles II in 1675, it is now a prestigious but largely honorary post. The Astronomer Royal in 1898 was William Christie (1845–1922; Astronomer Royal 1881–1910). Stent is fictional.

24 (p. 48) *Gorgon groups of tentacles*   The three Gorgons in Greek mythology, Medusa, Stheno and Euryale, had serpents for hair which turned those looking at them into stone.

25 (p. 53) *parabolic mirror of a lighthouse*   a method of transforming the light from a lantern into a beam

26 (p. 56) *electric lamps*   Electric lighting was still relatively new: London's first public electric lights were lit in 1878.

27 (p. 57) *The Times*   an iconic British newspaper of the centre-right, founded 1785

28 (p. 59) *Smith's monopoly*   A British stationer and newsagent founded in 1792, W. H. Smith & Son, as it was in Wells's time, was noted for its railway-station news-stands.

29 (p. 60) *two Maxims*   Hiram Stevens Maxim (1840–1916) was influential in the development of the machine gun, and his weapon was adopted by the British Army in 1889.

30 (p. 60) *four hundred men of the Cardigan regiment*   The 11th (or Prince Albert's Own) Hussars were notably led by the Earl of Cardigan during the ill-fated Charge of the Light Brigade (1854) in the Crimean War (1853–6).

31 (p. 61) *at the Horse Guards*   Horse Guards is a large building in central London that was until 1904 the offices of the Commander-in-Chief of the Forces – the head of the British Army.

32 (p. 62) *fishers of men*   Matthew 4:19: 'And he saith unto them, Follow me, and I will make you fishers of men.'

33 (p. 63) *Oriental College*   The British orientalist Gottlieb Wilhelm Leitner (1840–99) strove to found a European centre for the study of Oriental languages and cultures. He bought the buildings of the

former Royal Dramatic College in Woking in 1883, but the Institute did not last beyond his death in 1899. He commissioned the building of the Shah Jahan Mosque (1889), mentioned in the next sentence, which was the first purpose-built mosque in Britain.

34 (p. 64) *dogcart*   light horse-drawn vehicle for one or two people, originally used to carry sporting dogs

35 (p. 71) *the Potteries*   the area of the West Midlands around Stoke-on-Trent in England, historically famed for its pottery industry

36 (p. 71) *an ironclad*   late nineteenth-century armour-plated warship. Wells's story 'The Land Ironclads' (1903) transposes these ships on to land, anticipating the development of the tank in the First World War.

37 (p. 73) *valley of ashes*   Jeremiah 31:40: 'And the whole valley of the dead bodies, and of the ashes, and all the fields unto the brook of Kidron, unto the corner of the horse gate toward the east, shall be holy unto the LORD; it shall not be plucked up, nor thrown down any more for ever.'

38 (p. 74) *pitiless light of dawn*   Proverbs 4:14–19: 'Enter not into the path of the wicked, and go not in the way of evil men. Avoid it, pass not by it, turn from it, and pass away. For they sleep not, except they have done mischief; and their sleep is taken away, unless they cause *some* to fall. For they eat the bread of wickedness, and drink the wine of violence. But the path of the just *is* as the shining light, that shineth more and more unto the perfect day. The way of the wicked *is* as darkness: they know not at what they stumble.'

39 (p. 74) *pillars of fire*   Revelation 10:1: 'And I saw another mighty angel come down from heaven, clothed with a cloud: and a rainbow *was* upon his head, and his face *was* as it were the sun, and his feet as pillars of fire.'

40 (p. 75) *8th Hussars*   The 8th (King's Royal Irish) Hussars, as they were at the time of publication, was a long-established cavalry regiment that also took part in the Charge of the Light Brigade.

41 (p. 77) *sabbatical*   appropriate to the Sabbath

42 (p. 83) *the earthquake that destroyed Lisbon*   on 1 November 1755, among the strongest recorded. The majority of the city was flattened, and there were tens of thousands of fatalities.

43 (p. 85) *Sodom and Gomorrah*   cities destroyed in an act of divine judgement by God, and commonly used as metaphors for unrepentant wrongdoing

44 (p. 85) *The smoke of her burning goeth up for ever and ever*   Revelation 19:3: 'And again they said, Alleluia. And her smoke rose up for ever and ever.' Other versions of the Bible are closer to the curate's quotation, but none seems to replicate it exactly.

45 (p. 86) *The great and terrible day of the Lord! When men shall call upon the mountains and rocks to fall upon them and hide them – hide them from the face of him that sitteth upon the throne*   Joel 2:31: 'The sun shall be turned into darkness, and the moon into blood, before the great and the terrible day of the LORD come.' Revelation 6:15–6:16: 'And the kings of the earth, and the great men, and the rich men, and the chief captains, and the mighty men, and every bondman, and every free man, hid themselves in the dens and in the rocks of the mountains; And said to the mountains and rocks, Fall on us, and hide us from the face of him that sitteth on the throne, and from the wrath of the Lamb.'

46 (p. 87) *the relative strength of the earth's gravitational energy*   Gravity on Mars is only approximately 37.5% of the surface gravity of the earth. Therefore, a weight of 37.5 kilograms on Mars would equate to 100 kilograms on earth – two and two-thirds times heavier.

47 (p. 87) *St James's Gazette*   a Conservative London evening newspaper (1880–1905)

48 (p. 88) *theatre trains*   services timed to coincide with the end of performances and take audiences back to their homes in the suburbs

49 (p. 88) *the Southampton and Portsmouth Sunday League excursions*   services arranged to take crowds to and from football (soccer) matches in the Sunday (amateur) leagues

50 (p. 88) *Sunday Sun*   The British journalist and MP Thomas Power O'Connor (1848–1929) purchased the *Sunday Sun* in 1891. Two years later it was divided into the weekday evening *Sun* (1893–1906) and the *Weekly Sun* (1893–1901), published on Saturdays and Sundays. It was a cheap, popular and populist paper.

51 (p. 88) *the Referee*   a Sunday newspaper primarily covering sports, founded in 1877. Known in later years as the *Sunday Referee*, it was merged in 1939 with the *Sunday Chronicle*.

52 (p. 89) *Foundling Hospital*   established in Bloomsbury in 1739 by the philanthropist Thomas Coram (1688–1751) to care for babies found abandoned – predominantly, illegitimate children. The work of the charity continues, and the building is today a museum.

53 (p. 89) *omnibuses*   horse-drawn buses still, at this time. The first
motor omnibuses were not used in London until 1902.

54 (p. 89) *South-Western Company*   The London and South Western
Railway existed as a company from 1838–1922, operating lines far
into the south-west of England, as well as to major southern cities
such as Southampton and Bournemouth.

55 (p. 90) *the South-Western 'lungs'*   William Pitt the Elder (1708–78),
Prime Minister of Great Britain from 1766–8, is supposed to have
described parks and open spaces as 'the lungs of London'.

56 (p. 90) *Salvation Army lasses*   The Salvation Army is a Christian
charity with a pseudo-military method of organisation. It was
founded in 1865 by William (1829–1912) and Catherine (1829–
1890) Booth. They recruited young women, known as Hallelujah
lasses, to preach in the streets and assist the poor.

57 (p. 92) *Epsom High Street on a Derby Day*   The Derby, first run in
1780 and still run over the Epsom Downs course, is the most
prestigious of the five classic horse races on the flat in England.
Wells means simply that it is exceptionally busy.

58 (p. 94) *North-Western special trains*   The London and North
Western Railway (1846–1922) was noted for running services from
London Euston to the midlands and northern industrial cities of
Birmingham, Liverpool and Manchester.

59 (p. 98) *a Greater Moscow*   As Napoleon's troops entered Moscow
on 14 September 1812, Count Rostopchin ordered the Kremlin
and other prominent and strategic buildings to be burned or
levelled. Many other fires were started across the city to frustrate
Napoleon, probably also on Rostopchin's orders.

60 (p. 99) *kopjes*   (Dutch/Afrikaans) a small hill in an otherwise flat
area

61 (p. 99) *carbonic acid gas*   carbon dioxide

62 (p. 103) *pony-chaise*   another form of light horse-drawn carriage

63 (p. 105) *thirty pounds in gold*   A sovereign was a British gold coin
with a nominal value of one pound sterling, circulated until 1932.

64 (p. 108) *Vestry of St Pancras*   the local administration, named for its
historic meetings in the church vestry. This practice was outlawed
in 1850; the Vestry of St Pancras became the Metropolitan Borough
of St Pancras in 1900, following the London Government Act 1899.

65 (p. 109) *Lord Garrick . . . the Chief Justice*   The Lord Chief Justice was historically the second-highest judge of the Courts of England and Wales, with responsibility for the Criminal Division of the Court of Appeal. Lord Garrick is fictional, possibly a reference to the sort of gentleman who would be a member at the prestigious Garrick Club in London. The Lord Chief Justice in 1898 was Lord Russell of Killowen (1832–1900).

66 (p. 111) *Great Northern Railway*   The Great Northern Railway (1846–1922) ran trains from London King's Cross to cities including York and Sheffield.

67 (p. 112) *hosts of Goths and Huns*   both played significant roles in the collapse of the Western Roman Empire in the fourth and fifth centuries AD

68 (p. 113) *Pool of London*   the stretch of the River Thames in London from London Bridge to around Limehouse, the original part of the Port of London

69 (p. 113) *lightermen*   Lighters were flat–bottomed barges used to transfer cargo and/or passengers to and from anchored ships. Lightermen were the skilled operators of these crafts, using 'sweeps' (long oars) to propel them.

70 (p. 114) *Midland Railway Company*   The Midland Railway operated in from 1844 to 1922, running a number of lines centred on Derby.

71 (p. 114) *Committee of Public Supply*   echoes the Committee of Public Safety, for a time the *de facto* government during the French Revolution. It protected the newly-established republic against internal and external attack.

72 (p. 114) *Waltham Abbey Powder Mills*   The Royal Gunpowder Mills at Waltham Abbey was one of three such sites in the United Kingdom, purchased by the Crown in 1787.

73 (p. 117) *torpedo-ram*   a light, fast, armoured ship equipped with either of the titular weapons, for use where enemy ships could be approached without being sunk

74 (p. 119) *rained down darkness upon the land*   suggests Genesis 19:24: 'Then the LORD rained upon Sodom and Gomorrah brimstone and fire from the LORD out of heaven;' Exodus 10:22: 'And Moses stretched forth his hand toward heaven; and there was a thick darkness in all the land of Egypt three days;' Matthew 27:45: 'Now from the sixth hour there was darkness over all the land unto the ninth hour.'

75 (p. 124) *the destruction of Pompeii*   in AD79 by the eruption of the volcano Mount Vesuvius

76 (p. 124) *Hampton Court*   Hampton Court Palace is a royal palace in Richmond upon Thames, to the south-west of London but within Greater London. It was a royal residence from 1514 to 1737.

77 (p. 127) *coloured supplements*   British newspapers often had coloured supplements inserted in weekend editions, orientated more towards lifestyle than news.

78 (p. 131) *that distinguished anatomist, Professor Howes*   The British zoologist Thomas George Bond Howes (1853–1905) was an assistant to T. H. Huxley when Wells was taught by him. Howes wrote the introduction to Wells's *Text-Book of Biology* (1893).

79 (p. 132) *a certain speculative writer . . . November or December 1893 . . . Pall Mall Budget*   The writer is Wells. 'The Man of the Year Million' was first published in the London evening newspaper the *Pall Mall Gazette* (1865–1923) on 9 November 1893, and reprinted in the weekly *Pall Mall Budget* (1868–1920), which collected items from the *Gazette*, on 16 November 1893.

80 (p. 133) *red weed*   also appears in Wells's short story 'The Crystal Egg' (1897), published during the serialisation of *The War of the Worlds*

81 (p. 133) *Philips*   perhaps suggesting the British botanist William Phillips (1822–1905)

82 (p. 134) *telepathic theory*   The British author Frederic W.H. Myers (1843–1901) coined the term 'telepathy' in 1882. Wells criticised the concept in a review in *Nature* on 6 December 1894 of Frank Podmore's *Apparitions and Thought-Transference*.

83 (p. 134) *road-skates*   a roller-skate-type design that looked like a small bicycle under each foot

84 (p. 134) *Lilienthal soaring-machines*   Otto Lilienthal (1848–96) was a German aviation pioneer. He made many successful gliding flights, but died in a flying accident.

85 (p. 141) *We have sinned, we have fallen short*   Romans 3:22–3: 'Even the righteousness of God *which is* by faith of Jesus Christ unto all and upon all them that believe: for there is no difference; for all have sinned, and come short of the glory of God.'

86 (p. 141) *Oppressors of the poor and needy*   Psalm 12:5: 'For the oppression of the poor, for the sighing of the needy, now will I arise,

saith the LORD; I will set *him* in safety *from him that* puffeth at him.'
Compare Ezekiel 18:12.

87 (p. 141) *The wine-press of God*   Revelation 14:19–20: 'And the angel
thrust in his sickle into the earth, and gathered the vine of the earth,
and cast *it* into the great winepress of the wrath of God. And the
winepress was trodden without the city, and blood came out of the
winepress, even unto the horse bridles, by the space of a thousand
and six hundred furlongs.'

88 (p. 142) *Briareus*   in Greek mythology, one of the three Hekatonk-
heires, giants of supreme strength who overthrew the Titans

89 (p. 146) *Putney*   an historic crossing-point of the River Thames.
Notable instances include Cardinal Wolsey's in 1529 after falling
from Henry VIII's favour, and the bridge of boats built by
Parliamentary forces (Roundheads) in 1642. St Mary's Church in
Putney was also the site of the Putney Debates in 1647, at which
the Levellers, a faction within the New Model Army, rebelled
momentarily against the possibility of a new dictatorship in place of
the monarchy.

90 (p. 150) *Thomas Lobb*   The greengrocer shares a name with the
noted British botanist Thomas Lobb (1817–94).

91 (p. 153) *Royal Academy of Arts*   founded in 1768; an independent,
privately-funded organisation to promote appreciation of the visual
arts

92 (p. 156) *poetry swipes*   'Swipes' is weak or watery beer, so poetry
swipes suggests 'bad poetry'.

93 (p. 157) *mock-turtle soup*   Green-turtle soup is an expensive, rare
and in many countries illegal delicacy. Mock-turtle soup is an
approximation, using cheap parts of larger animals such as brains
and offal.

94 (p. 158) *the old palace*   Lambeth Palace, the London residence of
the Archbishop of Canterbury

95 (p. 158) *the Circus*   Piccadilly Circus

96 (p. 158) *the Langham*   The Langham Hotel (founded 1865) is a
grand establishment on Langham Place in Marylebone, London.

97 (p. 159) *parish points*   a non-monetary method of scoring, based on
the parishes of London

98 (p. 163) *mechanical Samson*   in the Bible a man of superhuman
strength, vulnerable only to untrustworthy women and the loss of
his hair (Judges 13–16)

99 (p. 163) *the Zoological Gardens* London Zoo, established by the Zoological Society of London in 1828

100 (p. 165) *Sennacherib* Assyrian king from 705–681BC, killed in mysterious circumstances

101 (p. 166) *Albert Hall* The Royal Albert Hall (opened 1871), a concert hall memorialising Queen Victoria's consort, Prince Albert

102 (p. 167) *The Last Man Left Alive* from the English poet Thomas Hood's (1799–1845) 'The Last Man': 'So there he hung, and there I stood / THE LAST MAN left alive, / To have my own will of all the earth: / Quoth I, now I shall thrive.'

103 (p. 168) *the Daily Mail* a British right-wing popular newspaper, founded in 1896. Half the price of its established rivals, it was also more populist in tone.

104 (p. 168) *advertisement stereo* presumably referring to stereo photography which creates the illusion of three-dimensionality

THE WAR IN THE AIR

105 (p. 181) *Bun Hill* fictional, but evoking Bromley, Kent, where Wells was born

106 (p. 181) *South of England Aero Club* Ballooning was a relatively new pastime. There was no South of England Aero Club, but the Royal Aero Club was founded in 1901.

107 (p. 181) *ballase* ballast

108 (p. 182) *Carnegie library* The Scottish-American steel magnate Andrew Carnegie (1835–1919) was in later life a noted philanthropist and patron of the arts.

109 (p. 183) *he was out of short frocks* It was common into the early twentieth century for very young boys to wear gowns or dresses.

110 (p. 183) *Boys of England American cigarettes* There appears to have been no such brand, but *Boys of England* (1866–99) was a popular periodical in the manner of the *Boy's Own Paper*, largely read by a working-class audience.

111 (p. 183) *Chips, Comic Cuts, Ally Sloper's Half-Holiday* Illustrated *Chips* (1890–1953), *Comic Cuts* (1890–1953) and *Ally Sloper's Half-Holiday* (1884–1916) were all comic-strip periodicals.

112 (p. 183) *the seventh standard* the top class in state schools of the time. Progression was by attainment rather than age.

113 (p. 184) *trick rider*   stunt rider

114 (p. 185) *teuf-teuffed*   an onomatopoeic representation of the sound of a motorcycle

115 (p. 186) *Mr George Griffith's 'Clipper of the Clouds'*   The British author George Chetwynd Griffith-Jones (1857–1906) wrote science-fiction stories as George Griffith. This reference conflates the translation of Jules Verne's *Robur le conquérant* (1886) with Griffith's work. The UK first edition gives 'Mr George Griffith's *The Outlaws of the Air* (1895)', which is indeed one of Griffith's novels.

116 (p. 186) *the halfpenny newspapers or by cinematograph records*   Halfpenny newspapers were aimed at the popular market; established broadsheets retailed for a penny. Newsreels, later made famous by Pathé, were often shown as part of a cinema programme.

117 (p. 187) *Brennan . . . gyroscopic monorail car*   The Irish-American inventor Louis Brennan (1852–1932) patented a monorail balanced by gyroscope in 1903.

118 (p. 187) *Royal Society*   the UK national academy of science, founded in 1663

119 (p. 188) *Home Counties Power Distribution Company*   Fictional at the time, although several companies were combined by the Electricity (Supply) Act 1919 into the London and Home Counties Joint Electricity Authority.

120 (p. 188) *the English Channel was bridged*   There had already in 1881–2 been a very preliminary and abortive attempt to tunnel below the Channel. The French engineer Aimé Thomé de Gamond (1807–76) surveyed the Channel extensively in the mid-nineteenth century, proposing crossings including a bridge, railway tunnels and even the creation of an artificial land isthmus.

121 (p. 189) *submarine crawler invented by Dr Alberto Cassini*   Cassini is fictional. Rather than a now-conventional submarine, this description suggests the early designs of the American engineer and naval pioneer Simon Lake (1866–1945), who built his first submarine in 1894.

122 (p. 190) *Aldershot*   The Hampshire town rapidly developed as a British Army garrison town in the late nineteenth century. From 1890 to 1906 the experimental School of Ballooning (from 1897 the Balloon Factory) was based there; experiments with airships were carried out from 1902.

123 (p. 191) *those Wright Brothers out in America*   Orville (1871–1948) and Wilbur Wright (1867–1912) were American aeroplane pioneers, usually credited with the world's first powered heavier-than-air flight at Kitty Hawk, North Carolina in December 1903.

124 (p. 191) *De Booley*   Given Bert's habit of transposing syllables, and the later reference, it seems likely that this is a corruption of Lebaudy. The Lebaudy Frères company, known primarily as sugar producers, produced the *Patrie*, the first French Army airship. It was completed in November 1906.

125 (p. 191) *Lydd*   On the Romney Marsh in Kent, an important artillery practice camp was sited at the town in the early years of the twentieth century.

126 (p. 194) *the Isaac Walton*   The British writer Isaak Walton (?1594–1683) was best known as the author of *The Compleat Angler* (1653), which he continued to revise for much of his life.

127 (p. 196) *The woman's soul leadeth us upward and on*   from Goethe's *Faust*, Part Two (1832)

128 (p. 197) *Daily Requiem*   fictional newspaper

129 (p. 202) *the Dog's Home in Battersea*   established in 1860, a famous UK establishment for rescuing and rehoming cats and dogs

130 (p. 204) *The Monroe Doctrine*   President James Monroe (1758–1831) declared in 1823 that European intervention in politics in the Americas would be viewed as aggression towards the United States.

131 (p. 205) *the Boer War*   i.e. the most recent conflict, the Second Boer War (1899–1902), in which the South African Republic fought against British Imperial forces

132 (p. 205) *Nineveh*   in ancient times, the capital of the Assyrian Empire. It is mentioned in the Bible: 'And Jonah began to enter into the city a day's journey, and he cried, and said, Yet forty days, and Nineveh shall be overthrown' (Jonah 3:4). The city was destroyed in 612BC; its site is near Mosul in modern-day Iraq.

133 (p. 205) *his lamps*   the headlights for his motorbike

134 (p. 206) *an Oxford intonation*   the affected pronunciation of someone educated at the University of Oxford, indicating a much higher class than Bert

135 (p. 209) *blackened Promethean figure*   Prometheus, in Greek mythology, stole fire from the gods to give it to mankind.

136 (p. 210) *Timbuctoo*   Timbuctoo (now usually Timbuktu), then in French Sudan, on the cusp of the Sahara Desert in modern-day Mali, was a byword for a distant and inaccessible place.

137 (p. 210) *Twaregs*   The twareg (more frequently tuareg or touareg) are a nomadic people who live in the Sahara.

138 (p. 211) *o–r–p–h*   orph, phonetic slang for off

139 (p. 212) *into a cocked hat*   To knock something into a cocked hat is to achieve something or defeat someone or something conclusively.

140 (p. 212) *The Bitter Cry of the Middle Class*   alludes to the Reverend Andrew Mearns's *The Bitter Cry of Outcast London* (1883), which drew attention to poverty in the slums of London's East End

141 (p. 213) *Scarlet Mr E's*   a noted concert troupe in the early years of the twentieth century whose members dressed as masked eighteenth-century highwayman, perhaps trading on the success of Baroness Orczy's (1865–1947) stage play (1903) and novel (1905) *The Scarlet Pimpernel*

142 (p. 215) *Eng!*   hang (it), a common expression of frustration

143 (p. 217) *tow beard*   a false beard

144 (p. 219) *'on the dibs'*   on the money, implying money obtained by dubious or nefarious means

145 (p. 220) *Kodak*   brand name for a simple and popular camera made by the Eastman Kodak company, founded in 1888

146 (p. 221) *Roman pie*   layered pie containing various meats and pasta

147 (p. 221) *self-heating tins of coffee and cocoa*   Bert uses one of these later in the chapter. It was at the time a fiction that has since been commercially developed.

148 (p. 222) *British ordnance maps*   The Ordnance Survey is the national mapping agency of Britain (founded 1791). The name speaks to the origins of the company in surveying Scotland after the Jacobite Rebellion of 1745.

149 (p. 222) *'Je suis Anglais. C'est une méprise. Je suis arrive par accident ici,'*   (French) 'I am English. This is a mistake. I arrived here by accident.'

150 (p. 222) *'Apportez moi à le Consuelo Britannique s'il vous plaît'*   in Bert's not-quite-correct French, 'Bring me to the British Consul, please.'

151 (p. 223) *Drachenflieger. Drachenballons. Ballonstoffe. Kugelballons* (German) Presumably these are names for and parts of various aircraft proposals – literally: 'dragon-flyer'; 'dragon-balloons'; 'balloon-material'; 'bullet-balloons'.

152 (p. 224) *'Voici Mossoo! . . . Voulez vous me directer là?'* In Bert's schoolboy French: 'Here, mister! I'm an English inventor. My name is Butteridge. B. U. T. T. E. R. I. D. G. E. I have here for sale the secret of the *flying machine*. Do you understand? To sell for cash right now, cash in hand. Do you understand? This is the machine that plays in the air. Do you understand? This machine does it like a bird. Do you understand? It balances? Yes, exactly? It beats the bird at what it does, at its own game. I want to sell this to your national government. Would you direct me there?'

153 (p. 226) *a prolate moon*   a full moon that looks egg-shaped because of atmospheric distortion

154 (p. 227) *Lorraine's*   Bert seems to misunderstand the French region Lorraine as the possession of a woman of that name.

155 (p. 230) *Têtes there, you!*   Bert translates literally from the English 'Heads (up)!' – Look out above you – into French.

156 (p. 232) *G. P. R. James* (1799–1860), a British author of popular historical romances that were widely parodied. These often featured a solitary horseman.

157 (p. 232) *Franconia*   An historic Duchy in southern Germany, after 1803 mostly part of Bavaria. The Bavarian monarchy was abolished after the First World War.

158 (p. 232) *his masters, the winds of heaven*   Ezekiel 37:9: 'Then said he unto me, Prophesy unto the wind, prophesy, son of man, and say to the wind, Thus saith the Lord GOD; Come from the four winds, O breath, and breathe upon these slain, that they may live.' It also evokes *Hamlet*: 'So excellent a king, that was to this / Hyperion to a satyr, so loving to my mother / That he might not beteem the winds of heaven / Visit her face too roughly' (1.2.139–42).

159 (p. 233) *Welt-Politik* (German) 'world-policy', the foreign policy that Kaiser Wilhelm II adopted in 1891. It signalled a move from pragmatic attempts to forestall a two-power war, to a focus on the enhancement of Germany's status.

160 (p. 234) *the Zeppelin airship that flew over Lake Constance in 1906* Ferdinand von Zeppelin (1838–1917) lived at his family's

manor near Constance (Konstanz), and conducted many of his test flights in the area.

161 (p. 234) *the Lebaudy navigables that made their memorable excursions over Paris in 1907 and 1908* See Note 124 above. The *Patrie* was lost in late 1907, but the French army was committed to continuing with the design: a sister ship, the *République*, flew several times in 1908–9.

162 (p. 234) *Pforzheim type* Pforzheim is a German city near the Black Forest; the technology is fictional.

163 (p. 237) *the Yellow Danger . . . the Black Peril* racist American and European attitudes fearing the potential power of Asian empires, underpinned by contemporary fears about miscegenation

164 (p. 237) *White Man's Burthen* 'The White Man's Burden' is an 1899 poem by British author Rudyard Kipling (1865–1936). Kipling's poem both endorses imperialism and warns about the costs involved, but was most often read uncritically as supporting supposedly beneficial racist imperialism.

165 (p. 239) *And never the twain shall meet* the first line of Kipling's 1889 poem 'The Ballad of East and West', usually used to justify racial segregation. As with 'The White Man's Burden', the poem continues more even-handedly: 'But there is neither East nor West, Border, nor Breed, nor Birth, / When two strong men stand face to face.'

166 (p. 239) *Quote Burns at them and Mill and Darwin* Each of these figures is associated with ideas about equality and liberty. The Scottish poet Robert Burns (1759–96) memorably expressed them in his 1795 poem 'Is there for Honest Poverty', known more commonly by the line 'A Man's a Man for a' that'; the British philosopher John Stuart Mill (1806–73) wrote *On Liberty* (1859), emphasising the importance of individuality in the relationship between authority and liberty; the theories of evolution demonstrated by the British scientist Charles Darwin (1809–82), first and most famously in *On the Origin of Species* (1859), contributed to undermining racist ideologies.

167 (p. 241) *Moltke* The Prussian general Helmuth von Moltke (1800–91) was chief of staff during the Franco-Prussian War (1870–1).

168 (p. 241) *Prince Karl Albert* fictional, but evoking the last German Emperor, Kaiser Wilhelm II (1859–1941)

169 (p. 242) *Black Prince*   Son of King Edward III of England (1312–77; reigned 1327–77), the Black Prince Edward (1330–76) predeceased his father. This meant that his son, Richard II (1367–1400; reigned from 1377 until being deposed in 1399) came to the throne as a minor.

170 (p. 242) *Alcibiades*   (c.450–404BC), an Athenian general and statesman who was a pupil of Socrates

171 (p. 242) *Nietzsche's Over-man*   a term used by the German philosopher Friedrich Nietzsche (1844–1900) in works such as *Thus Spoke Zarathustra* (1883; trans. 1886). The German 'übermensch' is often translated as 'superman'.

172 (p. 242) *Heligoland*   island off the coast of Germany which became a strategic naval base in the First World War

173 (p. 242) *The American yacht Defender*   In 1895 an American yacht named *Defender* won the America's Cup, the premier yacht-racing tournament.

174 (p. 242) *Rudolf Martin*   (1876–1916) German civil servant and author of the futuristic fantasy *Berlin-Bagdad: The German World-Empire in the Age of Airship Travel, 1910–1931* (1907). It was published in condensed form in the *Review of Reviews* and may have been an inspiration for Wells.

175 (p. 243) *Ja! Ja! . . . Selbst!*   (German) 'Yes! Yes! Mr Butteridge! Himself!'

176 (p. 243) *Besser*   (German) Better

177 (p. 244) *Mitbringen*   (German) bring him

178 (p. 244) *Kopf*   (German) head

179 (p. 244) *hals*   (German) neck

180 (p. 244) *Vorwärts*   (German) forward

181 (p. 245) *Woolwich Dockyard*   English naval dockyard on the south bank of the Thames, founded in 1512 as The King's Yard, Woolwich. It closed as a dockyard in 1869, but remained part of the larger Woolwich Arsenal site.

182 (p. 245) *Dummer*   (German) silly or stupid

183 (p. 245) *'tisn't a norfis*   i.e. it isn't an office

184 (p. 247) *Vaterland*   (German) Fatherland

185 (p. 248) *Rhodes scholar*   The mining magnate and imperialist Cecil Rhodes (1853–1902) endowed scholarships to enable international

students to study at the University of Oxford. The original beneficiaries were to be 'young colonists' from British colonies, the United States and Germany.

186 (p. 250) *the 'German Alexander'*   an analogy with Alexander III of Macedon, commonly known as Alexander the Great (356–323BC), whose conquests created one of the great empires of the ancient world. It also perhaps nods to the opening of the traditional marching song 'The British Grenadiers'.

187 (p. 250) *Hoch!* (German) literally high, or exalted, a toast to the nobility

188 (p. 251) *the Graf von Winterfeld*   probably modelled on Hugo von Winterfeld (1836–98), a long-standing and powerful officer in the Prussian Army

189 (p. 253) *a little cockney cad*   The strict meaning of cockney is someone born within the sound of Bow Bells, but more generally it suggests a member of the lower class: the East End of London was notorious for its slums in the early years of the twentieth century.

190 (p. 253) *hochgeborene*   (German) highborn

191 (p. 254) *Pooterage*   a Germanicising of Butteridge, but also evoking the bourgeois everyman Charles Pooter, protagonist of George and Weedon Grossmith's *Diary of a Nobody* (1892)

192 (p. 255) *an eagle's nest*   playing on the nautical crow's nest, an elevated lookout point

193 (p. 255) *Luftschiffe*   (German) airships

194 (p. 259) *The Daily Courier*   a widely-used name for a newspaper. the *Daily Telegraph* was founded in 1855 as the *Daily Telegraph and Courier*; there was a short-lived London society newspaper called the *Daily Courier* in 1896.

195 (p. 259) *Viel besser, nich wahr?*   (German) Much better, isn't it?

196 (p. 262) *the Ship Canal*   The Manchester Ship Canal, opened in 1894, connects Manchester to the Irish Sea by water, running out to the Mersey estuary.

197 (p. 263) *Siegfried Schmalz*   fictional, but suggesting 'schmaltz(y)', an American-English slang term for overly sentimental or florid art

198 (p. 263) *Eiserne Kreuz*   (German) Iron Cross, a military decoration

199 (p. 263) *Miles Standish*   (*c.*1584–1656) one of the Pilgrim Fathers who sailed to America on the *Mayflower*

200 (p. 263) *Karl der Grosse* (German) *Charles the Great* or, more commonly, Charlemagne (742–814), the founder of the Holy Roman Empire

201 (p. 263) *latitude 30° 50' N., longitude 30° 50' W.* a point in the North Atlantic Ocean, approximately 1,250 miles west from the coast of Morocco near Agadir

202 (p. 264) *Charlottenburg steel* fictional. Charlottenburg was historically an affluent city to the west of Berlin. It was transformed into a borough of Berlin in 1920.

203 (p. 266) *Barbarossa* most likely alluding to Frederick Barbarossa (1122–90), formally Frederick I, Holy Roman Emperor (1155–90). He became King of Germany in 1152, ruling until his death. It also evokes the fifteenth- to sixteenth-century family of Ottoman seamen.

204 (p. 270) *Susquehanna* The Susquehanna River in the USA flows out to Chesapeake Bay, the northern part of which is in Maryland, and the southern part in Virginia.

205 (p. 270) *Theodore Roosevelt* (1858–1919) US President (1901–9) at the time of the novel's publication

206 (p. 270) *Fürst Bismarck* (German) *Prince of Bismarck*, after the Prussian statesman Otto von Bismarck (1915–1898)

207 (p. 270) *Gott! Da waren Albrecht . . . und von Rosen!* (German) 'God! There's Albrecht – good Albrecht and old Zimmermann – and von Rosen!'

208 (p. 273) *Vogelstern and Preussen* (German) *Starbird* and *Prussia*

209 (p. 277) *the floating batteries of the Emperor Napoleon III in the Crimean War* The *Dévastation*-class ironclad floating batteries were built to bombard Russian coastal fortifications during the Crimean War (1854–5).

210 (p. 279) *Adler* (German) *Eagle*, a long-standing symbol on the German coat of arms

211 (p. 284) *In Madison Square about the Farragut monument* on Manhattan, New York. Rear Admiral David G. Farragut (1801–70) was famous for his command in the Battle of Mobile May (1864) in the American Civil War (1861–5), usually, but probably apocryphally, given as, 'Damn the torpedoes, full speed ahead.'

212 (p. 285) *Albany legislature* Albany is the capital of the state of New York.

213 (p. 285) *the Monitor and the Southern submarines of 1864*   The USS *Monitor* was the first ironclad warship commissioned by the Union Navy; it quickly became the name for a class of warship that could carry disproportionately large guns, designed for shallow waters. The *H. L. Hunley* was the first submarine (albeit one not wholly submerged) to sink a warship, the USS *Housatonic*, on 17 February 1864. It sank soon afterwards, killing all of the crew.

214 (p. 285) *The chief of the aeronautic establishment near West Point was Cabot Sinclair*   The United States Military Academy was founded at West Point, NY, in 1802. The Aeronautical Division, the US Signal Corps, was founded on 1 August 1907, and took delivery of its first Wright Brothers aeroplane at Fort Myer, Virginia on 1 September 1908. Cabot Sinclair is fictional.

215 (p. 287) *Sandy Hook observation station*   Sandy Hook is the northernmost point of coastal New Jersey, at the entrance to the Lower New York Bay and therefore a key coastal defence point. It was from 1874 to 1919 a military proving ground.

216 (p. 287) *Giffords and the one on Beacon Hill above Matawan*   Giffords was an area of Staten Island looking out towards Lower New York Bay. It is now known as Great Kills. Beacon Hill, about six miles inland from the north New Jersey shore, on the opposite side of the Raritan Bay, was named for its role as a lookout point and the site of a warning beacon indicating the proximity of British troops in the American Revolutionary War.

217 (p. 291) *Mayor O'Hagen*   fictional, but perhaps alluding to the Ulster Scots background of the contemporary Mayor of New York City, George B. McClellan Jr (1865–1940), who served from 1904 to 1909

218 (p. 291) *Monson Building*   not a building in New York, but on Ninth Square in New Haven, CT (the home of Yale University). It may also ironically evoke the British politician Lord Monson (*c.*1693–1748), who was President of the (British) Board of Trade (1737–1748).

219 (p. 292) *Elevated Railway of New York*   fictional. The now-disused elevated railway known as the High Line, on the Lower West Side of Manhattan, did not open until 1934.

220 (p. 297) *the great Dexter building*   fictional, but drawing on and perhaps replicating in New York the Dexter Building in Chicago (built 1887), which was at the time of publication a recent landmark building. It was destroyed by fire in 2006.

221 (p. 298) *Tiffany's*   founded in 1837, the famous jeweller's on Fifth Avenue in New York City

222 (p. 298) *Tammany Hall*   a building on Fourteenth Street, often used as a metonym for its occupants, the Society of St Tammany. The Society was influential in the Democratic Party and New York (City and State) politics, and helped immigrants, particularly Irish, succeed in US politics. In the mid-nineteenth century it was also notable for political corruption.

223 (p. 298) *Blut and Eisen*   (German) Blood and Iron! The Prince is given these characteristics as a title at the beginning of the next chapter.

224 (p. 303) *Colt-Coburn-Langley pattern*   fictional, but referring to real people. Samuel Colt (1814–62) founded Colt's Patent Firearms Manufacturing Company in 1855, following two earlier abortive concerns. He profited as a major supplier of arms to both sides in the American Civil War. Samuel Pierpont Langley (1834–1906) was an American astronomer and aeronautical pioneer. The name may also evoke Alvin Langdon Coburn (1882–1966), the early-twentieth-century photographer who had spent time in London in 1905–6, where he photographed Henry James, and whose fame was burgeoning as Wells wrote the novel.

225 (p. 307) *North Pole*   As Wells was writing, the North Pole was yet to be reached. The US explorer Frederick Cook claimed to have done it in April 1908, but this is not usually accepted.

226 (p. 308) *whether New York was our Moscow*   See Note 59.

227 (p. 310) *Ein feste Burg ist unser Gott*   (German) 'A mighty fortress is our God'

228 (p. 314) *Fifty centuries come to their Consummation*   Matthew 24:14: 'And this gospel of the kingdom shall be preached in all the world for a witness unto all nations; and then shall the end come.' In the Douay-Rheims version, it reads: 'And this gospel of the kingdom shall be preached in the whole world, for a testimony to all nations, and then shall the consummation come.'

229 (p. 319) *the English did at Alexandria, the Japanese at Port Arthur, the French at Casablanca*   The British bombardment of Alexandria's fortifications before the occupation of Egypt in 1882 led to riots and a massacre. The Russo-Japanese War (1904–5) began with a brutal attack by the Japanese on the Russian fleet at Port Arthur

(now Lüshunkou, China). French troops landed in Casablanca, Morocco, in 1907.

230 (p. 319) *Down in South America even they are fighting among themselves*   perhaps alluding to the Thousand Days' War, a civil war in Colombia (1899–1902)

231 (p. 320) *Tan Ting-siang*   a mid-nineteenth-century governor of Zhili, China

232 (p. 320) *Niaio*   ironically echoes the Mandarin Chinese *ni hao*, hello

233 (p. 321) *from Cape Horn to Nova Zembla, and from Canton round to Canton again*   Cape Horn is the southernmost point of Chile's Tierra del Fuego archipelago, the point where the Atlantic and Pacific Oceans meet and a key passage round the southern tip of South America for sea trade. Nova Zembla is the name both of a remote, uninhabited island in Nunavut, on the north east of Canada, and an alternative name for Novaya Zemlya, a Russian arctic archipelago which is the north-eastern point of Europe. There are many places named Canton on the American continent; it is also the former official name of Guangzhou, China. The context makes it equally plausible that Wells refers to the extremes of the American continent, or the world.

234 (p. 322) *the Communist insurrection of Paris, 1871*   To protest against the surrender of the city in the Franco-Prussian War, Parisians established a Commune. Tens of thousands of people were killed by the National Government in suppressing it.

235 (p. 324) *Universal Peace Conference in 1900*   There was a Peace Conference at The Hague, in the Netherlands, in 1899, at which the Hague Convention was established, setting out rules for the conduct of future wars.

236 (p. 325) *Winterhouse-Dunne aeroplanes*   fictional, but suggesting the British soldier and aeronautical pioneer J. W. Dunne (1875–1949), who was particularly active in 1907–8. His later book on precognition, *An Experiment with Time* (1927), was influential for Wells's work on *The Shape of Things to Come* (1933).

237 (p. 326) *Mohini K. Chatterjee*   perhaps alluding to the Bengali scholar and theosophist Mohini Mohun Chatterji (1858–1936). The Irish poet W. B. Yeats (1865–1939) wrote a poem about him entitled 'Mohini Chatterjee' (1895).

238 (p. 328) *Battle of Niagara* Wells evokes previous military encounters in the area. The Battle of Fort Niagara (1759) was part of the Seven Years' War (1756–63); Fort Niagara was captured in late 1813, during the War of 1812 (1812–15); the Battle of Lundy's Lane, also known as the Battle of Niagara Falls, was fought in July 1814 on the Canadian side of the river.

239 (p. 328) *Battle of Lissa* the first major sea battle between ironclads, made up of several small battles, during the Third Italian War of Independence (June–August 1866)

240 (p. 328) *Marconi pendants* popular form of industrial lighting

241 (p. 329) *Hohenzollern* the family name of Kaiser Wilhelm II (1859–1941), the last German Emperor and King of Prussia (1888–1918)

242 (p. 350) *Dummer Kerl!* (German) stupid bloke!

243 (p. 354) *Esel!* (German) Ass!

244 (p. 369) *comic, respectful niggers* a trope from popular fiction

245 (p. 370) *Tanooda* fictional, but echoes Canada

246 (p. 371) *Esperanto* devised in 1887, a synthetic language intended to facilitate international communication, drawing on aspects of key European languages

247 (p. 371) *not A shop, it is A store* playing on the difference between American and British English, but also suggesting a difference of scale

248 (p. 372) *mor'n a shillin'* more than a shilling. Until 1971 Britain had a duodecimal currency system: twelve pence in a shilling, and twenty shillings – 240 pence – in a pound.

249 (p. 379) *Last Word Trans-Continental Express* An express train called the *Transcontinental Express* travelled from New York City to San Francisco in 83 hours and 39 minutes in 1876 as a publicity stunt.

250 (p. 379) *Deyse* These

251 (p. 382) *the Roman Empire under the Antonines* Antoninus Pius (86–161; Emperor 138–161) and his adoptive son Marcus Aurelius (121–180; Emperor 161–180) were noted for their good governance.

252 (p. 385) *Jehad* i.e. Jihad, a Muslim war against non-believers

253 (p. 387) *the Purple Death* a common trope of the science fiction of the time, such as in the American author W. L. Alden's (1837–

1908) short story 'The Purple Death' (1895) and the British West Indian author M. P. Sheil's (1865–1947) *The Purple Cloud* (1901; revised 1929)

254 (p. 388) *Mogador* western Moroccan city, now known as Essaouira

255 (p. 389) *Düreresque* in the manner of the German painter Albrecht Dürer (1471–1528)

256 (p. 393) *drinking in the taproom* Historically, British public houses often had two bars: the public bar or taproom, often a primarily masculine space, and the saloon bar or lounge, which was better decorated and more orientated towards couples.

257 (p. 393) *Vigilance Committee* The term, denoting groups operating outside the law, is particularly associated with the American West during the mid-nineteenth-century Gold Rush.

258 (p. 396) *the Word* John 1:1: 'In the beginning was the Word, and the Word was with God, and the Word was God.'

259 (p. 396) *the Scarlet Woman* also known as the 'Whore of Babylon'. Revelation 17:3: 'So he carried me away in the spirit into the wilderness: and I saw a woman sit upon a scarlet coloured beast, full of names of blasphemy, having seven heads and ten horns.'

260 (p. 398) *Kentish men* There is a traditional distinction between Men of Kent and Kentish Men. Many myths and definitions exist, but perhaps the most common is that those born north and west of the River Medway were Kentish Men, while those from farther south east are Men of Kent. Wells was born in Bromley and so was a Kentish Man.

261 (p. 401) *custed marrers* custard marrows, also known as pattypan squash

262 (p. 401) *kerridges* carriages

263 (p. 402) *sammin* salmon

264 (p. 403) *sparrowgrass and chokes* asparagus and artichokes